It may be impossible to escape pollution in today's world . . . but it is possible to fight back.

This clear, comprehensive guide reveals how toxins can be hidden in unexpected places—and how we can defeat their harmful effects by detoxifying in simple, safe, effective ways. Discover how to combat the toxic effects of . . .

- pesticides
- gasoline fumes
- industrial chemicals
- over-the-counter medications
- upholstery and carpets
- unfiltered water
- household cleansers
  and more

CLEANSING
THE BODY, MIND AND SPIRIT

CLEANSING
THE BODY, MIND AND SPIRIT

Carolyn Reuben

BERKLEY BOOKS, NEW YORK

CLEANSING THE BODY, MIND AND SPIRIT

A Berkley Book / published by arrangement with
the author

PRINTING HISTORY
Berkley edition / November 1998

All rights reserved.
Copyright © 1998 by Carolyn Reuben.
Book design by Casey Hampton.
Interior illustration by Lisa Zdybel.
Cover design by Judith Murello.
This book may not be reproduced in whole
or in part, by mimeograph or any other means,
without permission. For information address:
The Berkley Publishing Group, a member of Penguin Putnam Inc.,
375 Hudson Street, New York, New York 10014.

The Penguin Putnam Inc. World Wide Web site address is
http://www.penguinputnam.com

ISBN: 0-425-16191-9

BERKLEY®
Berkley Books are published by The Berkley Publishing Group, a member of
Penguin Putnam Inc., 375 Hudson Street, New York, New York 10014.
BERKLEY and the "B" design are trademarks belonging to Berkley
Publishing Corporation.

PRINTED IN THE UNITED STATES OF AMERICA

10 9 8 7 6 5 4 3 2 1

NOTE TO READERS

This book is dedicated to
Lenore Wander,
with thanks for steadfast friendship.

CONTENTS

Acknowledgments   xi

Introduction   xiii

PART 1: SITE VISIT

1. The Need: What May Be Poisoning You?   3

2. The Process: The Body's Magnificent Detox
   Factory   11

3. The Equipment: A Tour Through the Detox Organs   19

4. The Damage: Measuring Levels of Toxicity   30

PART 2: FIRST STEP—SIMPLE, FREE, AND NEARLY FREE DETOX TECHNIQUES

5. Cleansing Feasts and Fasts   67

6. Touch   97

7. Thinking, Breathing, Moving, Bathing, Purging   126

PART 3: THE NEXT STEP—MODERATELY PRICED DETOX TECHNIQUES

8. Supplements from Earth and Sea   155

9. Herbs: Goodness from the Garden   168

10. Brushing, Slaking, Purging, and Sniffing   188

11. Special Detox Techniques: Heavy Metal and
    Parasite Removal   212

12. Home Sweet, Nontoxic Home   223

PART 4: COMMITMENT REQUIRED

13. Letting Others Help   251

14. Addiction and Substance Abuse Detox   275

    Appendix: *General References*   293

ACKNOWLEDGMENTS

With grateful heart I thank the following friends, associates, and total strangers who gave me their time and expertise during the writing of this book. The kindness is theirs, the mistakes are mine.

Those who provided information: Jeffrey S. Bland, Ph.D., CEO, HealthComm; Michael Cleveland, manager, Industrial Hygiene Services, Clayton Environmental Consultants; Ilisa Halpern, director federal affairs, American Public Health Association; Francene Lee; Terry Pollack, M.S., technical services, MetaMetrix Medical Laboratory; Corey Resnick, N.D., vice president, technical services, Tyler Encapsulations; Sherry Rogers, M.D,; Barbara Schiltz, R.N., HealthComm Intl.; and the staffs of Tower Books at the Watt Avenue and the Broadway locations in Sacramento.

Those patients who shared their personal stories: Michael Diamond, Debi Iannicelli-Ortiz, Susie Thackston Jackson and David Jackson, Mitch Lopez, Sally McCoy, Didi Carr Reuben, Katherine Stepanovich, Diana Stone, Lt. Col. Robert T. Wolfertz, and the wife of an armed forces veteran, all of whom generously shared with me their time and experiences.

Those professionals who provided interviews: Rosalind Anderson, Ph.D., Anderson Labs; Grant Born, D.O.; J. Alexander Bralley, Ph.D., chairman and laboratory director, MetaMetrix Medical Laboratory; Brian Cox, Colin Campbell & Sons, Ltd.; Denise Dalton; Bob Dash, Cell Tech; Kathleen DesMaisons, Ph.D., CEO, Radiant Recovery; Subhuti Dharmananda, Ph.D., director, Institute for Traditional Medicine; John Furlong, N.D., assistant director of Educational Services, Great Smokies Diagnostic Lab; Ross Gordon, M.D.; Jack Hank, executive director, American Board of Chelation Therapy; Carrol Hayward, president, Heidelberg International, Inc.; Jay Holder,

D.C., M.D., Ph.D.; Greg Kelly, N.D., technical advisor, Thorne Research; Kathi Keville, director, American Herb Association; Eleanor Lewallen, Mendocino Sea Vegetable Company; Galina Lisin, Herba Aromatica; Scott Luper, Tyler Encapsulations; Patrick McGrady, Jr., CANHELP; Cathy McNease, herbalist; Alexis Milea, chief, Standards and Technology Unit, California State Dept. of Health Services Office of Drinking Water; Robert P. Nees, president, Optimum Health Institute; Daoshing Ni, D.O.M., Ph.D., L.Ac.; president, Yo San University; Mary Oetzel, president, Environmental Education and Health Services, Inc.; Jona Plastino, L.Ac.; Jonathan Rastrick, N.D.,; Julia Ross, M.A., M.F.C.C. executive director, Recovery Systems; Herbert Schuck, N.D.; Mark Solomon, Ph.D., vice president, Optimum Health Institute; Murray Susser, M.D.; Morley Tadman, M.A., M.S., Optimum Health Institute; Sandra Weinrib, colonic specialist, Optimum Health Institute; B. C. "Bill" Wolverton, Ph.D.; James Woodworth, director, HealthMed.

Those who became my friends: David Aveni; Aster Black and Gorham L. Black, III; and Carol Stern, M.D.

In addition, I thank Denise Silvestro, my editor at Berkley, for inventing the project; Betsy Amster, my agent this time round, for inviting me on board; Cindy Palay Lyon, L.Ac., Jona Plastino, L.Ac., and Connie Taylor, L.Ac., for keeping Community Acupuncture Recovery Association afloat while I wrote it; Lisa Zdybel for her drawing; Sheila Moody, for a fine job of copyediting it; Casey Hampton, for attractively designing it; Roc Gantt, L.Ac., and Priscilla Monroe, N.D., for treating me when my physical body challenged me to continue it; and my amazingly patient, long-suffering husband and daughter, Allen and Natanya, for taking care of themselves and me until it was done. As always and eternally, I thank my parents, Betty Reuben and Jack Reuben, Ph.D., for way-of-life lessons in emotional and spiritual detoxification. Deep-felt gratitude to all.

INTRODUCTION

Detox suggests relief from either drug addiction or chemical exposure during work or warfare. The truth is, most of us are exposed repeatedly to an astonishing collection of toxins in our everyday life. Many health complaints are actually the body's way of signaling our need for detoxification.

IS YOUR COMPLAINT LISTED HERE?

Let's look at toxicity from the point of view of medical complaints. Here are some of the conditions that may be caused by an overload of toxins:

- acne
- allergies
- anxiety
- asthma
- attention deficit disorder
- autoimmune disorders
- back and neck pain
- bad breath
- bronchitis
- cancer
- clumsiness
- colitis
- poor concentration
- cough
- cramps
- cystitis
- depression
- digestive disorders

- dizziness
- endometriosis
- eczema
- eye irritation
- fatigue
- fuzzy thinking
- headaches
- high blood pressure
- high blood levels of both triglycerides and LDL proteins (low-density lipoproteins)
- hyperactivity
- infertility
- inflammatory joint disease
- irritability
- kidney disease
- liver disease
- lupus
- poor memory
- migraines
- mood swings
- nausea
- neuritis
- numbness and tingling in the hands and feet
- panic attacks
- prostatitis
- psoriasis
- psychosis
- postnasal drip
- recurrent infections
- rheumatoid arthritis
- sinus congestion
- Sjögren's syndrome
- skin abnormalities
- temporomandibular joint (TMJ) syndrome
- urethritis
- vaginitis

If you suffer from any of these conditions, it is possible that you will feel better if you rid your body of its toxic load.

PROCEED AT YOUR OWN SPEED

What you do to cleanse your inner landscape depends on how sick you are, how sick you are of being sick, and how much time you can devote to this endeavor. Since no one living today on this planet, not even a penguin at the South Pole, escapes pollution, even the simplest detox may reap unexpected rewards.

Remember, you don't have to do it all at once! Begin when you have the least pressure on you, such as during a four-day weekend or longer vacation time, when there's "downtime" at work right after the end of a major project, or when the children will be away from home at Grandma's or at camp.

Also think about what you can do on a daily basis to make small but important changes in what you eat and which products you use; even the addition of a few well-chosen nutritional supplements can help your liver handle the toxic world that much better.

WHAT'S IN THIS BOOK

An ordinary day in the life of You reveals the extent of pollution in and around you. After an overview of the foods, products, and drugs influencing your health, we dive inside the body for a tour of the parts that are affected by environmental poisons. We'll check out the various tests that can indicate toxicity, including many you can perform at home. Then, on to the core of the book, the variety of methods for cleansing your body of these chemical misery-makers. At the end of most chapters, and in the appendix, you'll find a resource section listing books, audiotapes, videos, medical clinics, spas, and products that can move you further along the route to better health and clearer thinking.

With your permission, my update of this book will include your experience in detoxifying. Please write me.

Thanks! Happy cleansing.

Carolyn Reuben
Sacramento, California

Write to:
>   Carolyn Reuben
>   c/o The Berkley Publishing Group
>   Publicity Department
>   375 Hudson Street
>   New York, New York 10014

CLEANSING
THE BODY, MIND AND SPIRIT

PART

1

SITE VISIT

THE NEED: WHAT MAY BE POISONING YOU?

If you can't eat it, don't breathe it.

—*Alfred V. Zamm, M.D.*

Just for fun, come take a walk with me through a typical day in the life of a typical American. Let's call this person You; You can be male or female and of any generation.

In bold print, I'll give you the possible contaminant or group of contaminants, followed by the possible health hazards of exposure. The effect of exposure on *you* depends on the health of your detoxification system, your daily intake of nutrients, your genetically determined level of sensitivity to that substance, how long you are exposed, what part of you is exposed, and the intensity of the exposure.

Circle the contaminants that are a part of your daily life. Be assured there *are* safe substitutions. You'll find out where to get them in the "Resources" sections at the ends of the chapters.

ONE DAY IN THE LIFE OF YOU

You wake up under no-iron sheets (**formaldehyde**—*fatigue, headaches, watery eyes, respiratory problems, skin rashes, sleep disturbance, cancer, birth defects*) after a night on a mattress made of foam (**polyurethane and toluene diisocyanate**—*conditions of the respiratory tract, eye, immune system, and skin*). Lucky you aren't sleeping on a water bed, or you'd have been inhaling other dangerous vapors (**vinyl and phenol**—*cancer, memory loss, headache, numb hands and feet, respiratory problems*). Your head rests on a foam pillow with a pillowcase of cotton and **polyester** (*respiratory, skin, and eye problems—*

3

except for those to whom cotton is an allergen; for them, polyester is often a source of relief from symptoms).

Among the other furniture in your bedroom is a bedstand, a desk, and a dresser, all made of particleboard and plywood (**formaldehyde and isocyanate resin**—*persistent cough, asthma, joint pain, anemia, skin conditions, memory loss, headaches).* There is also an easy chair, with a cushion of foam (**polyurethane**—*respiratory, eye, immune system, and skin conditions).*

The walls were recently covered with nonlatex paint (**diisocyanates, anhydrides, toluene, xylene, benzene, MEK, methyl isobutyl ketone, naphtha, formaldehyde, vinyl polymer, titanium dioxide, ethylene glycol, and potentially several hundred other toxic chemicals**—*central nervous system depression, eye irritation, liver damage, fatigue, headache, lung damage, kidney damage, cancer).*

You step down onto your synthetic wall-to-wall carpet (**4-phenylcyclohexane (4-PC), a by-product of combining styrene and butadiene in the latex backing; formaldehyde; xylene; benzene; toluene; and possibly around three dozen other toxic vapor-releasing chemicals**—*headaches, burning eyes and nose, thirst, depression, skin rashes, insomnia, respiratory distress, poor memory, joint pain, sore throats, difficulty concentrating, blurred vision)* and walk to the bathroom.

After using the toilet, you wipe yourself with chlorine-bleached white toilet paper and blow your nose on chlorine-bleached white tissues (**dioxin**—*cancer).* Next to the toilet are white, chlorine-bleached sanitary pads (**dioxin**—*cancer).* On the counter is a liquid soap containing synthetic surfactants (bubble former), emollients (oil), and emulsifiers (to join oil and water) (**diethanolamine (DEA) and triethanolamine (TEA)**—*through chemical reactions, they form cancer-causing nitrosamines; and* **alkoxylated alcohols.** *Ingredients ending with -eth, like laureth, or containing PEG (polyethylene glycol) or PPG (polypropylene glycol) or-oxynol, involve the creation of 1,4-dioxane, a cancer-causing chemical).*

You brush your teeth with toothpaste (**saccharin and FD&C Blue 1**—*possibly cause cancer;* **fluoride**—*cancer, numerous musculoskeletal, urinary tract, digestive tract, respiratory tract, and skin, hair, and nail disorders;* and **polysorbate 80**—*may be contaminated with 1,4-dioxane, a carcinogen)* and follow with mouthwash (**alcohol content of 25 percent or higher**—*tumors of mouth, tongue, or throat,* **saccharin, FD&D Blue 1, FD&C Green 3, and FD&C Yellow 5**—*possibly cause cancer;* and **polysorbate 60 or 80**—*may be contaminated with 1,4-dioxane, a carcinogen*).

In the shower, you use an antidandruff shampoo (**ammonia, coal-tar compounds, formaldehyde, nitrosamines, plastic (PVP), colors**—*carcinogens*). The shower water itself can be toxic (**aluminum**—*kidney and lung disorders, spinal cord and brain disease, skeletal pain;* **asbestos**—*cancer;* **cadmium**—*cancer, genetic mutations, nausea, vomiting, diarrhea, pain, reproductive tract damage, respiratory distress, headache, fatigue, anemia, loss of smell, hypertension;* **chlorine**—*cancer, particularly when chlorine reacts with organic material, such as decaying leaves, to form chlorinated hydrocarbons, such as trihalomethanes;* **fluoride**—*fuzzy thinking, mottled teeth, kidney disease, bone changes;* **industrial chemicals; lead, mercury, nitrates, organic solvents, pesticides, radon**—*cancer, birth defects, fatigue;* **parasites, bacteria, and viruses**—*infections, fatigue*). After you shower, you apply some moisturizer cream (**PEG and DEA**—*cancer;* and **mineral oil (Polycyclic Aromatic Hydrocarbons (PAH) and anthanthrene**—*cancer, acne*). Under your arms you roll on antiperspirant (**ammonia, formaldehyde**—*lung irritation, cancer;* **aluminum**—*kidney and lung disorders, spinal cord and brain disease, skeletal pain;* and **fragrance**—*allergies, cancer, headaches, irritability, poor concentration*).

In the makeup kit on the counter are mascara, blush, eyeliner, and lipstick, a veritable cornucopia of petrochemicals (**PEG, PPG, quaternium 15, formaldehyde, phenol, methyl ethyl ketone (MEK), ammonia, hydrous magnesium silicate (talc), colors, flavors, propellants, plastic resins, polyvinylpyrrolidine plastic (PVP), preservatives**—*cancer, allergies, nerve damage, respiratory distress, mucous membrane irritation, eye irritation, skin rashes*). In the cupboard is hair coloring (**coal tar dyes, ammonia**—*skin rashes, cancer;* **phenylenediamines**—*birth defects and cancer;* **Acid Orange 87, Solvent Brown 44, Acid Blue 168, Acid Violet 73**—*cancer;* and **lead acetate**—*birth defects, cancerous tumors, decreased mental functioning*). In the drawer by the sink are several shades of nail polish (**butyl acetate**—*conjunctivitis and other eye irritation*), but you reach for hair spray (**poly-

vinylpyrrolidone (PVP)—*the development of foreign substances in the lungs, kidney damage, fecal impaction*). Under the sink is a detergent (**chlorine**—*skin and lung damage*), a drain opener (**potassium hydroxide**—*pain, bleeding, skin rash, tumors*), and a tile cleaner (**phosphoric acid**—*skin and mucous membrane irritation*).

You return to the bedroom to get dressed. When you open the closet, a strong chemical smell reminds you of a suit you've been wanting to wear, which you picked up from the dry cleaner on your way home from work last night. You pull off the plastic bag over the suit and hanger, further releasing dry cleaning solvent vapors into the air (**perchloroethylene (PCE), trichloroethylene (TCE), naphthalene, toluene, xylene, formaldehyde, benzene, ammonia, chlorine**—*cancer, liver damage, respiratory tract irritation, kidney damage, drowsiness, headaches, skin and eye irritation*).

It's time for a quick breakfast! In the kitchen, you swallow a prescribed medication (**any drug uses up the liver's detoxification resources**). This drug is brightly colored (**artificial colors**—*hyperactivity in children, cancer*). You fill a bowl with a breakfast cereal (**BHT, BHA, artificial colors, artificial flavors**—*hyperactivity in children, cancer*). On goes milk from cows who have been consuming fodder laced with a variety of **pesticides** and **herbicides** (*nausea, muscle twitching, diarrhea, abdominal pain, profuse sweating, difficulty thinking clearly, dizziness, blurred vision, respiratory distress, cancer, birth defects, stillbirths, irregular heartbeat, and estrogen-stimulation effects, such as young girls developing breasts and pubic hair*). The coffee maker contains coffee decaffeinated with **methylene oxide gas** (*cancer*) and grown with **aldicarb** (*damage to nervous system, reproduction, immune system, endocrine system*). The warm, pungent drink drips through a white, chlorine-bleached coffee filter (**dioxin**—*cancer*). You splash into the brew some artificial creamer (**partially hydrogenated vegetable oil**—*atherosclerosis*). On a gas stove (**formaldehyde, sulfur dioxide, nitrogen dioxide, carbon monoxide, hydrogen cyanide, nitric oxide, and organic vapors**—*headaches, dizziness, fatigue, heart palpitations, asthma, personality changes, difficulty thinking, alterations in vision and hearing*), there's a frying pan containing several strips of sizzling bacon (**nitrites, nitrates, polycyclic hydro-carbons**—*cancer*.)

You prepare yourself lunch: bologna (**sodium nitrite**—*cancer*), bread (**EDTA**—*kidney damage, asthma, skin rashes*), some carrot sticks (**pesticides, particularly trifluralin, par-athion, and diazinon, as well as DDT left over in the soil from before it was banned**—*cancer, birth defects, learning difficulties*), a nonorganic banana (**diazinon, thiabendazole, carbaryl**—*nervous system damage, kidney damage*), and some candy (**artificial colors**—*hyperactive behavior in children, cancer*). Before closing the lunch bag you add a diet drink (**aspartame**—*may alter brain chemistry, contributing to sei-zures, allergic response, altered behavior in children; and* **caffeine**—*high blood pressure, increased heart rate, overstimulation of adrenal glands, nervousness, insomnia, ad-diction*).

Beneath the kitchen sink is spot remover (**toluene, ben-zene**—*cancer*), shoe polish and dye (**dichlorobenzene, methylene chloride**—*cancer*), and disinfectant (**cresol**—*respiratory, central nervous system, liver, and kidney damage; and* **phenol**—*skin rashes, gangrene, numbness, cancer*).

Walking outside to the car, you inhale automobile exhaust (**nitrogen oxides, ozone, sulfur dioxide, sulfuric acid, lead, carbon monoxide, acetaldehyde, formaldehyde, and partic-ulates, plus thousands of other compounds**—*respiratory damage, burning sensation in lungs, difficulty breathing, asthma, pneumonia, reduced oxygen in blood and cells, heart disease, leukemia, lymphoma, damage to bone marrow*).

At the office, you are exposed to a space heater (**carbon monoxide**—*headache, dizziness, shortness of breath, poor concentration, poor judgment, fainting*), a photocopier (**ozone**—*chest pain, fatigue, coughing*), colored markers (**ac-etone, cresol, ethanol, xylene, toluene, and phenol**—*respiratory system, liver, kidneys, and nervous system dys-function; cancer, skin ulcers and rashes; headache, nervous-ness, fatigue, confusion, insomnia, and teary eyes*) and a phone message pad made of carbonless paper (**polychlorinated bi-phenyls (PCBs)**—*irritation of eyes, skin, and respiratory tract; liver damage, cancer*).

You go for a drink from the fountain in the hall, possi-bly consuming agricultural and industrial runoff in the city's water supply (**benzene, trichloroethylene, dibutyl phthalate, vinyl chloride, carbon tetrachloride, dimethylformamide (DMF), cyclohexanone (CH), tetrahydrofuran (THF), de(2-ethylhexyl)phthalate (DEHP), cadmium, lead, fluoride, tetrachloroethylene, polychlorinated biphenyls, and pesticides and lead**—*cancer, high blood pressure, mottled teeth, bone changes, poor memory and lowered IQ, respiratory distress*).

After work, you stop at a local cocktail lounge for "happy hour" and inhale some four thousand chemicals from second-hand cigarette smoke, including **benzo(a)pyrenes, tar, carbon monoxide, nicotine, nitrosamines, hydrogen cyanide, phenols, aromatic hydrocarbons, radioactive polonium 210, and formaldehyde** (*cancer, emphysema, bronchitis, chronic cough, premature wrinkling, heart disease, addiction*).

Tomorrow, your home will be fumigated for termites using organochlorine insecticides (**chlordane** and **heptachlor**—*cancer*). Last month the problem was fleas (**chloropyrifos (Dursban)**—*poisoning, acute illness*). Your gardener regularly uses lawn care products containing a herbicide (**2, 4-dichlorophenoxyacetic acid**—*nonspecific toxicity*) and a fungicide (**ethylene bisdithiocarbamate (EBDC)**—*breaks down to ethylenethiourea (ETU), a probable carcinogen and possible cause of birth defects and thyroid problems*). You and several other neighbors use an organophosphate pesticide (**diazinon**—*neurobehavioral effects and birth defects*) on your lawns, which wafts through the air to all the yards on the block.

At the end of your day, you're back to bed.

This short scenario lists only a small fraction of the possibilities, which might also have included pesticides on school grounds and in classrooms, industrial solvents and other chemicals in the workplace, glues, solvents, and other chemicals involved with hobbies and leisure activities, additives and other toxic elements in pharmaceutical and over-the-counter drugs, genetic damage and liver disease from living near a polluted landfill, old mine, military base, or major industry, and food-borne pollutants such as parasites and fungi.

WHAT DO TOXINS DO TO US?

Since 1915, around four million new chemicals have been released into our environment, including around three thousand
chemicals allowed in foods during processing, around twelve
thousand chemicals used in food packing materials, and more
than thirty-four thousand pesticides. Chemicals originally
sprayed on crops end up in lakes, rivers, and oceans, contaminating fish. Chemicals sprayed on animal fodder, and drugs
fed to poultry, hogs, and cattle, end up in our meat. What do
these chemicals do to us? That isn't easy to say, since between
79 percent and 84 percent of all pesticides have not been appropriately tested for their ability to cause cancer, 90 percent
to 93 percent have not been adequately tested for their ability
to cause genetic mutations, and 60 percent to 75 percent have
been inadequately tested for their ability to cause birth defects.[1] Nevertheless, according to the National Academy of
Sciences, at least twenty thousand cancer deaths a year are due
to pesticide exposure, and the Environmental Protection
Agency lists chemical residues in food as one of the top three
greatest cancer risks in America today.

There are more subtle expressions of pesticide poisoning: a
Florida study in the late 1980s found the majority of male
panthers were born with one or more undescended testes, contributing to infertility. The animals had twice as much estrogen
as testosterone, which was assumed to be caused by pesticides,
which mimic estrogen in the body of animals and humans.[2] If
pesticides so clearly influence the sexual maturation of animals
due to these chemicals' mimicking estrogen, is it any wonder
that our young girls are entering puberty at ever-lowering
ages?

Given the pollution in which we live, and the toxins we are
exposed to, isn't it amazing that we survive at all? Our ability
to live with all these contaminants is due to our bodies' natural
detoxification system. The human body is a magnificent machine. Let's take a closer look at how it works to handle toxins.

REFERENCES

1. Household Hazardous Waste Project, *Guide to Hazardous
   Products Around the Home* (Springfield, Mo.: Southwest

Missouri State University's Office of Continuing Education, 1989), 138.

2. Nina Anderson and Howard Peiper, *Are You Poisoning Your Pets?* (East Canaan, Conn.: Safe Goods, 1995), 2.

TWO

THE PROCESS: THE BODY'S
MAGNIFICENT DETOX FACTORY

*We often think that when we have completed our study of
"one" we know all about "two," because "two" is "one
and one." We forget that we still have to make a study of
"and."*

—A. Eddington

You may be exposed to a harmful substance, a toxin, by eating
it, absorbing it, injecting it, inhaling it, or by creating it inside
yourself just in the process of living (for example, steroids,
bile acids, sex hormones, and fatty acids).

Sometimes years go by before you know you're suffering
from toxic exposure that is damaging your immune system,
gastrointestinal system, nervous system, endocrine system, reproductive system, or any other system of your body. Sometimes it is possible for a toxin to exist within tissues and cells
without causing serious harm. Whether your body is able to
protect itself or is damaged by exposure depends on the quantity of dangerous toxin, the length of time the toxin remains
in the body, the location of the toxin, your overall exposure
to other toxins (your "toxic load"), your inherited ability to
eliminate that toxin, your overall health and nutritional status,
and your current level of emotional stress, among other vari-
ables.

Luckily, to some extent our bodies can chemically rearrange
the structure of dangerous substances and release them before
they do irreparable damage. The body has a number of alternatives when confronted with a toxic substance. Vomiting and
diarrhea quickly eliminate poisons from fore and aft. The body
may store the toxin in fat cells and keep it out of general

11

circulation until you lose weight. Or it might transform the toxin into a form that can be eliminated safely through sweat, urine, or feces.

Actually, all of the above are occurring simultaneously. At this exact moment, your body is storing some toxins and transforming others. This process of transforming a toxin into a harmless substance involves two main biochemical pathways, a number of nutrient cofactors, and varying amounts of time.

PHASE I DETOXIFICATION

Phase I is often the first pathway used by the body for detoxification. What carries the reaction forward along the path are cytochrome P-450 enzymes. Enzymes are a kind of protein that speed reactions. The body has many thousands of enzymes, and each enzyme has a specific task to perform. At the end of the road, thanks to the cytochrome P-450 enzymes, toxins are more easily eliminated from the body or denatured by other chemical reactions.

SOME SUBSTANCES DETOXIFIED IN THE BODY BY CYTOCHROME P-450 ENZYMES

Caffeine, theophylline, propanolol (Inderol), amitriptyline (Elavil), clomipramine (Anafranil), codeine, phenytoin (Dilantin), ibuprofen, naproxen (Naprosyn), S-warfarin (Coumadin), diazepam (Valium), imipramine (Tofranil), acetaminophen, alcohol, lidocaine, erythromycin, cyclosporine, ketoconazole (Nizoral), testosterone, estradiol, and cortisone.

Unfortunately, the Phase I detox pathway itself can cause you problems! This happens because of the way the enzymes do their work.

Molecules like to have pairs of electrons in balanced orbit around their nucleus. However, the cytochrome P-450 enzymes do their detox work through oxidation-reduction reactions. An oxidation reaction means a molecule gives up one or two of its electrons to another molecule. A reduction reaction is the opposite: A molecule accepts electrons from another molecule. Another term for an oxidation-reduction reaction is a "redox" reaction.

Unfortunately, when a molecule gives up an electron, it is out of balance and searches for a convenient electron to kidnap to replace its missing electron. A molecule with a missing electron is called a free radical because the space normally filled by that other electron is temporarily "free." Problems arise when, in the process of refilling the space with a new electron, another molecule is burglarized and damaged. The damage that occurs molecule by molecule, by the theft of electrons, snowballs into major damage to cells and tissues.

In some cases, the damage is caused by atoms that aren't free radicals. The general name for these atoms is oxidants because they are often fragments of an oxygen atom. It's amazing how damaging oxygen can be. Oxygen causes metal to rust and oil to go rancid. Since it is oxygen that causes the rancidity, the process of making something go rancid is called oxidation. Rancid oil on a kitchen counter is one thing, but there is oil (called lipid) in the structure of every cell's membrane, which means that when oxidation occurs inside our own body, we, too, can go rancid.

In summary, Phase I detox starts the process of clearing out toxins, but often creates intermediate chemicals, such as oxidants, that are more dangerous than the original offending substance.

Recently, scientists have determined that oxidation in body tissues is the cause of many degenerative diseases, including cancer, heart disease, atherosclerosis, diabetes, cataracts, and more. Thanks to Phase II detoxification, some of this internal destruction by oxidants is neutralized.

PHASE II DETOXIFICATION

While they aren't the main stimulus for Phase II detoxification, it is certainly convenient that Phase II detox helps clean up the toxic intermediates formed during Phase I reactions. Phase

II also helps neutralize toxins that enter the blood directly from food, drugs, and environmental pollution.

However, Phase II reactions only occur successfully when the liver produces certain needed enzymes, and when there are adequate nutrients provided by your food. If you are missing these nutrients, you may be doubly damaged—first by the original toxin and second by the intermediate substances formed through Phase I detoxification, which build up dangerously when they are not being detoxed by your Phase II pathways.

Phase II detoxification takes place through conjugation. This is the addition of a molecule to the toxin to convert that toxin from fat-soluble to water-soluble. When a substance is fat soluble it may remain in the body inside the fat cells for a long time. If the body wants to get rid of a toxic fat-loving substance, it has to make the toxin water soluble by conjugation and then it can flush the toxin away in the urine, or sweat it out through the skin.

The body performs conjugation by a biochemical step-by-step process called a pathway. One drug may be detoxified by the work of one pathway, or simultaneously by the work of more than one. The five major Phase II conjugation pathways include *glucuronidation* (initiated by a sugar derivative called UDP-glucose), *sulfation* (initiated by the sulfur derivative called sulfate), *glutathione conjugation* (initiated by the amino acid glutathione), *glycination* (initiated by the amino acids taurine and glycine), *methylation* (initiated by biochemical families called methyl groups), and *acetylation* (initiated by certain enzymes).

PHASE II CONJUGATION PATHWAYS AND WHAT THEY DETOXIFY

Glucuronidation: acetaminophen, naproxen, benzodiazepines (including Valium), dilantin, aspirin.

Sulfation: serotonin, dopamine, corticosteroids, phenol, minoxidil, estradiol, vanillin, acetaminophen, tyramine, tyrosine, tannins.

Glutathione Conjugation: lead, mercury, arsenic, tetracycline, Tylenol, chlorobenzene.

Glycination: aspirin, sodium benzoate, toluene, phenylalanine.

Methylation: lead and other heavy metals, Paraquat, isoquinolines.

Acetylation: caffeine, hydralazine, isoniazid, mescaline.

Why are these pathways important to you? Here's one example: If you have a chronic pain for which you are taking daily aspirin, you may use up your glycine reserves in the process of metabolizing the aspirin day after day. Since many other toxins are detoxified through the glycine conjugation pathway, when you use up your glycine supply you may begin experiencing symptoms of toxicity from drugs or environmental chemicals that previously caused no distress. In chapter 4 you will learn of laboratory tests that can alert you to problems and inadequacies in your Phase I and Phase II detox pathways.

ANTIOXIDANTS: DEFENDERS OF THE INNER REALM

Antioxidants rescue our body from the damage caused by oxidants. Antioxidants are specific vitamins, minerals, amino acids, herbs, and other nutrients that are able to give up one of their electrons. In some cases they can do this without needing to steal another atom's electron. Depending on the situation, antioxidants can prevent damage, stop the continuation of damage while it's going on, and repair cells after damage has occurred.

The body needs constant and adequate levels of the full range of antioxidant nutrients, including vitamins A, C, and E, and the mineral selenium. Taking only one or two of these in supplement form won't provide the protection you need. They work together synergistically, helping each other stay active and effective. Other nutrients play supporting roles in this detox drama. They include vitamin B complex, the minerals calcium, magnesium, zinc, copper, and manganese, and certain amino acids.

AMINOS: THE OFT-FORGOTTEN NUTRIENTS

Amino acids string together like pearls on a chain, forming protein. You're actually eating combinations of amino acids each time you bite into a hamburger patty, an omelette, or a bean and cheese burrito. When proteins are broken apart, the body uses the individual amino acids to create other biochemical structures, particularly for detoxification.

For example, to detoxify ammonia, the body uses the amino acids ornithine and aspartate. To detoxify carboxylic acids, the body uses glycine, glutamine, and taurine. Steroid hormones are rendered less harmful to the body thanks to the amino acid methionine.

ENZYMES: LIFE IN THE RAW

One of the ways to enhance the use of amino acids for detoxification is to make sure your body does a good job of digestion. If you suffer from gas, bloating, and indigestion, you may need digestive aids along with your meals.

Our body uses two kinds of digestive aids from plants and from within our own digestive system: those that digest protein, and those that digest carbohydrates and fats. Which do you need? To find out, eat a meal of only protein (meat, poultry, eggs, fish), and wait at least two hours before eating anything else. If you experience gas, belching, distention, or stomach pain, you probably could use a couple capsules of betaine hydrochloride at the start of every strongly protein meal. You can purchase this commercial form of stomach acid at any health food store and some supermarkets. Sources of papain, an extract from papaya, or bromelain, an extract from pineapple, may also be used to help protein digestion. These or other "proteolytic" enzymes will help your stomach break down protein into its amino acid components.

Next, eat a meal of only fat and carbohydrates (a baked

potato, crackers, bagel, corn or potato chips, a granola bar) and wait at least an hour. Protein is digested in the stomach in a highly acidic environment; fats and carbohydrates, on the other hand, are digested in the small intestine using alkaline digestive juices secreted by the liver and pancreas. If you experience any distress after this carbohydrate meal, your digestion may improve if you take pancreatic enzymes during your next carbohydrate-rich meal. You can obtain pancreatic enzymes where nutritional supplements are sold.

It is possible that the source of your digestive problems isn't a lack of your own digestive aids, but rather a lack of those found in plants. If you eat few raw fruits and vegetables, or overcook the ones you do eat, you probably are deficient in plant enzymes such as amylase to digest carbohydrates, protease to digest protein, and lipase to digest fats. These important digestive aids are found in raw fruits and vegetables, and they are destroyed by high heat. You may be able to solve digestive problems by adding raw vegetable salads to your daily menus and eating more raw fruit. Plant enzymes help you digest protein, fat, and carbohydrates, as well as dietary fiber. Fruit and vegetables are excellent sources of antioxidants, as well.

IN SUMMARY

Phase I detoxification pathways sometimes create dangerous substances even as the detox process attempts to neutralize toxins. These new substances must be detoxified in a Phase II detoxification pathway. Phase II's main focus, however, is to take fat-soluble toxins and change them biochemically so they are water-soluble, and can be easily eliminated through the urine, sweat, and feces.

Phase I and II detox processes go on without your conscious attention, but you must participate by providing the body with helper nutrients, including amino acids, minerals, and vitamins that allow it to perform these biochemical sleights-of-hand.

For the nutrients to help in Phase I and Phase II detox, they must be well absorbed from the food you eat. To assure yourself optimum absorption of nutrients, you may want to take betaine hydrochloride just before a protein meal, or pancreatic enzymes just before a meal rich in carbohydrates and fats. Depending on how well your digestive tract works, you may need one or both of these categories of digestive aids. And if your diet is the usual vegetable-poor American fare, you may need plant enzymes from raw fruits and vegetables, as well.

RESOURCES

Books:

Jeffrey Bland, Ph.D., with Sara Benum, M.A., *The 20-Day Rejuvenation Diet Program* (New Canaan, Conn. Keats, 1997). Bland describes a program for minimizing oxygen radical damage, describes the process of detoxification, and advises you how to manage pain, to power immunity, and to balance hormones with proper nutrients.

Products:

If you will not add more fruits and vegetables to your daily diet, consider signing up for Juice Plus+ or some other company's raw-foods-in-a-capsule. Juice Plus+ and similar products juice and powder raw fruits and vegetables in a way that preserves their natural plant enzymes. Juice Plus+ offers two bottles of capsules: Orchard Blend is made from seven fruits and Garden Blend from eight vegetables plus plant enzymes, plant fiber, digestive aids, such as acidophilus, and some other plant nutrients. Adults take two capsules of each blend per day. The product is sold through multilevel marketing. For information, you can contact me in California via e-mail at creuben@pacbell.net or at the main office in Memphis, Tennessee, at (901) 366-9288 (ext. #2).

THREE

THE EQUIPMENT: A TOUR THROUGH THE DETOX ORGANS

Plant a radish, get a radish, not a Brussels sprout.
        —*from "Plant a Radish" in* The Fantasticks

The body is built for survival; nature gave you multiple means of self-defense and detoxification. These structures and systems include the nose, tongue and tonsils, saliva, breath, lungs, mucus, liver, stomach, small intestine, large intestine, feces, lymph, kidneys, urine, skin, semen, and menstrual flow.

Let's look at each of these, briefly, for their role in the detoxification process.

NOSE

Your nose has bristly hairs to stop the entrance of particles that might damage the lungs. It secretes mucus to stop dust and bacteria from entering the body, and a sneeze mechanism to reverse the direction of particles moving through the hair barrier.

TONGUE AND TONSILS

The taste buds particularly sensitive to bitter tastes are located at the back of the tongue, to set off an alarm that warns you of possible poisons and stops you from swallowing before it's too late. The tonsils at the sides of the throat are storage sites for the lymph system. Here residue from the process of metabolism and from battles with viruses and bacteria collects until the body can eliminate it.

SALIVA

The very thought of food, even before you put one spoonful in your mouth, causes salivary glands in your cheeks and under your tongue to secrete saliva. Saliva contains antibodies that attach to bacteria and other harmful substances. Saliva also contains enzymes that begin the digestion of carbohydrates.

The more you chew, the greater the quantity of saliva and the smaller the morsels of food. Thus, chewing long and well is important for good digestion and good self-defense against bacterial invaders.

BREATH

Whatever exits the body is used as a vehicle to release toxins, and the breath is no exception. Volatile organic compounds and other toxins in gas form can be released in every exhalation.

LUNGS

Cells across the surface of the lungs produce mucus, which coats the lung and protects it against harsh chemicals in inhaled vapors and smoke. In addition, particulate matter catches in this viscous mucus and is stopped from descending further into the innermost chambers of the lungs.

Tiny hairlike cilia line the respiratory tract. The waving cilia, coupled with strong upwards muscular contractions, propel the mucus and all that is trapped in it out of the lung, up the esophagus, and into the throat, where it can be spit out.

Grapelike bunches of miniscule sacs called alveoli at the innermost recesses of each lung allow an exchange of gas: inhaled oxygen moves into the blood, and carbon dioxide is released from the blood into the lung, from where it is exhaled.

The act of breathing does more than energize the body with oxygen. Breathing through the nose influences the nervous system, and through it your blood pressure, adrenal glands, and emotions. Yogis in India have known for centuries that simply putting your attention on your inhalation and exhalation helps you relax.

MUCUS

Mucus is your friend. It moistens and protects your entire digestive system. It helps food slide down your throat and it lubricates a woman's vagina during sexual intercourse. Mucus keeps hydrochloric acid from burning holes in your stomach and pancreatic enzymes from digesting the walls of your intestines. It moistens air in your nose, and it traps undesirable particles before they enter the lungs.

When you need boxes of tissues to wipe up excess mucus, your body is doing its best to protect you from some perceived toxin by entrapping it and floating it out. Instead of simply using drugs to stop the flow, begin a program of detoxification and immune system enhancement to stop excessive mucus production at its source.

LIVER

The liver is located on the right side of your torso, under your ribs. It performs over three hundred different jobs. Here are just a few: It creates enzymes to digest fats; metabolizes fats, proteins, and carbohydrates; stores vitamins A, B_{12}, D, E, and K until needed; creates immune system substances, like gamma globulin; stores extra blood; controls the amount of estrogen allowed to circulate in the blood; and checks out the blood for toxic substances, which the liver then neutralizes. Herbalist Christopher Hobbs writes in *Natural Liver Therapy*, "It is not called the live-r for nothing; it keeps us living."[1]

The liver is the body's major detox organ. In today's world, it is under constant assault, not only by the chemicals of daily life, but also from within, by hormones created from our own body's hyped-up reaction to chronic stress.

The good news is, the liver has amazing powers to regenerate. In fact, after reversible liver injury, the liver's ability to detoxify chemicals can *increase* to as much as 120 percent of normal! What's possibly even more amazing, the liver's power of regeneration is so strong that recently one donated liver was cut into two pieces, transplanted into two separate people (an infant and a middle-aged woman) and, given adequate nutrition and blood, is expected to regenerate and grow to full size, with full function in each of the recipients.

The liver protects us in two ways. It transforms fat-soluble chemicals (such as pesticides) with enzymes, using the Phase I and Phase II detoxification pathways described in chapter 2. It also filters material through special channels in its interior that contain immune cells that work like mini Pacmen to engulf and destroy bacteria and other undesirable substances.

Hobbs points out that herbs described as "blood purifiers" don't really clean the blood, but rather improve the function of liver cells and stimulate more blood to flow through and be filtered by the liver. In chapter 9 you will discover the best herbs to improve liver function.

STOMACH

The stomach is a muscular sac hanging in your upper abdomen between the esophagus and the small intestine. The stomach's intensely acidic digestive juice, called hydrochloric acid, kills some bacteria and denatures other substances that might injure you. The stomach also produces pepsin, a protein-digesting enzyme.

When stimulated by the presence of food, the stomach muscles contract and twist so that food is churned multiple times. The combination of churning, hydrochloric acid, and pepsin tears apart protein into its components, called amino acids. The body reuses these amino acids to build new substances, like enzymes and hormones, and to repair damaged tissues.

At this point in digestion, the churning mass is called chyme (pronounced "kime"). After anywhere from fifteen to forty-five minutes, food particles have been reduced in size enough and the chyme is acidic enough to stimulate the opening of the pyloric valve between the stomach and the small intestine. When the pyloric valve opens, chyme enters the duodenum, the upper section of the small intestine.

SMALL INTESTINE

The small intestine should really be called the narrow intestine because, although it is small in diameter (about the size of your big toe, according to Deepak Chopra, M.D.)[2] it is the largest intestine in length, measuring twenty feet, compared to the large intestine's six feet!

When food is finished being digested in the stomach, it is very acidic.

After chyme enters the duodenum, its acidity stimulates the pancreas to contribute pancreatic enzymes and the liver, via the gallbladder, to contribute bile. The pancreatic juices and bile turn the acidic mass of digesting food into a more alkaline mass of around 6 pH. It is now called chyle (pronounced "kile").

The small intestine's inner lining is covered with waving projections, called villi, which provide greater surface area for nutrients to be absorbed into the bloodstream. Absorption of nutrients is the small intestine's major job. When things go well, your food makes you alert, strong, healthy, and clear thinking. When you feel anything less, the small intestine may be the source of your distress.

In fact, although many think of the small intestine as nothing more than a vehicle for nutrients to pass into your cells, it can be, according to some experts, a major factor in the development of disease. The theories as to how this occurs include improper food combining (causing incomplete digestion, leading to putrification and nutritional deficiencies), abnormal balance of "good" and "bad" bacteria in the gut (causing systemic spread of the "bad" bacteria and bacterial by-products, which cause autoimmune reactions, like arthritis), proliferation of yeasts, particularly *Candida albicans* (and systemic spread of that infection, causing numerous symptoms), and "leaky gut syndrome" (the passage of not only bacteria and yeasts, but also toxic chemicals and incompletely digested particles of food into the bloodstream, leading to an immune system reaction that results in food allergies, chemical sensitivities, and a host of symptoms). These several explanations are not mutually exclusive, and all or some may occur in different people at different times.

It may take from three to five hours for chyle to pass

through the small intestine and into the large intestine. Greasy, fatty foods take longer to digest than fruits and vegetables. When you are emotionally upset, more stomach acid is produced, lowering the pH of the chyme as it enters the small intestine, forcing the small intestine to take longer to bring the pH up to the needed alkalinity for proper digestion of the fats and carbohydrates in the meal. Emotions also diminish the rhythmic peristalsis of the intestines, which is another reason transit slows through the system.

Eventually, chyle passes through the ileocecal valve into the large intestine.

LARGE INTESTINE

Deepak Chopra describes the large intestine as having a diameter about the size of your fist. Material moves far more slowly through the large intestine than the small intestine—it can take anywhere from four hours to three days to arrive at the rectum, the final segment of the digestive tract.

The large intestine, or colon, gracefully drapes its length of six feet or so across your abdomen, beginning at the lower right side as the ascending colon, crossing the midabdomen as the transverse colon, and dropping to the rectum as the descending colon. At the juncture with the rectum it is called the sigmoid colon.

As chyle moves through the colon, nutrients that weren't absorbed in the small intestine are now absorbed. By also reabsorbing water that was added in the stomach and small intestine, the colon dries out the chyle and forms feces, which are moved by contractions through the tube. In addition, B vitamins and vitamin K are produced by useful bacteria in the colon.

You probably have noticed that your bowel movements don't all smell or look the same. How you eat and what you eat have an immediate and intimate effect on the quality of your bowel movements and, like it or not, the quality of your bowel movements reflects the quality of your life. For example, if your bowel movements have a foul odor, that's a signal to you that your digestion needs help and you have too many toxins in your gastrointestinal tract. Look for more about this relationship in chapter 10.

FECES

Feces, stool, and bowel movements are all names for the waste material that is expelled from the rectum. At least four hundred different bacteria species have been identified in the colon, so it is no surprise that as much as half the weight of the feces is bacteria. In addition, feces are composed of indigestible roughage or food fiber, dead cells from the intestinal lining, mucus and other intestinal secretions, bile, and, in some cases, infective agents, such as parasites.

You can learn about yourself from observing your feces. A normal stool is soft but well formed, doesn't have a foul odor, and when you wipe yourself, there is little or no residue on the toilet paper. If your stool is loose, you may have an infection or an allergic reaction. If it is pale, you may not be absorbing your food properly, or you may have an obstruction of your bile duct. If you are not absorbing your nutrients properly (a condition called malabsorption), it isn't easy to flush the stool, and it may smell foul. Mucus may be caused by infections or irritation of the bowel from allergies or other causes. Dark feces can be colored by iron (in your diet or in medication), wine, or blood. Red feces can be caused by hemorrhoids, ulcerative colitis, or a tumor in the colon. Black blood in the feces may come from bleeding in the stomach or small intestine.

LYMPH

The lymph system is your body's garbage collection service. Lymph is clear, yellowish, and contains white blood cells—the scavengers of your immune system. The lymph moves through lymph vessels, which blanket the entire body, especially alongside blood vessels. The lymph network includes collection points of various sizes, called nodes or glands, located in your throat, armpits, chest, groin, and behind your knees.

Lymph collects toxins from cells and dumps the toxins into the blood. A healthy detoxification system relies on intact and active lymph nodes and the free movement of lymph throughout the body. However, modern life conflicts with this goal.

While the heart pumps blood, most of us have to go out of our way to exercise. Yet, exercise is what moves lymph. This means that a sedentary person's cells may detoxify inadequately because their lymph isn't moving properly through their body.

In addition, the two largest lymph collection sites are the appendix, located at the entrance to the colon, and the tonsils, located at the entrance to the throat. Unfortunately, toxic overload has sometimes so inflamed these two lymph glands that surgeons feel they have no alternative but to remove them. In the case of the appendix, there are often no commonly recognized warning signs that congestion is approaching this critical state, and the patient's life is in danger should the gland burst, spilling its toxic load of bacteria into the pelvic cavity.

With the tonsils, however, there is usually plenty of warning that toxicity is building in the system, since the patient has recurring ear infections, sore throats, and easily visible enlarged tonsils. Unfortunately, once the tonsil is removed, a major collection site for toxins from the neck and head is gone forever.

If body cells weren't so full of toxins, lymph glands such as the tonsils and appendix wouldn't back up like a clogged drain. Elsewhere in the system, clogging causes swelling of lymph vessels, a lessened ability of cells to receive proper nutrition, and a reduction in the effectiveness of the whole immune system.

Happily, as described elsewhere in this book, by changing your diet and by exercising, you can prevent and eliminate lymph congestion.

KIDNEYS

Kidneys are about four inches long, two inches wide and shaped like, no surprise, kidney beans! There is a kidney on each side of your middle back, below the ribs. Their major job is to filter blood, recycle some salts and other nutrients, and excrete undesired substances into urine. They perform this feat through the work of more than a million filtering units called nephrons.

Through secreting different enzymes and absorbing more or less of certain substances, the kidneys control your body's acid-alkaline balance, your blood pressure, the quantity of red blood cells produced in your bone marrow, and the amount of active vitamin D that is available to increase calcium levels in your bones.

URINE

Waste products that are released from the body in urine include uric acid, ammonia, trace metals, minerals, mucus, yellow pigment, and urea. Urea formation begins when proteins from food are broken down in the intestines to amino acids. These are absorbed through the intestinal wall into the blood and are carried to the liver. In the liver, unneeded amino acids are converted into urea and sent back through the blood to the kidneys. Another constituent of urea is cell proteins cast off from tissue damage after injury or surgery.

Although urine is sterile when it leaves you, it includes unwanted substances such as yeasts, organic chemicals, and traces of nutritional supplements and medications that were not absorbed by body cells.

SKIN

Your largest organ has three layers, each with its own function. The outer layer, the epidermis, consists of dead and dying cells, replaced over the course of a month with new cells born and rising from the base of this layer. The epidermis protects you against invasion by microorganisms and, by deepening pigmentation of the protective material called melanin, against damage by ultraviolet rays from the sun.

The innermost skin layer called the subcutaneous layer, contains fat, which insulates the body and protects the organs within from shock.

The middle layer, called the dermis, contains blood vessels, hair follicles, nerves, specialized sense cells, muscles, sebaceous (oil) glands, and sweat glands. The sweat glands contain water, salt, and waste products collected from the blood and released through pores in the skin or through hair follicles.

Bad circulation, poor nutrition, and an inability of the body to successfully release toxins in the feces or urine can lead to the secretion of toxins through the sweat glands. The skin can also reveal allergic reactions to certain plants, chemicals, medicines, insect bites, or foods, through red, raised bumps that may or may not be filled with fluid and may or may not itch.

SEMEN

The body uses every opportunity to clean house, and so semen, the fluid in which sperm are released, is yet another vehicle to remove bacteria, viruses, and other unwanted material. Toxic semen can affect the health of women exposed through unprotected intercourse. For example, some wives of Gulf War veterans reported persistently abnormal Pap smears until their husbands, who were suffering physical effects from war duty, started using condoms.

MENSTRUAL FLOW

A woman's body uses her menses like the man's body uses semen. It's a handy vehicle to eliminate unwanted by-products of metabolism, dead cells, and other bio-trash.

SIGNS OF TOXIC OVERLOAD

When you lose weight, the material that was being stored inside the fat cell is dumped into the lymph, carried to the bloodstream, biochemically altered in the liver, and either transferred to the kidney to be excreted in the urine or to the small intestine to be excreted from the large intestine in the feces.

When any of these systems are overloaded, a toxic condition results and symptoms appear. These may include itching, skin eruptions, foul-smelling gas and foul-smelling feces, bad breath, joint pain, fatigue, and several dozen other common complaints detailed in the introduction to this book. You can spend your life chasing symptoms, if you focus your attention only on the outcome of toxemia. By clearing up the core cause of the problem, you will cure your complaint permanently.

REFERENCES

1. Christopher Hobbs, *Natural Liver Therapy* (Santa Cruz: Botanica Press, 1995), 1.

2. Deepak Chopra, M.D., *Perfect Digestion* (New York: Harmony Books, 1995), 30.

FOUR

THE DAMAGE: MEASURING LEVELS OF TOXICITY

Truth rests with God alone, and a little bit with me.
—Yiddish saying

Men occasionally stumble over the Truth, but most pick themselves up and hurry off as if nothing had happened.
—Winston Churchill

You've surely read newspaper accounts of men who felt well and then suffered a fatal heart attack while jogging. It's tragic for their families and frightening for the rest of us. How could they not know their bodies were in such a dangerous condition?

According to M. Ted Morter, Jr., a chiropractor in Rogers, Arkansas, " 'Feeling good' and 'being healthy' are not necessarily the same."[1] Morter suggests that perhaps these apparently healthy joggers who die while exercising didn't ask their bodies the right questions.

In *Your Health, Your Choice,* Morter describes a simple test, using a strip of special paper and a sample of your urine, which lets you know if heavy exercise is safe and if you are truly healthy. You will learn to test yourself and analyze your own results in the following sections.

There are several other tests described in this chapter. They will help you learn about your state of well-being. Some are simple and free, and some are more involved and costly.

WHICH TEST IS NECESSARY?

Here are some questions to discuss with your health care provider as the two of you work out which tests are essential to your detox program.

1. What essential information will this test give me that cannot be gathered any other way?
2. How might the results of this test change my detox program?
3. Is it dangerous to my health to plunge ahead and experiment for a few weeks using a detox program of my own design, without this test?

For some people, the easiest tests may be all that are needed. And the easiest tests begin with a special roll of narrow yellow paper that measures pH.

SELF TESTS

1. pH

What is pH?

A change in your body pH is one of the most dramatic reactions caused by food; it influences the level of hydrochloric acid in your stomach, the quality of your heartbeat, the safety of vigorous exercise, the effectiveness of your liver, kidney, and intestines, the strength of your bones, and your body's susceptibility to chronic and life-threatening diseases. It is the one test that Morter recommends for an immediate readout on your state of health.

The term *pH* stands for "potential of hydrogen" and represents a scale of relative acidity and alkalinity of a solution. The scale reads from 0 to 14, with 7 as neutral. Water is neutral. Measurements from 1 to 6.9 are acid. The lower the number, the more acidic the solution. Vinegar is acid. So is the digestive juice in your stomach. Your stomach acid measures anywhere from 1 to 3.5. Measurements from 7.1 to 14 are alkaline. The higher the number, the more alkaline the solution. Bicarbonate of soda (baking soda) is alkaline. Your blood is slightly alkaline, being carefully maintained at a pH of 7.35 to 7.45. The pancreas is even more alkaline, at 8.0 to 8.3.

The pH scale is logarithmic, meaning each number is ten times higher than the preceding number. A pH of 3 is ten times more acidic than a pH of 4, and *one hundred times* more acidic than a pH of 5, so what appears as a minute change, say from 7.3 to 7.4, is actually quite significant and can cause a major shift in how your body functions.

The normal range of pH
Following are some of the normal pH ranges of several parts of the body.[2] Notice that all except the stomach are weakly alkaline. The stomach is quite strongly acid.

---

pH OF VARIOUS BODY SUBSTANCES

Bile as it leaves the liver	7.10–8.50
Bile in the gallbladder	5.50–7.70
Blood	7.35–7.45
Duodenum (large intestine)	4.20–8.20
Feces	4.60–8.40
Pancreatic juice	8.00–8.30
Saliva	6.50–7.50
Spinal fluid	7.30–7.50
Stomach acid	1.00–3.50
Urine	4.80–8.40

Why pH is important
The life of cells, enzymes, and other biological systems within your body depend on a delicate balance of acid and alkaline. Body fluids like to be weakly alkaline. The blood's pH, particularly, must be maintained between 7.35 and 7.45. If for any reason the blood's pH drops below 6.8 or above 7.8, that person has only hours to live.[3]

Because your cells produce acid just in the process of living, you are far more likely to be overly acidic than overly alkaline. In addition, negative thoughts contribute to your acid load. In fact, claims Morter, negative thinking is "the #1 acid producer in your body." However, the acid that is produced from thinking and from the processes of living can be easily detoxified and released via carbon dioxide through the lungs.

What is most problematic is the acid load created by a diet rich in protein foods like meat, dairy, eggs, and grains. These increase the acidity of your body by leaving an acidic residue, called ash, at the end of digestion. This acidic ash needs to be eliminated through the kidneys and bowels after being neutralized by mineral buffers such as calcium, magnesium, potassium, and sodium. These minerals combine with bicarbonate, and biochemically escort acids out of the body.

In *Cleanse and Purify Thyself,*[4] naturopathic physician Richard Anderson of Mt. Shasta, California, lists a number of ways we become deficient in these important minerals, including emotional stress, overeating, infections from bacteria, parasites, yeast, and other microorganisms, metal toxicity (such as mercury in dental fillings), and environmental pollution. Mineral deficiencies mean your body's acid elimination process cannot keep up with the acid production process, the cells' environment stays acid too long, and eventually your body cells malfunction: bones soften and joints hurt, body muscles feel tense and painful, the heart beats irregularly.

Strenuous exercise produces acid. If a jogger has been eating acid-producing foods and then exercises, it is possible to generate more acid during exercise than the body can eliminate, to the point where the body cannot function at all, and it dies. In these extreme cases, it isn't the meal alone or the exercise alone that kills the jogger, but the combination of the two in a body without appropriate alkaline reserves.[5]

How about you? It's time to test your pH and reveal your own alkaline reserves.

Supplies needed to measure pH

1. pen or pencil
2. notebook with lined paper

3. pH paper calibrated in two-tenths increments, registering between 5.5 and 8.0
4. one fresh lemon
5. a 2-day supply of pasta, bread, meat, nuts, corn, fish, rice, and lentils.

Note: Remember that one number on the pH strip is ten times more alkaline than the next lower whole number. That means it is going to take a major shift to show a change from one whole number to the next. Consequently, be sure you have bought paper calibrated in two-tenths increments from 5.5 to 8.0, as this paper will quickly reveal changes due to diet. One source is listed in Resources at the end of this chapter.

How to measure your pH

URINE

Urine contains the residues collected from body cells after twenty-four hours spent digesting and absorbing the nutrients in that day's meals. You may see a difference in your urine pH between one day and the next, depending on your diet. While monitoring your urine pH, take a reading first thing every morning. After sleeping for at least five hours, either catch some of your first morning urine in a cup, or use the flow itself, and dip a small (one- to one-and-a-half-inch) piece of pH paper into the urine. Compare the color of the wet paper with the chart provided in the paper packaging. Record in your notebook.

SALIVA

Your saliva provides another important measurement of pH. It tells you very directly about the environment in which your body cells live. The saliva pH doesn't change as quickly as the urinary pH, so you can measure saliva pH every two or three weeks. Record in your notebook.

If you don't savor sticking a piece of the chemical-soaked strip beneath your tongue, spit into a tablespoon and dip the pH paper in it. If you are healthy, your saliva pH will be at least 6.8 but according to Morter 6.2 is normal for Americans.

Monitoring your pH

Morter suggests the following protocol for collecting the data you need to evaluate your true level of health:

1. Begin by taking a baseline reading of your saliva pH first thing in the morning, after having your usual dinner and bedtime snacks and at least five hours of sleep the night before. Dip a piece of pH paper in your saliva. Write down this reading as "before meal" and date it in your notebook.
2. Take a baseline reading of your urine pH, and note the number and date in a different column in your notebook.
3. About four minutes after you eat breakfast, take another saliva pH reading, and write it down in your notebook as "after meal."
4. Take the lemon test, described in Anderson's book *Cleanse and Purify Thyself.* Anytime after not eating for at least two hours, take a saliva reading. Write it down as "Lemon Test—Before." Squeeze out the juice from half a lemon into a couple ounces of water. Drink it. Wait a couple minutes, then test your saliva again. Record your pH reading in a column titled "Lemon Test—After."
5. For two days, consume acid ash–forming foods only. *No fruits or vegetables.* During this two-day test, drink water only. No juices, alcoholic beverages, sodas, or coffee (if this is too stressful, limit your coffee consumption to one cup a day).
6. After two days of acid-forming foods, take your urine pH reading on the third morning. Write down this reading and date it in your notebook.

Analyzing pH results

What you are investigating is whether your body has adequate mineral reserves to buffer acidity. Mineral reserves keep your body fluids slightly alkaline, where they belong.

URINE

5.5–5.8: After two days of acid ash foods, your urine ought to be 5.5 to 5.8. This is because two days of only acid-producing food should have created a strongly acid ash, so acidic that if not buffered, it might damage your urinary tract. However, buffering minerals are moderately alkaline. The result of a strong acid ash combined with moderately alkaline minerals is still an acid ash, but an acidic ash that is too weak to harm the urinary tract.

6.0–8.0: If you have no alkalinizing mineral reserves available, the body will neutralize the acid ash with ammonia instead. Ammonia is strongly alkaline. The combination of strong acid ash and strong alkaline ammonia results in a urine pH that is highly alkaline. The higher the number, the more alkaline, indicating the more ammonia and the less minerals available to buffer the acid ash. Your pH paper will turn very dark, and your urine will smell like ammonia.

Note: When you are eating a lot of fruits and vegetables, your urine will also register alkaline, and the pH paper will turn dark. This is a healthy sign of a body with adequate mineral reserves. It is only when the alkaline pH follows two days of eating acid-forming foods that it is a sign of deficient minerals.

SALIVA

A healthy saliva is at least 6.2, and ideally 6.8. After eating a meal, you want to see a pH rise. This shows mineral reserves are being used. Even if your saliva is lower than 6.2, if after a meal the pH rises, you have some mineral reserves available, though you had better add more fruits and vegetables to your daily diet to raise your baseline saliva reading so it is more strongly alkaline. Otherwise, since the alkaline saliva begins the digestion of carbohydrates, if your saliva isn't a healthy alkalinity, you are not going to be digesting carbohydrates adequately.

If your saliva pH is the same before and after a meal, you need to replenish your minerals, and it is safer for you not to exercise vigorously until you do.

Morter describes the person whose saliva pH drops after a meal as being influenced by more than diet. This person has allowed his thoughts and emotions to control his well-being. Negative thoughts are, as already mentioned, an important source of acidity, and must be acknowledged and handled to protect you from disease. You cannot be healthy and maintain an attitude of fear, anger, or resentment.

What about the lemon test? If, after the six minute lemon test your pH was above 7, you have some alkaline reserves, with the higher the number the more minerals in the reserves. If your reading was below 7, you may want to handle any emotional stress that might be lowering your pH, get any infections diagnosed and treated, have your hair analyzed for any heavy metal toxicity, and liberally add fruits and vegetables to your daily diet to build up your alkaline reserves.

OTHER FACTORS INFLUENCING pH

Here are some other factors, besides acid foods, heavy metals, stress, and infections, that could be causing an acidic pH:

- Kidney disease or other kidney malfunctions
- Shallow breathing
- High altitude
- Lung damage from smoking or other causes

The connection between pH readings and detox programs

"Any type of cleansing will pull from one's alkaline reserves," writes Anderson, which is why he is adamant that participants in his Arise and Shine detoxification program (see chapter 13 for details) have clear indication, through pH testing, of adequate alkaline reserves before they undertake his protocol.

Eating your way to higher pH scores

Lost minerals can be replaced simply by changing your diet to more fruit and vegetables and less meat, dairy, and grains.

At first, explains Morter, your urine pH will drop even with the added fruits and vegetables. Don't be discouraged. After reaching 5.5, it will rise and you will know by this change that your level of organic sodium has built up enough for the body to use the sodium instead of ammonia to buffer acid ash.

"When you begin eating mostly alkaline ash foods," writes Morter, "you will be *getting better* as your urine pH drops from 7.0 to 6.4 and 5.5. You will be *getting healthy* when you are eating predominantly alkaline foods and your urine pH begins to rise to 6.4 and 7.0."[6]

2. STOOL

Like urine, your stool is another good indicator of your inner health. Take a few moments this week to carefully observe what comes out into the toilet. Use the following checklist to help you understand what you see.

1. Does it float?
   Stool with adequate fiber will float.
2. What is its shape and texture?
   Stool that is healthy will be easy to release, well formed, neither loose nor hard, and leave no residue on your anus.
3. What is its quantity?
   Stool of Africans who eat traditional diets of high-fiber foods is bulkier than the stool of people eating the usual highly refined diets of the Western world.
4. What is its transit time?
   A healthy body passes stool through the small and large intestine slow enough to allow adequate absorption of nutrients and production of B complex vitamins and vitamin K (over 10 hours) and fast enough to prevent constipation, headaches, hemorrhoids, and colon cancer. To test transit time eat beets and note how long it takes until you see red stools.

LAB TESTS

Why test?

From the symptoms you've noted through your self tests, you may suspect that your body is overloaded with poisons and needs a good housecleaning. Is there a way to find out scientifically just how seriously you need to detoxify? Yes! There are laboratory tests to prove to both you and your health care practitioner that a detox program might be a good idea. Some tests check your blood and some check your urine; there are tests that use your saliva, your stool, your muscle strength, and even one that looks for heavy metals in your hair.

Let's pretend

Before you take a closer look at the specialized tests that can reveal a need for detoxification, let's make sure you understand what they are measuring. Here's a brief story, in nontechnical terms, that describes the process of Phase I and Phase II detoxification pathways (which was introduced in chapter 2):

Let's pretend there are loose sticks, plastic pieces of various sizes, and small wheels lying on the floor around the room. You walk across them in bare feet, and not only does that hurt, but you lose your balance and fall. To prevent further injury, you pick up an instruction sheet and follow the steps to use up these loose toy pieces. What you create is a ferocious toy shark with pointed teeth. Many of the toy pieces went into this creation, and now there is less to trip over, but the shark begins to move! Its jaws are strong and its teeth are sharp. Oh, dear! In preventing injury from the toy parts, you have created an even more dangerous assailant. The toy shark chases you around the room. This is like Phase I detox.

Next, you grab more toy parts as you hop and twist across the floor out of jaw's way and, with these parts, you change the shark into a truck. The truck sits quietly without moving, and since, to create the shark and then the truck, you used up the toy parts that were lying loosely on the floor, you can at last walk safely across the room. This is like Phase II detox.

Once again, here's the more technical explanation: When the liver is confronted with a toxin, a group of enzymes known as the *cytochrome P-450 mixed function oxidases* leaps to attention. Different poisons inspire the activity of different members of this enzyme family. The appropriate enzyme rushes to the poison and introduces molecular oxygen into its structure to denature it. This is called oxidation. Unfortunately, this doesn't always denature the poison entirely. All too often, what results from the oxidation is an even more toxic "intermediate," like that shark in my previous example, which must itself be denatured during Phase II. And if the demand for Phase II overwhelms the body's ability to perform the Phase II processes, or the liver is diseased, or inadequate nutrients are available to perform the Phase II properly, the buildup of intermediates can be more harmful to the body than if detox hadn't ever taken place.

Phase II detoxification takes place through the work of enzymes and nutrients using a methodical, orderly process, manipulating the structure of toxic biochemicals step by step along any of six different "pathways." To neutralize a biochemical, the enzymes and nutrients may follow only one pathway, or more than one at a time. The names of the pathways are sulfation, glucuronidation, glutathione conjugation, acetylation, methylation, and glycination.

PRINCIPLES BEHIND TESTING

- Every individual has a genetically programmed ability to detoxify.
- The better the ability to detox, the less the symptoms of allergy, asthma, infections, and drug side effects.
- By supplementing specific nutrients, one can influence Phase I and Phase II detox and make up for genetic deficiencies.
- By checking for allergies and sensitivities, one can avoid those that are avoidable and, by lowering the total toxic load, help the body handle those that are unavoidable.

Principles of testing

One of the basic principles of testing the function of the liver and detox systems is that each person has a unique, genetically created ability to detoxify along the various pathways. You, for example, may have been born with less ability to perform sulfation than your own brother. If you both eat the exact same meals, yours may not provide you enough sulfur-containing foods to fuel your detoxification pathways adequately.

Even more striking than familial variations are the genetic variations between ethnic groups. Jeffrey Bland, Ph.D., a nutritional biochemist, often points out how much easier it is for the Irish to metabolize alcohol than the Chinese, because the Irish have more of the enzyme called aldehyde dehydrogenase. Deficiency of this particular enzyme causes the Chinese to flush and feel drunker sooner than the Irish.

Another tenet of testing is that when deficiencies in function are found, the individual can override these problems using nutritional supplements. For example, vitamins B, C, E, and bioflavonoids improve the activity of cytochrome P-450 enzymes during Phase I detoxification; the antioxidant glutathione and the amino acid cysteine improve the conjugation reactions of Phase II detox.

1. LIVER FUNCTION

Functional Liver Detoxification Profile

Is your liver doing its job of clearing toxic substances from the body? You must find out the answers to three separate questions: Do you have efficient detoxification happening during Phase I? Do you have efficient detoxification happening during Phase II? And can your liver detoxify the by-products of Phase I detox quickly, or is Phase II activity so slow there is a buildup of toxins created by Phase I activity?

The functional liver detoxification profile answers all three questions by challenging the liver with salicylate, acetaminophen, and caffeine, and measuring the organ's response in urine, blood, and saliva.

SALIVA

The Caffeine Challenge Test
Because caffeine activates a number of the cytochrome P-450

enzymes, caffeine can be used to test how well your body's Phase I P-450 enzymes can clear the caffeine from your saliva. The less caffeine found in the saliva, the more efficient your enzymes are at detoxifying.

URINE

The Benzoate Challenge Test

To measure the body's Phase II glycine conjugation pathway, you consume a bit of sodium benzoate (a common food preservative). When the liver's Phase II conjugation reaction occurs, a by-product called hippuric acid is created. The lab measures how much hippuric acid is in your urine. The more hippuric acid they find, the more effective your detox.

If this test reveals you're deficient in your glycine conjugation ability, you can take glycine to boost your reserves.

The Acetaminophen Challenge Test

The painkiller acetaminophen provides another test of Phase II conjugation. Acetaminophen uses three detox pathways. The first and most critical detox pathway begins with oxidation by Phase I cytochrome P-450 enzymes, which creates a very toxic intermediate called NAPQI. If NAPQI isn't detoxified by glutathione in a Phase II conjugation pathway, it destroys liver cells and poisons your nervous system. This is what happens to people who take an overdose of acetaminophen. They take so much of the drug, they use up their glutathione stores, and the NAPQI left over poisons them. When there is adequate glutathione to neutralize the NAPQI, it becomes a harmless biochemical called acetaminophen mercapturate. In addition to the Phase I and glutathione pathway just described, the acetaminophen is detoxified by two Phase II pathways, using sulfation and glucuronidation.

The acetaminophen challenge test measures levels in the urine of the by-products of these three detox pathways.

Is there any significance to you of such a test, if you don't use acetaminophen for pain relief? Yes! This test reveals how well your body performs sulfation, glucuronidation, and glutathione conjugation. Sulfation, particularly, is used to detoxify many different hormones and drugs, including estrogen, thyroid, steroids, and alcohol. What if you are a woman taking estrogen for hormone replacement therapy, and your body proves to have a very limited ability to conjugate toxins by sulfation, thereby limiting its ability to neutralize estrogen? You may have problems from a buildup of estrogen! What if you are a man taking minoxidil to promote hair growth? If you don't want side effects from an overdose of the drug, you need adequate levels of sulfate for Phase II detox. This is measured by the acetaminophen challenge test.

If your test shows you are deficient in sulfate, you can supplement your reserves with sulfur-containing foods, such as garlic, onion, cauliflower, Brussels sprouts, cabbage, and broccoli, and take supplements of magnesium sulfate or sodium sulfate. If you need a boost to improve your glucuronidation conjugation pathway, you can take zinc, pantothenic acid, or glycine supplements. And, if your glutathione levels are low, you can raise glutathione stores by taking lipoic acid, the amino acid cysteine, or the pharmaceutical N-acetylcysteine, and by eating cruciferous vegetables (such as Brussels sprouts, cabbage, cauliflower, and broccoli).

The Aspirin Challenge Test

When aspirin (salicylic acid) is detoxified by the liver, it follows three separate pathways, creating three different byproducts. Most of the aspirin is neutralized by glycination in a Phase II conjugation reaction that creates salicyluric acid as its harmless end product. Some of the aspirin is neutralized by a different Phase II conjugation reaction that creates salicyl glucuronides as the end product. And some of it goes through Phase I P-450 enzyme reactions to produce certain oxidized end products. The amount of these different by-products in your urine reveals how well your body can use the two Phase II detox pathways to detoxify the aspirin.

Porphyria

If you are a woman and your urine becomes dark red when left unflushed in the toilet or your skin blisters when exposed to sunlight, there is a strong likelihood you are suffering from porphyria, an abnormality of the liver's ability to break down red blood cells. See "Porphyria" under tests for chemical exposure on page 46.

Organic Acids
How well are you metabolizing protein, fat, and carbohydrates? Are you having emotional problems because of a B vitamin deficiency? Are your mood swings linked to a neurotransmitter imbalance? Do you have all the liver enzymes you need, and is your bowel doing its important job well enough? Do you have porphyria? These questions are answered in a urine test that measures organic acids.

This test will also reveal the end products of the breakdown of certain volatile organic compounds—chemicals that are found in gas form. Toluene and xylene, for example, are broken down by the liver to methylhippurate and hippurate, so if these compounds are found in the urine, it means you were probably exposed to a strong dose of toluene and xylene. You may be particularly sensitive to these common solvents, and be ill because of exposure, in spite of your urine levels of their metabolites being within what is considered normal range.

BLOOD

Liver enzymes
When special liver enzymes are elevated above normal, the liver may be damaged by toxins. When an enzyme called alkaline phosphatase is high, this, too, may indicate liver cell damage.

Assorted red flags
Other red flags indicating possible liver dysfunction are abnormally low or abnormally high cholesterol, elevated total protein, and elevated glucose. Abnormally high cholesterol, total protein, or glucose may also be signs of problems unrelated to liver dysfunction, and so must be evaluated in the context of your total symptom picture and other laboratory tests.

2. CHEMICAL EXPOSURE

If we lived in the Garden of Eden with organic food and immaculate skies and water, our body would still need to protect us from two distinct categories of assailants. The first is an assault by bacteria, viruses, yeasts, mold, and fungi. The second is the harmful buildup of metabolic waste created by the activity of millions of biochemical reactions and the tearing down, building up, remodeling, and dying of body cells and tissues. Unfortunately, in today's world we have a lot more to deal with than these two categories. Perhaps the major assault on our detoxification system at the end of the twentieth century and beginning of the twenty-first is industrial chemicals.

BLOOD

Hydrocarbon solvent screen
Blood testing can reveal excessive exposure to hydrocarbons, which are chemicals derived from petroleum, gas, or coal. Motor vehicle exhaust and gasoline, gas stoves and furnaces, pesticides, and many consumer products contain hydrocarbons.

Volatile organic compounds
A test for trimellitic anhydrides (TMA) measures some of the most common volatile organic compounds, including benzene, phenol, toluene, and styrene, among others. Doris Rapp, M.D., points out that your levels of antibodies against TMA may remain high for several months after falling ill from exposure to new carpet, roof insulation, or visiting or working in a print shop.[7]

Another blood test, called a general volatile screening test, measures the volatile organic compounds from aromatic chlorinated substances.

Formaldehyde
When formaldehyde, a potential carcinogen, is attacked by oxygen (a process called oxidation), formic acid results. Measuring formic acid levels reveals if you've been a smoker, lived with a smoker, or worked in a smoke-filled environment,

since they are often abnormally high due to inhaled tobacco smoke.

Porphyria
Porphyria involves a deficiency of the enzymes needed by the liver to break down red blood cells. This leads to an excessive buildup of biochemicals called porphyrins in body tissues. Symptoms include abdominal pain, leg cramps, muscle weakness, hypersensitivity to odors, hypersensitivity to sunlight, pigmentation of the face, anemia, and psychiatric problems. It is a disease that occurs mainly in women, and can be misdiagnosed as fibromyalgia or as caused by silicone breast implants.

This disease can be inherited. It can also be caused by psychiatric drugs, infections, crash dieting, and exposure to chemicals and other toxins. It is accurately diagnosed if a twenty-four-hour blood and urine porphyrin level remains elevated. If the disease is inherited, the abnormal enzymes remain stable, while in cases of chemical sensitivity, the level changes according to exposure.

3. IMMUNE FUNCTION

Your liver may be happily detoxifying every chemical in sight, but you still need a healthy immune system to back it up, or you're as fragile as a healthy wingless dove who will be attacked by the first predator to come around.

BLOOD

White blood cell count
A conventional blood panel reveals your total white blood cell count, which can help separate a bacterial infection from a viral one, and an individual suffering from chemical sensitivity from one with a viral infection (a white blood cell count of at least 5,000 suggests a viral infection). White blood cells are your defense team. They include B cells, T cells, and other specialized cells that together identify, attack, destroy, and devour what the body perceives to be its enemies. When these

immune cells are too busy fighting allergens that aren't really dangerous, your defense force is less effective when truly dangerous invaders come along.

B cells

B cells are specialized lymph cells found in lymph nodes, the digestive tract, the spleen, and bone marrow. B cells make antibodies. An antibody is created whenever something enters your body that the immune system identifies as "not you." It may be a virus, a bacterium, a fragment of ragweed pollen or cat dander, a clump of partially digested wheat that is larger than expected, or any of thousands of other "invaders."

One antibody is created for each invader, and once the antibody exists, it can react and attach to the invader more quickly the next time that invader appears. That's why allergic reaction's often worsen over time.

T cells

Having adequate levels of T cells is critical not only to staying well, but to staying alive! There are several kinds of T cells. One kind is called "natural killer cells" and serve as cancer cell finders and eliminators. If your body is overwhelmed with environmental toxins, the natural killer cells may be low in number.

Another kind of T cell is the T suppressor cells, also called T5 cells. These white blood cells are responsible for stopping the B cells from creating antibodies. Industrial chemicals like formaldehyde and pesticides stop T suppressor cells from controlling B cells. When this happens, your body produces too many antibodies when they aren't needed, and you become overly sensitive to your environment, reacting with respiratory disorders, digestive complaints, skin problems, pain in joints or headaches, or any number of other hypersensitivity reactions to plants, animals, or the toxins of twentieth-century life.

People with cancer and AIDS have the opposite problem. They have so many T suppressor cells, they destroy their own defense system. Health, then, is a proper balance of T and B cells.

4. NUTRIENT LEVELS

You can't build a house that lasts if all you have to work with is sand and straw. Whatever you provide for your body as fuel and building materials, in the food you eat and the water you drink, is all your cells have for their creation, development, and repair.

TASTE

One of the easiest of all tests is for zinc status. Zinc is important for proper functioning of sex glands, healthy skin, cardiovascular fitness, stimulation of the immune system, essential fatty acid metabolism, healing of wounds and fractures, proper growth of the body, tooth decay prevention, healthy hair, good appetite, and an excellent sense of taste and smell.

Metagenics, Inc., offers a zinc status assay in the form of liquid zinc sulfate in a base of distilled water (see "Resources" at the end of this chapter). To discover your zinc status, you hold two teaspoons of the solution in your mouth for at least ten seconds. If the liquid can be tasted, you probably don't need zinc. If you cannot taste it, or there is a delayed perception of taste, you probably do need more zinc.

BLOOD

Enzymes
Specific enzymes help specific nutrients fulfill their role in detoxification. By measuring levels of enzymes in the blood, you can find out which nutrients are efficient and which are not.

For example, the enzyme glutathione peroxidase measures the efficiency of selenium during detoxification. The red blood cell enzyme transketolase measures vitamin B_1 (thiamine) and glutathione reductase measures vitamin B_2 (riboflavin). Methylmalonic acid measures vitamin B_{12} levels, 1-N-methyl nicotinamide measures B_3 (niacin), formiminoglutamic acid can reveal a folic acid deficiency, and glutamate pyruvate transaminase, another red blood cell enzyme, can indicate the effectiveness of vitamin B_6 (pyridoxine) in the detox process.

Vitamin B_6 is an interesting anomaly. You may actually test high in B_6, but still have a problem. According to environmental health specialist Sherry Rogers, M.D.[8], an abnormally high level of vitamin B_6 may indicate an inability to convert B_6 into pyridoxal-5-phosphate, an enzyme that allows vitamin B_6 to be used by the body. If so, you will need the pyridoxal-5-phosphate as a supplement rather than B_6. People who are chemically sensitive also need a supplement of pyridoxal-5-phosphate rather than vitamin B_6.

Nutrients

Discovering the status of antioxidants, such as vitamins A, C, and E, and antioxidant helper enzymes is similarly possible by measuring by-products of free radical activity in the blood. In addition, minerals such as magnesium and the full spectrum of B vitamins in the B complex are involved in Phase I and Phase II detoxification pathways, so if they are deficient in the blood, you probably have a decreased ability to adequately detoxify poisons.

Often, health depends not on individual levels, but on the proportion of one nutrient to another. For example, the proportions of zinc to copper and of calcium to magnesium are of critical importance. Also, what appears in the blood may be misleading, as the nutrient may or may not be deficient in the cells and tissues elsewhere in the body. So it's a good idea to read up on the signs of deficiency, and compare your health complaints with symptoms known to be associated with deficiency of the nutrients measuring low in your blood test. If they match, it's likely that the test accurately indicates what you need to correct.

For example, if your blood test suggests you are low in zinc, and you can't taste food well and so are always jazzing up your dishes with spices, salsa, salt, or ketchup, have white spots under your nails, and take a long time to heal from wounds, there's a high likelihood you really do need zinc!

Excellent sources of this information include *Encyclopedia of Nutritional Supplements* by Michael T. Murray, N.D. (Rochlin, CA: Prima Publishing, 1996) and *Antioxidants: Your*

Complete Guide by Carolyn Reuben (Rochlin, CA: Prima Publishing, 1995).

Amino Acids

Blood tests can also provide a complete picture of your amino acid levels. Your emotional state as well as your overall health can be influenced by imbalances in amino acid levels. Amino acids are used in normal brain function and in the process of detoxification. Learning disabilities and behavioral problems in children are sometimes linked to abnormal amino acid profiles.

Amino acids work synergistically with certain vitamins and minerals. After an amino acid assay, a good laboratory should recommend specific other nutrients as part of the therapy for amino acid deficiencies.

See *The Healing Nutrients Within* by Eric R. Braverman, M.D. and others (New Canaan, Conn.: Keats, 1997) for detailed information on amino acids.

URINE

Magnesium

By giving you an oral dose of magnesium, and measuring the output of magnesium in your urine, your health care provider can find out how efficient magnesium is as a participant in the detox process. According to Doris Rapp the magnesium loading test accurately reveals how much magnesium the cells actually need.[9]

If you excrete much of the magnesium given to you, this shows your cells are loaded properly with the mineral and don't need any more. If little or none of the magnesium is found in your urine, your cells are hungry for the nutrient. Low magnesium levels may be related to tics, twitches, and crampy muscles anywhere in the body, heart irregularities and spasms, visual problems, poor appetite, headaches, dizziness, anxiety, and even hyperactive behavior.

5. ADRENAL FUNCTION

The adrenal glands look like a triangular blob of Play-Doh dropped atop each kidney. Hormones secreted into the blood from the inner core of each gland stimulate organs, just as the nervous system does when under stress, readying the body to handle an emergency. When these hormones enter the blood-stream, they increase the body's metabolic rate (how fast and well you process food and burn energy), the pumping action of the heart, and the movement of food through the digestive system. They also increase blood pressure by tightening mus-cles around your blood vessels.

Hormones secreted into the blood from the outer shell of each adrenal gland include cortisol, aldosterone, and andro-gens. Cortisol controls the breakdown of carbohydrates, fats, and protein into usable nutrients. Cortisol also increases sugar in the blood and glucose and amino acids in cells, and reduces the effect of stress on the body. Aldosterone prevents too much sodium from being lost in the urine, and it controls electrolyte balance in the blood (the organic minerals the body uses to help maintain a proper pH). Androgens act similarly to the male sex hormone testosterone in influencing the development of muscles and bones and the growth of body hair.

SALIVA

The Cortisol Measurement Test

Simply swishing a cotton swab under your tongue four sepa-rate times during a twenty-four-hour period, putting each swab in its own small vial, and having a laboratory read the amount of cortisol in the saliva samples reveals the daily high and low of your cortisol.

Normally, cortisol is highest during the morning and lowest at night. If your measurements are either reversed or higher than normal at all hours, your adrenal glands need help. Over-stressed lives create overstressed adrenal glands, and over-stressed adrenal glands lead to many different kinds of physical and emotional complaints.

6. ALLERGIES

About 70 percent of allergies are inherited. The others are a sign that your liver isn't functioning optimally. In either case, your immune system needs help differentiating between friend and foe.

SKIN

Scratch and RAST tests
Anyone with allergies may be familiar with provocation tests in which specific dilutions of toxins are scratched on the surface of the skin or injected under the skin and, if there is a wheal (a red, circular, raised reaction) at the site (indicating antibodies have been created against the substance), the test is positive. However, the same dose is usually injected into everyone. Sometimes people have no reaction, even though they are actually allergic to the substance. They simply need a stronger dilution to cause their body to respond.

A RAST (radioallergosorbent test) measures antibody reactions in the blood, but this test, too, can be falsely negative, because the test looks for an antibody called immunoglobulin E (IgE), which applies to airborne allergens, such as dust, animal dander, mold, and pollen. Unfortunately the vast majority of food allergies involve a different antibody, called immunoblobulin G (IgG). IgG responses are usually delayed, from one hour to three days after exposure to the offending food.

Serial Endpoint Titration (SET)
The SET test searches for the lowest dose of extracts of dust, mold, and pollen that cause you to react. Successively greater doses of a potential allergen are injected under your skin and with each injection the physician waits and observes until a dose is found that makes you react with redness and swelling at the site. A slightly lower dose than the one that caused a reaction is the most your body can tolerate at this time. This is the dose the physician uses in an injection to desensitize you.

Provocation-Neutralization Tests

For chemical and food sensitivities, the provocation-neutralization method involves injection of progressively greater doses of suspected allergens into the upper layers of the skin every ten minutes. If a wheal appears, or if symptoms of discomfort occur, such as asthma, headaches, pain anywhere, congestion, hyperactive behavior, or a change in the patient's voice, thinking ability, legibility of writing, or lung function, the physician knows that this is the provocation dose. If no reaction occurs, a slightly higher dose is injected.

Once the provocation dose is found, fivefold stronger concentrations of the allergy extract are injected every seven to ten minutes, until a certain dose is reached that completely neutralizes the reaction, the skin returns to normal, and all the symptoms of discomfort disappear. This is called the neutralization dose, and it becomes the treatment for the allergic reaction.

The benefit of this kind of testing and treatment is that it involves exact doses appropriate for each individual patient, rather than the single standardized dose administered to all patients that is the conventional approach. In addition, the appropriate dilutions for a number of different allergens can be combined into one injection, or made into drops that are taken under the tongue. This is especially useful for children.

PULSE

About forty-five years ago, an allergist (and former president of the American College of Allergists) named Arthur F. Coca, M.D., published *The Pulse Test*, in which he noted that some people show no obvious reaction to a food except that their heart rate and pulse rate increase.[10] Coca suggested people take their own pulse before eating something and then every thirty minutes after, for at least an hour. If you do this and find at least a fifteen-beat unexplained increase in pulse, you probably have an allergy to something you have just eaten.

MUSCLE STRENGTH

Some practitioners use muscle testing to diagnose sensitivities. It isn't as reliably reproducible, but when done by someone who has a knack for it, results can be useful. Muscle testing is a handy technique to do at home too. It is said that geniuses use only 10 percent of their brain, and the rest of us use even less. That means there is an enormous storehouse of information in our brain biocomputer that is never accessed. Muscle testing is one way to access more information from yourself than is available to your conscious mind.

O Ring
To use muscle testing on yourself, touch the ends of your left little finger and thumb together, like a ring. To become familiar with this system, ask yourself a question with a known answer. For example, if your name if Joan, ask yourself, "Is my name Joan?" See if you can open the ring of fingers by placing the right index finger and thumb into the ring and pushing your index finger against the little finger and right thumb against your left thumb. It should be difficult or impossible to break the ring that you have formed with your left thumb and little finger. Now ask yourself a question with a "no" answer. Ask yourself, "Is my name Herman?" It should be quite easy to break open the ring.

Once you are comfortable using your fingers as biofeedback devices giving you correct "yes" and "no" answers, you can use the method to find out why you are feeling uncomfortable after a meal. Ask, for example, "Is my discomfort from something I ate?" If the answer is a strong ring—i.e., "yes"—ask "Was it the . . . ?" one by one naming each food eaten, until the culprit or culprits are revealed.

If the answer at the beginning was "no"—it wasn't something you ate—then perhaps it was something you inhaled or touched (someone's perfume? a cleaning agent?).

Arm Length
To test yourself another way, you can simply extend your two arms side by side in front of you. Notice if your fingers are lined up evenly; they must extend to the same distance before you can start the test. If they aren't even, shake out your arms,

have someone massage your shoulders, and notice if you are using any product that might be irritating your nervous system (such as hair spray, perfume, or freshly applied deodorant).

Once your fingers are in line, place a suspected item near or on your body and hold up your arms again. If you are sensitive to the item near you, one of your shoulders will twist in a way that places the fingers of the hand on that side noticeably past the fingers on the other hand.

Arm Strength: Arm Outstretched[11]

This test requires two people: one person is the tester and one is being tested. Children aged four and up can be tested, and soon will be testing you. My daughter has been a proficient tester of family members since she was five years old. Any muscle can be used for testing, as long as you can see a difference between the muscle locking in place and releasing.

One muscle often used for testing is the pectoralis major clavicular, which holds the arm up and away from the body. The tester places one hand, usually her left, on the tested's right shoulder to stabilize the person, and the other hand (the right hand, in this case) on the tested's left arm which is raised directly in front of her (the arms can be switched whenever one arm feels tired). The tested has her arm parallel to the floor. (If the tested lies down, her arm will be straight up in the air during the test. In this case, the tester doesn't need to hold on to the tested's shoulder.)

The tester's hand is a couple inches above the tested's wrist, about where a watch is worn. The tester warns the other that she is about to test, by saying, "Ready?" The tested nods, and tightens her arm muscles as the tester presses downward firmly, *without jerking*. It is important for the tester to remember she isn't testing her strength against the tested's strength, but instead she is testing the tested's strength *not* holding something, compared to the arm's strength when the tested *is* holding something.

Without holding anything, the tested should have strong results. The tester should feel that arm lock into place. The tester should press downward *only* to the count of "one thousand, two thousand" and no longer!

Now the tested should take a possible allergen in her right hand, or place it next to her or in her lap. Some of the most common foods that cause allergic reactions include wheat, corn, soy, peanuts, cheese, chocolate, eggs, strawberries, artificial sweeteners, and artificial colors. However, you may also be sensitive to an individual vitamin (i.e., if you have a hard time digesting wheat, you may be sensitive to the B complex. If you have a hard time with orange juice, you may be sensitive to vitamin C).

If the tester and tested are unclear what "strong" and "weak" feel like, the tester should first ask aloud, "What is your sign for sensitive?" and see what happens when testing. Then she should ask, "What is your sign for not sensitive?" and see how different it feels.

The more you practice this technique, the more comfortable you will feel in testing and being tested. Since children cannot reach above an adult's outstretched arm for good leverage, an adult being tested should sit or lie down, and the child should stand to do the testing.

Arm Strength: Arm Against the Side

Sometimes a tested's arm muscles are so strong, the tester cannot feel a difference when pressing downward. In this case test using the latissimus dorsi muscle. The latissimus is a large back muscle that holds the arm against the side.

The tester stands facing the side of the tested and places one palm against the tested's waist or hip. The tested holds her arm against her side, pressing her arm against the tester's hand. The tester slides her other hand between the back of her own hand and the tested's arm, with the tester pressing her palm against the tested's downstretched arm.

The tester asks, "Ready?" and when the tested agrees, the tester simultaneously pushes against the tested's waist or hip with the one hand, while pulling firmly, without jerking, against the tested's arm with the other, trying to pull the downstretched arm away from the tested's hip. (If the tester doesn't push against the tested's body with one hand, the tested will not be stabilized and the pulling action will simply pull the tested off balance). Go through the same procedure to find out whether something held in the tested's hand is an allergen for that person.

7. TOXIC METALS

Not everything natural is good for us! Certain metals have no safe levels in the human body, though the level that actually causes symptoms will vary from individual to individual. Toxic metals include lead, cadmium, mercury, arsenic, aluminum, and nickel. These toxic metals collect in our fat cells and in bone, brain, nerves, glands, and hair. Symptoms of toxicity include muscle weakness, high blood pressure, hyperactive behavior, learning disabilities, fatigue, headaches, painful joints, frequent infections, skin disorders, gastrointestinal complaints, and vision and hearing problems. When aluminum was found in the brains of Alzheimer syndrome victims during autopsy, controversy erupted over the link between aluminum excess and brain function. It still has not been resolved.

HAIR

A small sample of hair from your head or, if you are bald, from your body or pubic area can be tested for the presence of the full spectrum of heavy metals. See the appendix for a laboratory that provides this service.

BLOOD

An FEP (free erythrocyte protoporphyrin) test suggests possible lead poisoning. Since if it is positive it may also indicate zinc deficiency or anemia, you will want to have a blood serum test to confirm a lead overload. Any reading over 10 mcg/dl is considered harmful, and action must be taken. Chelation therapy (see chapter 13) is the recommended treatment for lead poisoning.

8. DIGESTIVE FUNCTION

Do you have leaky gut syndrome? This is one of the common denominators for a wide range of complaints, including allergies, gas, bloating, fatigue, systemic yeast infections, and arthritis. Sherry Rogers, M.D., goes so far as to claim leaky gut as the most common cause of all autoimmune diseases.[12]

Leaky gut refers to a pathological change in the lining of the intestinal tract. The tract, when healthy, is composed of tightly knit cells, an arrangement that allows only a small range of molecular sizes through the wall to the bloodstream.

After taking certain medications, suffering certain infections, being irritated by food allergies, eating a long-standing diet of nutrient-deficient and low-fiber foods, or being fed solid food earlier than six months of age, the cell walls become flaccid and lose their ability to restrict large molecules from entering the bloodstream.

As a result, the immune system is alerted by Kupffer's cells in the liver about the existence of large, unidentified objects floating in the bloodstream. They may be simply overly large molecules of hearty whole wheat bread, but they are the wrong size, according to the body's early warning system; they are thus identified as potentially dangerous invaders, and the alarm sounds. The white blood cells attack, the B cells create antibodies against the invasion, and an allergic or autoimmune reaction may take place.

The result may be arthritis, allergies, autoimmune diseases, or infection. As Jeffrey Bland, Ph.D., and Sara Benum state in *The 20-Day Rejuvenation Diet Program,* "The intestinal tract must be continuously exposed to nutrients of the right type in order to maintain its proper function as a barrier of defense against toxins and bacteria."[13]

URINE

Lactulose and Mannitol Excretion
Lactulose is a large-sized molecule that is similar to sugar. Normally, it isn't easily passed through the small intestine's lining into the bloodstream, to be excreted in the urine. However, if you swallow lactulose and you have a leaky gut, a laboratory will find lactulose in your urine.

Mannitol is another kind of sugar. It is much smaller in size than lactulose, and normally should be easily absorbed into the bloodstream from the small intestine. However, if the usual method for pumping nutrients through the gut lining and into the bloodstream (active transport) doesn't work very well, the level of mannitol passing into the urine will be less than expected. This means your gut lining isn't letting through needed nutrients, and you are probably nutritionally deficient.

In summary, if your lactulose is high and your mannitol level is low, you are probably suffering from an inability to properly absorb into the body the good nutrients you do eat, and exclude the toxins you don't want circulating in your bloodstream.

Grant Born, D.O., of Grand Rapids, Michigan: "My mother was Darla, the girl with the long curls in the 'Our Gang' comedies. She jogged until she was eighty. A few years later she came back from Florida, where they had told her her knee was bone on bone. Her right wrist was also degenerative. She was told she had to have a knee replacement.

"I had her take a test for gut function. We use a sugar, lactulose (not lactose), which is such a huge molecule it is not normally absorbed. We also test for mannitol, which is a heavy sugar that should be absorbed one hundred percent.

"My mother's test showed she had what is called leaky gut. Foreign substances considered poisonous to the body, called xenobiotics, were leaking through to her bloodstream. If you don't get rid of the xenobiotics, they attack the joints.

"I put her on glucosamine sulfate to regrow some of her joint lining, and Ultraclear Sustain [a nutritional powder designed by Jeffrey Bland specifically to treat leaky gut syndrome] for a month. She walked across the Mackinac Bridge in our yearly Labor Day Governor's Walk, as she has done for over twenty-five years. She had been afraid she couldn't do it, but she did it in one hour forty minutes this year. Her wrist is also back to normal."

Note: Glucosamine sulfate is found in the body, helping form ligaments, tendons, synovial fluid, and other body tissues. It is available from numerous nutritional products manufacturers. Ultraclear

Sustain is available from Metagenics in San Clemente, Calif. (800/ 692-9400).

Sulfate to Creatinine Ratio

A low level of sulfate compared to creatinine in your urine reveals the level of oxidative stress you are experiencing. Oxidative stress means there is damage to body cells and tissues by wayward oxygen molecules. These oxidants should be neutralized by enzymes and nutrients called antioxidants, such as vitamins A, C, E, the mineral selenium, and particular herbs, such as ginkgo biloba, milk thistle, and bilberry.

STOOL

Comprehensive Digestive Stool Analysis

Do you have leaky gut syndrome? Poor absorption of nutrients? Parasites? Perhaps you don't have parasites, but you have an unhealthy ratio of harmful bacteria to helpful bacteria. How about an overgrowth of the *Candida albicans* yeast? This test answers these questions and others regarding the cause of chronic digestive complaints.

Finding help

Not every physician is familiar with the spectrum of tests available. Even practitioners of complementary medical specialties, including nurse practitioners, naturopathic doctors, chiropractors, and licensed acupuncturists may not consider themselves experts in this field. Also, not every medical practitioner believes that a patient's symptoms might be caused by toxic exposures. You may have to spend time requesting referrals from people you know and questioning several medical professionals before you find someone who can work with you.

What you want is a medical professional who, if not formally trained in detoxification techniques, is willing to listen with respect and interest to your desire to follow a detoxification program, and who will offer advice based on current scientific research, not on his or her prejudice and knee-jerk negativism. At the very least, be sure the person you choose is interested in learning more, and is licensed in your state to request laboratory tests. The best laboratories have professional staff that can explain to your medical provider the significance of your test results.

In severe cases of environmental illness, you may need to travel to one of the thirty-five hundred medical experts who have taken specialized training with the American Academy of Environmental Medicine (see the appendix for referral information).

So, at this point you should know how toxic you are, and hopefully you're ready to do something about it. Are you going to put one toe in the water, or dive into the deep end? Detoxification can involve anything from simply drinking more water to a complete overhaul of your daily life, with possibly a hundred variations in between.

Don't get too frantic about needing to choose! After all, you don't do an excellent job of cleaning your car and say, "Well, that's that! I'll never have to clean this vehicle again." Detoxification techniques are like different methods of doing an internal cleaning job. You do it when needed, as diligently as needed at that time.

Don't be discouraged! Walk any chosen detox path with reverence, knowing that forward and backward movement is inevitably a part of life. Whatever the skips and bumps in the road, you can begin changing who and what you are at any moment. After all, you are not supposed to be a completed work of art. You are a work in progress.

Now, if you're a stalwart soul who's ready to plunge forward along the detox pathway, the next chapter begins the journey.

RESOURCES

If your local pharmacy cannot provide you with pH paper in two-tenths-inch increments, you can purchase it from MicroEssential Laboratory, 4224 Avenue H, Brooklyn, NY 11210 (718/338-3618; fax 718/692-4491).

To find out if you need more zinc, obtain Zinc Tally from Metagenics, 971 Calle Negocio, San Clemente, CA 92673 (800/692-9400; 714/366-0818).

REFERENCES

1. M. Ted Morter, Jr., *Your Health, Your Choice* (Hollywood, Fla.: Lifetime Books, 1992), xviii.

2. Morter, 55.

3. *Encyclopedia and Dictionary of Medicine, Nursing, and Allied Health*, 4th ed. (Philadelphia: W. B. Saunders, 1987), 952. Also Morter, 132.

4. Richard Anderson, N.D., *Cleanse and Purify Thyself*, rev. ed. II (self-published, 1994), 118. Available from Arise and Shine Herbal Products, P.O. Box 1439, Mt. Shasta, CA 96067 (916/926-8867).

5. Morter, 63.

6. Morter, 103.

7. Doris Rapp, M.D., *Is This Your Child's World?* (New York: Bantam, 1996), 349.

8. Sherry Rogers, M.D., *Tired or Toxic?* (Syracuse, N.Y.: Prestige Publishing, 1990), 176.

9. Rapp, 387.

10. Arthur F. Coca, M.D., *The Pulse Test* (New York: Tor Books, 1996). To order, call 800/221-7945.

11. Devi S. Nambudripad, D.C., L.Ac., R.N., Ph.D., *Say Goodbye to Illness* (Buena Park, Calif.: Delta Publishing, 1993). To order, call 714/523-0800.

12. Sherry Rogers, M.D., *The E.I. Syndrome* (Sarasota, Fla.: SK Publishing, 1995), 547.

13. Jeffrey Bland, Ph.D., with Sara Benum, M.A., *The 20-Day Rejuvenation Diet Program* (New Canaan, Conn.: Keats, 1997), 129.

PART 2

FIRST STEP— SIMPLE, FREE, AND NEARLY FREE DETOX TECHNIQUES

FIVE

CLEANSING FEASTS AND FASTS

Every time we eat we are talking to our genes.
—*Jeffrey Bland, Ph.D.*

A short fast on diluted fruit or vegetable juices gives an ill person a welcome opportunity to eliminate his toxic wastes. If, then, the blood chemistry is altered by the proper selection of food, the person will be restored to health.
—*Henry Bieler, M.D.*

Food, glorious food, sung about, written about, discussed, and experienced with anticipation and gusto by just about everyone. When we don't have enough, getting some is all we can think about. When we've overindulged, we can't imagine ever being hungry again, until the next day dawns and we eagerly await our next meal!

Food is one of the first techniques of detoxification discussed in this book, because it is a technique that is accessible to everyone. If you swallow only non-nourishing "junk food" your stomach feels full and you may even be overweight, but your cells are malnourished and you will suffer any of a variety of physical complaints. You will also have to detoxify from pesticides, food coloring, food additives, and the wrong kind of dietary fat. Thus, nourishing the body means more than putting away three meals a day. The quality of those meals is all important, as explained in this chapter.

In addition, some believe that temporarily abstaining from nourishment may allow the body the luxury of releasing toxins stored in fat cells. Fasting has a time-honored tradition, but how you fast, and for how long, is still debated among health experts. Honor your intuition as you decide whether to use cleansing feasts or fasts.

EATING

Eating satisfies many needs. If asked, most people will agree-that they eat to pass time with friends, to avoid feeling uncomfortable emotions, or to stop the sensation of hunger. It is probably safe to say that missing from just about everyone's list of reasons to eat is "talking to our genes." Yet, according to nutritional biochemist Jeffrey Bland, of Gig Harbor, Washington, every mouthful is a veritable conversation between the "you" who was born into this world, the "you" you are today, and the "you" you may become tomorrow.

Not so long ago, scientists believed your genetic inheritance was determined the moment sperm met egg. Now scientists know that looks, personality, health problems, and the ability to recover from those problems can be intimately influenced by nutritional deficiencies, food sensitivities, and a toxic environment.

In *The 20-Day Rejuvenation Diet Program,* Bland explains this food-to-genes conversation in greater depth.[1] Here's one example: A person inherits genes that interfere with the proper processing of cholesterol. On a low-fat diet, the person might live a long life, but the person in our example consumes a high-fat diet. Before long, the quantity of fat in his diet overwhelms his ability to process it, and his circulatory system clogs with cholesterol, causing an early death from a heart attack.

Another person has a genetic tendency to develop cancerous cells. If that person chooses to live in clean air, away from smokers and industrial pollution, drinks pure water and eats organic produce—or at the very least she supports her body cells with strong daily doses of antioxidants to counteract the weak defense of her own cells against chemical assaults in food, water, and air—she may die of old age. Otherwise, her genes will speak the loudest. The choice is hers.

WHAT YOU EAT

One of the pioneers in recognizing the influence of diet on health was a dentist named Weston Price. During the first third of the twentieth century, he visited and photographed fourteen different native peoples who had not yet been introduced to the Western diet. He found their jaws wide and their teeth well spaced, strong, and healthy. Twenty years later, he revisited some of the same communities, and photographed the extended families who had since been eating foods made with white flour, white sugar, and other standard Western fare. The children's teeth were in need of dental work, and their overall health was noticeably poorer than their parents' had been at their age. The grandchildren had narrow, overcrowded jaws, crooked teeth, cavities, and the poorest health of all, including degenerative diseases and tuberculosis.[2]

During the 1940s, Price met Francis M. Pottenger, Jr., M.D., who had experimented with nine-hundred cats over three cat generations, and found that heated, pasteurized milk and well-cooked meat caused nutritional deficiency diseases and degenerative changes in the cats' skeletons. Most upsetting was the discovery that the nutritional deficiencies of one generation caused increasingly detrimental changes in the health of the following generations, to the point that the third generation was infertile, of fragile health, and often deformed.[3]

The research of Price and Pottenger handily supported each other. They illustrated in humans and animals the sad fact that just about every aspect of us, from our facial structure to our trips to the allergist, are dictated more by what our mothers and grandmothers chose to eat and chose to feed us in infancy and earliest childhood, coupled with what we've done with ourselves since then, than by the chance convergence of genes from Mom and Pop.[4]

Take a look at your own family tree. Do you find some signs of a deficient diet becoming more and more pronounced in each succeeding generation? Look for the following signs:

- fatigue
- thin, splitting, peeling nails
- dry, dull, thin hair
- irritability and emotional unpredictability
- weak ligaments, leading to:
  flat feet
  weak ankles
  hyperextendable wrist, elbow, shoulder, and knee joints
- frequent colds
- frequent accidents due to poor coordination

- slow maturation
- narrow dental arch, leading to:
  impacted teeth
  incorrect bite
  crooked teeth
- crowded sinuses, leading to:
  incomplete drainage, causing sinus and ear infections
- fertility problems
- difficult pregnancies, labor, and deliveries
- birth defects
- soft, spongy bones
- allergies with symptoms present in respiratory tract, gastrointestinal tract, and skin

---

Debi Iannicelli-Ortiz, of Waterbury, Connecticut (who had trouble getting pregnant): "My medical doctor was going to do exploratory surgery and take out my ovary. I had cysts that kept coming and going and coming and going. I had a lot of pain. [My naturopathic doctor] put me on an antiestrogen diet, a detox diet: no meat, no chicken, none of the cabbage and Brussels sprouts vegetables, no dairy, no soda, no caffeine, no sugar, no salt, no alcohol. Just fish, green vegetables, potatoes, brown rice, fruit, and spelt flour bread. Nothing refined. I felt really good when I was on it. After three weeks, the cyst burst. I had a really heavy period. The next month I got pregnant."

WHICH DIET IS BEST?

There is no one best diet for everyone. Every diet book that becomes a best-seller is full of success stories. Yet, you can line up these books on four sides of your desk, one side extolling protein, another carbohydrates, a third advocating eating vegetables raw, and a fourth insisting good meals are cooked meals.

The fact is, they are all the best diet for someone, but maybe not for you. The best diet for you depends on what part of the world your ancestors originated, the nutritional and environmental conditions of your grandparents and parents, your own current life condition, and perhaps your blood type.

My recommendations on eating to detox are based on the work of two men who questioned common wisdom and found exciting answers of their own. The first is M. Ted Morter, Jr., a chiropractor in Rogers, Arkansas, whose book *Your Health, Your Choice* explains the relationship between fruits and vegetables, the acidity of the body, and health.[5] The second is a naturopathic physician in Portsmouth, New Hampshire, named James D'Adamo, whose book *The D'Adamo Diet* reveals the connection between blood type and the best diet and exercise regimen for the individual.[6]

THE IMPORTANCE OF pH

At the end of digestion and assimilation, after many of the nutrients, water, and other useful parts have been removed, there are ashes. In other words, ashes are indigestible metabolic trash. The ashes from meats, nuts, dairy, eggs, and grains are acid, while the ashes from almost all fruits and vegetables (except for cranberries, prunes, and plums) are alkaline. Even lemons and pineapples, which are acidic in the mouth, leave an alkaline ash at the end of the digestive process.

The body is happy about alkaline ash, because in this ash are the organic minerals sodium, calcium, potassium, and magnesium, which the body uses to maintain its alkalinity. It does this by combining a mineral with bicarbonate. This combination neutralizes, or buffers, acid.

In contrast, although there are also minerals left in acid ash, like sulphur and phosphorus, these minerals make the body more acidic.

ACID ASH FOODS

- meat
- fish
- poultry and eggs
- dairy products
- wheat products, including wheat germ, bread, crackers, pasta
- oatmeal
- corn
- rice
- cranberries
- currants
- prunes
- plums
- winter squash
- walnuts
- peanuts and peanut butter
- dried peas
- lentils
- honey
- sunflower seeds
- (white sugar and olive oil acidify the body though they create a neutral ash)

ALKALINE ASH FOODS

- fresh and dried fruits and berries
- vegetables
- dried beans and green soy beans
- goat's milk
- millet
- molasses
- sweet potatoes and white potatoes
- sauerkraut

Printed with permission of Lifetime Books, Your Health, Your Choice *by Dr. M. Ted Morter, Jr., p. 85.*

Organic sodium is the best mineral for alkalinizing the body, and the best sources of organic sodium are fruits and vegetables. The table salt (sodium chloride) that you may liberally sprinkle on your food isn't useful for this purpose. That salt is inorganic, and the bonds between the sodium and chloride are too tight to release the sodium for alkalinizing purposes.

You can easily test yourself for your body's acid/alkaline balance, using a strip of chemical-impregnated paper obtainable at pharmacies and medical supply houses. See chapter 4 for a complete explanation about pH testing.

Maintaining the proper acid/alkaline balance of the blood and body cells is so important, your body will borrow organic sodium from other organs if you need more than you are getting in your diet. However, this can sometimes cause problems. As Morter explains, if your body retrieves organic sodium from the bile while it is being held in the gallbladder, the cholesterol that is also a part of the bile becomes overly concentrated and forms stones. And if the bile becomes acidic instead of alkaline, it is going to arrive in the duodenum (the beginning of the small intestine) as an acid juice, mix with the already acidic material arriving from the stomach, and burn a hole in the unprotected wall of the duodenum. This is why the vast majority of ulcers occur in the duodenum, not the stomach, and why removing your gallbladder may stop the pain of gallstones but won't solve the original problem of a diet deficient in fruits and vegetables.

If you don't have enough organic sodium to keep the body appropriately alkaline, even after borrowing sodium from wherever it could be borrowed, the body will go to the second best buffering agent, which is calcium. As the body uses up its calcium store, osteoporosis develops, or worse. You can't expect your body to use a backup system for long without breaking down. The current epidemic of degenerative diseases isn't just caused by the aging of our population; it's caused by the kind of life that our aging population lives, and the kind of food it doesn't eat! Why else would we now be seeing arthritis, cancer, and atherosclerosis in children?

Morter is not demanding that everyone become a vegetarian, but he does insist that everyone needs fruits and vegetables in their diet, in varying amounts, explaining, ''When you eat *more* vegetables and fruit than acid ash–producing foods, your body can maintain the necessary reserve of usable sodium.''

Of course, in addition to organic sodium, fruits and vegetables contain the known and not-yet-discovered vitamins, minerals, and other substances needed for good health. Recently, for example, research worldwide has proven the importance of vitamins A, C, and E, plus betacarotene and the mineral selenium, to keep us free from heart disease, cancer, cataracts, and other degenerative diseases.

So, what is the right ratio of plant food to animal food for you? That's the question answered by D'Adamo.

THE IMPORTANCE OF BLOOD TYPE

When James D'Adamo, N.D., began his medical practice as a naturopathic physician in the 1950s, he believed everything he had been taught about the best diet, namely, to totally replace meat with grains, beans, and vegetables. He was therefore disconcerted to find many patients feeling ill when they ate this way, although he and his family felt great on this type of diet.

Over years of careful observation and study, D'Adamo developed a theory that defined the ideal diet and exercise program for each individual according to that individual's blood type. In addition to the four main blood types (O, A, B, and AB) he added six subgroups that combine features of the main types (Oa, Ao, Ob, Ba, Bo, and Ab). He explains his theory in *The D'Adamo Diet*. More recently, his son Peter, a naturopathic physician in Greenwich, Connecticut, has expanded upon and provided the scientific basis for the theory in *Eat Right 4 Your Type*.[7]

Following is a summary of the D'Adamos' findings, including a summary of what *not* to eat. (For a complete list of foods that are allowed, see Peter D'Adamo's book. In it he differentiates the allowed foods into those that are neutral and those that really help each blood type feel great.)

Many of the forbidden foods for your blood type at first glance seem odd, such as the whole wheat forbidden to Type Os. In *Eat Right 4 Your Type*, Peter D'Adamo explains that his and his father's categories are influenced by the existence of substances called lectins. Lectins are proteins that act like Super Glue, attaching one thing to another. Lectins on the surface of a germ allow the germ to attach to a slippery wall within your body. Lectins on antibodies help your immune cells chain germs together, to allow for easier removal.

Lectins in foods that are incompatible with your blood type may resemble another blood type, causing your blood to clump in a way that leads to unpleasant consequences. Lectins destroy red and white blood cells, cause irritable bowel syndrome, restrict blood flow in the kidneys, irritate the nervous system, contribute to hyperactivity, and mimic rheumatoid arthritis. For example, Type A blood sees milk as if it were a transfusion of Type B blood! Type O blood reacts to the lectins in wheat, which causes problems with a Type O person's digestive tract and blood.

Peter D'Adamo challenges you to carefully follow the diet designed for your blood type for two weeks, to see what changes may occur in your health. For specific details, see his book.

Type O

Almost three-quarters of the world's population has Type O blood. Peter D'Adamo suggests you think "Old" when you think O, for this blood type hearkens back to the hunter-gatherer days of human life, before dairy foods and domesticated grains. The Type O body is like an engine in idle, needing high-energy food and then needing vigorous exercise to burn off that energy.

Since pork may be contaminated with chemicals and bacteria, conventionally raised beef injected with steroids and chemicals, veal polluted with chemicals and ethically reprehensible because of the inhumane treatment of the calves, and tuna and swordfish contaminated more than other fish with mercury, that leaves most other types of seafood, plus lamb, venison, free-range beef, and poultry as the meats relatively safe and important to eat.

You Type O's who have been told to avoid fat to treat or prevent heart disease: If the D'Adamos are right, the villain on your plate is more the bun than the hamburger! Here is how grains influence Type Os, according to Peter D'Adamo. The lectin in wheat, called wheat germ agglutinin (WGA), mimics insulin by binding to the insulin receptor on fat cells. The body will normally control insulin's enthusiastic removal of carbohydrates from the blood and the creation of fat cells; however, when WGA is on board, there is no feedback control. The WGA-loaded fat cell scavenges carbohydrates in the blood without stopping, turning it all into fat. Thus, eating wheat causes weight gain among people with Type O blood.

You may want to drink soy milk and eat soy cheese, particularly if you are African-American, Asian, or Jewish, as a high rate of lactose intolerance in these populations makes dairy products undigestible for you. If you simply must eat some dairy, choose butter, goat cheese, feta, farmer's cheese, or mozzarella.

SOME FORBIDDEN FOODS FOR BLOOD TYPE O
(FROM *EAT RIGHT 4 YOUR TYPE*)

MEAT: pork

FISH: pickled herring, lox (smoked salmon)

DAIRY: cheese (except feta, goat, mozzarella, and farmer), all other dairy except butter

OILS: corn, peanut, safflower, cottonseed

NUTS/SEEDS: peanuts, cashews, Brazil, pistachios, poppy seeds

BEANS: kidney beans, navy beans, lentils

CEREALS/BREADS: wheat, oats, corn

VEGETABLES: cauliflower, cabbage, red or white potatoes, alfalfa sprouts, mushrooms, mustard greens, eggplant

FRUITS: avocados, blackberries, oranges, olives, tangerines, cantaloupe, honeydew, strawberries

SPICES: cinnamon, nutmeg, pepper, vanilla, any kind of vinegar

CONDIMENTS: ketchup, pickles

BEVERAGES: coffee, distilled liquor, black tea, soda pop

Type A

Type A blood arrived somewhat later than Type O, and after humans began farming (Peter D'Adamo suggests thinking "Agriculture" for A). According to the D'Adamos, scientific studies confirm that people with Type A blood tend to produce less hydrochloric acid than Type Os, and so have more trouble digesting heavy protein meals. In addition, highly acidic foods irritate the stomach of Type As, which means avoiding 100 percent whole wheat products, dairy, and meat. Since most of the D'Adamos had type A blood, their family thrived on a vegetarian diet.

If you're a Type A, D'Adamo recommends you do a slow transition to vegetarianism, and include soy products as staples in your diet ("Type As take note," writes Peter, "the path to your good health is paved with bean curd!"). As a transition, eat sprouted wheat bread at home until you're ready to give up wheat entirely, and order fish instead of steak when dining out. If you must have meat, eat turkey, chicken, or Cornish hens. To start reducing your symptoms of ill health, add one more serving of cooked vegetable and one more raw vegetable in a salad, with one less serving of ice cream and meat over the next few weeks. Don't switch your eating habits in a day. Give your body a chance to get used to the change.

One interesting feature of the ideal Type A diet is D'Adamo's recommendation that you drink coffee (because it increases stomach acid, among other benefits), red wine, and green tea.

SOME FORBIDDEN FOODS FOR BLOOD TYPE A (FROM *EAT RIGHT 4 YOUR TYPE*)

MEAT: best to avoid

FISH: best to avoid

DAIRY: best to avoid including whey (a by-product of cottage cheese, whey is dried and added to crackers and breads to sweeten and thicken dough). If you must have some dairy, eat yogurt, kefir (liquid yogurt), ricotta, moz-

zarella, string cheese, feta, farmer, or goat cheese. No
milk is best, but if you must have some, choose raw
goat's milk.

OILS: corn, safflower, sesame, cottonseed, peanut

NUTS/SEEDS: Brazil, cashews, pistachios

BEANS: garbanzo, kidney, lima, navy, red

CEREALS/BREADS: wheat

VEGETABLES: cabbage, eggplant, mushrooms, peppers, olives, potatoes, tomatoes, yams

FRUITS: oranges, tangerines, cantaloupe, honeydew, mangoes, papayas, bananas, coconut

SPICES: pepper, vinegar, gelatin

CONDIMENTS: ketchup, mayonnaise, Worcestershire sauce

BEVERAGES: beer, distilled liquor, seltzer water, soda pop,
black tea

Type B
Type B blood appeared after Type A, and seems to combine
the best of the older blood types (think "Balance" for B,
writes Peter D'Adamo). Where the Type O needs the intensity
of a meat diet and the Type A needs the easy digestibility of
plant foods, a Type B can eat vegetables, lamb, turkey, and
seafood (but should avoid chicken).

The choice of what to eat may depend on the Type B's
personal history. If allergies and respiratory problems are par-
amount, eliminating dairy is a good idea. If fatigue is the main
problem, more meat protein may be needed.

SOME FORBIDDEN FOODS FOR BLOOD TYPE B
(FROM *EAT RIGHT 4 YOUR TYPE*)

MEAT: pork, chicken

FISH: anchovies, shellfish, smoked salmon, bass

DAIRY: American, blue, and string cheese, ice cream

OILS: canola, corn, peanut, cottonseed, safflower, sesame, sunflower

NUTS/SEEDS: cashews, filberts, pine nuts, pistachios, peanuts; poppy, pumpkin, sesame, and sunflower seeds

BEANS: black, garbanzo, pinto, black-eyed peas, lentils, soy

CEREALS/BREADS: amaranth, barley, buckwheat, corn, kamut, kasha, rye, wheat, couscous, wild rice, artichoke pasta, soba noodles

VEGETABLES: artichoke, Jerusalem artichoke, corn, pumpkin, radishes, tomatoes, mung sprouts

FRUITS: coconut, persimmons, pomegranates, rhubarb, avocados, olives

SPICES: allspice, almond extract, barley malt, cinnamon, tapioca, pepper, gelatin

CONDIMENTS: ketchup

BEVERAGES: distilled liquor, seltzer water, soda pop

Type AB

Only up to 5 percent of the population carries the newest blood type, called AB. Depending on your inheritance you will have a unique combination of the qualities and needs of Type A and Type B blood. In some cases, you have a superiority to both blood types. For example, you can eat tomatoes without health effects, unlike either the Type As or the Type Bs. Like Bs, you can indulge in some dairy and, to a limited extent, some grains. However, like As, you don't produce enough stomach acid to indulge in a lot of meat, and you should particularly avoid smoked and cured meats, which add to your risk of stomach cancer.

You can eat most vegetables, and will do well to add tofu to your weekly menus. Dairy is fine for an AB, unless you find yourself suffering too many respiratory infections or other signs of over-production of mucus.

SOME FORBIDDEN FOODS FOR BLOOD TYPE AB
(FROM *EAT RIGHT 4 YOUR TYPE*)

MEAT: pork, chicken, duck, Cornish hens, beef, veal, venison

FISH: anchovies, flounder, haddock, halibut, pickled herring, smoked salmon, shellfish, all bass

DAIRY: if you have symptoms of excess mucus, avoid dairy products

OILS: corn, sesame, cottonseed, safflower, sunflower

NUTS/SEEDS: filberts; poppy, pumpkin, sesame, and sunflower seeds

BEANS: black, garbanzo, kidney, lima, black-eyed peas

CEREALS/BREADS: kamut, corn, buckwheat, kasha, soba noodles, artichoke pasta (you may have spinach pasta and whole wheat each once a week)

VEGETABLES: artichoke, Jerusalem artichoke, corn, mushrooms, peppers, radishes, mung and radish sprouts

FRUITS: avocados, mangoes, papayas, and other tropical fruits; oranges, olives

SPICES: allspice, almond extract, anise, barley malt, gelatin, tapioca, vinegar, pepper

CONDIMENTS: pickled foods, ketchup, Worcestershire sauce

BEVERAGES: distilled liquor, soda pop, black tea

CHANGING YOUR DIET

THOSE IN DIRE NEED OF SWIFT CHANGE

Although most people will feel healthier if they slowly change their diet in the direction it needs to go (more meat for the Type O, more vegetables for the Type A) there is one type of person who needs to switch right away.

If you have a serious or life-threatening disease, and if the morning after you have eaten a lot of protein your pH is 8.0 (strongly alkaline), you need to raise your alkaline reserves immediately by eating raw fruits and vegetables both whole and juiced. It may takes many weeks for the body to build up its alkaline reserves to a safe level. For more about pH and health, see chapter 4.

A SLOW TRANSITION

If today is the day you are starting to eat healthy, write on your calendar reminders of the week-by-week transition to whole, natural foods, so you can see the progression and not become impatient or discouraged.

Week One: The first few days, make one meal a day of

brown rice and cooked vegetables, and another one a vegetable omelette instead of a Big Mac. After a few days, make sure you have a raw foods salad, at least one fruit, and one more cooked vegetable each day. At each meal, take digestive enzymes to help your body absorb the unfamiliar whole foods. You will find enzymes in health food stores and some drugstores. Betaine hydrochloride at the beginning of a meal helps digest meat and other forms of protein. Pancreatic enzymes taken after a meal help digest bread, sugar, vegetables, and fruit.

Week Two: Continue the eating changes described above.

Week Three: Eat one meal a day that is only fruit and/or cooked vegetables. Begin to reduce the amount of ''health inhibitors'' like coffee, chocolate, colas, salt, cigarettes, and sugar you consume.

Week Four and onward: Slowly continue to reduce the amount of health inhibitors you consume, while increasing the amount of fresh fruits and vegetables. By now, you should be familiar with the food list for your blood type, and be dropping the forbidden items from your weekly menus. I encourage you to look at the D'Adamo book for detailed descriptions of the diet for your blood type.

Having fruit alone for breakfast, according to M. Ted Morter, will shorten the time you need to successfully condition your body to a new eating regimen.

Remember, even though Type Os may need meat on a daily basis, people in this group still need the nutrition and enzymes found in fresh fruits and vegetables. If you are the typical American, you may go days without much more than a lettuce leaf for your vegetable quotient! Even the U.S. government's conservative recommendation is five to nine servings of fruits and vegetables *daily* to help prevent heart disease, cancer, and other common degenerative diseases.

Vegetarians, too, may need to revise their diets, reducing the amount of grains and dairy (which are acid ash–producers and low on the priority list of every blood type).

If you leap into a healthy regimen with both feet the first week, you may feel ill from the metabolic shock to your system! Diarrhea, headaches, fatigue, and irritability are all signs you are changing your diet too fast. Slow down. ''Your objective,'' explains Morter, ''is to be healthy and pain-free as long as you live." Take a good six weeks or longer for this transition, and you will be able to keep your healthy eating plan for life.

WHAT IF YOU FEEL LOUSY EATING WELL?

When you clean house, you use garbage bags large enough to contain your trash and kitchen scraps. If your trash overflows, you have a stinking mess on your hands. Likewise, if you are diligently cleaning your inner landscape and the accumulated toxins overflow the capacity of your skin, lungs, kidneys, and bowel to release them, you are going to be one unhappy, uncomfortable person. The cause is toxic material circulating in your bloodstream. To feel better fast, do the following:

- Drink more water (to dilute the toxins as the body releases them).
- Eat red meat (to slow the cleansing).
- Review your thoughts and beliefs. Negative thoughts produce an acid condition, and poison you from the inside out.

EATING FOR A TOXIC-FREE BODY

In summary, you can modify your inherited health destiny by careful use of dietary technology.

You cannot simply follow the recommendations of the diet book author on your favorite talk show, no matter how many degrees follow his or her name. You have to ask, Is this new diet healthy for me, given my genes, my blood type, my life?

Food is one of your best choices in detoxifying the body, because its action is so immediate. Barry Sears, Ph.D., says it best: "Once food is broken down into its basic components (glucose, amino acids, and fatty acids) and sent into the bloodstream, *it has a more powerful impact on your body—and your health—than any drug your doctor could ever prescribe.*"

FASTING

Stopping consumption of food has a noble history as a healing technique, stretching back at least to biblical days and possibly well beyond. Our ancestors watched animals abstain from eating when ill, noting that increased appetite was a sign an animals had recovered its health.

Yet fasting remains a controversial method of detoxification. Gig Harbor, Washington, nutritional biochemist Jeffrey Bland claims that fasting can, paradoxically, deplete the body's store of nutrients that are essential for detoxification. Since the body is constantly producing dangerous free radicals just in the process of living, and produces even more during detoxification, the body must have a constant supply of antioxidant nutrients for self-protection. If food is denied the body for any period of time, Bland believes the detoxification process is impaired, the liver and immune system may be harmed, and the body may suffer from even more severe effects of toxic exposure than necessary. According to Bland, there is also research linking fasting to increased biological aging.

Other problems associated with fasting are the possibility of water and electrolyte loss, particularly if you cause yourself to sweat from exercise or a sauna and don't replenish your fluids. A severe loss of sodium or potassium can cause an altered heartbeat and other serious consequences. In addition, if your fat cells are contaminated with heavy metals, industrial chemicals, or pesticides, rapid release into the bloodstream during a fast can poison you and cause organ damage.

In contrast, Joel Fuhrman, a medical doctor in Belle Mead, New Jersey, has supervised over a thousand fasts and insists fasting improves abnormal liver function, reduces blood pressure, clears clogged arteries, eliminates asthma, and can put autoimmune diseases such as lupus into remission. Fuhrman carefully describes how to safely fast in *Fasting and Eating for Health: A Medical Doctor's Program for Conquering Disease* (St. Martin's Press, 1998).

Intelligent fasting does not necessitate giving up either electrolytes or antioxidants. A quite satisfying method of fasting is the consumption of nutrient-rich fruit and vegetable juices instead of plain water.

Avoiding solid foods gives the body organs a break. The usual loading of the intestines with acidic foods—such as dairy, meat, and eggs—ceases, and the intestines have a chance to normalize the body's acid-alkaline balance. The body also has a chance to get rid of old, damaged cells and break down and eliminate undesired substances that were being stored until just such an opportunity. For example, during my twenty-one-day juice fast, a long-standing lump disappeared from the lymph gland underneath one arm.

During a fast, the liver also has a chance to rest. When the liver is overworked filtering toxins in the blood, it cannot create and shunt adequate and appropriate bile to the gallbladder. Fat-soluble nutrients, such as vitamins A, D, E, and K, may not be properly assimilated, which can cause problems with circulation, eyes, bones, and skin.

In *Enzyme Nutrition,* Dr. Edward Howell suggests that during a fast the body becomes amenable to the action of enzymes, which can remove excess calcium where it is no longer needed, such as in cases of arthritis and arteriosclerosis, although, warns the doctor, "one cannot stay on a fast long enough to effect a 'cure' in deforming arthritis."[8] He does note that the obvious benefits of a fast include a drop in blood pressure and improvement in lung conditions.

As for aging, in contrast to Bland's position, there is significant scientific evidence linking regular fasting with extended lifespan, at least in fish and rodents. In one experiment, mice who were fasted every third day lived 40 percent longer than mice given unlimited access to food. Among the most delightful sources of information on this topic are the works of UCLA gerontologist Roy Walford, M.D., Ph.D., who writes with great wit and eclectic wisdom in *Maximum Lifespan* and *The 120 Year Diet.*

Fasting was a favorite healing technique of Dr. Herbert M. Shelton, who, in 1928, founded the Natural Hygiene Health School in San Antonio, Texas. The philosophy of Natural Hygiene is based on a diet of fresh fruits and vegetables, whole grains, and clean water, and it emphasizes the healing powers of nature. During his long life (1895–1985), Shelton authored over forty books and spread what was at the turn of the century the nearly heretical idea that fresh air, bathing, exercise, and diet were all inextricably linked to health.

Today, there are nearly a dozen Natural Hygiene Health Spas where clients can detoxify under the supervision of experienced personnel. Each spa offers individualized fasting programs, juice diets, and other Natural Hygiene–based methods of detoxification. In Santa Barbara, California, Dr. Philip C. Royal directs Hygiea-West Health Spa's fasting program. The program's literature claims, "There is no easier way to make the transition to a more healthful lifestyle than by fasting." However, Royal and other experts caution the eager new faster that no one should fast more than three consecutive days without professional advice and supervision.

The classic Natural Hygiene fast uses only distilled water. During the weeks before and after the fast, the diet is restricted to fruits, vegetables, nuts, seeds, potatoes, dressings, and whole-grain breads and pastries. After studying the Natural Hygiene philosophy, Dean D. Kimmel wrote *6 Weeks to a Toxic-Free Body*, in which he emphasizes the importance of eating oranges, grapefruit, tomatoes, grapes, and apples to eliminate stored toxins during these important weeks.[9]

Nutritionist Willa Vae Bowles claims water may do a good job of cleaning out the body, but it is juiced fruits and vegetables that provide the body with vitamins, minerals, chlorophyll, enzymes, and trace elements that can rebuild and repair. According to Bowles, analysis of blood before and after a fast reveals increased red blood cells and other parameters of improved blood quality. "If the fast is long enough," writes Bowles, "toxins are eliminated, the skin clears, eyes brighten, heart rate is reduced, wounds are healed and all body tissues are rejuvenated."[10]

BEFORE YOU BEGIN ANY FAST

As you consider the possibility of fasting for detoxification, remember that you don't have to make it an all-or-nothing proposition. After checking with a health professional to rule out any personal health conditions that might veto a fast, you might choose to fast one meal a day, or one day a week. You can fast with water alone, fruit juices alone (though this isn't recommended for extended periods of time), vegetable juices alone, fruit and vegetable juices, or one single food for a full day, such as only melons or grapes one day, or only salad, or only soft cooked rice. Such partial fasts are a good way to introduce the method if you've never fasted before, and want to see how it works for you.

WHAT TO EXPECT

The benefits of fasting occur thanks to the body's ability to use stored reserves when external sources of energy are not forthcoming. The reserves least important to the continuation of life are used first, meaning body fat. An obese individual may have up to 65 percent of body weight as fat. If the fast lasts so long that the fat tissue is used up, the body proceeds to use muscle tissue for energy. If the fast isn't halted in time, starvation occurs and the body cannibalizes its own vital organs, leading to death.

A healthy fast, then, is long enough to offer rest for overworked kidneys, intestines, and liver, without lasting so long that organ function is impaired. Even a healthy fast may involve some unpleasant symptoms, however, including weakness, nausea, headaches, bad breath, offensive body odor, foul-smelling urine or stool, skin eruptions, erratic pulse, tiredness, abnormally high or low temperature, and loss of sexual desire. All of these symptoms are caused by the release of toxins into the bloodstream from their storage sites in body fat, as the fat is metabolized for energy.

It isn't all bad, as you may also experience a feeling of euphoria, improved ability to think clearly, improved ability to perform on tests, and weight loss.

Don't expect that in a three-day fast you will be able to rid your body cells of all the toxins they have been storing for decades. You may need to repeat a short fast a number of times over a couple of years, or undergo an extensive fast with careful medical supervision in order to achieve your personal health goals. Nevertheless, there is benefit to resting the organs, eating lightly and healthily, drinking much more water than you are probably drinking now, and taking a day or two to focus on your body with an intensity of purpose and a commitment to your well-being. The emotional, and even spiritual, benefits of fasting may surprise you.

WHO SHOULD NOT FAST

How long you fast—and how many fasts you undertake in any span of time—depends on how toxic and how sick you are.

Do not fast if you are quite thin, are in frail health, are malnourished, are pregnant or nursing, or have cancer, tuberculosis, severe heart disease, kidney disease, collagen disease, or advanced diabetes.

Do not use an all-fruit or fruit juice fast if you are hypoglycemic (low blood sugar) or have any degree of diabetes.

Do not fast if you plan to end your fast with a pizza party (I know, because I did it when I was young and foolish—and were my intestines unhappy!). Coming off a fast is a part of the whole process, and you need to make it a slow transition, hopefully to an improved daily diet.

Do not fast when you or someone else in your household has deadlines or is involved in an emotionally draining experience of any kind.

Do not fast in the heart of winter, when staying warm and dry will be difficult.

Do not fast until you have discussed your plans with a health practitioner who has supervised fasts undertaken by others, to make sure fasting will be safe for you.

PREPARING FOR A FAST

Plan to fast during a stress-free time. Be sure you can relax and focus on yourself.

For three to five days before your fast, eat lightly and emphasize fruits and vegetables in your daily diet. Eliminate heavy protein foods such as meat, fish, and dairy.

The purpose of this fast is to cleanse your body cells, so abstain from caffeinated beverages, smoking, stimulants, or other nonessential drugs.

DURING THE FAST

Avoid vigorous exercise and sweating. Sweating in a sauna or steam bath during a fast is acceptable, but only under supervision of an expert, and only if you can do so without taxing your energy reserves in any severe way. Profuse sweating can seriously affect your electrolyte balance and cause heart irregularities, as well as reduce water-soluble vitamins such as the B complex and vitamin C.

Since it is the introduction of food that stimulates the contractions of the colon to eliminate bowel movements, constipation is a normal consequence during a fast. To prevent the body from reabsorbing toxins from the bowel into the bloodstream, enemas are an essential component of a fast lasting longer than three days; some experts recommend it for shorter fasts as well.

Help yourself through the detoxification process by dry brushing your skin and by getting massaged. Vigorous massage will move lymph, the body's garbage disposal system, more efficiently through the lymph drainage system and into the intestines, from which point the lymph and all the toxins it has accumulated are flushed out of the body. Be sure the massage of arms and legs is *toward* the heart. This protects the one-way valves in veins from being damaged.

If your fast includes organic vegetable juices, you may be consuming adequate vitamins and minerals to protect you against the ravages of free radicals. If there is any doubt, you can avoid the problem by taking supplemental nutrients during your fast.

AFTER THE FAST

As mentioned before, breaking your fast ought to be intelligently orchestrated. The body is vulnerable at this time. Your stomach has shrunk and your intestines and digestive enzymes have been on vacation. They certainly can't handle a heavy load of greasy grains, cheese, and meat.

Choose something light, like vegetable soup. Eat slowly, chewing well, to allow digestive juices a chance to jump into action.

Meal by meal, day by day, move up to cooked vegetables, fruit slices, and then yogurt, before progressing to more complex meals of mixed foods.

Come off a fast according to how many days you were on

the fast itself. For example, after a three-day fast take three days to return to your ordinary meal schedule.

MAKING NORMAL SPECIAL

Returning to a "normal" diet ought not be a return to fast food and thoughtless consumption of processed, dyed, greasy pseudofood that Westerners call meals. These meals may be usual, but they are not normal. Now that you have experienced the heightened awareness that comes with fasting, each day's menu is a chance to nourish those freshly cleaned cells in a way that makes mealtime special.

When possible, buy organic produce. As one convert to health food said, "The only side effect of organic food is you are healthy." If you can't find it locally, you can order it from suppliers listed under "Resources" at the end of this chapter.

Include a raw salad each day, mixing a variety of vegetables and lettuces (excluding iceberg, which is practically devoid of nutrition and a waste of space on your plate). Check out the vegetables you've never experienced, to add variety of taste and nutrients to your weekly menus.

Reserve one day every so often for juices only, to once again give your intestines a chance to rest and regenerate.

RECIPES FOR A NOURISHING JUICE FAST

Bieler Broth: Dr. Henry G. Bieler was a physician in Capistrano Beach, California, who believed food was the very best medicine. In fact, he described his fifty years of culinary therapies in a paperback book titled *Food Is Your Best Medicine.*[11] His famous recipe for Bieler Broth was a favorite remedy of health-conscious Hollywood stars like actress Gloria Swanson. The broth alkalinizes an overly acidic body. In a large pot of water, cook 1 pound each of green beans, celery, and zucchini until tender. Add 1 bunch of parsley, and cook about three more minutes. Put the cooking water and cooked vegetables through a blender. Drink about 6 ounces of the broth every hour during your fast.

Garden Delight: Mix a glass of carrot juice, a dash of beet juice, a dash of cucumber juice, and even less parsley juice. Drink 5 ounces for each meal.

Garden Delight Plus: Juice 1 cucumber, 1 green pepper, 1 tomato, 2 carrots, 4 celery stalks, and a few sprigs of parsley or spinach.

Citrus Dream: Blend ½ cup each orange juice, pineapple juice, and apple juice with 5 strawberries, 1 frozen banana, 5 slices frozen papaya.

Morning Charge: Add 1 cup of any juiced green vegetable to ½ cup apple juice.

Celery Soup: Blend ¼ cup celery juice, ¾ cup fennel juice, ½ avocado, ⅛ teaspoon lime juice.

Carrot Soup: Blend 3 cups carrot juice, 2 teaspoons cumin, 1 avocado.

CCP: Juice 3 celery stalks, 2 cucumbers, 1 green pepper.

V-10: Juice 1 cucumber, 1 tomato, 1 shallot, 1 celery stalk, 1 green pepper, 2 carrots, 2 parsley sprigs, 2 spinach leaves, 1 small beet, 1 cabbage spear. Add pinch of cayenne for spicy taste.

Except for Bieler Broth, the above recipes are adapted from Michael Blair Schleyer's great raw foods cookbook, The High Integrity Diet: Gourmet Vegetarian Delights Made from Raw and Sprouted Foods *(self-published, 1987); it has 300 recipes. For your own copy, send $27 (includes tax, postage, and handling) to Greensland Publishing, P.O. Box 254531, Sacramento, CA 95825-4531.*

RESOURCES

For organic food:

In the mail-order section of *The Safe Shopper's Bible* (New York: Macmillan, 1995), authors David Steinman and Samuel S. Epstein, M.D., list sixty-two sources in twenty-four states for organic vegetables, fruits, grains, honey, wines, baby food, dairy products, eggs, and meat. Most sell nationwide by mail. Here are just a few of them:

Blooming Prairie Warehouse, 2340 Heinze Road, Iowa City, IA 52240 (319/337-6448). Organic produce for a nine-state Midwestern area.

Ecology Sound Farm, 42126 Road 168, Orosi, CA 93647 (209/528-3816). Organic fruits.

Organic Foods Express, 11003 Emack Road, Beltsville, MD 20705 (301/816-4944). Organic produce.

Walnut Acres, Penns Creek, PA 17862 (800/433-3998 or 717/837-0601). Organically farmed produce, nuts, grains and products since 1946!

Benson Natural, Second and State, Osmond, NE 68765 (402/748-3309). Organic beef and pork.

Garden Spot Distributors, Box 729A, New Holland, PA 17557 (717/354-4936). Organic meat and poultry products, including luncheon meats, hot dogs.

Canadian Organic Growers, P.O. Box 6408 J, Ottawa, Ontario, Canada K2A 3Y6 (416/253-5885). Sells a directory of organic food sources in Canada.

For general information on a healthy diet:

"The New Green Diet: How to Shop for the Earth, Cook for Your Health, and Bring Pleasure Back to Your Kitchen," a delightful brochure with recipes by famous chefs and advice by Mothers and Others for a Livable Planet, 40 West 20th Street, New York, NY 10011 (212/242-0010).

Mothers and Others is a nonprofit advocacy organization dedicated to providing practical solutions to environmental problems by promoting ecologically sound consumer behavior. They have designed the Shoppers' Campaign for Better Food Choices to help consumers demand better quality food, less pesticides, and more safe, affordable food choices.

The brochure is free. Their *Green Guide for Everyday Life* newsletter, published fifteen times a year, is $20.

For more information about the D'Adamo diet:

James D'Adamo, N.D., 44-46 Bridge Street, Portsmouth, NH 03801.

Peter D'Adamo, N.D., 56 Lafayette Place C, Greenwich, CT 06830 (203/661-7375), or P.O. Box 2106, Norwalk, CT 06852-2106, or on the Internet at http://www.dadamo.com. Contact him for audiotapes, a home blood testing kit, and other information.

Roy Walford, M.D., Ph.D., *Maximum Lifespan* (New York: Norton & Co., 1983) and *The 120 Year Diet* (New York: Pocket Books, 1991).

For information on fasting:

American Natural Hygiene Society, P.O. Box 30630, Tampa, FL 30630 (813/855-6607; fax 813/855-8052; Internet http://www.anhs.org; e-mail anhs@anhs.org). Contact the society for its catalog of audio- and videocassettes and books. Membership ($25) includes subscription to *Health Science* magazine and discounts on seminars and purchases from the catalog.

Books:

Paavo Airola, N.D., Ph.D., *How to Keep Slim, Healthy and Young with Juice Fasting* (Sherwood, Ore.: Health Plus, 1971).

Airola was a prolific writer and lecturer about natural healing. This short book gives successful stories of how juice fasting helped a variety of conditions, how to do it without ending up wrinkled and baggy, and why bowel cleansing is an important part of any long fast.

John Heinerman, *Heinerman's Encyclopedia of Healing Juices* (West Nyack, N.Y.: Parker Publishing, 1994). "The reader of this book will be surprised and impressed by how so many lowly fruits and vegetables can be so helpful to the ailing," writes Lendon H. Smith, M.D., in the introduction. In it you'll learn how to choose produce, and how and why to use eighty-three different juices for healing purposes, including numerous personal stories of healing with juices. Heinerman is a medical anthropologist who has written over three dozen books, including *The Science of Herbal Medicine*.

Paul C. Bragg, N.D., Ph.D., and Patricia Bragg, N.D., Ph.D., *The Miracle of Fasting* (Santa Barbara, Calif.: Health Science, 1996). Paul Bragg was one of the most popular natural health advocates early in the Back to Nature movement. He ate two meals a day, without snacking, and he fasted one day each week, as well as seven to ten days three or four times a year. This book is for people who can overlook the small type and jarring layout in order to appreciate its wealth of golden information.

Dean D. Kimmel, *6 Weeks to a Toxic-Free Body* (Brooklyn, N.Y.: Corbin House, 1992). Kimmel describes the Natural Hygiene philosophy of healing, which is basically vegetarian, with intermittent fasting on distilled water and juices. This small paperback is for someone who seeks a guide that is succinct and well organized.

Richard Anderson, N.D., N.M.D., *Cleanse and Purify Thyself* (self-published, 1994). Anderson created the Clean-Me-Out Program, which incorporates fasting, taking your urine pH daily, and consuming specific herbal and nutritional supplements to move the bowels and detoxify. If you don't find the book, you can order it and his products from Richard Anderson, N.D., Arise and Shine Herbal Products, P.O. Box 1439, Mount Shasta, CA 96067 (916/926-0891).

Equipment:

Since 1921, Vita-Mix Corporation has been manufacturing a high-quality juicer that does lots more than just tear apart produce. We use ours a couple times a week to grind whole wheat berries into fresh flour for our bread-machine baking. On cold evenings we've made soup right in the Vita-Mix, adding the ingredients and letting the whirling blades create enough friction as it cuts up the veggies that it heats our meal. And many warm mornings I throw in a frozen banana, frozen strawberries, Rice Dream (an unsweetened, naturally sweet, nondairy "milk" made from brown rice), and liquid minerals or powdered nutrients for a power-packed smoothie when my daughter announces she doesn't feel like eating a big breakfast.

Buying a Vita-Mix is a major investment. They retail for about $550. You can buy one from the company, or at state fairs or home shows. You can get a better deal if someone you know (or you) wants to become a distributor. Otherwise you may have to forgo a vacation this year, in exchange for having the Vita-Mix in your family forever.

Vita-Mix Corporation, 8615 Usher Road, Cleveland, OH 44138 (800/848-2649).

Another beloved kitchen appliance is my trusty Champion juicer. I bought mine used for $50, twenty-one years ago. They retail for $215 in Sacramento but prices vary across the country. You can often find used Champions for sale on natural food store bulletin boards, at garage sales, or in newspaper ads. Not only does it juice with or without pulp, but it is incredibly simple to clean.

Plastaket Manufacturing Company, 6220 East Highway 12, Lodi, CA 95240 (209/369-2154; fax 209/369-7455).

REFERENCES

1. Jeffrey Bland, Ph.D. with Sara Benum, *The 20-Day Rejuvenation Diet Program* (New Canaan, Conn.: Keats, 1997), 17.

2. Weston Price, *Nutrition and Physical Degeneration* (La Mesa, Calif.: Price-Pottenger Nutrition Foundation, 1939; reprinted in 1970).

3. Francis M. Pottenger, Jr., M.D., *Pottenger's Cats: A Study in Nutrition* (La Mesa, Calif.: Price-Pottenger Nutrition Foundation, 1983).

4. The works of Weston Price, D.D.S., and Francis M. Pottenger, M.D., are disseminated through a nonprofit organization called the Price-Pottenger Nutrition Foundation, 2667 Camino del Rio South, #109, San Diego, CA 92108-3767 (619/574-7763). Send a legal-size SASE with 55¢ postage for information on the foundation.

5. M. Ted Morter, Jr., *Your Health, Your Choice* (Hollywood, Fla.: Lifetime Books, 1992).

6. James D'Adamo, N.D., *The D'Adamo Diet* (Toronto: McGraw-Hill Ryerson, 1989).

7. Peter J. D'Adamo, N.D., *Eat Right 4 Your Type* (New York: G. P. Putnam's Sons, 1996).

8. Dr. Edward Howell, *Enzyme Nutrition* (Wayne, N.J.: Avery Publishing Group, 1985), 134.

9. Dean D. Kimmel, *6 Weeks to a Toxic-Free Body* (Brooklyn, N.Y.: Corbin House, 1992).

10. Willa Vae Bowles, "How to Purify Your Bloodstream," *Total Health* (February 1987): 35.

11. Henry G. Bieler, M.D., *Food Is Your Best Medicine* (New York: Random House, 1965).

SIX

TOUCH

The human significance of touching is considerably more profound than has hitherto been undestood.

—Ashley Montagu
Touching: The Human Significance of the Skin

Touch is one of the least recognized factors in health. Yet, since the 1940s, researchers have proven that in humans as well as in animals the sense of touch is one of the most important factors in proper growth, development, and sociability, and a lack of enough touching during infancy and youth leads to physical and mental disorders.

In this chapter, you will learn how to capitalize on touch as a form of diagnosis and healing. You will take off your shoes and socks, explore the hills and furrows of your own anatomy, and test your muscle strength in your search for detoxification through the magic of touch. Be aware as you search for just the right spot on the soles of the feet or elsewhere along the body surface, that being precise isn't as important as touching with a loving intention.

REFLEXOLOGY

Steady, even pressure on the feet can influence all the major body systems. This is the basis for the technique of healing called reflexology.

According to Laura Norman, author of *Feet First,* ancient people in Asia, the Middle East, and Eastern Europe worked on the feet to help the body heal.[1] They recognized areas on the soles, sides, and tops of the feet that reflected the status of both individual body organs and whole systems. They found that pressure on those areas reflexively stimulated the body to heal those corresponding body parts.

During the 1930s, a physiotherapist named Eunice Ingham was able to use the ancient art of foot massage to treat patients for a wide variety of ailments. She organized the information into a coherent system and taught it to others through charts and books, such as *Stories the Feet Can Tell* (Ingham Publishing, 1984). One of Ingham's students, Mildred Carter, furthered public education with books on foot and hand reflexology (see "Resources" at the end of this chapter). Laura Norman began her work training in the Original Ingham Method over twenty years ago, and in the intervening years she has developed her own training program at the Laura Norman Reflexology Center in New York City.

More than seven thousand nerves are stimulated by touching the feet, Norman contends, and an educated touch can deepen relaxation to the point that all systems, including the liver, kidneys, lymph, skin, and colon, function more efficiently. As a result, Norman lists reflexology's benefits as providing an ongoing sense of pleasure, relaxation, elimination of stress, increased mental alertness, better circulation of blood, more tempered emotional responses, and a rebalancing of the body's biochemistry and metabolism.

"Gravity," writes Norman, "pulls toxins downward. Inorganic waste materials such as uric acid and calcium crystals can build up in the bottoms of the feet." According to Norman, such deposits can be felt and broken up by finger pressure.

Reflexology is based on ten energy zones running the length of the body from head to toe, five on each side. These zones are three-dimensional fields that extend beyond the skin. Thus, working on any one zone on the foot can influence the function of any organ, gland, or tissue within that particular zone.

Why? How? That isn't clear. It may be partly due to enhancing relaxation, which helps the body function better on all levels, or to energy transmission. In the section on acupressure, later in this chapter, I describe the body's energy zones as an electrical circuit. Perhaps, as some researchers postulate, there is a primitive wireless communication system (our body's cellular phone system) in addition to transmission along nerves.

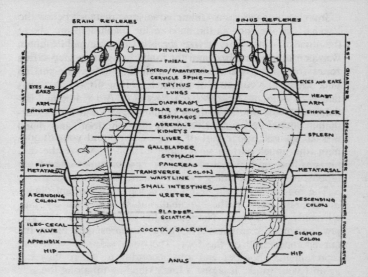

For now, practical results are what motivate those who press and those who are pressed to continue reflexology treatments.

FINDING REFLEXOLOGY ZONES

If you massage the entire foot—the toes, the sole, the top of the foot, and around the ankle—you can give your whole body a reflexive treatment. If you are interested in honing in on specific areas, imagine an outline of your trunk superimposed against the bottoms of your feet.

Imagine a line across your foot at the level of the highest point of your arch. This is like your waist. Run your thumb up the center of your foot from your heel toward your toe; where it stops, caught at the lower border of the ball of the foot, is the solar plexus. This is the apex of a bowed line that represents the diaphragm. Another way to find it is to squeeze the foot, and see where a hollow appears at the lower border of the ball of the foot.

Imagine a space approximately the same distance below the "waist" on the foot as the ends of the diaphragm are above the "waist" line. This is like the level of your public bone. Between the lowest line and the waist line are located reflex zones for your lower abdomen, including the lower part of your kidneys, your small intestines, colon, ureters, bladder, ileocecal valve, and appendix. Between the waist line and the diaphragm line are located the reflex areas for your upper abdomen, including liver, gallbladder, stomach, pancreas, spleen, adrenal glands, upper part of your kidneys, and your duodenum (the upper part of your large intestine). Above the diaphragm line, on the ball of the foot, is your upper chest from nipples to neck, including lymph system, lungs, and heart.

The big toe holds the reflex areas for the important glands in the brain, such as the hypothalamus, pineal, pituitary, parathyroids, and thyroid. The rest of the toes help treat eye, ear, jaw, and neck problems. The spine is represented along the curved inner side of the foot. The outer sides of your feet represent the shoulder and arm according to where they fall against your trunk: Imagine a line extending up along the side from the lines along the sole you've identified previously. From the base of the toes to the diaphragm line is your shoulder and upper arm. From the diaphragm line to your waist line is your elbow, lower arm, wrist, and hand. From the fifth metatarsal (the bone sticking out along the outer edge of your foot at approximately the waist line) to the heel line includes the hip, knee, and leg.

Your sex organs are represented around your inner and outer ankles. Around the outer ankle are the ovary and testicle reflex areas. Around the inner ankle are the reflex zones for the uterus, prostate, vagina, penis, and bladder. A particularly useful area for treatment of the prostate or uterus is pressure starting from a point located twice the width of your four fingers above the inner ankle down to below the ankle.

The fallopian tubes, vas deferens, seminal vesicles, and lymphatic nodes in your groin are represented atop your foot, in a narrow ribbon from below one ankle extending across the foot to the other side of the ankle on that foot. Also atop your foot, between the first and second toes, is the area representing lymph nodes in your neck and chest. Between your fourth and fifth toes where they attach to the foot is the area representing the lymph nodes under your arms. In three separate locations on the foot's upper surface to each side and directly in front where the leg attaches to the foot, are the areas representing lymph drainage for the groin.

Lymph is an important part of your waste removal system. Lymph removes unusable proteins, dead cells, viruses and bacteria, and excess fluids that have been excreted from cells or that exists between cells, moves them into holding tanks called lymph nodes, and drains this cellular refuse into the large intestine to be eliminated in the feces. Therefore, massage of the lymph drainage reflex zones are particularly important parts of any detoxification program.

The breasts' reflex area is also on the upper surface of the foot, in the area between the second, third, fourth, and fifth toes. Right at the junction of the first and second toes and the foot is located a special area related to your vocal cords. And between the second and third toes, at their junction with the foot, is the area for treating the inner ear.

All the above areas are reflex zones, located on the foot and able to reflexively treat areas elsewhere in the body. In contrast, there is an area on the heel that is actually a branch of the sciatic nerve; it may be tender when pressed.

GIVING YOURSELF A REFLEXOLOGY TREATMENT

Take your foot in your hands and explore the skin surface. What you feel may astonish you. Some places you press hurt, and some feel ticklish. Some places give and some resist. On a different day, after working the spots, the painful places may not feel uncomfortable at all. This work assumes that you are actually influencing the course of your body's biochemistry and well-being.

Use your fingertips, the sides of your fingers, your thumb, knuckles, side of your hand, flat of your hand, and ball of your palm to press, squeeze, tap, rub, encircle, twist, rotate, punch, wring, slap, karate chop, stretch, slide across, vibrate against, rock, bounce, jiggle, and glide up and down one foot and then the other. Remember to work on the toes, too, individually and in groups.

Focus in on a particular area, then incorporate that area into a movement that includes the whole foot. Make firm, emphatic movements and soft gentle movements, holding the foot with one hand and stimulating the skin with the other. You can also hold the foot with both hands and work with your thumbs simultaneously.

Following are some specific ailments that suggest a toxic condition, and some of the possible areas you might want to press on your feet to help your body detoxify. Be creative and inventive. You can only help yourself if you do more locations than those listed below. And, if you can't remember where a body part's reflex zone is, don't worry. If you find a sore spot on the foot, rub it.

Conditions	Reflex Zones to Press
Allergies	Liver, lung, intestines, all lymph, thyroid, pituitary
Asthma	Ileocecal valve, adrenals
Bad breath	Intestines, liver, teeth/gums
Drug/alcohol/cigarette addiction	Lungs, diaphragm, heart, brain, pituitary, kidneys, liver
Gas/indigestion/hemorrhoids	Intestines, pancreas, liver, stomach, sciatic, lower spine
Kidney conditions	Kidneys, bladder, ureters, adrenals, lower back, parathyroids, lung, liver
Liver toxicity or disease	Liver, gallbladder, heart, thoracic spine, lung

Menopause/menstrual issues	Liver, thyroid, pituitary, brain, kidneys, uterus, ovaries
Prostate problems	Bladder, adrenals, prostate, lymph in groin, lower back, sciatic, pituitary
Respiratory infections	Lungs, diaphragm, all lymph, spleen, intestines, thymus, middle third of toes, adrenals
Skin conditions	Lungs, intestines, adrenals, thyroid, pituitary, kidneys

---

ACUPRESSURE

I was standing in line at the cash register of a sporting goods store. The cashier was telling another young woman behind the counter that her headache had lasted for hours and she was miserable.

When my turn came, I handed her my merchandise, and asked if she would like me to possibly help her headache. Eagerly, she agreed. So, I took her hand in mine and began to press firmly in the center of the web between her thumb and index finger. It was sore and she yelped in discomfort. "How's your headache?" I asked. Astonished, she reported it was gone.

Another name for acupressure is contact healing. Contact is made by pressing on special sites on the body. These sites were first described over twenty-three centuries ago in China. One irreverent legend has the discovery linked to warfare: After a fierce battle, the commanding officer tells an old soldier's wife, "The bad news is, your husband's riddled with arrows. The good news is, his arthritis is gone!"

Acu*puncture* is the stimulation of these specific points on the skin by the insertion of super-thin needles. Acu*pressure* is the stimulation of the skin surface. Acupuncture is the domain of licensed professionals. But you are the perfect person to perform acupressure. Besides finger pressure, you can use heat or electronics to stimulate acupoints, or tape magnets, small hard seeds, or tiny metal balls on the skin on those same locations. One acupressurist uses a tool carved from a thirty-thousand-year-old mastadon bone! Whatever tool you use, the purpose of both the puncture and the pressure is to influence organs, glands, and body processes to work better and to return to a state of comfort and well-being.

POINTS FORM CHANNELS

Both acupuncture and acupressure are based on the belief that energy flows along mappable pathways that form an intricate grid on the body. Imagine there is a trolley car hooked up to your body's electrical grid. Let's call it the acupressure trolley car. The trolley car moves along one street after another, until after passing along twelve different streets it eventually circles back to the place it began, and starts to circle all over again. Imagine that from three to five A.M. it passes along Lung Street, then it turns onto Large Intestine Street, where it runs from five to seven A.M. It makes another turn and moves along Stomach Street from seven to nine A.M. and so on through the twelve streets.

Here's the full schedule of appearances of the acupressure trolley car:

Street Name	Time of Passage
Lung	3–5 A.M.
Large Intestine	5–7 A.M.
Stomach	7–9 A.M.

Spleen	9–11 A.M.
Heart	11 A.M.–1 P.M.
Small Intestine	1–3 P.M.
Urinary Bladder	3–5 P.M.
Kidney	5–7 P.M.
Pericardium	7–9 P.M.
Triple Warmer	9–11 P.M.
Gallbladder	11 P.M.–1 A.M.
Liver	1–3 A.M.

Each of these streets runs in your body, and has a specific number of acupressure points located along it, like stops along the route. In acupressure language a street is called a channel or a meridian. Each channel has a specific and unchanging number of acupuncture points. So, for example, the Lung Channel always has eleven points, in approximately the same location along a similar route on everyone. The ancients discovered that each of the channels is intimately connected with a particular organ or body process, as described by its name. However, there isn't a simple correspondence between the channel and the organ: for example, the "Spleen" Channel is used to treat digestive problems more often than diseases of the spleen.

There are two extra streets that support a second trolley car line. Their names are Governing Street and Conception Street. The trolley car circles through them constantly. The Governing Channel runs from the perineum up the spine and over the skull to the upper lip. The Conception Channel runs up the torso from the pubic bone to the lower lip. All other channels are located on both the right and the left sides of the body.

You notice two odd "organs" in the above list: Pericardium and Triple Warmer. The Pericardium Channel represents the outer covering of the heart. In Chinese medicine, this is considered a separate "organ" with the job of protecting the heart. The Triple Warmer is considered a function, rather than a specific organ. It represents the areas of the body from the pubic bone to the navel, the navel to the diaphragm, and the diaphragm to the neckline. Its function is to warm the body, govern the process of metabolism and water distribution, and supervise the overall working of the organs in its boundaries.

ENERGY ON BOARD

The lone passenger on the acupressure trolley cars is energy. The ancients called this energy *Qi* (pronounced "chee"), which can be explained as the force behind the organization of the universe. It is both within you, contained in channels, and outside you, in everything you see and touch.

Our trolley cars' electrical grid is fired up at a central control station. Along the routes, substations boost the signal to keep it going strong. In your body, the acupressure points are your substations. By pressing them, you can help your inner trolley make all the right connections and pass through each section of the route on time.

When we are well, we have plenty of Qi and it circulates unimpeded. When we use up our Qi, or our Qi is blocked by injury, infection, improper eating, excessive worry, or emotional distress, there is some kind of physical consequence: pain, dysfunction, or disease. The more serious and complicated the imbalance of Qi, the deeper and more serious the condition that results.

Is there a discomfort you repeatedly suffer at a specific time of day? Do you often have a headache an hour or two after lunch? Perhaps your small intestine cannot properly digest your meal, causing stagnation of energy along the Small Intestine Channel, which happens to end along the side of your scalp. Do you awaken at three or four A.M. with a cough? Perhaps your Lung energy is deficient and needs support. Do you have difficulty falling asleep, or do you awaken with a headache between one and three A.M.? Perhaps your Liver energy is overstimulated, and needs balancing.

By comparing your own symptoms with the chart of the

times the individual channel energies are strongest (pages 104–05), you may have a clue as to what system needs your attention. You may help yourself in any of these cases with improved nutrition, herbal medicines, breathing exercises, yoga, increased water consumption, acupuncture, or acupressure.

WHAT IS A POINT?

Although the details of how acupressure influences the body are still being studied, it seems to involve electrical energy. If you wanted to find an acupressure point "scientifically," you can use a simple device that measures electrical resistance. It fits in the palm and emits a tone when the device passes over a spot where electricity more easily enters the skin compared to surrounding skin. Sure enough, these spots are just where the ancient Chinese described the acupuncture points.

Most acupuncturists and acupressurists don't use a device to find the points, except, perhaps, in the ear, where the distance between points is so minute. On the body, it is easier to learn point location by body landmarks. Usually, point locations are described in relation to bones, tendons, or where muscles cross. You can often find them in an indentation.

Distances from these geographical landmarks are measured in *cuns*, which I prefer to call "body inches": one inch on your body is the distance across your thumb's knuckle. The distance across all four fingers is considered three body inches and the distance across your index and middle fingers is 1.5 body inches.

Don't get overly hung up about the inches. When you are approximately near the acupressure point, search with your fingertip for a sore place, and assume that's the correct spot. After some experience, you may be able to feel heat or other sensations in your fingertips when you are over the right spot.

PERFORMING ACUPRESSURE ON YOURSELF

Even if you don't remember the points, acupressure can help. Rub your thumb or fingers along your skin. When you find a tender place on an indentation, or "valley," between muscle fibers, press! Consider soreness a call for help. You can use one finger or thumb, or any combination that feels comfortable for you.

Press firmly, without gouging yourself, and hold your finger on the sore spot. Imagine yourself closing an energy leak. Imagine warmth in whatever organ needs this assistance, a warmth that comes from renewed energy to repair itself. When the tenderness is gone, remove your finger.

Alternatively, you can massage in a tight circle. If you want to draw energy into you, and tonify an energy-deficient area, massage clockwise. If you want to draw energy away from the area—for example, in cases of pain and spasm—massage counterclockwise.

San Francisco acupuncturists Harriet Beinfield and Efrem Korngold explain duration of treatment this way: "Stimulation of a single point can last thirty seconds, five minutes, or be continued for twenty minutes in one-minute sequences with rests in between."[2] You may need several treatments. Acupressure usually takes longer than acupuncture, and acupuncture rarely does the whole job after only one treatment.

Find a time that is convenient, and repeat the treatment until there is no more tenderness at any time at the treated sites. Consider taking a bath instead of a shower, and pressing points then. Or press while you're sitting on the subway or taking a short break from your work. You may want to do it as you lie in bed awaiting sleep.

POINTS FOR SPECIFIC CONDITIONS

Sometimes you will press on a point because it is along a channel that runs through an area you want to treat, and your goal is to move energy along the channel. Other times, you will press on a point because that particular point has special powers you want to harness.

Please note: If you are pressing on a point around the pain and it isn't getting better, switch to one of the suggested points that is distant from the pain, and rub counterclockwise to draw excess energy away from the painful site. And please see a medical professional for a diagnosis; be sure there isn't an underlying condition that needs medical attention in addition to, or instead of, acupressure.

Following are some acupressure protocols for common conditions shared by people who need to detoxify. Excellent books giving acupressure protocols for many other conditions can be found in "References" at the end of this chapter.

Caution: Certain acupressure points are forbidden during pregnancy, as they can contribute to an unwanted miscarriage. Do *not* press points on your abdomen, particularly along the Conception Channel from your navel to your pubic bone. To remind you, these points are printed in bold in the following pages.

According to Daoshing Ni, an acupuncturist, herbalist, and president of Yo San University in Santa Monica, California, while massages during pregnancy are great stress relievers, a pregnant woman is safest receiving frequent, gentle, and short (half hour at the most) full body massages rather than infrequent, firm, hour-long massages.

Headache

Many headaches are caused by tension in the muscles of the head, neck, and shoulders. The tension not only contracts the muscles around the nerves, but squeezes blood vessels carrying oxygen to the brain.

There are other causes of headache that need more than acupressure: high blood pressure, constipation, dental problems, uterine disease, food or environmental allergies, tumors, hemorrhage, toxemia from inflamed kidneys, arteriosclerosis, sinus infections, anemia, and abnormal placement of the neck bones or skull bones. If headaches plague you, see your primary care practitioner for a medical checkup.

Migraine headaches are the most painful and may have added distressing symptoms like nausea, vomiting, and visual disturbances. The pain seems to stem from instability of the blood vessels, so that vessels in the head, particularly near the temples, are significantly dilated. Yet, many studies show a constriction of blood flow to the brain. An accumulation of stresses is also often involved. In addition, migraines are often initiated by allergies, particularly to foods high in tyramine (such as chocolate and certain cheeses), caffeine-containing drinks and drugs, alcohol, citrus fruits, food additives (such as monosodium glutamate, or MSG), artificial colors, and certain drugs (such as oral contraceptives and a hypertension medicine called reserpine).

Besides common points that relax tense muscles, specific treatment depends on the location of the headache. You don't have to use all of the suggested points. See which combinations or single points work for you.

ALL HEADACHES

Carotid Stroking

Put a thumb on one side of your neck and your four fingers on the other. Stroke gently downward, from your jaw to your shoulderbone. According to Dr. J. V. Cerney, author of *Acupuncture Without Needles*,[3] this helps stimulate the Stomach Channel, the autonomic nervous system, and the carotid sinus (an area of the carotid artery particularly influenced by changes in blood pressure). This movement, says Cerney, relieves headaches due to congestion, blood pressure malfunction, or emotional causes.

SCM Grab

Grab the muscle along both sides of the neck deep enough to pull it away from the neck. It is uncomfortable, but often quickly relieves headaches.

Hair Pulling

My favorite fifteen-second cure for headaches. Grab your hair in a large chunk between all your fingers, lift, and twist. Then move to another place nearby, grab, lift, and twist. Cover the entire scalp, particularly over the area that hurts.

If you are bald, press your fingertips against your scalp, and move the scalp back and forth without moving your fingers from that spot. Shift your fingers an inch or two, and twist the scalp back and forth again. Continue across the scalp this way, paying particular attention to the area above the pain.

FRONTAL HEADACHES (ABOVE THE EYES)

Before you spend time doing acupressure, remember to eat something! You may have low blood sugar, since headaches here are connected to the Stomach Channel.

Large Intestine 4 (He Gu—Adjoining Valleys)
The Chinese pronounce this point "huh goo" and the Japanese "ho koo." It stimulates the immune system, relieves constipation, and is called the "master point" for the head and upper body. It is about halfway along the first metacarpal bone of the index finger, at the highest point of the web when the thumb and index finger are touching. **Avoid during pregnancy**.

Gallbladder 14 (Yangbai—Yang White)
Relaxes the stomach, relieves stress. One body inch above the eyebrow, in a depression directly above the pupil, about a third of the way to the hairline.

Urinary Bladder 2 (Zanzhu—Gathered Bamboo)
Opens nasal sinuses. At the medial end of the eyebrow (side closest to the nose), in a notch (feel gently with your fingertips and you'll feel a slight indentation in the eye socket).

Stomach 44 (Neiting—Inner Court)
Good for inflammatory conditions involving the stomach and mouth. At the beginning of the web of skin between the second and third toes.

Gallbladder 21 (Jianjing—Shoulder Well)
Alleviates pain in the neck and shoulder. Midway along the top of the shoulder, at the highest point. It is often uncomfortable when pressed (most of us have tension there)!

VERTEX HEADACHES (AT THE TOP OF THE HEAD)

Gallbladder 20 (Fengchi—Wind Pool)
Alleviates pain in head and neck, improves function of eyes and ears. Drop your head, and run your fingers along the base

of your skull, starting with both hands at your spine. Your fingers fall into both the points in indentations halfway between the spine and the bottom of your ear.

Governing Channel
Press with your fingertips, hold, then release along the channel, beginning at your hairline in line with your nose, moving along the top of your skull and down to the bottom of the skull where it meets your spine. Now press parallel to this midline, with fingers on the skull and palm against your temples. Squeeze your scalp. Move along these parallel lines, looking for painful points to press, hold, and release.

Liver 3 (*Taichong*—Great Pouring)
Treats pain in the head and other conditions of the uterus and liver, and reduces feelings of anger. Between the bones of the first and second toes, in the tender area atop the foot about one or two body inches from the edge of the web. You can use the heel of one foot to press this area on the other foot, and then switch. **Avoid during pregnancy.**

TEMPORAL HEADACHES (AT THE SIDE OF THE HEAD) AND MIGRAINES

Gallbladder 20 (*Fengchi*—Wind Pool)
Alleviates pain in head and neck, improves function of eyes and ears. Drop your head, and run your fingers along the base of your skull, starting with both hands at your spine. Your fingers fall into both the points in indentations halfway between the spine and the bottom of your ear.

Extra Point (*Taiyang*—Great Yang)
Imagine a line between the outer edge of your eye and your eyebrow. The point is about one body inch from the center of that line, in an indentation at the temple.

Liver 3 (*Taichong*—Great Pouring)
Treats pain in the head and other conditions of the uterus and liver, and reduces feelings of anger. Between the bones of the first and second toes, in the tender area atop the foot about

one or two body inches from the edge of the web. You can use the heel of one foot to press this area on the other foot, and then switch. **Avoid during pregnancy.**

Gallbladder 41 (*Zulinqi*—Near Tears on the Foot)
Moves Qi in the Liver and Gallbladder Channels. In the groove between the bones on the top of the foot, just before the webbing of the fourth and fifth toes.

OCCIPITAL HEADACHES (AT THE BACK OF THE HEAD)

Gallbladder 20 (*Fengchi*—Wind Pool)
Alleviates pain in head and neck, improves function of eyes and ears. Drop your head, and run your fingers along the base of your skull, starting with both hands at your spine. Your fingers fall into both the points in indentations halfway between the spine and the bottom of your ear.

Governing 16 (*Fengfu*—Wind's Dwelling)
Relieves congestion in the Governing Channel, alleviates pain in the neck and head. One body inch above the natural hairline at the nape of the neck, in the hollow directly below the occipital bone of the skull.

Urinary Bladder 10 (*Tianzhu*—Heaven's Pillar)
Relieves pain along the Urinary Bladder Channel. A half body inch above the natural hairline, and a little over one body inch to each side of the spine.

Urinary Bladder 64 (*Jinggu*—Capital Bone)
Relieves headache and stiff neck. Also lower back and leg pain, and removes blocked Qi in the Urinary Bladder Channel. In the depression on the outside of the foot midway from heel to little toe beneath the protruding bone of the fifth metatarsal.

Liver 3 (*Taichong*—Great Pouring)
Treats pain in the head and other conditions of the uterus and liver, and reduces feelings of anger. Between the bones of the first and second toes, in the tender area atop the foot about

one or two body inches from the edge of the web. You can use the heel of one foot to press this area on the other foot, and then switch. **Avoid during pregnancy.**

Digestive upsets

This complaint covers constipation, loose stools, bloating, gas, abdominal pain or a burning sensation after eating, mucus or undigested food in the stools, acid regurgitation, and loss of appetite.

Large Intestine 4 (Hegu—Adjoining Valleys)
The Chinese pronounce this point "huh goo" and the Japanese "ho koo." It stimulates the immune system, relieves constipation, and is called the "master point" for the head and upper body. It is about halfway along the first metacarpal bone of the index finger, at the highest point of the web when the thumb and index finger are touching. **Avoid during pregnancy.**

Conception 12 (Zhongwan—Middle Cavity)
Helps digestion. Halfway between the xyphoid process (lowest point of the breastbone) and the navel. Do not use within two hours of eating a meal. If you can, lie on your back with your knees bent, and press gradually into the point at a forty-five-degree angle toward your diaphragm. Breathe deeply. Allow your inner organs to relax. **Avoid during pregnancy.**

Stomach 36 (Zusanli—Three Measures on the Leg)
One of the best points for strengthening and balancing the body. Improves digestion and relieves constipation and diarrhea. Three body inches below the outer hollow of the knee, one toward the outer side of the shinbone. If necessary, you can use the heel of one foot to press on the point on the opposite leg.

Pericardium 6 (Neiguan—Inner Gate)
Helps relieve anxiety and heart palpitations. The best point to relieve nausea during pregnancy or travel. Two body inches up the arm from the midpoint of the crease of the wrist.

Spleen 4 (*Gongsun*—Grandfather's Grandson)
An important point for helping improve digestion and relieving pain along the Spleen or Stomach Channels. One body inch behind the joint of the big toe, on the transverse arch of the foot. In *Acupressure's Potent Points,* Michael Reed Gach suggests pressing your left Spleen 4 with your right heel while pressing your right Pericardium 6 with your left thumb, breathing deeply, then switching sides and holding these points another minute.[4]

Stomach 25 (*Tianshu*—Heavenly Pivot)
Improves function of the intestines. Two body inches to each side of the navel. **Avoid during pregnancy.**

Liver conditions

In Chinese medicine, the Liver controls the smooth flow of both Qi and Blood, which directs the ebb and flow of a woman's menstrual cycle, procreation, the harmonious transition through menopause, and the nourishment of muscles, tendons, ligaments, and the eyes. The liver is our miracle organ, the only one that can regenerate when damaged or cut, which is quite useful in a modern world full of toxins! Because the liver produces bile, which is needed to digest fats and absorb fat-soluble vitamins, the liver is involved in digestion and assimilation. Its paired organ in acupuncture theory is the gallbladder, which means if there is a problem with one organ there is probably a problem with the other.

When these functions of the liver are disturbed, you may experience muscle cramps or weakness, stiffness that is worse after resting and better with motion (as blood begins to circulate), numbness in the extremities, pain that travels from one spot to another, stubbornness, digestive upsets, uneven sugar metabolism, infertility, menstrual pain or other menstrual complaints, symptoms of menopause, and eye conditions, such as dry eyes, cataracts, and glaucoma. You may also suffer migraines, with heat in the head and cold extremities.

If the Liver Qi or Blood is stuck, you may experience stabbing pain, clots during menstruation, ovarian cysts, or lumps and tumors, such as fibroids or even cancer. If the Liver cannot control the Qi, you may have a short temper and habitually flare up with strong emotion. Even the Western language, using the term "flare up," suggests the Chinese concept of Liver Fire Rising, causing a red face and angry disposition.

Liver Massage

Begin with direct massage, through the skin. Your liver is located beneath the ribs on your right side. If it is enlarged by illness, it can stick out beyond the ribs. Use your fingertips curled under the ribs on your right side to press gently, then hold. Move slowly toward the midline of your body, holding at each place as you count to three. Go to where the ribs turn upwards toward the breastbone. According to Dr. J. V. Cerney, when you curl your fingers around the ribs and press into the abdomen here, you are helping to both stimulate gallbladder activity and "chase the gas out of the hepatic flexure of the large colon."[5]

If the gallbladder is functioning below par, you may have a referred pain between your shoulder blades. It is a good idea to see a physician for a Western medical exam, to rule out a need for emergency treatment of heart, liver, or gallbladder. Once you know you are in no immediate danger, and if you are alone, lie back on a golf ball, pressing the ball into the pain. If someone else can help, have that person press his or her thumbs into the painful place, while you are lying on your stomach on a bed, couch, or on a towel on the floor.

Whenever doing self-massage on acupressure points, hold the point until the pain disappears, or, if it won't disappear, repeat the pressure the next day and the next until it does disappear.

Liver 2 (Xingjian—Walk Between)

Treats conditions in the head, eyes, and liver. In the web between the first and second toes. You can use the heel of one foot to press this area on the other foot, and then switch. **Avoid during pregnancy.**

Spleen 6 (Sanyinjiao—Three Yin Junction)

The crossing point of the Spleen, Kidney, and Liver Channels, giving it particular importance in Chinese medicine. Treats menstrual and menopausal symptoms, male and female infertility, and digestive disorders. Three body inches up from the inner ankle, in the muscle at the edge of the tibia bone. **Avoid during pregnancy.**

Gallbladder 34 (*Yanglingquan*—Yang Tomb Spring)
Helps remove edema, fights infection, and treats conditions of tendons and bones. With the leg bent at the knee, the point is just in front of and below the rounded head of the fibula, in a hollow to the outside of the knee next to the stomach 36 (see page 114).

Sinus congestion, nasal congestion, and allergies
In Chinese medicine, anything related to the respiratory system is also considered connected to the digestive system, for the Lung Channel and the Large Intestine Channel are an intimate pair. That's why some of the points for nasal congestion are on the Large Intestine Channel. Other points are located over the nasal sinuses, and pressure on these points stimulates drainage.

The four pairs of caverns called sinuses are behind, to the sides, and above the structure of the nose. They help warm air en route to the lungs, but they are mostly famous for being congested with mucus, which for some is a mere annoyance and for others the source of head pain and chronic distress. The congestion is a result of either an infection or an allergy. Whether the offender is a microorganism or a pinch of pollen, the body's response is to attempt to surround, immobilize, and wash out the invader with, first, a mild flood of clear or white mucus. If the battle rages on, there will be losses on both sides and the body count of invaders and immune system fighting cells will rise, causing the mucus to turn yellow, then green with the heat and intensity of the war within.

To eliminate congestion, chase your symptoms away and strengthen your fighting force with acupressure, rest, stress reduction, exercise, more vegetables/vegetable juices, less sugar/grains/dairy, and by expressing the tears and other strong emotions that are locked inside.

Extra Point (*Bitong*—Nose Passage)
Relieves congestion in nasal passages. In the depression below the nasal bone, at the upper end of the smile line. Press firmly in and upward to each side of the nose.

Extra Points (unnamed)
Treat infection in head or body and relieve nasal congestion.
These extra points are located along the upper and lower edge
of the cheekbones. Squeeze the cheekbone between thumbs
and fingers pressing firmly, particularly on areas of discomfort.

Urinary Bladder 2 (*Zanzhu*—Gathered Bamboo)
Opens nasal sinuses. At the medial end of the eyebrow (side
closest to the nose), in a notch (feel gently with your fingertips
and you'll feel a slight indentation in the eye socket).

Large Intestine 20 (*Yingxiang*—Welcome Fragrance)
Opens nasal sinuses. A half body inch lateral to the nostril, in
the smile groove.

Large Intestine 4 (*Hegu*—Adjoining Valleys)
The Chinese pronounce this point "huh goo" and the Japanese
"ho koo." It stimulates the immune system, relieves constipation, and is called the "master point" for the head and upper
body. It is about halfway along the first metacarpal bone of
the index finger, at the highest point of the web when the
thumb and index finger are touching. **Avoid during pregnancy.**

Governing Vessel 20 (*Baihui*—a Hundred Meetings)
Press here for headaches, dizziness, sleep disturbance. Touch
the top of each ear with a finger. Run the fingers up the scalp
to meet at the top of the head directly back from the nose.

ALLERGY ELIMINATION

*One night my husband, Allen, was watching TV with a
look that I knew meant something was wrong. He con-
fessed he'd had a headache ever since hugging me earlier
in the evening. We had been standing in the kitchen at
the time. "What had you eaten before we hugged?" I
asked. "A piece of dark chocolate," he answered. There
was more chocolate still in the drawer. I retrieved the bar
and put it on his stomach. He held it there with one hand,
and raised the other hand in the air at a right angle to*

his body. "Ready?" I asked. He nodded. I pressed his upraised arm and it collapsed to his thigh with little resistance. He turned so I could massage the acupressure points on his head and back that eliminate a food sensitivity. He lifted up his arm again. This time, no amount of pressure could budge that arm. "Do you still have a headache?" I asked. "No!" he said. "It's gone!" He was glad to be relieved of a headache, and I was glad to know it wasn't the hug that caused it!

A substance that causes an allergic reaction is called an allergen. Sometimes you don't know what allergen sparked the reaction; all you know is that you are suffering from nasal congestion, asthma, a rash, a sinus headache, aching joints, fuzzy thinking, memory loss, irritability, or other symptoms of distress.

Doris Rapp, M.D., a pediatric allergist and author of *Is This Your Child?* and *Is This Your Child's World?*, suggests paying attention immediately after eating something or being exposed to something new, and answering what she calls the Big Five questions:[6]

1. Is there a change in your *thinking* ability?
2. Is there a change in your *breathing* ability?
3. Is there a change in your *drawing* or writing ability? (Write your name or draw something and see if it looks different than usual.)
4. Is there a change in your *appearance*? (Are your ears red? Are there dark circles under your eyes?)
5. Is your *pulse* rate faster?

Once you know what you are allergic to, the usual treatment for a food allergy is to avoid eating that food. The usual treatment for inhaled allergens, such as pollens, is a series of injections of dilutions of the offending substance, until the body learns to tolerate that substance.

There is an alternative to either avoidance or injections that is quick and effective for almost any allergy or sensitivity. With this new method, allergens reveal themselves through muscle testing and are eliminated by acupressure. As I tell my own patients when I teach them how to do it, I wouldn't decide whether to take insulin or not based on muscle testing, but for situations that aren't life threatening, and when done by someone who has a knack for it, results can be useful.

MUSCLE TESTING POINTS THE WAY

Your body is constantly receiving information about the world around you. Much of it is never brought to your conscious attention. That means there is an enormous storehouse of information in your brain biocomputer. Muscle testing is one way to access that information.

If you were a sleuth looking for a murderer and had found a button at the crime scene, you would pay very careful attention to the buttons on the clothing of every person you interviewed. Without this clue, the buttons on a person's coat would probably be furthest from your attention as you questioned a suspect.

In the same way, muscle testing allows you to discover files in your brain's biocomputer that otherwise you might never have known existed.

TREATING YOURSELF FOR MINOR ALLERGIES

Warning: This procedure for allergy elimination is to be used on allergens that cause minor reactions only, not serious or life-threatening allergic reactions. Do not use this technique if you suffer from asthma, or if your throat closes or your heartbeat changes when you are exposed to some food or environmental substance! In these cases, seek professional help from people who have been trained in this form of allergy relief. Look under "Resources" at the end of this section for referrals.

STOPPING AN ALLERGIC REACTION

If you suffer from serious reactions to certain foods, keep some Alka Seltzer Gold (make sure it says "Gold" on the orange package) with you. Drinking a tablet dissolved in water may help you to quickly stop an allergic reaction if you drink this aspirin-free source of buffering minerals as soon as you start to react.

You can only treat yourself if you are *not* pregnant. If you know you are pregnant or might be pregnant, do not treat yourself. See "Resources" at the end of this section for a referral to a professional. The points used to treat yourself may cause contraction of your uterus, and are forbidden during pregnancy until labor.

Assuming you are not pregnant, and as long as you don't have a severe or life-threatening reaction, you can work the acupressure allergy elimination system on yourself.

First, see if you are allergic to common foods and nutrients. Collect small samples of the following:

- multivitamin (no minerals)
- multimineral (no vitamins)
- B complex
- vitamin C
- oranges
- strawberries (fresh or frozen, but no sugar added)
- whole milk or butter
- whole wheat (100 percent) flour
- corn on the cob, frozen corn (nothing added, not even salt), popcorn (uncooked is fine), cornmeal, or cornstarch
- soybeans
- peanuts
- pumpkin pie spice combination (cinnamon, nutmeg, ginger)
- Italian spice combination (rosemary, basil, oregano, thyme)

1. Go through the following testing procedure to find out your body's signals for a "yes" and a "no." Make a ring with your thumb and little finger. Attempt to pull your fingertips apart by inserting the thumb and index finger of the other hand into the ring, and pushing apart. Ask yourself, "What is a 'yes'?" See if your fingers stay

tightly together or pull easily apart. Next, ask "What is a 'no'?" Do your fingers stay together or pull apart? To work as feedback, you need to consistently have the same response to each question. For me, strong muscles (I can't pull my fingertips apart) means the answer "yes" and weak muscles means "no."

2. Hold the substance in a ceramic, metal, cardboard, or glass (*not* plastic) container on your lap and make your ring with thumb and little finger. See if you can open the ring. Compare your finger strength when the substance is at least a foot away from you.

3. Ask yourself, "Is this substance OK for my body?" and try to break the ring of two fingers. Assuming strong muscle reaction is a "yes" for you, if you cannot break through, your body is telling you that "yes," it is OK for you. If you can easily break through the ring, your body is telling you "no," this substance isn't OK for you.

4. Ask yourself, "How many times a day do I have to treat myself to eliminate this sensitivity? One?" Try to break the ring. If the answer is "yes" (i.e., the ring is strong), go on to "Two?" and try to break the ring. As long as the answer keeps being "yes" keep asking a higher number, until the answer is "no" (i.e., you can easily break through the ring). The number of times you have to treat yourself was the previous number.

For example, let's say you ask, "How many times a day do I have to treat myself? One?" The ring is strong, so you ask, "Two?" The ring is strong, so you ask "Three?" The ring is strong, so you ask, "Four?" and your index finger breaks through the ring. Your body is telling you you need to treat yourself three times to eliminate that allergy.

Double check with this handy personal lie detector test and make sure you get a consistent answer for the required treatment. (If you can't get a consistent answer, or you feel too unsure of yourself to do this treatment on your own, use a trained professional. See "Resources" at the end of this chapter).

Next, ask how many days you have to treat yourself.

When you know how many times a day and how many days, you can begin your first treatment.

5. Hold a sample of the offending food in your lap, as before.
6. For one full minute, rub briskly the following two acupressure points on each side of your body (for a total of four points):

   • Between your thumb and index finger, at the highest point of the web when you press your thumb and index finger together.
   • Between your big toe and second toe, on the top of your foot.

Each time you treat yourself, be sure to have the sample on your lap, in your pocket, or otherwise on your body.

At the end of the allotted treatments, check to see if you are still having the old reaction to the substance. If you are, contact a professional who has studied NAET (Nambudripad Allergy Elimination Technique) to help you (see "Resources," below). If you aren't, congratulations! You can eliminate your allergies yourself with this easy system.

RESOURCES

Books on reflexology:

Eunice D. Ingham, *Stories the Feet Have Told Thru Reflexology* (St. Petersburg, Fla.: Ingham Publishing, 1963).

Stephanie Rick, *The Reflexology Workout* (New York: Harmony Books, 1986).

Mildred Carter, *Helping Yourself with Foot Reflexology* (West Nyack, N.Y.: Parker Publishing, 1969) and *Hand Reflexology: Key to Perfect Health* (West Nyack, N.Y.: Parker Publishing, 1975).

For allergy elimination and practitioner referrals:

The allergy resolution technique you read about in this chapter is my personal interpretation of a system I originally learned from Dr. Devi Nambudripad, a brilliant and innovative émigré from India who is a registered nurse, acupuncturist, and chiropractor with a medical practice in Buena Park, California. Medical professionals can register for weekend courses in NAET (which is far more comprehensive than described in this book, and entails treatment of emotional as well as physical sensitivities), by calling her office Monday, Wednesday, Friday, or Saturday mornings at 714/523-8900.

To obtain an updated list of trained practitioners of this allergy elimination technique who practice in your area, send $5 to Pain Clinic, Dr. Devi S. Nambudripad, D.C., L.Ac., Ph.D., 6714 Beach Boulevard, Buena Park, CA 90261 (714/523-0800).

To purchase *Say Goodbye to Illness*, a 344-page book written by Dr. Devi Nambudripad describing the technique and its origins (with numerous examples of successful treatments), send a cashier's check for $25, postpaid, made out to Pain Clinic at the above address.

Another good reference on the Nambudripad Allergy elimination Technique is *Winning the War Against Asthma & Allergies* by Ellen W. Cutler, D.C. (New York: Delmar Publishers, 1998), available in bookstores.

Books on other self-care protocols for allergy elimination:

Prof. Steven Rochlitz, *Allergies and Candida with the Physicist's Rapid Solution* (Mahopac, N.Y.: Human Ecology Balancing Sciences, 1993).

The Natural Medicine Collective with Gary McLain, *The Natural Way of Healing Asthma and Allergies* (New York: Dell, 1995).

Doris J. Rapp, M.D., *Is This Your Child?* (Buffalo, N.Y.: Practical Allergy Research Foundation, 1992).

Doris J. Rapp, M.D., *Is This Your Child's World?: How You Can Fix the Schools and Homes That Are Making Your Children Sick* (New York: Bantam, 1996).

REFERENCES

1. Laura Norman, *Feet First* (New York: Fireside, 1988), 17.

2. Harriet Beinfield, L.Ac., and Efrem Korngold, L.Ac., O.M.D., *Between Heaven and Earth: A Guide to Chinese Medicine* (New York: Ballantine, 1991), 253.

3. Dr. J. V. Cerney, *Acupuncture Without Needles* (West Nyack, N.Y.: Parker Publishing, 1974), 87.

4. Michael Reed Gach, *Acupressure's Potent Points* (New York: Bantam, 1990), 212.

5. Cerney, 66.

6. Doris, J. Rapp, M.D., *Is This Your Child's World?* (New York: Bantam, 1996), 44.

SEVEN

THINKING, BREATHING, MOVING, BATHING, PURGING

Anything can cure somebody. Nothing cures everybody. Nothings works forever. People change.
—Jeanne Achterberg, Ph.D.

People change. It may seem obvious, but we tend to forget that we may need one kind of detox at one time in our lives, and another way to cleanse, later. This can be disconcerting if we've invested a lot of time, energy, money, and emotion into one particular technique and expect it to last a lifetime. It won't.

What is much more practical is to rely, first, on the most ordinary of activities. In this chapter you are introduced to the way primary activities of daily life can be harnessed for your detox needs. The very first discussed is the power of thought to make a difference in your state of being. Along with thought you can use the cleansing power of the fuel of life itself: oxygen. Your every breath is another chance to detox! And, from there, you move along. Literally. You might call it muscle power, or exercise as a cleansing ritual.

After the three detox systems needing nothing outside of yourself for assistance, you dip into another of life's necessities, and use it for purification. You will recline in restful tranquility submerged in a watery solution of special salt, hop in and out of a stimulating hip bath, and learn a variety of ways to purge from the bowels of your inner self whatever toxic residues may be lurking there.

THINKING

This section focuses on the power of thought, for thoughts are so powerful, toxic thoughts can poison your life as surely as chemical pollutants.

In researching endorphins—those biochemicals that influence moods, perceptions of pain, and other important characteristics—Candace Pert, Ph.D., and others at the National Institutes of Health discovered that the same cellular lock-and-key pattern determining emotional states occurs not just in the brain, but in numerous body organs: when you are sad, your liver is sad, your kidneys are sad, and so on; when you are merry, so is your heart, your pancreas, and your other organs.

During the 1980s, a professor of psychiatry at Stanford University set out to disprove the notion that the right mental attitude can influence the course of a disease. David Siegel, M.D., recruited people with metastatic breast cancer; he put fifty in a weekly, ninety-minute support group. Thirty-six patients served as the controls. Members of the treatment group talked about their cancer and their feelings, and bonded with others in the group. They were taught self-hypnosis and pain control techniques, but they were not told that this group time would alter the course of their cancer.

To Dr. Siegel's surprise and the surprise of the medical community, after ten years, three support group patients were still alive, and the survival time of the other support group participants had been around thirty-seven months, compared to nineteenth months for the controls.[1] The cynics had to admit that maybe there was something to the notion of "mind-body medicine" after all!

The cancer patients at Stanford were able to express all the fear, disappointments, anger, and other unsociable feelings that were so hard to express with their families. Apparently, it is the expression of the emotion, whatever that emotion is, that is so cathartic and beneficial. And it isn't only cancer patients who need this release.

Dean Ornish, M.D., has proved that clogged arteries can be unclogged without drugs or surgery. In *Dr. Dean Ornish's Program for Reversing Heart Disease*,[2] Ornish describes his comprehensive plaque-reversal lifestyle: low-fat eating, no smoking, moderate daily exercise, yoga stretches and breathing exercises, and meditation. Only through years of experience did Ornish discover that exercise and diet weren't quite enough. A permanent and successful change in heart health had to include releasing toxic attitudes like hostility, competition, cynicism, and self-centeredness. To do this, Ornish provides his program participants a caring support group to help them quite literally "open the heart" to others and details the healing power of attitude in his newest book, *Love and Survival* (San Francisco: HarperCollins, 1998).

YOUR BIOCOMPUTER

Ann Wigmore, author of *The Wheatgrass Book* (Wayne, N.J.: Avery, 1985), said it best: "Your thoughts are a purchase order to the universe." What you picture in your mind is what your body will create for you, just as surely as if you typed your wishes into nature's computer.

I told myself for twenty-five years that when I weighed 125 pounds, I'd get married. When I found the man I wanted to marry, in a matter of months, without dieting, my weight dropped from 140 to 125 for my wedding day. Three years later, I told the universe in a daily request that we needed a new car. The fifteen-year-old station wagon I'd been driving was getting unreliable. I detailed what I wanted: how big, how strong a motor, how many people could ride in it. It had to be American-made (because my trusted mechanic only works on American cars), of a color and style agreeable to the whole family. Within a month a woman missed the curve on the street in front of my office and at full speed smashed her Jaguar into the back of my parked wagon. Although she escaped injury, my car was totalled.

With credit, we bought a new minivan, which I loved, but my husband said, "Honey, you forgot to ask for the money to buy the car!" So my daily request changed to "Without anyone dying to provide it, we will have enough money to pay off the car before my next birthday" (which was three months away). Within a couple weeks my husband heard from a major corporation he'd been wooing for five years. They finally decided to underwrite his product development proposal.

How cars and money relate to detoxification is this: If you

aren't convinced about alternative healing methods, do what all great actors and all healthy children do: pretend. The body doesn't know the difference between thought and reality.

Don't believe me? Think of a lemon slice gushing tart juices. Is your saliva flowing yet? Pretend you're an optimist, pretend you can see your body cleansed and fine-tuned and humming along with all the organs functioning their best, your skin clear and soft, your joints moving easily and comfortably, your digestive system happy to absorb and use nutrients.

THE POWER OF A SMILE

While you're at it, look beyond the bright side, to the funny side of your life. When the author of Proverbs 17:22 stated, "A cheerful heart is good medicine" he (or she) hadn't seen the research to back him (or her) up, but it exists: Laughter lowers cortisol, one of the stress hormones produced by your adrenal glands. It increases beta endorphins, the biochemicals that elevate your mood, reduce feelings of pain, and enhance feelings of contentment. Laughter relaxes you, decreases blood pressure, reduces heart rate, and make you feel better.[3] If you're still wondering what all this has to do with detoxification, remember the immortal words of Phyllis Diller: "A smile is a curve that sets everything straight."

According to John Diamond, M.D., when you lift the corners of your mouth, the muscles you are using (zygomaticus major) work on the thymus gland in your upper chest. Since the thymus is intimately linked to the health of your immune system, Diamond claims that smiling is good for your immune system.[4] Even fake smiling. So, "fake it 'til you make it" and begin your detox with a smile.

BREATHING

If, instead of breathing automatically, you learn to control your breath, you may discover a power within you for health and for healing that is greater than you ever imagined.

When you were an infant, you breathed with your body: your stomach rose as you inhaled, and dropped as you exhaled.

This a true full breath. As an adult, however, you probably breathe shallowly in the chest, because most people worry more about their abdomen sticking out than the quality of their inhalation and exhalation.

Nevertheless, breath can be a great part of your detox program: it's free, always available, and useful for cleaning out your cellular waste. Through breathing, the blood carries oxygen to oxygen-hungry cells and removes carbon dioxide, a waste product of respiration. Since detoxification is about removing waste material efficiently, you can start detoxing with the very simple act of conscious breathing.

For example, when volunteers were taught a breathing exercise, which they then performed for twenty minutes a day for a total of ten days, they were able to produce a significantly greater amount of carbon dioxide, and they used significantly more oxygen, than before their breath training.[5]

Breathing influences the body's balance of alkalinity/acidity (see chapter 4 for a more detailed explanation). Your body fluids, except those in the stomach, are alkaline. Your body works best when that alkalinity is maintained. Richard Anderson, a naturopathic physician and founder of the Arise and Shine body cleansing system, details the importance of all this in his informative manual *Cleanse and Purify Thyself.*[6] According to Anderson, breathing deeply keeps the body alkaline, while habitual shallow breathing makes the body more acidic. Since the blood must be maintained as alkaline, the body buffers the acidity of shallow breathing by using certain buffering minerals. If the bloodstream is low in buffering minerals, the body borrows them from various sites, which can cause problems: If minerals are removed from the bile, the bile becomes too acidic and serious bowel disease can result. If the body takes minerals from the bones, osteoporosis and arthritis may result.[7] Thus, breathing deeply to keep our blood alkaline is our number one detox technique.

THE ART OF BREATHING

Although air can reach the lungs equally well from nose or mouth, breathing through the nose is far preferable. As described on page 19, the nose is engineered with extraordinary

care. Dirty air is at least partially cleaned by the hairs in the
nose. Frigid air is warmed to body temperature as it passes
through the blood vessel–lined interior of the nose. Hot air is
cooled as it passes through the chambers of the nose, and in
the end arrives in the lungs at approximately body temperature.

Breathing is a powerful tool. Doing it right can make you
feel better, look better, and be better. Here are two of the
easiest breathing techniques to get you started.

Observation

The simplest breathing exercise is to observe your inhalation
and exhalation. Nothing more. Let your body breathe unim-
paired by worry over the width of your waistline. This alone
can help calm your frazzled nerves and put you in a state of
relaxed attention, ready to think clearly and act decisively.
If you cannot stand doing nothing, stare at the second hand on
your watch for three minutes while feeling the rise and fall of
your abdomen and the sensation of air tickling your nose,
throat, and lungs.

Cleansing

Here's a morning ritual using a cleansing breath: Lean over,
hands on thighs, knees bent. Forcefully blow out all the air in
your lungs. While holding your breath, snap your abdominal
muscles firmly against your internal organs, as if you could
tap your navel against your spine. Do this about ten times, or
however many times feels comfortable. Take a deep breath,
letting your abdomen out as far as it will go, then again blow
out firmly and thoroughly, collapsing your abdomen inward.
This time, as you hold your breath, make your abdomen move
in a circle. The internal organs are getting a great massage
as you work in one direction and then the other. You may find
you are pushing old, stale air out of the deepest recesses of
your lungs. Remember to take deep breaths after your abdominal workout.

SAGE ADVICE

Ancient sages in both India and China developed exercises to
return people to proper breathing. In India, the breathing ex-

ercises were an important part of the spiritual and physical discipline of yoga. The breath is associated with a life force, called *prana,* and its control is called *pranayama.* "Pranayama," states Georg Feuerstein in his *Encyclopedic Dictionary of Yoga,* "is recognized as one of the chief means of rejuvenating and indeed immortalizing the body."[8] Studies of *pranayama* have proven that the yoga breathing techniques can reduce asthma,[9] improve heart function, relieve emotional distress, and correct indigestion.[10]

A simple yoga exercise is alternate nostril breathing: Breathe deeply several times, allowing your stomach to extend as you inhale. Close your left nostril with the thumb of your left hand. Place your left middle finger comfortably against your forehead. Inhale deeply with your right nostril. Close your right nostril with the ring finger of your left hand, count to six, open your left nostril, and exhale deeply through your left nostril. Close the left nostril again, release your ring finger, and again inhale through your right, holding your breath for the count of six. Exhale through your left nostril. Repeat this pattern a total of three times.

Now, inhale through the left nostril, and open the right to exhale. Repeat a total of three times, inhaling through the left, holding, and exhaling through the right. Finally, drop your hand, and with open nostrils breathe in and out deeply and evenly for three full breaths.

Using this alternate nostril breathing when you feel tired or fuzzy-minded brings you to a state of alertness and mental clarity.

Disciplined breathing was an important skill among the ancient Chinese, too. They called the life force *Qi* (pronounced "chee"), and their spiritual/physical discipline that incorporates breath control is called *Qi gung.* They, too, found that through training they could use breathing to influence their nervous system, heart rate, blood flow, digestive system, and many other supposedly automatic functions.

Nancy Zi, a singer and singing teacher, developed a series of exercises based on the wisdom of *Qi gung.* In *The Art of Breathing,* Zi suggests you imagine your lungs are a vertical accordion and with each breath the lower edge drops, creating space into which air flows.[11] When you breathe this way, it may feel as if air enters your abdomen, but of course it doesn't really leave the lungs. Yet, when you breathe deeply, your inhalations and exhalations include contracting and releasing muscles of the front, sides, and lower back of your trunk, so the body, as well as the lungs, breathes with each breath.

Breathing well is a way to cleanse yourself both emotionally (by releasing tension) and physically. The detoxifying effect of breathing occurs with each exhalation. So remember to exhale deeply and fully.

EXERCISE

"Whether you are young or old," I wrote in *Antioxidants: Your Complete Guide*, "exercise improves your muscle tone, reduces your risk of heart disease and cancer, reduces cholesterol, keeps your bones strong, thickens your skin to prevent sagging, helps you sleep better, controls your weight, improves your self-esteem, increases the activity of a virus-fighting protein called interferon, and is a useful tonic for depression."[12] Exercise, then, should be an enjoyable part of every detox regimen.

IMPROVED CIRCULATION

Exercise increases circulation of blood by stimulating the growth of capillaries, your smallest blood vessels. As more capillaries spread deeper into your muscles and body tissues, they provide a ready stream for even more waste to be withdrawn from body cells, transported through the kidneys, and excreted in the urine.

Vigorous exercise releases toxins stored in fat cells. According to James Woodworth, executive director of HealthMed, a detoxification program in Sacramento, California, "Oil-based chemicals, drug residuals, and heavy metals tend to lodge in the body fat. These chemicals are released back in the bloodstream as the fat is utilized during physical exercise." The body dumps these undersirables through the urine, bowel, sweat, and sweaty oil glands. (Read more about HealthMed in chapter 13.)

EXERCISE AND FREE RADICALS

There is one downside to exercise, and that is its creation of free radicals. It's been called "the exercise paradox." Exercise is good for you, yet exercise increases your body's production of dangerous molecules called free radicals that have been linked to muscle damage, heart disease, cancer, and a long list of other unwanted conditions.[13] Free radicals are molecules with one electron missing. This makes them unstable and highly reactive. They attack fat globules in cell walls, in the nucleus, and elsewhere in the cell. In each case, damage results.

Exercising outdoors exposes you to sunlight and extremes of heat and cold, generating greater free radical production. In addition, inflammation, a common experience of serious outdoor exercisers, stimulates the production of free radicals as part of your immune response.

Controlling free radical damage

Your body needs some free radicals as a part of your immune defense force (they can kill viruses and bacteria as well as healthy tissue). Damage occurs when free radical production outstrips your body's ability to control them. Since the damage is often caused by fragments of oxygen in a process called oxidation, those substances that protect the cell from free radicals are often called "antioxidants." They help us in three ways: by stopping some free radical production, by limiting what is produced to controllable levels, and by repairing damage. Antioxidants include vitamins A, C, and E and the mineral selenium. Exercisers also need coenzyme Q-10.

In one experiment, a German researcher looked at the damage to the DNA of five men, aged twenty-nine to thirty-four, who ran on a treadmill until exhausted. When they took 800 IU (international units) of vitamin E twice the day before the treadmill workout and once the day afterward, there was a noticeable reduction in damage. Furthermore, when the five men took 1,200 IU of vitamin E daily for the two weeks before their treadmill effort, there was no damage in the DNA of four of the men and less damage in the DNA of the fifth. The lesson from this study is clearly the need for sustained exposure to the right antioxidant dose, to adequately protect the body from free radical harm.

In addition to vitamin E, exercisers need vitamin C. This vitamin improves the health of connective tissue, reduces wound healing time, relaxes cramped muscles, and reduces inflammation and limb pain. Vitamin C is particularly important to take with vitamin E, as the two work synergistically: When vitamin E is used up as it fights free radicals, vitamin C helps regenerate the E, so the E fights free radicals longer.

Another important antioxidant nutrient for serious exercisers is coenzyme Q-10. This is found in greatest concentration in the liver and heart, and in lesser concentration in every cell of the body. CoQ-10 helps the mitochondria, the energy factory found inside each cell, to produce the power of life.

DAILY SELF-PROTECTION FOR EXERCISERS

Vitamin A	5,000 IU
Vitamin E	400 IU regularly; 800–1,200 IU for heavy workouts
Vitamin C	1 to 3 grams
Coenzyme Q-10	30 mg

WATER

If you've ever stirred sugar into tea, you've seen nature's most popular solvent at work. The solvent is water, and it composes about 60 percent of your body weight if you are a man under age 40, and about half your weight if you are a woman in that age group. In older populations, there is a gradual decline in the total amount of water compared to body weight.[14]

Water is essential to all life on earth. It not only serves as a bank holding reserves of inorganic salts, organic materials, and dissolved gases within body cells, it is a core building block for those cells and serves as the environment in which cells are nourished and survive. In fact, maintaining a proper balance of water in the body is a daily necessity. You cannot obtain enough water from your food to stay alive. You need to drink a certain amount of water each day to keep your body machinery humming in health or you'd eventually become poisoned from the buildup of the waste products of metabolism and the natural losses from your bowel, your urine, your breath, and your sweat.

As a solvent, water makes solids dissolve. You are going to use this solvent both outside and inside yourself to dissolve out cellular dirt and metabolic wastes and to flush out whatever hazards are hidden or hardened in the undulating landscape of the inner you.

EPSOM SALTS BATH

Epsom salts is a colorless crystal of magnesium sulfate. It is called Epsom after the city in England where it was first used. When dissolved in water and swallowed, it causes the bowels to release stool. Dumped in bathwater, it draws toxins, infection, and inflammation out of the body. It does this by osmosis.

Osmosis is the movement of water (or any solvent) from an area of higher concentration to an area of lower concentration through a selectively permeable membrane. The magnesium salt in the bath is stopped from moving into your body by your skin (a selectively permeable membrane), but the water inside your body is able to move into the bathwater through your pores. So, out comes the fluid built up around an injury, or toxic irritants dissolved in body fluids that are attacking joints in conditions of arthritis.

Dump around three pounds of Epsom salts into a steamy hot bath, and relax in the water for ten to twenty minutes, submerging as much of your body as you can. Rinse off in the shower.

Caution:

- Do not take an Epsom salts bath if you have a weak heart or hypertension.
- Do be sure to drink lots of water before and after the bath.

- All salts are drying, including magnesium sulfate, so after your Epsom salts bath, nourish your skin with sesame oil or a good-quality moisturizer.

COLD HIP BATH

According to Raymond Dextreit, a French natural medicine practitioner, hip baths accelerate the discharge of waste products. A cold hip bath is particularly good for constipation, but is also useful for a multitude of conditions. The cold water stimulates the nervous system, improves blood circulation, and causes an increase in peristalsis (the rhythmic contractions that move feces through the intestines).

In *Our Earth, Our Cure,* a compilation of the best of Dextreit's forty-three books, the naturopath recommends the following procedure for a cold hip bath:[15]

- First, make sure the bathroom itself is warm. If the room isn't warm, keep your upper body covered during your hip bath.
- The first time, sit in the tub for a few minutes in a small amount of lukewarm water.
- On each succeeding day, sit in cooler water, until it is around 64°F.
- Keep the water level no higher than just above your pubic bone.
- If the water feels very cold, sit for no longer than three minutes.
- After the bath, massage your skin vigorously. You can use a towel, your hand, or a dry brush massager.

Caution: Never take a hip bath under any of these conditions:

- if you are menstruating
- if you are seriously fatigued
- if the bath causes you palpitations or other heart reactions
- if you feel your whole body is chilled

BOWEL CLEANSING

In general, we can say that the blood is only as clean as the bowel, and since the blood circulates through every organ in the body and reaches every cell in the body, toxins in the blood due to a dirty bowel contaminate the entire body. To properly cleanse the body tissue we must start by a thorough cleansing of the bowel.
—Bernard Jensen, D.C.

An enema is the introduction of water into the colon to cleanse the bowel and help improve bowel function. I bet you're thinking you'll skip this detox option, but consider this: the quality of your blood depends on the kind of substances that are dumped into the bloodstream through your intestinal walls. If you have a quick transit time of waste (eight to twelve hours), your bowel movements are large and well-formed, and your digestion is accompanied by a minimum of gas and bloating, your waste-removal system is functioning well, and you can probably assume that mostly it's good nutrition that is being transported through the intestinal lining into your bloodstream.

However, if you have to use a lot of wiping to clean yourself after a bowel movement, or if the output each day isn't anywhere near the quantity of food you've consumed (for example, if you go more than a day without a bowel movement), or if you suffer from gas and hemorrhoids, you have a waste removal problem that must be solved. Otherwise, your intestines are going to continue to seep toxic substances into your bloodstream and counteract all the good you do with your detoxification program.

Of course an enema, or a series of enemas, is only a temporary solution to a systemic problem. If your bowels aren't working well, you must discover the cause and solve the problem. Here are some reasons why your bowels might be lazy:

- food allergies (the most likely suspects are grains and dairy)
- excessive consumption of white flour, white sugar, overcooked vegetables, and other denatured, poor-quality, low-fiber foods

- dehydration (how many hours has it been since you drank a "water glass" full of water?)

Giving yourself an enema

It may sound disgusting, insulting, and unpleasant to give yourself an enema. However, folks have been doing it for at least thirty-five hundred years! Colon cleansing was mentioned in the Ebers Papyrus, a medical text of ancient Egypt. Hippocrates, a fifth-century B.C. Greek physician, used enemas to treat fever. And the Essenes, a biblical-era religious sect, reportedly used a long-necked gourd for cleansing the colon. Luckily, your tools will be more easily controlled and a lot more hygienic.

How often should you administer an enema? You're hoping I'll say do it just once, and never again. Sorry. The answer is: how many enemas you need depends on your condition. Whenever you have a severe headache or a fever; or you are suffering from a serious health challenge; or you know you've been exposed to toxins; or you have binged for some time on white flour, white sugar, and hydrogenated oils, you may want to give yourself at least one enema and maybe more to clean yourself out.

Check with your local medical equipment store for an enema set containing a plastic two-quart bucket with an outlet, and a long flexible tube to attach to it. The bucket is transparent, allowing you to see the water level as it drops. If you can't find the bucket locally, see "Resources" at the end of this chapter, or use a standard rubber enema bag from your drugstore. It comes with tubing and a hard plastic tip.

Whether it's a bucket or bag, the kit should include a clamp that can stop water flow. You may also want a lubricant. Use K-Y Jelly or some other nontoxic substance, such as cooking oil or a pierced vitamin E capsule. Don't use petroleum jelly. When you are working this hard to detox, you don't want petroleum products inside polluting you!

Attach the tubing to the bucket or bag. Keep the tubing clamped as you fill the bucket or bag with lukewarm water. If you have a serious health challenge, you may want to use distilled or filtered water. Hang the bucket or bag about one and a half feet above your hip. A good spot is a bathtub faucet. One woman used a shoestring and the hook that came with her enema kit to attach her bag to the shower enclosure handle.

If your bathtub is long enough for you to lie in it comfortably, run hot water in the tub until the porcelain feels toasty warm (let the water out before you step in). Or lay several thick towels on your bathroom rug, and on top of them lay a plastic sheet, an inexpensive painter's tarp, or a waterproof paper sheet from a home health care equipment store.

Release the clamp so water flows out the end of the tube and into the empty tub. This pushes out any air that was in the tube. Now, clamp it again, near the open end.

Lubricate the end of the tube, if you need to in order to insert it. Kneel in the tub, or on the floor next to the tub on your soft pile of towels, with the tube in your hand. Insert into your rectum four to five inches of the narrow tubing that is attached to the bucket, or as much of the tip that goes with the bag as is comfortable. Now lie down on your left side, knees bent.

Open the clamp. Water will flow into your colon. If you feel uncomfortable, bend the tube so it's double in your hand. This is the quickest way to stop the water flow until you are ready to let more in. If you need to free your hand to massage your abdomen, close the clamp.

When you have reached your limit or when the bucket is empty, clamp the tube. (This is to stop backflow. Also, there may still be water inside the tube, even if the bucket is empty.) Remove the tube from your body, and drop the tube into the bathtub.

See if moving your hips from side to side, contracting your buttocks in a rhythmic manner, or telling yourself to relax while consciously relaxing your shoulders, neck, and lower anatomy, will allow you to keep the water inside for a bit longer.

Massage your abdomen up on the left, across, and down the right, which is the opposite direction of the movement of feces. You want to encourage your bowel walls to release any impacted feces. To this end, also move to your right side, and onto your back, massaging in all positions.

Release the water into the toilet. Now you can help the release by massaging up the right side, and down the left.

You may want to repeat the procedure until what you release is clear water.

Be sure to clean the equipment thoroughly with hot soapy

water, and air dry. Be sure to clean the bathroom surfaces involved in this procedure thoroughly with soap or disinfectant.

Caution:

- Drink plenty of water the day you give yourself an enema, to replenish your body's water and electrolyte supply.
- An enema should not be used as a replacement for correcting constipation that results from improper eating habits. It should also not be used if you are pregnant or have had surgery on your bowel.
- Use great care in giving an enema to children and infants, to avoid puncturing through their intestinal wall. In fact, the best ways to correct children's digestive problems is not enemas at all. Instead, it's better to help children deal with the stress in their life, give them acidophilus to replenish the helpful bacteria that inhabit their gut, and avoid giving them foods that irritate their digestive tract, such as milk products, eggs, wheat, corn, peanuts, and/or soybeans.

Different kinds of enemas
You might say there are different soaks for different folks. Here are a few of them.

- Hot water (104°–110°). Causes blood flow to increase to the abdomen. Useful for diarrhea, intestinal parasites, and other bowel problems, as well as pain in distant sites, including headache.[16]
- Lukewarm water. Useful for most enemas.
- Charcoal. Draws out toxins. Dissolve one tablespoon of charcoal in eight ounces of lukewarm water. Available in capsules or bulk in health food stores or have your pharmacy contact Starwest Botanicals at (800) 800-4372 or (916) 853-9354 in Rancho Cordova, California. Keep the bucket not much higher than your shoulders, so the charcoal water enters the rectum gently, and can be held inside until absorbed. According to Agatha Thrash, M.D., and Calvin Thrash, M.D., in *Home Remedies*,[17] a charcoal retention enema is an excellent treatment for toxicity from snakebites, kidney failure, drug overdose, or any other

toxic state, or for inflammations or infections.
- Bentonite clay. Clay can soothe an irritated digestive tract. Bentonite clay, writes naturopath Richard Anderson, "can absorb 180 times or more its own weight in toxins, bacteria, and parasites."[18] In *Healthy Healing,*[19] Linda Rector-Page, N.D., Ph.D., recommends using a half cup of clay per enema bag or bucket.
- Garlic. Destroys parasites, viruses, and bacteria. In *Healthy Healing,* Rector-Page suggests blending six garlic cloves in two cups cold water.[20] Strain. Add to one quart of water for the enema.
- Acidophilus. One of the bacteria that live harmoniously in our digestive tract, helping us absorb nutrients and counteracting the overgrowth of illness-causing bacteria. Since acidophilus and another species called bifidobacteria are the most prevalent form of bacteria in a healthy intestinal tract, you don't have to worry about using too much acidophilus. In general, use four to six ounces of powder in the quart bucket or enema bag.

IMPLANTS

The purpose of an implant isn't to clean out the bowel; it's to move some healing substance into your bloodstream through the lining of the colon. You can do that by holding the fluid inside you. Aim for approximately fifteen to twenty minutes. This is a goal to strive for over time! At first, you may last less than five minutes.

Remember that all these detox techniques are to be done more than once, so don't become upset when you don't get the immediate results you desire. Real life is an approximation of the ideal.

Coffee implant

It may be shockingly new to you, but coffee implants have been used successfully since their introduction by Dr. Max Gerson in the 1930s. Gerson used them with his cancer patients to help the liver release toxins, the gallbladder release bile, the intestines work more effectively, and the body to function at a more efficient level.

"When cancer cells are broken down, they are extremely toxic," says Patrick McGrady, Jr., whose CANHELP service links cancer patients with useful therapies worldwide.[21] "Whenever you use anything to kill cancer cells, you should use coffee enemas, even with chemotherapy."

Caffeine is the main active ingredient in coffee used for these purposes. According to Dr. Ian Gawler, "Caffeine introduced into the rectum by enema is absorbed by the rectal veins into the portal vein, passing from there directly to the liver. There it stimulates bile flow. Bile is a major means of eliminating toxic material from the body."[22]

Gawler, an Australian veterinarian, used coffee enemas regularly to eliminate the pain from his bone cancer as well as to help his body detoxify. In fact, a number of cancer survivors report the same phenomenon: their pain is relieved by a coffee implant.

Use only freshly ground coffee, preferably organically grown. Use two tablespoons of coffee to one pint of water. Boil, then simmer ten minutes. Strain it and decant through a mesh strainer. Do not filter. Filtering removes palmitates, which are chemicals that stimulate a powerful enzyme in the body, called glutathione-s-transferase, to fight cancer.

Give yourself a plain water enema while the coffee is cooling, so you will be empty enough to be able to hold the coffee inside you for ten to fifteen minutes. When the coffee is cooled to body temperature, pour it into your enema bucket or bag.

Use the same procedure as with a water enema (page 139) to get the coffee inside you. Reading may draw your attention away from a need to evacuate. You will also want something to raise your hips, such as a folded-over pillow covered with a piece of plastic, or an upside-down backrest, also covered with plastic.

The longer you retain the coffee, the more of it will be absorbed into your body. Release the fluid when you need to, or at the end of twenty minutes.

Susie Thackston, age 43, Agoura Hills, California: "The first time I used a coffee enema was to try to break a cycle of repeated bronchial infections. I related the infections to having had a shot of BCG [a vaccine given to Thackston as partial treatment of her breast cancer], but they may just have been due to my immune system being down fighting the cancer. Nothing worked, so I finally did the coffee enema and the next day, I felt better. I found if you do the enema in the morning, you feel better later that same day.

"Over the course of the next year or two, whenever I felt the bronchial thing come on, I would do the coffee enema and the infection would never get full blown. Over the last couple of years, David and I use a coffee enema whenever we come down with anything longer than twenty-four hours, and it will perk us right up! (Pun intended. . . .)"

Susie's husband, David Jackson, age 52: "One morning I had some kind of fever. I felt disoriented, had the shakes, my nose was congested, and I had pains in my intestines. This went on until four in the afternoon. I was going to take some painkillers, but instead did the coffee enema. The pain stopped, and believe it or not my nose became uncongested."

Wheat grass implant

Grass? Yes! The young, green, grass stage of the amber waves of grain, cut and ground in an old-fashioned, cast-iron meat grinder to release a dark green juice, pungent with chlorophyll. Or wheat grass pushed with a wooden plunger into the waiting jaws of an electric wheat grass juicer. Or wheat grass quick dried into a powder and added to water.

Wheat grass is rich with nutrients: one hundred grams of wheat grass (about one-fifth of a pound) has over 23,000 IU of vitamin A, 32 grams of protein, 100 micrograms of folic acid, 34 grams of iron, 51 milligrams of vitamin C, and 543 milligrams of chlorophyll. Being a living food, it also contains enzymes, the workhorses of our body's biochemistry.

Chlorophyll has been called "green magic" by one medical doctor.[23] It has been scientifically proven to control the growth of bacteria, stimulate repair of damaged tissues, relieve pain, reduce inflammation, eliminate odors, and heal both internal and external wounds and ulcers. It promotes regular bowel movements and reduces gas. Researchers have found that chlorophyll from wheat grass and other cereal grasses as well as green vegetables can counteract the cancer-causing effects of a number of toxic substances in our food and environment, such as radiation, coal dust, tobacco, charcoal-broiled meat, and red wine.[24]

In one study, a product called Kyo-green was tested for its benefit on the immune system and as a cancer fighter. Kyogreen is a powdered drink containing wheat grass, young barley leaves, chlorella (an alga), and kelp. Laboratory data suggest these green substances can help protect us against mutations and cancer, and improve our immune function.[25]

You may find the grass for sale at a local health food store, juice bar, or farmers' market. You can also buy it from a distributor, and have it sent to you (see "Resources" at the end of this chapter). Wait to buy it until you have obtained a means of juicing it. Wheat grass juice is difficult to extract because of the toughness of the grass stem. Do not use your usual juicer to make wheat grass juice, or you can blow out the motor. If you are going to use wheat grass regularly, you will either want to purchase a juicer made specifically to grind wheat grass or use an old cast-iron meat grinder that is tough enough for the job.

Wheat grass is easy to grow yourself. Juice bars may charge you a dollar an ounce. By growing it yourself, you can have wheat grass juice for pennies an ounce. For directions, see *The Wheatgrass Book* by Ann Wigmore,[26] or contact distributors. (See "Resources" at the end of this chapter.)

First, prepare two to two and a half ounces of wheat grass juice. Next, give yourself a warm water enema. This washes you out and prepares your colon to hold onto the implant.

After expelling the water, wait until the colon feels relaxed. Clean the enema bag or bucket and tubing. If you are using powdered grass, add two tablespoons powder to half cup water. If you are using fresh wheat grass juice, pour the couple of ounces you made or bought into the bucket, bag, or, perhaps even more convenient, a bulb syringe.

If you are using a bucket or bag, release the clamp and allow a small amount of juice to flow into a cup, to eliminate air in the tube. Reclamp, and pour the extra juice back into the bucket or bag. Attach the bucket by one handle so it tips forward. If you are using an enema bag, if possible have the bag tipped, too, so the juice will flow into the tube.

If you are using a bulb syringe for the implant instead of a bucket, squeeze the bulb and keep your hand squeezing it while you withdraw the tip, to avoid the liquid returning into the bulb.

Lie on your back, with your hips up on a plastic-covered pillow or upside-down backrest. Hold the implant as long as possible before releasing it into the toilet. The longer you hold it, the more will be absorbed.

SWEATING

As long as you replace lost fluids and minerals, sweating is a safe and pleasant method of detoxification. The sweat carries in it unwanted material that wasn't eliminated by bowel, bladder, or breath. Using sweating in addition to nutritional support, people have reported relief from any number of conditions, from arthritis pain to the multitude of symptoms called Gulf War syndrome.

Your skin contains about three million sweat glands.[27] Most release water, salt, and minute quantities of other dissolved substances directly onto the skin surface. These glands, called eccrine glands, are mostly found on your palms and soles, but also on your upper lip, forehead, neck, chest, and to a lesser extent on other parts of your anatomy. A second form of sweat glands, the apocrine glands, are found mostly under the arms and in the pubic region. These secrete hormonelike pheromones that play a role in sexual attraction. In this section, however, we are interested in plain old unglamorous sweating.

The blood vessels lying beneath the surface of the skin feed unwanted material into your sweat glands. However, about 99 percent of sweat is water, so you need to carefully replace what you sweat out. How much water you need to drink to replace what you've sweated out depends on how big, round, and heavy you are (a six-foot-two man weighing 280 pounds is going to need to drink a lot more water than a five-foot-one slender woman). Experts studying athletic performance encourage athletes to replace the water they sweat out by drinking an equal amount of water, to prevent stress on their heart and loss of body heat.[28] That's good advice for non-athletes, too.

How much you actually sweat depends on more than your body weight and shape. Different people have different numbers of active sweat glands. Some people are termed *atopics* by dermatologists. These folks tend to have allergies, like hay fever, and don't sweat as much as others. Atopics need to watch out, because they can easily become overheated.

Anyone can oversweat when conditions demand more of sweat glands than they are used to. Numerous men in Vietnam, for example, suffered severe prickly heat (miliaria), an irritating skin rash caused by the overloaded demands on the sweat glands in that intensely hot, intensely anxiety producing environment. If your glands are not given enough time to regenerate after a prickly heat episode, you can suffer heat stroke.

Cell washing

In *Inner Cleansing*, Carlson Wade describes a simple cell-washing ritual:[29]

1. Sit in a steamy hot bath for about fifteen minutes. Make sure you are perspiring.
2. Let the water out, and for about three minutes stand under a cool shower. You should feel a pleasant sting. The hot water opened your pores, releasing toxins into the water. The colder water closes your pores to keep out pollutants. You can further support your detox by drying yourself with a rough towel.

If you belong to a health club, you can use the club's sauna or steam room to wash out your cells.

For further information about a doctor-supervised sweat-based detoxification system, see HealthMed in chapter 13.

In these few chapters we have covered some of the simplest and least expensive forms of detoxification available. Let's move on to techniques that may be just a bit more demanding in terms of finances and methodology.

RESOURCES

Books and journals:

Joan Borysenko, Ph.D., and Miroslav Borysenko, Ph.D., *The Power of the Mind to Heal* (Carson, Calif.: Hay House, 1994). Anything Joan Borysenko writes is suffused with love, devotion to truth, and compassion. As always, this one's enlightening, comforting, and inspiring.

Allen Klein, *The Healing Power of Humor: Techniques for Getting through Loss, Setbacks, Upsets, Disappointments, Difficulties, Trials, Tribulations, and All That Not-So-Funny Stuff* (Los Angeles: Jeremy P. Tarcher, 1989). Thought-provoking, and the jokes are pretty good, too.

Gerald Jampolsky, M.D., *Love Is Letting Go of Fear* (Berkeley: Celestial Arts, 1979). This book drew me out of a deep depression some years ago, by allowing me to view the world and my place in it through a different lens. It is full of cartoons that make it fun and easy to skim and still get the messages of hope and joy in living.

Paul Pearsall, Ph.D., *The Pleasure Prescription: To Love, to Work, to Play—Life in the Balance* (Alameda, Calif.: Hunter House, 1996). Pearsall, a therapist, is married to a Hawaiian and weaves his lessons for creating a peaceful, calm, unhurried, loving lifestyle of true family values and the most life-enhancing work ethic with the thread of a Polynesian worldview.

Clinics in Dermatology, vol. 14, no. 6 (November–December 1996). The entire issue of this medical journal is devoted to balneology, the study of the therapeutic effects of bathing!

For wheat grass:

Sungrown Organic Distributors, 2325 Hollister Street, San Diego, CA 92154 (800/995-7776).

For wheat grass juicers and enema buckets:

Optimum Health Institute Store, 6970 Central Avenue, Lemon Grove, CA 91945-3346 (619/464-3346). Call for price.

Hippocrates Health Lifechange Center, 1443 Palmdale Court, West Palm Beach, FL 33411 (407/471-8876).

REFERENCES

1. David Siegal, "Psychosocial Aspects of Cancer Treatment," *Seminars in Oncology* 1 (Suppl 1), S1-36–S1-47 (Feb. 24, 1997).

2. Dean Ornish, M.D., *Dr. Dean Ornish's Program for Reversing Heart Disease* (New York: Ballantine, 1992).

3. Allen Klein, *The Healing Power of Humor* (Los Angeles: Jeremy P. Tarcher, 1989)., 19.

4. John Diamond, M.D., *Your Body Doesn't Lie* (New York: Warner, 1989).

5. Yet Aun Lim et al., "Effects of Qigong on Cardiorespiratory Changes: A Preliminary Study," *The American Journal of Chinese Medicine*, 1993; 21 (1): 1–6, As listed in *Clinical Pearls 1993*, edited by Chelsea J. Carter, et al. (Sacramento, Calif.: ITServices, 1994), 94.

6. Richard Anderson, N.D., N.M.D., *Cleanse and Purify Thyself* (self-published, 4th ed., 1994).

7. Anderson, 119.

8. George Feuerstein, *Encyclopedic Dictionary of Yoga* (New York: Paragon House, 1990), 267.

9. Virendra Singh et al., "Effect of Yoga Breathing Exercises (Pranayama) on Airway Reactivity in Subjects With Asthma," *The Lancet* June 9, 1990; 335: 1381–1383.

10. Breath Control, "Yoga," in *Alternative Medicine*, the Burton Goldberg Group, comp. (Fife, Wash.: Future Medicine Publishing, 1995), 471.

11. Nancy Zi, *The Art of Breathing* (Glendale, Calif.: Vivi Company, 1997).

12. Carolyn Reuben, *Antioxidants: Your Complete Guide* (Rocklin, Calif.: Prima, 1995), 160.

13. Gunter Speit, M.D., et al., *Mutation Research* April 1995; 346: 195–202. As reported in "The Exercise Paradox" by Jack Challem, *Let's Live*, August 1996: 39.

14. "Water, Electrolytes and Acid-Base Balance" by H. T. Randall in *Modern Nutrition in Health and Disease*, Sixth Edition (Philadelphia, PA: Lea & Febigir, 1980), p. 355.

15. Raymond Dextreit, *Our Earth, Our Cure*, trans. Michel Abehsera (New York: Swan House, 1974), 58. A newer edition was published by Carol Publishing Group in 1993.

16. Agatha Thrash, M.D., and Calvin Thrash, M.D., *Home Remedies* (Seale, Ala.: Yuchi Pines Institute, 1981), 78.

17. Ibid.

18. Richard Anderson, N.D., N.M.D., *Cleanse and Purify Thyself* (self-published, 4th ed., 1994).

19. Linda Rector-Page, N.D., Ph.D., *Healthy Healing* (Sonora, Calif.: Healthy Healing Publications, 10th ed., 1996), 446.

20. Ibid.

21. CANHELP, Patrick McGrady, Jr., 3111 Paradise Bay Road, Port Ludlow, WA 98365-9771 (360/437-2272; fax 206/437-2272).

22. Ian Gawler, D.V.M., *You Can Conquer Cancer* (Melbourne: Hill of Content, 1984), 93.

23. H. E. Kirschner, M.D., in *Nature's Healing Grasses* (Riverside, Calif.: H. C. White, 1960), quoted in *Cereal Grass* [see note 23], 42.

24. Ronald L. Siebold, ed., *Cereal Grass*, (New Canaan, Conn.: Keats, 1991), 44–48.

25. Benjamin Lau, H.S., M.D., Ph.D., et al., "Edible Plant Extracts Modulate Macrophage Activity and Bacterial Mutagenesis," *International Journal of Clinical Nutrition*, July 1992; 12(3): 147–155, as published in *Clinical Pearls 1992*, compiled by Kirk Hamilton PA-C (Sacramento, Calif.: ITServices, 1993), 128.

26. Ann Wigmore, *The Wheatgrass Book* (Wayne, N.J.: Avery, 1985), 65.

27. Charles B. Clayman, ed., *The American Medical Society Encyclopedia of Medicine* (New York: Random House, 1989), 958.

28. Edward F. Coyle and Scott J. Montain, "Benefits of Fluid Replacement with Carbohydrate During Exercise," *Medicine and Science and Sports and Exercise*, 1992; S324–S330. In *Clinical Pearls 1993* [see note 5], 149.

29. Carlson Wade, *Inner Cleansing* (West Nyack, N.Y.: Parker Publishing, 1992), 158.

PART 3

THE NEXT STEP—MODERATELY PRICED DETOX TECHNIQUES

EIGHT

SUPPLEMENTS FROM EARTH AND SEA

The term nutritional supplementation *includes the use of vitamins, minerals, and other food factors to support good health and prevent or treat disease.*

—*Michael T. Murray, N. D.*

The basis of health isn't dramatic advances in pharmaceuticals or surgical procedures, it's that eighth glass of water today, the fruit salad for dessert, the frequent vigorous exercise, the optimistic attitude, and the supportive circle of friends. Yet, there comes a time when ordinary life choices just aren't enough, and for better health you need something extra.

Your liver may be genetically less efficient at processing pollutants than someone else. Your lungs and immune system may be genetically extra sensitive to natural pollens and molds. It could be the toss of the genetic dice, a traumatic accident, living or working with smokers or other environmental pollution, or just the gradual accumulation of wear and tear.

Alternately, you may be in excellent health and simply desire to remain that way. As you will read in this chapter, even an excellent diet may no longer provide you with enough basic nutrients to maintain that level of excellent health. Whatever the cause of poor health, nutritional supplements can come to your rescue, if you choose the ones which provide the relief you need or which will prevent disease.

When we think of supplements, we think of individual vitamins like vitamin C. However, supplementation includes special foods such as seaweed and algae, which provide your body a broad platform of nutrition on which to stand.

NUTRITIONAL SUPPLEMENTS

In an ideal world, the farmer's fields would be dark, loamy, and nutrient-dense. Plants would suck these minerals up, along with pristine water that had fallen from azure skies, and the plants would be picked at the peak of ripeness. You would eat this succulent body fuel raw or lightly steamed, satisfying your body cells' every need with exquisite precision.

A century ago, this idyllic situation very nearly existed: the food grown in America was local, picked ripe, and rich with health-providing nutrients. Heart disease and cancer were rare among adults, and even rarer among children. If those folks had been able to stop premature deaths from infectious diseases, they would have lived long and healthy lives.

Today, though we have solved to a great extent the problem of infectious diseases shortening life span, we are, as a people, suffering from cellular pollution and malnutrition. These conditions allow for a sickly life that stretches longer, but with degenerative ailments that bring pain and infirmity over the years.

Our country's nutrient story is so different today, that even a vegetarian living on greens and grains may not be getting adequate vitamins and minerals, and it is rare to find anyone who feels physically well. Thus, you need nutritional supplements to properly nourish your cells and, as you will read in this chapter, a little boost from seaweed and blue-green algae can help too.

For decades, farmers and the public alike have been led to believe that greater crop yields means greater nutrition for the masses, yet this is simply not true. When the U.S. Department of Agriculture evaporated off the extra water swelling up plants grown on synthetic fertilizers, they found that these grains, fruits, and vegetables contained significantly less protein, vitamins, and trace minerals than plants organically grown or allowed to grow wild. In some cases the synthetically fertilized plants contained only half the nutrients of the organic produce!

Michael Colgan, Ph.D., studied the nutritional content of food in his native New Zealand. He and his staff bought a variety of common foods from different suppliers, and measured beta-carotene (provitamin A) content. The RDA (Recommended Dietary Allowance) for beta-carotene is 5,000 IU (international units). Colgan's staff found that the quantity of beta-carotene in 3.5 ounces of carrots varied from 70 IU to 18,500 IU![1]

The Colgan team bought oranges at a local supermarket, and the fruit looked, smelled, and tasted perfectly normal—but it contained *no* vitamin C! In contrast, they obtained fresh-picked oranges from a grower, and found 180 milligrams of vitamin C per orange (compared to the 80 milligram frequently listed on nutrition tables for an orange).

Even if you start out with a raw food bursting with vitamins, by the time you store a head of lettuce at room temperature for one day, it has lost half its vitamin C. A head of lettuce in the refrigerator for three days loses the same amount. If you cook a vegetable, another 25 percent of the vitamin C content disappears and up to 70 percent of the vitamin B_1 (thiamin). When a pot of dried beans is canned, three-fourths of their vitamins B_5 and B_6 disappears.[2]

And what do we eat just about every day? For most of us, it's not beans. It's milled white flour conveniently and deliciously camouflaged as croissants, bagels, pasta, bread, cupcakes, cookies, muffins, and cereal. These staples of our diet are made with flour that has had its B_5 and B_6, phosphorous, and magnesium removed during the milling and not replaced, even when the label claims the white flour used has been enriched. And, what has been replaced are only fractions of the original nutrients (e.g., enriched flour contains .77mg of zinc, while whole-wheat flour contains 3.19mg).[3]

So the next time you hear a so-called expert insisting you can obtain all the necessary life-protecting nutrients you need from your daily diet, ask him where he shops!

WHY ARE OUR CROPS NUTRIENT-POOR?

The availability of artificial fertilizers with high nitrogen content allows farmers to grow the same crop one year after the next without allowing the field to lie fallow. This means organisms in the soil are not given time to replenish the land with nutrients.

Over fifty years ago, Dr. William Albrecht of the University of Missouri demonstrated the difference in crop health between plants organically grown and those synthetically fertilized. Albrecht grew two vines side by side, one in organic soil and one in synthetically fertilized soil. The vines eventually intertwined. When bugs attacked, they only infested the plant growing in the chemically treated soil, even though this plant's vine was entwined with the healthy plant's.[4]

While Albrecht was conducting experiments on the health of various soils, the U.S. Senate was declaring America's soil nutritionally a disaster. In document 264, published in 1936, the Senate claimed, "No man of today can eat enough fruits and vegetables to supply his system with the minerals he requires for perfect health because his stomach isn't big enough to hold them." The cause, the document claimed, was the fact that our food was raised "on millions of acres of land that no longer contain[s] enough of certain minerals."[5]

What was considered bankrupt nutrition back then was a bowl of spinach containing over 150 milligram of iron. Today, that bowl may contain 1 milligram of iron![6] Or take selenium, a mineral that protects you against heart disease and cancer. Wheat from selenium-poor New Zealand can contain one-thousandth the amount of the mineral that wheat from selenium-rich South Dakota can contain.[7] How important is this? When researcher Raymond Shamburger, Ph.D., compared the geographic distribution of cancer and heart disease to that of selenium, he found that people living in selenium-poor states were three times more likely to die from heart disease than those living where selenium was abundant. The same was true for cancer. People living in Lima, Ohio, had the lowest levels of selenium in their blood of any of the cities studied, and they had the highest rate of cancer.[8]

GETTING ENOUGH

In *Your Personal Vitamin Profile,* Michael Colgan helps you figure out what you, personally, need in the way of nutritional supplements. Following are some basic suggestions for improving your daily intake of nutrients, beginning with some particularly nutrient-rich foods:

Seaweeds for multiple minerals: Use dulse or kelp flakes as you would salt, or cook with kombu, hijiki, or arame and then throw away the seaweed and consume the soup or other liquid substance in which the seaweed was boiled.

Brewer's yeast for chromium and the full B complex: Take twelve tablets a day, or a tablespoon of powder hidden in tomato juice.

Blue-green algae, chlorella, or spirulina: Each form of nutrient-dense plant has its dosage recommended on the container. Generally, you begin slowly and build up; for example, beginning with blue-green algae, you take one tablet with each meal for one week, then two tablets each meal for a second week, and then four tablets per meal (they are very small tablets). With chlorella, the recommended dosage is fifteen tablets per day.

With these whole food supplements, you may begin to feel detoxification symptoms, such as headaches, nausea, skin eruptions, fuzzy-headedness, or achiness in muscles or bones. Drink more water! Cut back and let yourself build up slowly to larger doses. The goal is to detox without feeling ill. It took you years to congest, so you can be gentle on yourself and take at least a couple months to decongest!

You should, however, get down to basics right away. Lay the groundwork with a diet rich in organic fruits and vegetables and whole grains (if you can digest them), and take a multivitamin and extra vitamin C daily. Make sure your multi has vitamins A, C, D, E, and the full complement of B (B_1, B_2, B_3, B_5, B_6, B_{12}, inositol, biotin, PABA, choline, and folic acid). It should also contain beta-carotene, which turns into vitamin A in your body.

It is possible for a single vitamin pill to contain all the known vitamins. Minerals, on the other hand, are naturally big, and unless the label on your mineral tablets recommends you take several pills, you are not getting enough. A multivitamin/mineral manufacturer may have put some minerals into the formula for marketing purposes, but if the recommended dosage is only one or two a day, there couldn't be enough minerals in the tablets for your needs. Any multimineral tablets worth taking are big and bulky and require that you take six to eight pills a day to obtain a useful dose.

If you just can't stand taking so many mineral tablets, get your minerals from foods, such as sea vegetables, blue-green algae, or spirulina, as described above. Then, in addition to these, take particular supplements for your health condition.

Here are some of the ways the body shouts its need for supplementation (the nutrients possibly needed are in parentheses):

- The skin on the back of your arms feels rough and bumpy (vitamin A).
- Your gums bleed when you brush your teeth, or you bruise easily (vitamin C, bioflavonoids, and possibly zinc).
- Poorly formed, light-colored stools (vitamin C and copper).
- Little or no sense of taste or smell (zinc).
- Thyroid deficiency (zinc and copper, as well as vitamin B_6).
- Difficulty digesting fatty foods (fat-soluble vitamins A and E will also be poorly digested).
- Eczema—red, scaly, itchy skin (zinc, along with a source of essential fatty acids, such as flaxseed oil, and vitamin B_6).

SEAWEEDS

For most Americans, mention seaweed and they'll think of smelly dark whips strewn along the beach in untidy piles where the tides abandoned them. Definitely not appetizing. Yet the Japanese dine on a wide variety of sea plants that, when properly prepared, can both delight your tastebuds and release you from the grips of two devastating toxins: radiation and heavy metals.

Residual radiation from World War II; above-ground nuclear tests in the years following the war; nuclear accidents, such as at Chernobyl and Three Mile Island; and radon emanating from within the earth itself can be sources of radioactive materials, such as strontium 90. This pollutant binds with calcium, then accumulates in food sources like dark greens and milk. When you consume the food, that calcium becomes part of your bone structure, and the radiation attached to it begins damaging your bone marrow.

Brown kelp (sodium alginate) stops strontium 90 from being absorbed by binding to it, creating an insoluble compound, called strontium alginate, which is eliminated from the intestine. The alginate-containing seaweeds may also help the body to release previously absorbed radiation and repair the damage caused by previous radiation doses.

Kelp also provides an indigestible fiber that increases the bulk of stool and speeds transit time through the intestines without irritating the intestinal lining. In addition, kelp inhibits bile acids from being absorbed, reducing the risk of cancer and lowering cholesterol. It is thought that the consumption of kelp by Japanese women contributes to their low risk for breast cancer.[9]

"Use seaweed as a bodyguard," advises Susun Weed in *Healing Wise*. The algin in seaweeds prevents the body from absorbing toxic metals, such as lead, arsenic, mercury, tin, and cadmium, and helps the body eliminate those already absorbed. The high level of protein, vitamins, and minerals in seaweed, as well as the magnificent algin, makes this gift from the sea a treasure chest of healing powers. Weed believes that daily use of seaweed's "splendid feast of nutrients" improves the function of the cardiovascular, endocrine, digestive, and nervous systems, leading to healthier hair, increased sexual desire, better digestion, reduced allergies, easier menstruation and menopause, a healthy prostate, appropriate weight, and greater energy.[10]

Judith Benn Hurley, author of *The Healing Herbs*,[11] suggests your first seaweed experience be nori, which comes as a roasted and tasty flat sheet. My daughter and I like to break off pieces of nori and chew it as a snack (just remember to brush it off your teeth before smiling in public!). It is a useful wrapper for white rice, as in sushi. You can also just break it up into a bowl of steamy noodles or soup.

Other seaweeds include the flat, broad strips of kombu; the thin, miniature branches of hijiki; and red, crinkly dulse, which, like kelp, can be purchased in shakers to be used instead of salt.

Get in the habit of dropping a piece of kombu into cooking water, and then removing it before serving the dish. You don't have to actually eat the seaweed, since some of its beneficial dose of minerals will have been transferred to the water.

ALGAE (BLUE-GREEN ALGAE, CHLORELLA, SPIRULINA)

These products come in very easily swallowed tiny tablets that even a child can take.

Linda Rector-Page, N.D., author of *Healthy Healing,* claims blue-green algae contains "the most potent source of beta-carotene available in the world today, and the richest food sources of vitamin B_{12}."[12] Of particular note is the GLA (gamma-linolenic acid) present in the algae. GLA is an essential fatty acid sorely lacking in most American diets, and important for healthy endocrine, cardiovascular, and digestive functions. Algae have a reputation as a source of energy and an assist to the immune system when called upon to rebuild and repair the body. Eating algae—and other forms of seaweed—protects you from radiation and heavy metals.

Blue-green algae are rich in protein, fiber, chlorophyll, enzymes, and the vitamins and minerals needed for a healthy body. They are wild-harvested from the unpolluted waters of Upper Klamath Lake, Oregon. Other algaes include chlorella and spirulina. Much of the commercial spirulina is grown in carefully monitored and nourished man-made pools.

Each alga has its proponents and its sales force, its literature and its promises. You can compare the nutritional content of the three in detail in the table following.

The fact is, any species of algae is a power-packed, nutrient-dense food, high in blood-cleansing chlorophyll and energy-boosting protein. You'll want to take algae as a regular part of your diet for long periods of time, so try one for one bottle's worth, and then another, comparing taste, odor, enzyme action (digestibility), and effect on your energy level. Your own body will tell you which is best for you.

NUTRITIONAL VALUE OF THREE KINDS OF ALGAE

	Blue-Green	*Chlorella*	*Spirulina*
Ash	7%	3%	7%
Carbohydrate	27%	23%	18%
Moisture	6%	5%	5%
Nucleic acid	4%	3%	4.5%
Protein	60–69%	60%	65%
Total lipid	3%	9%	5%

MINERALS

	Blue-Green	*Chlorella*	*Spirulina*
Calcium	140.0mg	22.0mg	100.0mg
Chlorine	46.0mg	n/a	44.0mg
Chromium	40.0mcg	n/a	28.0mcg
Copper	60.0mcg	10.0mcg	120.0mcg
Iron	6.4mg	13.0mg	15.0mg
Magnesium	16.0mg	32.0mg	40.0mg
Manganese	0.3mg	n/a	0.5mg
Phosphorus	51.0mg	90.0mg	90.0mg
Potassium	100.0mg	90.0mg	120.0mg

Sodium	38.0mg	n/a	60.0mg
Zinc	0.3mg	7.0mg	0.3mg

VITAMINS

Ascorbic Acid (vitamin C)	5.0mg	1.0mg	0.5mg
Biotin (a B vitamin)	3.6mcg	19.0mcg	0.5mcg
Carotene (becomes vitamin A)	2,000.0RE	550.0RE	2,300.0RE
Choline (a B vitamin)	2.6mg	n/a	n/a
Cobalamin (vitamin B_{12})	8.0mcg	1.3mcg	3.2mcg
Folic Acid (a B vitamin)	1.0mcg	2.7mcg	1.0mcg
Inositol (a B vitamin)	n/a	13.2mg	6.4mg
Niacin (B_3)	0.65mg	2.38mg	1.46mg
Pantothenic Acid (B_5)	130.0mcg	130.0mcg	10.0mcg
Pyridoxine (B_6)	67.0mcg	140.0mcg	80.0mcg
Thiamin (B_1)	0.03mg	0.17mg	0.31mg
Vitamin E	1.2IU	0.1IU	1.0IU

ASSOCIATED FOOD SUBSTANCE

Chlorophyll   300.0mg   200.0mg   115.0mg

RESOURCES

Seaweed sources:

Eleanor and John Lewallen, Mendocino Sea Vegetable Company, P.O. Box 1265, Mendocino, CA 95460 (707/937-2050). Northern California coastal seaweeds. Seaweed from Northern California is clean, thanks to the tireless political efforts of the Lewallens and others. Also available from them is their own *Sea Vegetable Gourmet Cookbook and Wildcrafters Guide* (Mendocino Sea Vegetable Co., 1996). $19.95 plus $4.50 for tax and shipping.

Eden Foods (800/248-0320). Importers of Japanese seaweeds nationwide. Their customer service department can direct you to a store near you.

Good Eats catalog, (800/490-0044; Internet www.goodeats. com). Minimum order is $20 for their wide variety of seaweeds and numerous other healthy foods.

Harvest Time, 3565 South Onondaga Road, Eaton Rapids, MI 48827 (800/628-8736; fax 517/628-3325). Wholesale food distributor in Michigan, selling to buyers clubs in Michigan and by catalog to other states. Minimum order is $35.

Blue-green algae, chlorella, and spirulina are available at natural foods stores. You may also find quality-controlled brands sold through multilevel marketing organizations, such as blue-green algae's Cell Tech. Cell Tech's number is 800/800-1300.

I married into a family of algae enthusiasts. In fact, it was my stepdaughter who introduced me to algae. If you don't have a contact in your circle of acquaintances selling any, you can get information about the product from her, Leah Green, at 360/297-2280.

Books:

R. A. Kay, "Microalgae as Food and Supplement," *Critical Reviews in Food Science and Nutrition* vol. 39, 1991. A scientific discussion.

Dr. John W. Apsley, II, *The Genesis Effect: Spearheading Regeneration with Wild Blue Green Algae* vol. 1 (Northport, Ala.: Genesis Communications, LLC, 1995). Enthusiastic discussion of the use of algae for antiaging and health purposes.

Karl J. Abrams, *Algae to the Rescue: Everything You Need to Know About Nutritional Blue-Green Algae* (Studio City, Calif.: Logan House, 1996). A chemistry professor looks at the scientific basis for the health claims about algae.

REFERENCES

1. Michael Colgan, Ph.D., *Your Personal Vitamin Profile* (New York: Morrow, 1982), 31.

2. Colgan, 34.

3. Michael T. Murray, N.D., *The Healing Power of Foods* (Rochlin, Calif.: Prima Publishing, 1993), 376.

4. Dr. John W. Apsley, II, *The Genesis Effect: Spearheading Regeneration with Wild Blue Green Algae* (Northport, Ala.: Genesis Communications, LLC, 1995), 13.

5. Apsley, 37.

6. Apsley, 39.

7. Carolyn Reuben, *Antioxidants: Your Complete Guide* (Rocklin, Calif.: Prima, 1992), 48.

8. Reuben, 49.

9. Daniel Mowrey, *The Scientific Validation of Herbal Medicine* (New Canaan, Conn.: Keats, 1986), 88.

10. Susun Weed, *Healing Wise* (Woodstock, N.Y.: Ash Tree Publications, 1989), 223.

11. Judith Benn Hurley, *The Healing Herbs* (New York: William Morrow, 1995), 362.

12. Linda Rector-Page, N.D., Ph.D., *Healthy Healing* (Sonora, Calif.: Healthy Healing Publications, 10th ed., 1996), 183.

NINE

HERBS: GOODNESS FROM THE GARDEN

AN OATH TO HERBS

I pledge allegiance to the herbs
and to the chemical-free drugs
for which they stand;
one natural medicine inspired of God,
with value and good health for all.
                              —John Heinerman

Herbs are especially exciting detoxifiers because they are readily available, and if they aren't free in your own front yard or the empty lot down the street, they are as close as the nearest supermarket, nursery, or health food store.

In his *Essential Book of Herbal Medicine*,[1] herbalist/researcher Simon Y. Mills defines the common thread weaving together all herbal remedies as their power to ease the removal of waste from the body. When one eliminatory function is malfunctioning, Mills explains, there is greater reliance, and therefore greater burden, on the others, which can lead to more malfunctions as each system breaks under the added toxic load. Thus, improving elimination is a key quality of all the detox herbs discussed in this chapter.

For the novice herb taker, here are some important guidelines:

- Read carefully and fully about any herb you take. Quality of guidebooks vary, so read more than one.
- If you don't see any improvement in your condition within two months, stop the herbal remedy and seek professional guidance. ''Contrary to popular belief,'' Mills avows, ''most herbs do not take months to work.''

- A professional herbalist has not just read a few books on the subject. Make sure the person you pay for advice has a degree as an acupuncturist or naturopath, or has years of specialized training in the field of herbology.
- When a remedy you are using particularly for detoxification feels successful, after a couple weeks stop it and see if your old symptoms return. If the symptoms are really gone, discontinue the remedy unless specifically recommended to continue treatment. If symptoms return, go back on the treatment for another couple weeks and check again. For serious health conditions, you need the advice of a qualified herbalist, who may want you on herbs for several months.
- If you are pregnant or nursing, get professional guidance before taking herbs, except for the following few, which are considered safe during pregnancy: dandelion for fluid retention or liver distress; psyllium seed for constipation; and chamomile for morning sickness. Some herbs are considered abortifacients, meaning, they bring on menstruation. However, if you are thinking about using them to end an unwanted pregnancy, consider that it isn't easy to force out an embryo with herbs, and even if you do, you might retain part of the tissue inside, with serious health consequences to you. Or, you may not cause an abortion at all, but damage the fetus instead.
- Buy organically grown or wildcrafted herbs if possible, and buy small amounts that will stay fresh rather than large quantities that may lose potency before being used.

HERBS AND YOUR LIVER

Mills, who is associated with several British research and professional institutions, including the National Institute of Medical Herbalists and the Centre for Complementary Health Studies at Exeter University, believes the treatment of liver conditions is a core concept of medical herbalism. "The modern herbalist," he writes, "often finds signs that liver and bowel disorders coexist with other syndromes, particularly those which are sometimes referred to as 'toxic': migraine headaches; chronic skin disease; allergies; inflammatory and other bowel disease (and constipation, of course)."[2]

PLANTS TO IMPROVE LIVER/GALLBLADDER FUNCTION

Every culture has its liver-loving herbs: The Western world has used lemon, dandelion, milk thistle, burdock, chamomile, rosemary, garlic, yellow dock, algae, artichoke, and grape leaves. The Far East has used ginger, bupleurum, turmeric, licorice, shizandra, astragalus, seaweed, and reishi mushrooms, among others.

In some cases, as with milk thistle for mushroom poisoning, the benefit is obvious in a matter of hours. In others, it may take days or weeks to feel the difference. Yet there will be a difference. All these herbs have scientific verification as useful and even life-preserving in the treatment of toxicity. Of all the possible plants, I've picked out a few to discuss here that are easy to find and to use.

Even though I am a licensed acupuncturist and am trained in Chinese medicine, I only list a couple Chinese herbs. I believe that nature uses local plants to solve local health problems, meaning, there are plants grown in America that do the same job just as well as those more exotic varieties from across the Pacific. However, I also believe in using whatever works, whatever its source, and so I bless the universal intelligence that allows us to wriggle out of our self-made health messes with the gentle and forgiving kindness of the world's plants and flowers. Use whatever appropriate herbs are most easily available to you.

LEMON (*CITRUS LIMON*)

The lemon is a year-round blessing, for every season is lemon season, as you discover if you have a lemon tree in your yard. Lemons contain limonene, which helps dissolve gallstones and may even have anticancer properties. As with other bioflavonoids, the limonene is found in the white inner lining of the rind.

Sipping lemonade throughout the day will calm your nerves and help flush toxins out of your system, say Mildren Jackson, N.D., and Terri Teague, N.D., in their *Handbook of Alternatives to Chemical Medicine.*[3]

For a lemonade without sugar, use this recipe suggested by Jay Kordich, "the Juiceman," which I found in Michael T. Murray's *The Healing Power of Foods:*[4] Juice four apples and a quarter of a lemon (including the skin), and serve over crushed ice. As with all citrus fruits, the thinner the skin, the greater the juice content. Roll a lemon gently along a table with the flat of your hand to increase the juice yield no matter how thick the skin.

Jackson and Teague also suggest placing a raw lemon over swelling caused by blood poisoning to help relieve pain and draw out the inflammation. According to Jean Carper, lemon extract can kill roundworms and fungi.[5]

Elson M. Haas, M.D., describes lemons as "a cleanser, purifier, rejuvenator, and detoxifier, especially for the liver, as they help in fat metabolism." Haas enjoys drinking the juice of half a lemon in a glass of water a half hour before meals to stimulate gastric juices and improve digestion.[6] As Haas points out, citrus is a common additive to dishwashing detergent, to "cut grease" and so the lemon may support gallbladder function in as-yet undiscovered ways.

Careful Use of the Liver Flush
A "liver flush" using lemon juice and olive oil is a popular method of forcing your gallbladder to contract vigorously. The gallbladder contains bile, a strong liquid that digests fats. When the liver secretes bile into the gallbladder, it also releases stored toxins. Flushing out the gallbladder with vigorous contractions stimulates the liver to secrete more bile and toxins into the empty gallbladder.

Naturopathic physicians Michael Murray, N.D., and Joseph Pizzorno, N.D., authors of *The Encyclopedia of Natural Healing,* warn against this detox technique if you have gallstones. The stones could become stuck inside the bile duct, stopping the release of bile from the liver and leading to the liver being poisoned by its own wastes. This is a potentially life-threatening condition necessitating immediate surgery.

If you do not have gallstones, a flush may be useful as part of a detox program. I found a very interesting and unique recipe for a liver flush in *The Body Smart System* by Helene Silver.[8] She suggests combining the juice of one or two lemons and an orange with a teaspoon of grated ginger, a pinch of cayenne, one to three cloves of garlic crushed, and a tablespoon each of cold-pressed safflower oil and cold-pressed olive oil. For the flush to work, you need to drink it in the morning and not eat for at least two hours. The ingredients have strong tastes, so you might enjoy the experience more if you start conservatively and add to the minimum amounts as desired.

DANDELION (*TARAXACUM OFFICINALE*)

It was Ralph Waldo Emerson who said, "A weed is a plant whose virtues have not yet been recognized." He might have been speaking about the dandelion. Its bright yellow flowers and spikey leaves (like lion's teeth, from whence came its name: *dent-de-lion* in French) are rooted out with ferocious zeal by most American gardeners, who might instead be harvesting its every part with great care if they only recognized its numerous virtues.

Here's a list of some of those virtues, as described by Susun Weed in her book *Healing Wise*:[9]

- stimulates bile flow
- dissolves kidney and bladder stones
- nourishes the liver and strengthens its function
- nourishes the stomach and strengthens its function
- stimulates production of breast milk
- stimulates release of urine
- kills bacteria and fungi
- reduces swellings
- stimulates the appetite (a quality of all "bitter" herbs— dandelion was one of the five bitter herbs mentioned in the biblical book of Exodus)
- softens feces, increases fecal bulk, and lubricates the intestinal lining so bowel movements are regular and easy

"The liver," Weed reminds the reader, "does more than five hundred functions and deserves a lot of love and cherishing." Dandelion is a great cherisher. Dandelion fights all kinds of infections of the respiratory tract and can help reduce swollen lymph glands. Fresh dandelion greens are rich in antioxidants that attack those pesky metabolic Darth Vaders called free radicals. Fresh dandelion root helps relieve chronic constipation and some skin eruptions. Menstrual cramps sometimes disappear with regular use of a tincture or fresh root infusion.

Another French name for dandelion is *pissenlit* (*en lit* means "in bed") and graphically describes one other dandelion triumph: the herb is an excellent diuretic, which has even been used along with other treatments in cases of heart failure, to help relieve excess fluids while maintaining potassium levels.[10] And through its diuretic action, dandelion helps reduce swollen breasts and water retention in cases of premenstrual syndrome.

Dandelion leaves improve digestion by increasing stomach acid. This is, therefore, an especially important salad green for those with Type A blood, who tend to be weak in stomach acid (see chapter 5). It does this by tickling alert the bitter taste receptors on the tongue, causing the release of a digestive hormone called gastrin. Gastrin increases stomach acid, pepsin, pancreatic digestive juices, bicarbonate production, and bile flow.

Dandelion also increases insulin and other important substances to improve both digestion and absorption of nutrients. It is important to note that this benefit does not occur if you swallow a capsule of dandelion. Your tongue needs to sense the dandelion leaf itself.

Tea made from dandelion leaves, both taken internally and applied in a poultice to the skin, can help heal weepy rashes, eczema, and acne.

In 1952, a German study found those suffering gallbladder problems felt relief within a few days of taking the German over-the-counter remedy called Hepatichol. The drug is actually a mixture of herbs, mostly dandelion.

When you cut into a dandelion stalk, leaf, or root with your fingernail, white sap drips out. Susun Weed calls the sap "an eraser" because, she claims, it can help erase warts, corns, calluses, hard pimples, bee stings, old sores, and blisters.[11]

If you have access to a lawn or field of dandelions (which you know hasn't been sprayed), dig the roots in early spring and pick the leaves in spring or early summer. You'll know you've found dandelion and not one of its close relatives, like chicory, if the leaf is totally hairless along the midrib. Freeze for later use what you won't cook right away. If fresh herb is unavailable, check out your local health food store for tea, capsules, or liquid extracts. One to two cups of tea, one to three dropperfuls of extract, or around four capsules a day is probably adequate. Dandelion is nontoxic.

BURDOCK (*ARCTIUM LAPPA*)

Also called gobo root. Burdock has a reputation as a "blood cleanser," which probably means it helps the liver and digestive organs function better. "Burdock," writes Kathi Keville in *Herbs for Health and Healing*,[12] "has been used around the world to inhibit and slow the growth of cancerous tumors." Thus, it also acts on your immune system.

David Hoffman in *The New Holistic Herbal*[13] advises preparing the root as a poultice to help heal wounds and ulcers, and for skin conditions, such as eczema and psoriasis. He cautions, however, that internal use of this and other medicinal herbs is essential for truly healing skin diseases.

According to Kathi Keville, one reason for burdock's success in the realm of women's health is the fact that the liver deactivates estrogen, "especially the carcinogenic form, which tends to settle in breast and uterine tissue."[14]

Using Burdock
Fresh root is best. Look for it in supermarkets where Asian vegetables are sold, as well as in health food stores and farmers' markets. Ask your produce person to obtain some roots for you if the market doesn't already carry burdock. Scrape off the outer layer, chop, and soak in water with a bit of vinegar added to preserve its color and crispness. After fifteen minutes, add to stir-fry, salads, omelettes, or casseroles.

To make an infusion of burdock root, place a handful of chopped root in a pint jar, fill it with boiling water, cap it, and let it sit eight hours at room temperature. Weed suggests using the burdock infusion for these purposes:

- to soak limbs aching from varicose veins, sciatica, bursitis, rheumatism, or sprains
- to pour on your scalp after shampooing to eliminate dandruff
- to drink to relieve sore throat or any respiratory condition
- to drink so it can help your liver neutralize heavy metals, industrial chemicals, food additives, and the waste from normal life
- to drink while you fast so your intestines won't go on strike
- to place on a piece of soft cloth pressed against your skin for acne, psoriasis, erysipelas, and other skin conditions

According to Judith Benn Hurley, author of *The Good Herb*, burdock root and dandelion root "are beginning to be known as 'the party herbs' since some folks take them in tablet form the day after drinking a few too many."[15]

If you can't find the raw root, take one to six dropperfuls of tincture in a glass of water per day, depending on need.

One caveat: This herb draws out heat from inflammations and infections. Don't use it if you have cold conditions, such as feeling chronically chilled and craving hot food and beverages.

MILK THISTLE (*SILYBUM MARIANUM*)

Many lives cut short by poisoning might be saved if only American doctors know what German doctors do about the talented milk thistle. German research in the 1970s proved that an extract of the herb protects the liver against the death-cap mushroom (*Amanita phalloides*) as well as chemical toxins, such as carbon tetrachloride.

Since it improves liver function, milk thistle is particularly useful to counteract the effects of long-term drug use, whether the drugs were taken for medicinal reasons or because of addiction.

According to Kathi Keville, director of the American Herb

Association and author of *Herbs for Health and Healing,* the flavonoids in milk thistle are some of the most potent liver-protecting substances now known.[16] Of particular importance is silymarin, which inhibits the damage of free radicals, leukotrienes, and other metabolic marauders.

Silymarin can prevent toxins from penetrating into the cell by taking their place in key openings along the cell wall. Thus silymarin serves as a liver guard.[17] It is also a help in cases of hepatitis, fatty infiltration of the liver, cirrhosis, and gallbladder disease.

As Michael Murray, N.D., and Joseph Pizzorno, N.D., point out in their *Encyclopedia of Natural Medicine,* silymarin stimulates protein synthesis, which means it not only protects the liver from damage, but it prods a damaged liver to repair and regenerate itself![18]

On another front, milk thistle seeds increase milk production and are safe for breastfeeding mothers[19] (have you noticed how the names of plants often clue you to their use or something peculiar about them?).

Taking milk thistle

For medicinal purposes, take any one of the following: one to two milliliters of tincture three times a day; one to two capsules of powdered seeds per day; or buy whole seeds, grind them in a coffee grinder, and use liberally on potatoes, cereal, soup, or any other multitextured dish.

ARTICHOKE (CYNARA SCOLYMUS)

Another thistle family member useful for liver detox is this curious plant some find not worth the effort to eat, and others consider a special delicacy. European doctors have known of the plant's benefit for the liver for at least two hundred years and regularly prescribe an artichoke extract when treating jaundice, hepatitis, and other liver complaints. It has only been during this century, however, that the active ingredient, cynarin, was discovered and studied. In one study, Polish workers exposed to carbon disulfide were given artichoke extract for two years and then tested. Their blood had none of the pathological changes usually found after carbon disulfide poisoning.[20]

Cynarin from artichoke leaves not only helps protect and regenerate the liver, it also stabilizes blood sugar, releases fluids and reduces swelling, provides nourishment to the cells, stimulates the flow of bile, counteracts arteriosclerosis, reduces cholesterol, and improves the function of the stomach. In addition, extracts of artichoke have been used for infantile itching, hives, and eczema.[21]

Pay the extra coins for organic artichokes. If your goal is a healthy liver, why add pesticides to your toxic load? Choose heavier artichokes, whatever the size. All sizes are mature. With scissors snip off the barbed tips of each leaf, and with a sharp knife cut the bottom of the stalk to remove the toughest part. Then boil the artichokes in an open saucepan for at least a half hour, until a leaf easily slides away from the stalk. Remove water and turn the vegetables upside down to drain. Eat artichokes hot or cold. Pull off a leaf, and either dip the pudgy end of the leaf into a tiny bit of flavored vinegar or mayonnaise or eat it naked. Scrape this area along your teeth to release the tasty pulp onto your tongue.

The purple-tinged innermost leaves at the top of the stalk are inedible, but after you scrape them away, you have a tender stalk with a shallow bowl-like "heart" that is not only edible, but, for some, the prize of the whole artichoke-eating event.

GARLIC *(ALLIUM SATIVUM)*

The first-century Greek physician Dioscorides extolled garlic as a cure for worms, as well as a diuretic, antiasthmatic, and tonic. American Indians a continent away also found garlic expelled worms. In fact, the smelly bulb is useful for roundworms, pinworms, ringworm, tapeworms, and hookworms.[22]

Garlic was applauded in the Bible, discussed by the Egyptians, and consumed by Vikings and Phoenicians. So should we be surprised that a modern physician like Albert Schweitzer would find it useful against typhoid fever in the jungles of Africa? After all, 1 milligram of garlic's allicin is equivalent to 15 standard units of penicillin.[23]

Allicin and its cousin allyl sulfide give garlic its odor and provide its firepower against parasites and other dangerous microorganisms, including viruses, yeasts, and fungi. Thanks to these sulphur compounds, the herb is also useful against fever, inflammation, and bronchial congestion, and lowers blood pressure by dilating blood vessels. Garlic has another great trick: it attaches to lead and mercury in your intestinal tract, and helps the body discharge these toxic metals.[24]

If you just don't dig garlic, there's hope. Onions have the same powerful sulfur compounds, and protect the body from bacteria and heavy metals in similar ways.

Although deodorized garlic capsules can help lower cholesterol levels in the blood and reduce blood pressure, it is the smelly part of the plant's makeup that has the power to detoxify.

GINGER (*ZINGIBER OFFICINALE*)

Ginger inspires strong loyalty and equally strong revulsion. You either love it or you hate it. As far as detox talents are concerned, ginger is unique. It prevents the destruction of other medicinal herbs by the liver, allowing them to remain in the blood and do their good work for longer than they would otherwise. Ginger also improves the intestine's ability to absorb other herbs and move their medicinal elements into the bloodstream.[25]

TURMERIC (*CURCUMA LONGA*)

The yellow pigment curcumin is what colors curry and what gives this spice its medicinal punch. Curcumin protects the liver in a way similar to silymarin in milk thistle and cynarin in artichoke, and like cynarin, it also lowers cholesterol and increases bile flow. This last talent is particularly important, because if bile builds in the gallbladder or, worse, in the liver itself, a state of congestion leading to autointoxication results, damaging the liver.

Curcumin is a powerful anti-inflammatory and pain reliever. It accomplishes this by reducing the body's prostaglandin activity and by sensitizing the body to cortisone, making the anti-inflammatory hormone more effective.[26]

SCHISANDRA (*SCHISANDRA CHINENSIS*)

In Mandarin, schisandra is called *wu wei tzu*, which means "five flavors," because, it is said, the skin and fruit are sweet and sour, the kernels are pungent and bitter, and all together it has a salty taste. In addition to reducing liver damage in cases of liver disease, this climbing vine can reduce swelling, improve bowel function, treat insomnia and night sweats, and strengthen the lungs. It is considered a tonic, strengthening the function of all organs.

In one Chinese study, schisandra was given to one group of patients with hepatitis, while another group received vitamin E and liver extract. After six months, almost 75 percent of those given schisandra had normal blood tests compared to those in the vitamin group, who improved less and took longer to show improvement.[27]

BUPLEURUM (*BUPLEURUM FALCATUM*)

According to master herbalist Subhuti Dharmananda, Ph.D., "Bupleurum formulas are among the most important in Chinese herbalism because they treat liver disturbance—a very common problem."[28] Bupleurum root is the medicinal part of the plant, and it is useful for lowering fevers, improving digestion, bringing on menstrual periods, relieving muscle pains, and reducing diarrhea.[29]

THE FORMULA IS EVERYTHING

Chinese herbalists do not prescribe single herbs (though they are studied that way in scientific regimens based on the protocols for investigating Western drugs). So you would never be told to buy some bupleurum (or schisandra or any other single herb) for your condition. Rather, you would find it as the major ingredient of a formula prescribed specifically for you, with one herb counteracting the possible side effects of another. However, even one herb alone can make a difference in your health. Just be open to learning more with time and experience.

If your town has herbalists, acupuncturists trained in herbs, naturopaths, chiropractors trained in clinical herbology, or even a good supply of herb books at the local library, bookstore, or health food store, you can find good guidance to initiate you on the herbal path of healing.

METHODS OF TAKING HERBS

In the old days, patients would use an earthenware pot and simmer their collection of twigs, leaves, roots, and seeds for an hour or so, filling their residence with the pungent smell of their herbal formula. I think modern technology has saved many a household the distress of those aromas, now that herbs are sold in powder granules, capsules, and tinctures!

Your herbalist will have his or her favorite sources of ready-made formulas, many imported from China, Taiwan, or Japan. One company, Brion, in Irvine, California, has for many years encapsulated personalized herbal prescriptions the practitioner has formulated for individual patients.

Under "Resources," which follows, you'll find a list of books on Chinese herbal formulas that offer the concepts behind the prescriptions.

You can dilute herbs with hot water as a tea, or extract them into alcohol or glycerine as tinctures. You can macerate them and apply them to the skin as a poultice. You can dry and grind them, then stuff them into capsules or sprinkle them on food. They're versatile. They're condiments. They're food. Yet, they also influence the workings of the body's biochemistry as drugs do.

Eventually, America will create a special category for herbs, as Germany and other countries have, so the general public can have access to healing plants and at the same time be protected by government standards for quality control.

You don't have to become an expert herbalist to start using herbs. At the beginning, stick to the tonics and the liver detoxifiers described in this section. You'll soon discover that certain herbs feel like old friends. Read a variety of authors until you understand why those herbs call to you, enabling you to respond with an educated embrace.

RESOURCES

For information and referrals:

Yellow Pages. Remember this handy resource! One brief phone call to a couple of people listed under Acupuncture or Herbs in your local phone book will give you more useful information than the referral given by the secretary in a national organization who is just repeating a name on a membership list.

American Botanical Council, P.O. Box 201660, Austin, TX 78720 (512/331-8868; 800/373-7105 for subscription orders; fax 512/331-1924; Internet www.herbalgram.org; e-mail abc@herbalgram.org). Nonprofit education and research organization. Copublishes *HerbalGram* magazine with the Herb Research Foundation and provides information on herbs, including scientific reprints, to the public. Four issues for $25.

American Herb Association, P.O. Box 1673, Nevada City, CA 95959 (916/265-9552; fax 916/274-3140). Twenty-page newsletter, *AHA Quarterly*, is $20 per year. Directory of mail-order products is $4. Directory of herb education opportunities is $3.50.

American Association of Oriental Medicine, 433 Front Street, Catasauqua, PA 18032 (610/433-2448; fax 610/264-2768; e-mail aaom1@aol.com). A trade organization of acupuncturists, many of whom are also herbalists. AAOM will refer you to someone practicing near you.

American Association of Naturopathic Physicians, 2366 Eastlake Avenue East, Suite 322, Seattle, WA 98102 (206/323-7610; fax 206/323-7612). Send $5 for national list of naturopathic physicians, who are trained to use herbs and other nonsurgical, nonpharmaceutical therapies.

For courses in herbalism:

American School of Herbalism, 603 34th Avenue, Santa Cruz, CA 95062 (408/476-6377). A two-year, part-time (two evenings a week) herbology study program; the Western herbs are taught by Christopher Hobbs and the Eastern herbs by Michael Tierra. Hobbs has numerous herb books and pamphlets to his credit. Tierra, too, has penned numerous books, including the classic *Way of Herbs* and *Planetary Herbology*. Their program is two-track, for beginners and advanced students.

The Art and Science of Herbology, Rosemary Gladstar, P.O. Box 420, East Barre, VT 05649 (802/479-9825; fax 802/476-3722; e-mail jcatsage@plainfield.bypass.com). A ten-week course on the foundations of medical herbalism.

Australasian College of Herbal Studies, P.O. Box 57, Lake Oswego, OR 97034 (800/487-8839). Among their eleven course offerings is a popular one on aromatherapy.

Rocky Mt. Center for Botanical Studies, Mindy Green, P.O. Box 19254, Boulder, CO 80308-2254.

Aromatherapy and Herbal Study Course, Jeanne Rose, 219 Carl Street, San Francisco, CA 94117 (415/564-6785; fax 415/564-6799). The Grand Dame of popular herbalism America.

The Institute of Medical Herbalism, P.O. Box 1149, Calistoga, CA 94515 (707/942-1250). Specifically for health care professionals who would like to begin including botanicals in their practices.

Books:

Shatoiya de la Tour, *The Herbalist of Yarrow: A Fairy Tale of Plant Wisdom* (Sacramento, Calif.: Tzedakah Publications, 1994). "As meaningful for adults as it is for the children it was written for, *The Herbalist of Yarrow* bears, in the tradition of every true fairy tale, a message quite pertinent and auspicious for our modern world," writes Rosemary Gladstar, author of *Herbal Healing for Women*, in this book's foreword. If you have a young daughter, granddaughter, niece, or neighbor who is at all sensitive to nature, gift her with this book. Neither you nor she will ever look at a plant in the same way again. In addition, scattered through the pages are sidebars with real-life recipes for herbal-based medicinals. The publisher is defunct but the book is still in print, and can be ordered from the author if you can't find it locally. See Dry Creek Herb Farm, under "For raw herbs," following, for address.

Michael Castleman, *The Healing Herbs* (Emmaus, Penn.: Rodale Press, 1991). When I see Castleman's name on a book, I know it will be well-researched, interesting, and useful.

Ron Teeguarden, *Chinese Tonic Herbs* (Tokyo: Japan Publications, 1986). Easy to read and use, this is one of the most accessible explanations of some of the most commonly prescribed traditional Chinese herbs.

Daniel Reid, *A Handbook of Chinese Healing Herbs* (Boston: Shambhala, 1995). Useful reference that describes the Western and traditional Chinese medical uses of 108 herbs, thirty-six healing herbal formulas, suppliers, schools, and how to get started using Chinese herbs for yourself.

Li Shih-Chen, compiler, and R. Porter Smith, M.D., and G. A. Stuart, M.D., translators and researchers, *Chinese Medicinal Herbs* (San Francisco: Georgetown Press, 1973). This work was originally published in 1578.

Subhuti Dharmananda, Ph.D., *Chinese Herbology: A Professional Training Program* (Portland, Ore.: Institute for Traditional Medicine, 1992). You can contact the institute at 2017 SE Hawthorne, Portland, OR 97214.

Susun S. Weed, *Healing Wise* (Woodstock, N.Y.: Ash Tree Publications, 1989). Weed's herb books speak to you in a multiplicity of voices: scientific, playful, dramatic, and wise.

Simon Y. Mills, *The Essential Book of Herbal Medicine* (London: Penguin, 1991). Mills holds the field of herbalism up to scrutiny from both the Western academic and the traditional Chinese points of view.

Kathi Keville, *Herbs for Health and Healing* (Emmaus, Penn.: Rodale Press, 1996). Rich with useful information and lore. Written in Keville's usual unpretentious, approachable style.

Judith Benn Hurley, *The Good Herb: Recipes and Remedies from Nature* (New York: William Morrow, 1995). How to use medicinal herbs in everyday (yummy-looking) dishes, and why.

David Hoffman, *The New Holistic Herbal* (Rockport, Mass.: Element, 1990). A guidebook with sections on treatments for body systems and common conditions (including cancer) plus the preparation and action of herbs and details about individual plants.

Linda Rector-Page, N.D., Ph.D., *How to Be Your Own Herbal Pharmacist* (Sonora, Calif.: Healthy Healing Publications, 1991). Rector-Page writes for people who are strong on self-care. All her work is immediately practical. It is as if there's an unwritten banner across every one of her publications proclaiming, YOU CAN DO IT!

For herbal formulas:

Chinese herbs, since they are usually in prescribed formulas, are often sold only to licensed practitioners. If you are prescribed a formula in raw herb form and would prefer to take it as a powder or capsule, you can ask your practitioner to contact Brion Herbs, 9200 Jeronimo Road, Irvine, CA 92618 (714/567-1214; 800/333-4372; fax 800/557-1260; e-mail brionc@sunten.com).

Alternatively, your herbal practitioner can now obtain Chinese formulas produced as herbal concentrates. Have the herbalist contact JR Laboratories, P.O. Box 33381, San Diego, CA 92163-3381 (800/669-3954; fax 619/294-3954).

For raw herbs:

Nature's Herb Company, 1010 46th Street, Emeryville, CA 94608 (415/601-0700). A source of raw herbs, including the makings of the Lincoln Hospital Sleep Mix discussed in chapter 14.

China Herb Company, 6333 Wayne Avenue, Philadelphia, PA 19144 (215/843-5864).

Oak Valley Herb Farm, Kathi Keville, P.O. Box 2482, Nevada City, CA 95959. Tinctures, aromatherapy products, and essential oils only.

Penn Herb Company, 10601 Decatur Road 2, Philadelphia, PA 19154 (800/523-9971 from 8:30am to 5pm EST).

Cata Corporation, 3131 West Alabama Street 300, Houston, TX 77098 (800/267-7116, 24 hours a day; or 713/529-9397).

Bronson, 1945 Craig Road, P.O. Box 46903, St. Louis, MO 63146-6903 (800/235-3200; fax 314/469-5741). A relatively inexpensive mail-order source of herbs in capsules.

Dry Creek Herb Farm and Learning Center, 13935 Dry Creek Road, Auburn, CA 95602 (916/878-2441; 916/878-6772). Sells supplies and herbs through mail order. Herb lessons on site. Gift shop office open 9–4 PST Thurs.–Sun. Catalog costs $2. Owner Shatoiya de la Tour's fairy tale, *The Herbalist of Yarrow*, is available for $15.95 plus $4.75 shipping and handling, plus sales tax of 7.75% for California residents. Or look for it in your local bookstores and health food stores.

REFERENCES

1. Simon Y. Mills, *Essential Book of Herbal Medicine* (London: Penguin, 1991).

2. Mills, 106.

3. Mildren Jackson, N.D., and Terri Teague, N.D., *Handbook of Alternatives to Chemical Medicine* (Oakland, Calif.: self-published, 1975), 86.

4. Michael T. Murray, N.D., *The Healing Power of Foods* (Rocklin, Calif.: Prima, 1993), 145.

5. Jean Carper, *The Food Pharmacy* (New York: Bantam, 1989), 223.

6. Elson Haas, M.D., *Staying Healthy With Nutrition* (Berkeley: Celestial Arts, 1992), 301.

7. Michael Murray, N.D., and Joseph Pizzorno, N.D., *Encyclopedia of Natural Medicine* (Rocklin, Calif.: Prima, 1991).

8. Helene Silver, *The Body-Smart System* (Sonora, Calif.: Healthy Healing Publications, 1990).

9. Susun Weed, *Healing Wise* (Woodstock, N.Y.: Ash Tree Publications, 1989), 131–162.

10. Mills, 110.

11. Weed, 150.

12. Kathi Keville, *Herbs for Health and Healing* (Emmaus, Penn.: Rodale Press, 1996).

13. David Hoffmann, *The New Holistic Herbal* (Rockport, Mass.: Element, 1990), 186.

14. Keville, 152.

15. Judith Benn Hurley, *The Good Herb* (New York: William Morrow, 1995), 363.

16. Keville, 115.

17. John Heinerman, *The Science of Herbal Medicine* (Orem, Utah: Bi-World Publishers, 1979), xxvii.

18. Michael Murray, N.D., and Joseph Pizzorno, 353.

19. Hoffmann, 215.

20. Keville, 116.

21. Francesco Bianchini and Francesco Corbetta, *Health Plants of the World* (New York: Newsweek Books, 1977), 30.

22. Daniel B. Mowrey, Ph.D., *The Scientific Validation of Herbal Medicine* (New Canaan, Conn.: Keats, 1986), 230.

23. Mowrey, 122.

24. Carolyn Reuben, *The Healthy Baby Book: A Parent's Guide to Preventing Birth Defects and Other Long-term Medical Problems Before, During, and After Pregnancy* (New York: Jeremy P. Tarcher/Perigee, 1992), 90.

25. Keville, 117.

26. Keville, 47.

27. Keville, 116.

28. Subhuti Dharmananda, Ph.D., *Chinese Herbology* (Portland, Ore.: Institute for Traditional Medicine, 1992), 133.

29. Li Shih-Chen, compiler, and F. Porter Smith, M.D., and G. A. Stuart, M.D., translators and researchers, *Chinese Medicinal Herbs* (San Francisco: Georgetown Press, 1973), 76.

TEN

BRUSHING, SLAKING, PURGING, AND SNIFFING

The big question in life, is, "What do you do for yourself?" Everybody is looking for a good doctor. I'm looking for a good patient.

—*Bernard Jensen, D.C.*

This chapter moves you progressively deeper into your anatomy, from brushing the skin surface, to slaking your body's thirst by drinking more water, to purging toxins from your lower intestine via colonic irrigation, to influencing the entire system, inside and out, by sniffing the cleansing scent of certain essential oils.

A skin brushing is a pleasure you can perform every day, if you so desire. Drinking more water is harder for some people than others. You may need to put reminders around where you work, eat, and relax. A colonic isn't something you will experience often, but it has its own unique rewards. Aromatherapy has become so popular recently, what used to be an esoteric science is now noticeably present in the cosmetic sections of large department stores and drug stores as well as health food stores. If you want to know why you might use any of these varied means of detoxification useful, read on.

SKIN BRUSHING

Bernard Jensen, D.C., Ph.D., a prolific teacher and author, calls skin brushing "one of the finest of all baths."[1] According to Jensen, skin brushing removes the top layer of skin, which is composed of dead cells, and with it, various residues of acid waste. The brush massage also stimulates blood lymph circulation in the under layers, which are alive and growing. Improved blood and lymph circulation helps mobilize toxin release and cleanup.

PERFORMING A DRY BRUSH MASSAGE

Use a natural bristle brush. Avoid nylon. You can purchase body brushes in the cosmetics department of a large department store as well as in health food stores and pharmacies.

Use the few moments waiting for your shower water to heat up to brush away toxins from your dry, naked skin. Press firmly toward the heart, brushing briskly, though gently, in all directions. Brush everywhere on the body surface except the face. There are special cosmetics brushes for the more delicate tissues of the face.

Since you are literally brushing off layers of skin, be scrupulous about sweeping or vacuuming the bathroom floor and cleaning the rug regularly.

WATER: DRINK MORE!

In its most pristine state, water is odorless, colorless, tasteless, and absolutely essential for all forms of life. However, in a world enamored with diet sodas, steeped leaves, and a certain dark, pungent, bean extract, water is often a forgotten essential.

You began as a life form in the dark primordial waters, and you maintain within your genetic structure the need to preserve, ration, and distribute water to every cell, tissue, and organ. It is in water that all your body's biochemical reactions take place. Containing water, your blood, lymph, and cerebrospinal fluid slosh about their appointed tasks. Through water, dissolved substances, both desirable ones and toxic ones, move from place to place in the body. Releasing water, your kidneys, intestines, lungs, and skin excrete unwanted toxins through urine, feces, water vapor, and sweat.

To rid itself of toxic waste, your body must urinate away at least a pint a day. Most adults eliminate about three times that amount. This water must be replaced or the body is forced into what F. Batmanghelidj, M.D., calls "drought management." In *Your Body's Many Cries for Water*,[2] Dr. Batmanghelidj reports his discovery that the body does not always signal its need for water with a dry mouth. You may, for example, be dehydrated and develop a peptic ulcer. Dr. Batmanghelidj has used only water to treat over three thousand people suffering from peptic ulcers.

Alternatively, you may have morning sickness, fatigue, asthma, or other allergic reactions due to histamine release, or chronic pain. In fact, according to Dr. Batmanghelidj, "chronic pains of the body that cannot be easily explained as injury or infection should *first and foremost* be interpreted as signals of chronic water shortage in the area where pain is registered— *a local thirst.*"[3] These pains include rheumatoid arthritis, angina, low back pain, heartburn, intermittent claudication (leg pain upon walking), migraine, and hangover headaches.

If water deprivation is the true cause of your pain, drinking two and a half quarts of water in twenty-four hours for several days (before resorting to analgesics), will cause the pain to disappear. In the case of peptic ulcers, the pain disappears in a matter of minutes. In the case of asthma, you may need two quarts or more of water daily for several weeks before your asthma improves. And cut orange juice to one glass a day as, according to Dr. Batmanghelidj, the high level of potassium in orange juice can stimulate extra histamine production, causing bronchial constriction.

When researchers in North Carolina investigated the relationship between the source of water, the amount consumed, and exposure to a toxic by-product of chlorination (trihalomethane) and the risk of miscarriage, preterm delivery, and low birth weight, they discovered the most important variable was how much water the pregnant women drank! Those women drinking four or more glasses of water per day had the best outcome, and those drinking no water per day had the worst outcome.[4]

Adequate water also helps eliminate the water-soluble environmental toxins that reside in your body fluids. Many toxins in modern life are fat-soluble, and these are deposited in the fat that widens your waistline and hugs your hips. (Even thin people carry toxins in fat, because there are fats, called lipids, incorporated into the membrane surrounding every cell). Tox-

ins in fat won't be washed away in your urine until you break
down the fat cells during weight loss. However, toxins that are
water-soluble *will* be flushed out in your urine and feces even
if your fat remains.

HOW MUCH AND WHEN?

Six to eight eight-ounce glasses of water per day is the minimum amount your body needs for optimum functioning.

By observing the results of several thousand peptic ulcer
patients, Dr. Batmanghelidj has determined the best time to
take water is a half hour before each meal and two and a half
hours after each meal. "This," he writes, "is the very minimum amount of water your body needs. For the sake of not
shortchanging your body, two more glasses of water should be
taken around the heaviest meal or before going to bed."

Unlike some health advisors, Dr. Batmanghelidj does not
fear diluting digestive juices. In fact, he suggests that drinking
water around mealtimes "prevents the blood from becoming
concentrated as a result of food intake," since the concentrated
blood will draw water to it from surrounding cells.

Caution: There should be an obvious increase in urination
commensurate to your increased intake. Be sure your kidneys
are functioning well enough so your body doesn't retain the
excess water, and so they can handle the released toxins flushing through them.

KEEP IT PURE

Drinking two quarts of water per day is a simple and inexpensive treatment for toxicity. However, you don't want to
replace old toxins with new. So, although you may wonder
why this section isn't included in part 2, since drinking water
is certainly one of the least expensive and simplest of detox
methods, it can be pricey if you need to filter your water before
you drink it.

The federal government has had a Safe Drinking Water Act
in place for twenty-five years, but it takes the cost of controlling the pollutant into consideration when setting the limits for

carcinogens in drinking water, it does not give authority to the
Environmental Protection Agency to stop the contamination of
underground water sources if local governments allow indus-
tries and developers to pollute them, and it has no authority
over private wells. So you may find less than pristine water
gushing from your home tap.

It is estimated that about ten thousand of some 2 million
underground oil and gasoline tanks across the United States
are currently leaking, adding to the agricultural runoff of pesticides, herbicides, fertilizers, and organic wastes, road salt,
and industrial chemicals that pollute our rivers and lakes.
There is also danger to the deep underground sources of water,
our aquifers, springs, and wells.[5]

The Environmental Protection Agency, for example, found
819 cities exceeding federal levels for lead in drinking water,
affecting some 30 million people across the United States.[6]
That isn't surprising, since more than six hundred thousand
tons of lead are released into the atmosphere *every year* in the
United States alone.[7] Chlorine is added by city treatment facilities to eliminate toxic bacteria, but when chlorine combines
with leaves and other organic material in the water, it creates
a carcinogenic compound called trihalomethane.

In agricultural areas, nitrites from fertilizer and a chemical
potpourri from pesticides and herbicides are commonly found
in groundwater. Where industry is located, groundwater can
be contaminated with industrial waste, including trichloroethylene and perchloroethylene (commonly used in dry cleaning
clothes). In addition, landfills and other sources of concentrated toxins release industrial chemicals into groundwater
through the earth around and beneath the dump. The U.S.
Agency for Toxic Substances and Disease Registry has determined that the health of approximately 11 million people is in
danger due to their living close to toxic dump sites.

For some, there is danger of inhaling a form of radiation
called radon when they bathe, do dishes, or wash clothes. Radon is emitted naturally from some geologic deposits of ura-
nium ore. Areas particularly radon-rich are parts of Arizona
and North Carolina and an area in Appalachia called Reading
Prong, including sections of New York, Pennsylvania, and
New Jersey.

Unfortunately, exposures to hazardous substances in water

can have terrible consequences. For example, TCE (trichloroethylene) in drinking water can cause birth defects, kidney disease, stroke, liver problems, skin rashes, and speech and hearing impairments in young children.[8] Evaluating the effects of water contamination on birth outcome in New Jersey, the U.S. Agency for Toxic Substances and Disease Registry compared monthly exposures to tap water for over eighty-one thousand births (and, among those, almost six hundred fetal deaths) and found birth defects associated with mothers' consumption of tap water containing common industrial chemicals, such as trihalomethanes, carbon tetrachloride, trichloroethylene, and benzene.[9]

In some cities, municipal water supplies have been polluted with bacteria, viruses, or protozoans. In 1993, for example, if the residents of Milwaukee had drunk their famous beer instead of tap water, four hundred thousand of them might have avoided being stricken with severe gastrointestinal illness from water contaminated with the parasite *cryptosporidium*.

Some communities and some state legislatures have themselves created a toxic condition of public drinking water. Since fluoride, a chemical ion that is found most often as sodium fluoride (NaF), will draw magnesium out of bones and teeth, and the body will replace the missing magnesium with calcium and extra fluoride, and since this makes the teeth harder, some public officials believe that fluoridating drinking water will reduce tooth decay. Unfortunately, there is scientific evidence suggesting fluoride is a dangerous industrial waste product with serious health consequences:

- Hip fracture rates are greater for men and women living in fluoridated communities, because fluoride-permeated bones are not only harder, but more brittle.[10]
- Two Chinese studies found the IQ of children influenced by their level of exposure to fluoride.[11]
- A number of children and adults have died as a result of accidentally consuming too much fluoride. Have you noticed the FDA-required warning on fluoride-containing toothpaste? It reads "Keep out of reach of children under six years of age. If you accidentally swallow more than used for brushing, seek professional help or contact a poison control center immediately!"

• Neither Japan nor most of the nations in Europe fluoridate their water.

In fact, scientists from the National Federation of Federal Employees, Local 2050 who work at the Environmental Protection Agency in Washington, D.C., stated, "As the professionals who are charged with assessing the safety of drinking water, we conclude that the health and welfare of the public is not served by the addition of this substance (fluoride) to the public water supply."

Ironically, a study published in 1987 of the dental records of over 39,000 American children conducted by the National Institute of Dental Research found almost identical levels of tooth decay in those drinking fluoridated water compared to those not drinking fluoridated water.

The usual retort to those who worry about pollution is the claim that the dose is so minute you shouldn't be concerned. As David Steinmen points out in *Diet for a Poisoned Planet,* "There is no safe level of a cancer-causing chemical or of a chemical that causes cell mutations, birth defects, or illnesses."[12]

Consequently, Joseph W. Weissman, M.D., urges you to drink tap water "only for survival when good water is not available and you are in danger of dehydration. Otherwise, it is for external use only—for bathing, laundry, and household cleaning."[13] Weissman suggests holding down even these exposures, by taking short, cooler baths and showers, ventilating the bathroom afterward, avoiding long exposure to chlorinated pools, and laundering in well-ventilated rooms.

GOING ON THE BOTTLE

Bottled water may be an adequate alternative to tap water, if it is really filtered before being bottled, which may or may not be the case. Ask for a water analysis from the bottler, and compare it with an analysis provided you by your municipal water company. Consider, too, that keeping even an excellent quality water in a plastic container means eventually molecules of plastic are going to leach into the water. Do you really want to taste plastic in your drinking water?

For all the prior reasons, filtering your cooking and drinking water is probably a good idea. There are three main kinds of water filters: charcoal, reverse osmosis, and distillers. If you have a serious health challenge, you may want to combine charcoal filtration with one of the other two types to provide yourself the purest possible water.

FILTERS AND THEIR USES

- *Activated carbon block filters* remove chlorine, asbestos, viruses and bacteria, pesticides, heavy metals, and some fluoride.
- *Reverse osmosis filters* remove asbestos, fluoride, heavy metals, radioactive elements (like radium and strontium 90), minerals, pesticides, nitrates, salts, and some viruses and bacteria. Different filters have different membrane sizes.
- *Distillation units* destroy bacteria and viruses and remove inorganic chemicals, fluoride, asbestos, trace minerals, heavy metals, dissolved solids, and nitrates.

The filters found in hardware and grocery stores attached to plastic pitchers may use activated and silverized carbon to reduce sediment and improve taste, and an ion exchange resin to magnetically pull chlorine and lead from the water. They do not contain enough carbon or the right kind of carbon to do more.

For excellent discussions of the pros and cons of different filtration systems, see *Nontoxic, Natural, and Earthwise* by Debra Lynn Dadd,[14] *Choose to Live* by Joseph Weissman, M.D.,[15] and *The Safe Shopper's Bible* by David Steinman and Samuel S. Epstein, M.D.[16]

If you can't afford a water filter at this time, here are two good techniques for minimizing exposure to toxins:

- In the morning, let your tap water run at least two to three minutes uninterrupted, to allow lead and other heavy

metals leached out during the night to be flushed from the
pipes.
• Fill a large, open-topped pitcher with water, and let it sit
  on your kitchen counter, or outside (covered with a small
  piece of screen or a strainer), or in your refrigerator, to
  allow the chlorine to evaporate before you use the water
  for drinking or cooking.

If you live in a big city you are more likely to have a higher
quality water than if you live in a small town or drink from a
private water source, thanks to a bigger budget for a more
sophisticated treatment facility. Even so, it may be to your
family's best health interest to invest in a filter as soon as you
are able.

COLONICS

A colonic is the flushing of the lower bowel with water, using
a specialized machine that pumps water into you from one
hose and withdraws the water, accompanying feces, and other
material from the bowel through a second hose. The process
is often called colonic irrigation. It is performed by someone
who does colonic irrigations professionally. That person may
be hired by a chiropractor or another health professional, or
work independently.

The American Medical Association has no official position
on this technique for cleansing the lower bowel, but colonics
are not considered standard medical procedures. As usual with
unconventional health care measures, colonic irrigations have
advocates who adamantly swear they derive benefit from this
procedure as well as detractors who just as adamantly swear
colonics are of no benefit or are even dangerous.

Nevertheless, if you are careful who you go to for your
colonic, and make sure it is appropriately hygienic, you probably won't be harmed by the pleasant sensation of inner clean-
liness. You may even find it useful.

Sandra Weinrib, a colonic specialist at the Optimum Health
Institute in Lemon Grove, California, shared an interesting
thought: ''We brush our teeth daily, but we still go to the
dental hygienist every few months for a special cleaning,'' she

said. "Far more dirt passes through the colon than the mouth!"

THE MILIEU

The colon is between four and a half and six and a half feet long. The material that enters it from the small intestine must climb against gravity up the ascending segment to reach the transverse segment, and then drop down the descending segment to reach the sigmoid colon and rectum, from where it is released.

If you don't exercise or drink enough water, and you eat a diet missing fiber, vitamins, and minerals, the colon's muscle-powered peristaltic action can't successfully move the material through this twisty tube. If you have a lot of anger, that doesn't help, either. Exercise tones your abdominal muscles and improves blood circulation. Water helps prevent dry, hard stools. Fiber serves as a broom, sweeping the material in the colon from beginning to end. Vitamins and minerals support the job of nerves that tell the muscles to contract and carry out the proper peristaltic action of the colon as it twists corkscrewlike to move everything along. Anger (and any other strong emotion) shuts down this system.

If you end up with stool going nowhere, bacteria continue to multiply in this dark, moist, nutrient-rich environment. Gas, bloating, and a buildup up of toxic by-products results.

There are less serious, but nonetheless aggravating problems, too. When feces build up in the colon, the pressure on veins in the rectum causes hemorrhoids. About sixty percent of Americans suffer from this uncomfortable condition. Is it true that in this case a good inner cleanse will help prevent autointoxication? "The scientific evidence isn't there, but my experiential evidence is that it is true," says Santa Monica, California, physician Murray Susser, who brackets his enthusiasm with warnings about overenthusiasm for the procedure.

Susser has worked in several offices where colonics were offered. "If the bowel is toxic, people often feel dramatically better after one colonic," he says, "but it rarely lasts more than several days." If the person's problem involves an overgrowth of yeast or infestation of parasites, he explains, these are not going to be permanently washed out by water.

Nevertheless, there are some conditions for which colonics seemed of more permanent benefit. Earlier in his career, for example, Susser worked with a physician who gave colonics to patients suffering from diverticulosis, a ballooning of the large intestine into pockets. According to Western medical experience, this is an incurable condition caused by deficient fiber in the diet, and managed by avoiding foods that irritate the intestinal lining. Susser watched patients receive as many as three colonics a week for four weeks. Then, their before- and after-treatment X rays were compared. "Every case improved," Susser recalls, "and in some cases looked cured."

Colonics, Susser believes, are also a useful adjunct to prepare people for bowel or pelvic surgery. However, he has one problem with the often-repeated justification for the need for colonics, the idea that mucus builds and hardens along the walls of the colon. He recalls observing several dozen autopsies of people who died from a variety of conditions, and in none of them were there signs of the black mucoid buildup which is the standard description of the inside lining of the toxic bowel.

Dr. Grant Born, a Grand Rapids, Michigan, osteopath, has had a similar experience. "In the thirty-one years that I have been in medicine, I've done thousands of colonoscopies (the observation of the inside of the colon using a fiberoptic instrument). We don't observe that black ropey stuff. If you ask gastroenterologists, who make their living looking at the colon day in and day out magnified on a screen, they'll tell you they don't see it."

According to Born, the lack of obvious hardened gunk on the large intestine wall doesn't contradict the fact there can be and often is toxic material inside that ought to be eliminated. "If you give someone colonics a couple times a week, you will reduce toxins," he says, "but you need to get rid of problems higher up in the system. It's the small intestine that needs to be addressed." He wants to know if the problem originates with too little stomach acid, too great a toxic load on the liver, too acidic digestive juices, or too leaky a gut (allowing toxins through the gut walls into the bloodstream).

The whole purpose of detoxifying is to make the whole body well, so any investigations that help treat the root cause are important. Meanwhile, what if you have congestion, like a cold, and want to clear out the lower bowel immediately, while those investigations are taking place? The benefits of going to a colonic specialist include the ease with which the whole procedure takes place (compared to the hassles and cleanup needed in your bathroom when you give yourself an enema), the deeper cleansing, and the benefit to the muscles of the lower bowel of their reflex reaction to the stream of water pushing against it.

What is hanging around in your colon waiting to be expelled? Jayne de Felice, who supervises the colon specialists at Optimum Health Institute, thinks you'd be surprised. She's seen parasites of all shapes and sizes, old chunks of white cementlike barium, large chunks of undigested watermelon, whole mung beans, and other foods that weren't chewed.

Colonics aren't for everyone. Don't have a colonic if you are pregnant, have had surgery within the past year, have an abdominal hernia, have a fistula (an abnormal opening between an internal organ and the skin or between two organs), uncontrolled high blood pressure, ulcerative colitis, inflamed diverticulitis, or colon cancer.

In this day of AIDS, hepatitis, parasites, and other communicable conditions, you do have to take some common-sense precautions when you choose where to have your irrigation. Here is de Felice's list of questions to ask any potential provider of colonics before you make the appointment, to insure yourself a safe, pleasant, and healing experience:

1. Do you use disposable, prepackaged hoses and speculums (the part that inserts)? This is absolutely necessary.
2. Do you have a pressure gauge? They should.
3. What is the maximum amount of pressure you allow on a fill? No more than 2 psi (pounds per square inch) is the right answer.
4. Do you use purified water? They should.
5. Does your equipment have a viewing tube? It ought to. Seeing what comes out is not only the most fascinating and unique part of the experience, but also useful so the provider can gauge how well you are releasing material.
6. Do you massage the colon? Hand massage is the right answer. You want her to massage your abdomen a bit,

but gently, and not with a vibrator. She needs to feel what level of pressure you prefer.

7. Do you have questions for me? She ought to. She needs to know if you have a condition for which a colonic is not advised.

8. Will you do an implant of wheat grass juice, if I want it? This is a question for those who want it.

Everyone needs a sewage system, but not a cesspool. When you're stuck with one, you may want to help yourself clean out with a colonic irrigation. You *can* detox without one. But they are convenient for limited use during an intense period of detoxification, or for regular seasonal cleanings. If proper hygiene is maintained and they are performed by a well-trained specialist, they are pleasant and safe.

Naturopath Jonathan Rastrick, of Middlebury, Connecticut: "I have several machines here, and nurses who do colon therapy. That aids in the detox mode. It gets the liver to dump [toxic material] into the biliary tract [gallbladder] and bowel. We need to be sure it is moved out of there or else the patient will autointoxicate. If the person is on a detox, if they feel really bad, where there is a temporal headache, anger, and other symptoms, colonic therapy can speed things up and help with elimination."

AROMATHERAPY

A scratch-and-smell history book allows students to scratch the appropriate page and discover what a real "love apple" was a couple centuries ago, when a man and woman each kept an apple underneath an armpit and exchanged them as mementos of their love. That isn't exactly what proponents of aromatherapy have in mind, but it does illustrate the power of aroma to arouse emotions.

Aromatherapy is the use of scents from essential oils to improve your health and psychological well-being. It is a medical therapy as old as history and as fresh as the daily news.

We know that frankincense, myrrh, cinnamon, and other essential oils were familiar to the people of the Bible, and that Egyptians over four thousand years ago used essential oils for treating illnesses and embalming the dead. The fact is, you probably use essential oils yourself, every day. Does your toothpaste have peppermint oil in it? Does your household cleaner have the scent of pine? Does that mosquito-repellent candle on your picnic table smell like citronella? Did your grandfather, like mine, tell you to add drops of eucalyptus oil to a bowl of boiling water and lean over it, covering your head with a towel, so the fragrant steam would open your nasal passages when you had a cold? These are all examples of aromatherapy.

Handkerchiefs are handy when you use aromatherapy. Let's say you have at least forty minutes more to wait in the auto repair shop, but your head begins to pound with a doozy of a headache. You whip out your tiny bottle of lavender oil, pop a few drops on your hanky, inhale deeply, and violà. Lavender oil is also used for panic attacks, asthma, and mild seizures, as well as headaches, according to Dr. David G. Williams, editor of *ALTERNATIVES for the Health Conscious Individual*.[7]

There was a time when medical science scoffed at the idea of transmitting medicinal products through the skin or nose. Of course, if any of the scoffers had stuck a clove of garlic in their sock, they would have had to taste their words. For those for whom personal experience is nothing and scientific research all, scientific research has proven that transdermal (through the skin) delivery of drugs is both possible and, as proven by the now commonplace patches for nicotine and estrogen, quite successful. And in another study, students who took tests in rooms sprayed with air fresheners consistently outscored students tested in unsprayed rooms.[18] So don't think that aromatherapy is non-scents! Those scents affect your body and your mind.

GETTING IT TO THE BLOODSTREAM

There are two methods for getting scents into the brain, where they are going to accomplish their task, whatever it may be.

One is through the skin and one is through the nose. Of course, if you soak in a bath or receive a massage involving essential oils, unless you clamp a clothespin on your nose you're also going to be inhaling the oil's vapors.

The sense of smell is curious. Unlike taste, touch, sight, or hearing, the sense of smell is relayed directly through nerve channels to the brain's cortex. It is here, in the cortex, where each essential oil is interpreted and it is from here that the body is directed to alter core physiological processes, such as heart rate and blood pressure. Proponents of aromatherapy claim that essential oils can, in fact, calm you, arouse you, regulate your menstrual period, increase your secretion of neurochemical pain-relievers, allow you to think better or sleep sounder, and in ways sometimes subtle, sometimes dramatic, change your life.[19, 20]

Watch out. Others know the power of scent, and may use it for their financial gain: Realtors knows the scent of fresh baked bread will help sell a house. A researcher in Las Vegas piped pleasant scents into the Hilton and people gambled longer, raising the hotel's gaming revenues by 45 percent. In another study, clerical workers set higher performance records for themselves in scented offices than they did in unscented ones![21]

RULES FOR SAFE AROMATHERAPY

Generally, aromatherapy is safe, pleasant, and beneficial. However, since essential oils are so concentrated, and have biological effect, you do need to pay attention to a few safety rules:

- Essential oils are powerful because they are incredibly concentrated. (It takes over a hundred pounds of rose petals to create one cup of rose oil.) So, except for tea tree oil and lavender oil, never apply an undiluted essential oil directly to the skin.
- *Never* swallow an essential oil, unless specified in a recipe from a reputable source, and even then be careful.
- Dilute essential oils by adding two to four drops of the oil to two teaspoonfuls of cold-pressed and unrefined hazelnut, avocado, olive, or almond oil. If you don't have any-

thing else, your canola cooking oil can be used. For
children, the elderly, the ill, and pregnant women, use only
one drop per teaspoon.

· To keep oils from going rancid, add a capsule (100–200
IU) of vitamin E and store in the refrigerator, preferably
in an opaque, dark, glass container (see "Resources" at
the end of the chapter, for a source). Use citrus within one
year, other oils within three years.

· After diluting it, test the oil by applying it on a small area
of your skin and waiting twelve hours to make sure your
skin doesn't become irritated. Any irritation caused by an
essential oil (be it on the skin or in the eye) is relieved
with straight vegetable oil, not water.

· Oils that are safe during pregnancy are: rose, jasmine,
lavender, neroli, ylang-ylang, chamomile, spearmint,
frankincense, geranium, sandalwood, and citrus.[22]

MEDICAL USES OF SELECT ESSENTIAL OILS

adrenal gland rejuvenation	pine, spruce, basil, rosemary
air passage clearing	eucalyptus
anti-inflammatories, toxin elimination	grapefruit, juniper
blood pressure reduction	neroli, clary sage, lavender
depression relief	neroli (orange blossom)
detoxification	angelica, juniper, fennel
digestion enhancement	mint, cardamom
food absorption enhancement	rosemary

headache treatment, stress relief	lavender
liver tonic	carrot
mental clarity improvement	peppermint, rosemary
nausea blocking	ginger, peppermint
pituitary/thyroid/adrenal boosting	jasmine, ylang-ylang
stomach acid enhancement	black pepper, juniper
virus fighting	cinnamon, thyme
yeast fighting	tea tree, lavender, geranium

When choosing an oil, check what books recommend and then check your own reaction to the oil. Don't overwhelm your sniffer by trying too many scents at once. No matter what the experts say about a scent, aromatherapy is a uniquely personal experience that begins and ends with you.

Perhaps an easy way to begin is to add around ten drops (no more!) of an essential oil into your bath for a medicinal soak. Relax, inhale, and enjoy.

RESOURCES

For water filters:

Elson Haas, M.D., reveals in his book *Staying Healthy with Nutrition* that he uses the MultiPure carbon block filter in his kitchen. My MultiPure is in the bathroom, because my husband doesn't like the countertop model's tube stretching across the kitchen sink from faucet to counter. If I'd known I would someday marry him, I'd have purchased an under-counter model! One other gripe: Someone should invent a filter that cleans itself. I don't like having to spend around $40 every six months to replace mine (they need to be replaced every 400–1,000 gallons).

Contact MultiPure Corporation at 800/622-9206. The company will direct you to a distributor in your area (and if there is none, you may consider becoming a distributor yourself, for good discounts on the unit and replacement filters), or look in your local Yellow Pages. One friendly distributor in New York City is Luis Reyes at 800/700-0802. He'll mail you a unit.

Amway and NeoLife also sell carbon block filters. Look in your local Yellow Pages for a nearby distributor.

Kerri Bodmer, editor of *Women's Health Letter*, uses and recommends the Doulton Ceramic Water Filter, which removes parasites, sediment, lead, chlorine, and, with the addition of an optional ultraviolet attachment, viruses. Call 800/728-2288 for information.

For a variety of water filter options, including shower heads, reverse osmosis units, carbon block filters, and more, contact Nigra Enterprises, 5699 Kanan Road, Agoura, CA 91301 (818/889-6877). Jim Nigra represents a variety of companies, and recommends the system that best fits your needs and budget.

Dasun Company, P.O Box 668, Escondido, CA 92033 (800/433-8929; fax 619/746-8865). Portable water purification systems. Also shower filters.

NSF International, P.O. Box 1468, Ann Arbor, MI 48106 (313/769-8010). For fifty-three years NSF (formerly called National Sanitation Foundation) has been testing and certifying water filters and other products that handle food or water. For $6, including shipping and handling, they'll send you a forty-page consumer booklet detailing what to look for in a water filter and how to determine the quality of your home water supply.

For testing your water:

National Testing Laboratories, 6151 Wilson Mills Road, Cleveland, OH 44143 (800/458-3330; 216/449-2525).

Suburban Water Testing Laboratories, 4600 Kutztown Road, Temple, PA 19560 (800/433-6595; 215/929-3666).

For information about clean water issues:

Check the Internet by typing FLUORIDE as your search topic.

Clean Water Action, 4455 Connecticut Avenue NW, Washington, DC 20008 (202/895-0420). This organization runs a Home Safe Home pollution prevention campaign and works at state and local levels on water quality issues. Information is available to the public from the group's research and education division.

Water Quality Association, 4151 Naperville Road, Lisle, IL 60532 (630/505-0160). A trade organization representing firms designing and manufacturing water treatment equipment. You can ask them for manufacturers of equipment near you or obtain general information on water quality issues.

EPA Safe Drinking Water Hotline, 9am–5:30pm EST (800/426-4791).

National Safety Council's National Lead Information Center (800/424-5323; 800/424-LEAD). Offers a "Protect Your Family from Lead in Your Home" pamphlet, info on lead abatement regulations, and has specialists available for individual consultation. Information is available via fax, mail, or e-mail.

Citizens for Safe Drinking Water, 3243 Madrid Street, San Diego, CA 92110 (800/728-3833). A source of information on the dangers of water fluoridation.

For information about the hazards of colonics:

"Hazards of Overuse of Enemas and Colonic Irrigation," *FDA Consumer*, June 1984.

For a qualified colon therapist near you:

International Association for Colon Therapy (210/366-2888).

Books and newsletters on aromatherapy:

Chrissie Wildwood, *The Encyclopedia of Aromatherapy* (Rochester, VT: Healing Arts Press, 1996).

Kathi Keville and Mindy Green, *Aromatherapy: A Complete Guide to the Healing Art* (Freedom, Calif.: The Crossing Press, 1995).

Jeanne Rose, *The Aromatherapy Book: Inhalations and Applications* (Berkeley: North Atlantic Books, 1992).

Jeanne Rose, *Guide to [375] Essential Oils* (San Francisco: Herbal Studies Course, 1995).

Jeanne Rose, *Herbs and Aromatherapy for the Reproductive System* (Berkeley: Frog, 1995).

Jeanne Rose, ed., *The World of Aromatherapy* (Berkeley: Frog, 1996). Contains articles by thirty-five of the world's top authorities on aromatherapy.

You may order the books by Jeanne Rose from her, if you don't find them in stores. See "Courses on Aromatherapy," following.

ALTERNATIVES for the Health Conscious Individual, edited by Dr. David G. Williams, Mountain Home Publishing, 2700 Cummings Lane, Kerrville, TX 78028 (210/367-4492). Twelve issues a year for $69.95. An interesting, iconoclastic eight-page medical newsletter focusing on one topic, discussed in great depth, each month. Frequent discussions of herbs and aromatics.

Scentsitivity. Described as "an aromatic journal" published by the National Association for Holistic Aromatherapy (NAHA). Call 415/731-4634 for information.

Courses on aromatherapy:

Aromatherapy and Herbal Studies Course, Jeanne Rose, 219 Carl Street, San Francisco, CA 94117 (415/564-6785; fax 415/564-6799). Two aromatherapy courses are available.

Australasian College of Herbal Studies, P.O. Box 57, Lake Oswego, OR 97034 (800/487-8839). Among their eleven course offerings is a popular one on aromatherapy.

Michael Scholes School for Aromatic Studies, 117 N. Robertson Boulevard, Los Angeles, CA 90048 (800/677-2368; 310/276-1191). Correspondence courses, seminars, teacher training, and their own line of organic essential oils called Laboratory of Flowers.

Aromatherapy supplies:

Peppermint and eucalyptus oils are usually on the shelves of conventional drugstores. You can also find these and other essential oils at any health food store. The following companies will provide you with catalogs of their lines of essential oils:

Oak Valley Herb Farm, Kathi Keville, P.O. Box 2482, Nevada City, CA 95959. Tinctures, aromatherapy products, and essential oils. Catalog $1.

The Vitamin Shoppe, 4700 Westside Avenue, North Bergen, NJ 07047 (800/223-1216; 201/866-7711). M–F 7am–11pm, Sat. and Sun. 9am–5pm EST for phone shopping.

Jeanne Rose Aromatherapy, 219 Carl Street, San Francisco, CA 94117 (415/564-6785). Essential oils.

Aura Cacia, P.O. Box 399, Weaverville, CA 96093 (800/437-3301). 9am–5pm PST.

Aroma Vera, 5901 Rodeo Road, Los Angeles, CA 90016 (800/669-9514). M–F 7am–6pm PST.

Penn Herb Company, 10601 Decatur Road 2, Philadelphia, PA 19154 (800/523-9971). 8:30am–5pm EST.

Cata Corporation, 3131 West Alabama Street 300, Houston, TX 77098 (800/267-7116, 24 hours a day; 713/529-9397).

Aroma Land, 1326 Rufina Circle, Santa Fe, NM 87505 (800/933-5267; 505/438-0402).

Lavender Lane, 7337 Roseville Road #1, Sacramento, CA 95842 (916/443-4400; fax 916/339-0842). Bottles, jars, scoops, droppers, and cosmetics-making kits as well as essential oils, pearls, gels, powders, and clays.

REFERENCES

1. Bernard Jensen, D.C., Ph.D., and Sylvia Bell, *Tissue Cleansing Through Bowel Management* (Escondido, Calif.: self-published, 1981), 132.

2. F. Batmanghelidj, M.D., *Your Body's Many Cries for Water* (Falls Church, Va.: Global Health Solutions, 1992).

3. Batmanghelidj, 25.

4. David A. Savitz, et al., "Drinking Water and Pregnancy Outcome in Central North Carolina: Source, Amount, and Trihalomethane Levels," *Environmental Health Perspective* 1995 June; 103 (6): 592–6.

5. Herbert L. Needleman, M.D., and Philip J. Landrigan, *Raising Children Toxic Free* (New York: Avon Books, 1994), 208.

6. Environmental Protection Agency, "819 Cities Exceed Lead Level for Drinking Water," *EPA Environmental News* publication no. A-107 (May 11, 1993), R110.

7. Kathi Keville, *Herbs for Health and Healing* (Emmaus, Penn.: Rodale Press, 1996), 115.

8. Congressional testimony before the Subcommittee on Commerce, Trade, and Hazardous Materials of the U.S. House of Representatives May 23, 1995, by Barry L. Johnson, Ph.D., Assistant Surgeon General, Assistant Administrator of the Agency for Toxic Substances and Disease Registry.

9. F. J. Bove et al., "Public Drinking Water Contamination and Birth Outcomes," for the Agency for Toxic Substances and Disease Registry, U.S. Dept. of Health and Human Services. In the *American Journal of Epidemiology*, 1995 May 1; 141(9): 850–62.

10. Christa Danielson, M.D. et al., "Hip Fractures and Fluoridation in Utah's Elderly Population." In the *Journal of the American Medical Association*, 1992 August; 12: 746–748.

11. L. B. Zhao et al., "Effects of high fluoride water supply on children's intelligence." In *Fluoride*, 1996; 29(4): 190–192.

12. David Steinman, *Diet for a Poisoned Planet* (New York: Harmony Books, 1990), 205.

13. Joseph Weissman, M.D., *Choose to Live* (New York: Grove Press, 1988), 62.

14. Debra Lynn Dadd, *Nontoxic, Natural, and Earthwise* (Los Angeles: Jeremy P. Tarcher, 1990), 50–57.

15. Weissman, 54–62.

16. David Steinman and Samuel S. Epstein, M.D., *The Safe Shopper's Bible* (New York: Macmillan, 1995), 175–177.

17. Dr. David G. Williams, ed., *ALTERNATIVES for the Health Conscious Individual* vol. 6, no. 17 (November 1996), 130.

18. *Journal of Applied Social Psychology* 24: 1179–1203, as reported by Jacqueline Krohn, M.D., M.P.H., in "Re-

search Reports and Literature Reviews," *The Environmental Physician*, Winter 1996, 18.

19. Chrissie Wildwood, *The Encyclopedia of Aromatherapy* (Rochester, VT: Healing Arts Press, 1996), 9–11.

20. Kathi Keville and Mindy Green, *Aromatherapy: A Complete Guide to the Healing Art* (Freedom, Calif.: The Crossing Press, 1995), 13–17.

21. Keville and Green, 13.

22. Keville and Green, 21.

ELEVEN

SPECIAL DETOX TECHNIQUES: HEAVY METAL AND PARASITE REMOVAL

You will observe with concern how long a useful truth may be known and exist, before it is generally received and practiced on.

—*Benjamin Franklin*

Heavy metal toxicity and parasites seem like somebody else's problems. That's why they are unexpected. "Wipe your feet!" your mother may have nagged you when you raced into the kitchen from the yard. She didn't say "Prevent unnecessary exposure to lead dust by brushing it off your shoes on the porch!" Or she may have nagged you at mealtime to "wash your hands!" She didn't say "Prevent an infestation of creepy crawly things that comes from touching unwashed produce or uncooked meat!"

Nevertheless, living in our polluted world presents your body with numerous opportunities to allow unwanted metals and living guests to find a home. Fortunately, as you will read in this chapter, there are natural substances that help you draw out the metals and flush out the parasites. These toxins may be unexpected, but you're prepared!

HEAVY METALS AREN'T A BAND

Some copper is good for you, but too much copper (from water pipes or growth enhancer in poultry and pig feed) can cause mental disturbances.

Lead looks pretty in leaded glass, but lead in your body

from lead-contaminated calcium in nutritional supplements and antacids, from drinking water contaminated by lead solder in water pipes, from residues in the soil from the days of leaded gasoline which is dragged into the home on shoes, from lead in lead-containing glazes on mugs and plates, or from the air around lead smelters or other industrial sources, can result in lowered intelligence, learning disabilities, and impaired visual-motor functioning in children, and kidney malfunction, diminished mental functioning, and hypertension in adults.

Mercury is useful to reveal a fever when locked inside a glass thermometer, but when it leaches out of amalgam fillings in your teeth,[1] or when you consume mercury in the flesh of swordfish, striped bass, shark, buffalo fish, or northern pike,[2] it may build up to levels that poison your nervous system, causing tremors, gum pain, unsteady gait, weight loss, and emotional instability, among other symptoms.[3]

You can detoxify your body using specific foods and nutritional supplements as well as a medical treatment that pulls the heavy metals out of your body and dumps it into your urine for removal.

SUPPLEMENTS THAT DETOX HEAVY METALS

Detoxifying yourself from lead, copper, or mercury overload involves taking certain antioxidants daily, for several months. Most are vitamins and minerals. One is a plant, milk thistle (the botanical name is *Silybum*), which is discussed on page 175. It has special powers to help the liver function better, and so is a useful assistant whenever the body needs help detoxifying anything. The minerals and vitamins listed on the following pages help remove the heavy metals by taking their place in body structures, allowing the toxic metal to be eliminated in the urine and bowel.

In 1996, California's Attorney General Dan Lungren filed suit against nine major drug companies and some supplement manufacturers for marketing calcium products, including antacids, that contained unsafe levels of lead. According to national lead experts, there is *no* safe level for lead. In 1997, the Food and Drug Administration (FDA) recommendation was that children be exposed to no more than six micrograms (mcg) from all sources. Women of childbearing age in the United States have an average daily intake of lead of up to nine micrograms per day from food alone, not including supplements or antacids.

According to California's Proposition 65, manufacturers must warn consumers of any products that would provide more than 0.5 mcg per day. When the Natural Resources Defense Council had half a dozen or more samples of twenty-five different products tested, it found lead levels per maximum daily dosage of elemental calcium ranging from 0.44 mcg in Tums 500 chewable calcium supplement to 20.75 mcg in Source Naturals Calcium Night.

In February 1997, the NRDC announced a settlement with Leiner Health Products Group, one of the major calcium manufacturers, providing the manufacturer would henceforth market supplements containing no more than 0.5 mcg per maximum daily dose. By the time you read this book, I am hopeful the other manufacturers will have changed their calcium sources, so rather than list the companies cited, I suggest you do the following:

- Call the manufacturer of your favorite calcium supplement, and ask if the company tests for lead. If it doesn't, choose a brand that does. If it does, ask how much lead its brand contains.
- Never purchase bone meal as a source of your minerals. In fact, avoid any supplement with calcium in it from animal bones.
- Find out more information about lead, calcium supplements, and the progress of the NRDC's petition of the FDA to establish a national standard strictly limiting the presence of lead in calcium supplements and antacids to 0.5 micrograms per day by contacting the NRDC at its Web site http://www.nrdc.org or call one of its offices: New York (212/727-2700); D.C. (202/783-7800); Los Angeles (213/934-6900).

That said, here are the useful products that, over months of use, will pull the unwanted lead and other heavy metals out of your body:[4]

- Milk thistle (silymarin), as recommended on label
- Lipoic acid, 100 mg three times a day[5]
- Vitamin E, 400 IU
- Calcium, 1,000 mg
- Phosphorus, 400 mg
- Manganese, 20 mg
- Zinc, 30 mg
- Bioflavonoids, 1,000 mg
- Cysteine, 1–3 g
- Selenium, 200 mcg
- Vitamin C, 3–10 g or to bowel tolerance

Bowel tolerance for vitamin C has been studied extensively by Los Altos, California, physician Robert Cathcart. He discovered that people suffering from severe infections can take much more vitamin C before their bowels complain with cramping or diarrhea than people who are healthier As your body becomes healthier, you have to keep reducing your dosage to prevent loose stools. So if you have a problem for which you are taking vitamin C, build up your dosage until you get loose stools. You then know that the next dose you must cut back. Regulate your intake according to what your stools can take.

FOODS THAT DETOX HEAVY METALS

Besides antioxidants, eating seaweed (such as algae, kelp, dulse, or any other sea vegetable) and soy products (such as soy nuts, soy milk, tofu, or miso soup) also helps eliminate toxic metals from the body. When you make miso soup, avoid boiling the miso. Instead, first boil water, turn off the heat, and then add a tablespoon of miso paste per cup, and mix the paste evenly in the water. By avoiding boiling the miso, you protect the digestive enzymes in it from being denatured.

CHELATION THERAPY FOR DETOXING
HEAVY METALS

Chelation therapy involves the intravenous drip of a special amino acid blend. It is uniquely suited to remove toxic lead deposits in the body. However, it costs around $100 per treatment, and so is explained in greater detail in part 3 (chapter 13), where I discuss more expensive and involved detox therapies.

CHARCOAL

To prove a point, a scientist named Touery swallowed 15 grams of strychnine, ten times the dose that will kill a man, and survived. He performed this feat of magic before the august body of the French Academy of Medicine in 1831. What saved him was the charcoal he swallowed with the poison. In 1913, another brave scientist swallowed 5 grams of an arsenic compound and reputedly survived, because the arsenic, too, was mixed with charcoal.

"Charcoal is without a rival as an agent for cleansing and assisting the healing of the body," explain Agatha Thrash, M.D., and Calvin Thrash, M.D., in *Home Remedies*.[6] Grains of charcoal, the doctors write, are able to protect the body from "gases, foreign proteins, body wastes, chemicals, and drugs of various kinds." Charcoal can prevent toxins from building up in the blood in cases of liver disease. It stops itching from long-term dialysis, and it seems to bind blood fats in the intestines, helping lower cholesterol and triglycerides in patients with kidney failure.

Other uses of charcoal taken internally include stopping bad breath, diarrhea, and poisoning by a great number of toxic substances, including aspirin, acetaminophen, heavy metals, gasoline, opiates, narcotics, stimulants, antibiotics, pesticides, radioactive substances, poisonous mushrooms, and industrial chemicals.

Charcoal should be in the first aid kit at every summer camp. As a poultice (on a Band-Aid or double-thickness facial tissue or paper towel, held in place by an Ace bandage or plastic wrap), charcoal can draw the pain and swelling out of bee, wasp, or yellow jacket stings, even stopping an anaphylactic shock reaction. If applied quickly, charcoal can even prevent severe ulceration from the bite of a brown recluse spider.[7]

Charcoal poultices may reduce or eliminate pain and inflammation from infections, but be sure the charcoal isn't touching newly broken skin, or the skin may discolor permanently. Pain can also be relieved by charcoal poultices applied to any body location, including the throat, ears, joints, lungs, and abdomen.

Charcoal works by adsorbing toxic substances, meaning, it pulls them onto its surface. About one tablespoon of charcoal adsorbs about 3–7 grams of toxic material, so take about twice the dose of charcoal as the weight of the toxin consumed.

Making Your Own Charcoal

It would be convenient if you could simply burn your morning toast to start your day off right, but, according to the Thrashes, burnt toast is "apparently entirely worthless" for detoxing. Charcoal for medicinal purposes can be made from burned wood, coal, bone, coconut shells, black walnut shells, fruit pits, corn cobs, rice hulls, or even waste from distilleries and paper mills—but not from charcoal briquettes, as they probably contain undesirable fillers and chemicals for speedy lighting. Buy charcoal as capsules or in bulk (for under $20 you can purchase a capsulating machine, which allows you to fill one hundred capsules at a time fairly easily. Ask your local health food store about it). In Sacramento, bulk charcoal costs two dollars an ounce, and a bottle of one hundred capsules costs $4.87.

Inside water filters, you'll find "activated" charcoal. This has first been burned, then infused with air or steam at high temperature, causing the internal structure of the charcoal to fragment into a complex and intricate network, significantly increasing the surface area.

Caution: Tannic acid, found in tea, decreases the effectiveness of charcoal. Don't take charcoal and drink tea at the same time.

PARASITE REMOVAL

"Parasites," states Joan Priestley, M.D., of Anchorage, Alaska, "are epidemic in America." Parasites are plants or animals that live in or on and feed off of their hosts. Common parasites in North America are head lice, mites, fleas, tapeworms, hookworms, round worms, pinworms, trichina worms, fungi, and yeast. The problem of parasites, says Priestley, is far more widespread than most people realize. For example, Murray Susser, a physician in Santa Monica, California, specializing in chronic fatigue and other immune dysfunction conditions, claims testing has revealed that approximately a third of the patients in his medical practice have parasites.

Priestley tells the story of an herbalist of her acquaintance, a woman dedicated to clean living and a strictly healthy diet, who has been using and prescribing herbal remedies for twenty years. Still, claims Priestley, during an herbal detox aimed at parasites, this woman "passed something two feet long and squirming!" It's enough to give you pause.

You don't have to travel abroad to contract parasites. You can get them by eating food handled by someone with the condition, by drinking contaminated water, and by eating uncooked meat or poorly washed fresh fruits and vegetables, particularly if you lack sufficient hydrochloric acid in your stomach to kill parasites consumed with food. Some symptoms of parasite infestation include fatigue, diarrhea, abdominal pain, pain between the shoulder blades, stiff neck, headaches, and nausea.

In 1990, the Great Smokies Diagnostic Laboratory in Asheville, North Carolina, studied the stool of sixty-seven patients who lived in the upscale community of Elmhurst on Long Island, New York, and who complained of diarrhea and/or abdominal pain. To the lab staff's great surprise they found that fifty-one of the patients harbored at least one parasite. It was such a high percentage, the lab director sent the diagnostic slides to the federal Centers for Disease Control for double-checking. The CDC confirmed Great Smokies' findings.[8]

What happened in Elmhurst doesn't necessarily mean that it's happening in your town, but if you or anyone in your family is suffering from diarrhea, abdominal pain, chronic flatulence, foul-smelling stool, anal itching, abdominal bloating, or any other abnormal condition of the digestive system, it is a good idea to get tested. You will be asked to provide a stool sample, and the lab does the rest.

NATURAL REMEDIES

There are a number of natural remedies for parasites:

- *Black walnut green hull extract* (the green hull encircling the actual nut), has been used by American Indians as well as Asians for centuries to expel various parasites. It is particularly useful for ringworm and tapeworm, perhaps because of its high tannin content. In *The Woman's Encyclopedia of Natural Healing*,[9] Gary Null, Ph.D., recommends drinking a few drops of tincture in a glass of pure water first thing in the morning and at the end of the day. Hulda Clark, Ph.D., N.D., in *The Cure for All Cancers*,[10] has a much more extensive protocol, increasing dosage as the days progress.
- *Wormwood leaves* (*Artemisium absynthium*) is a useful treatment for roundworms and pinworms. The wormwood can be purchased in capsules, which helps avoid its bitter taste.
- *Garlic*, because of its sulfur-containing allicin and other powerful chemical constituents, has proven itself against yeast, fungi, bacteria, and viruses as well as worms. Unfortunately for your social life, only the fresh, raw garlic, and not the deodorized kind, works in this way (although deodorized garlic is good for cardiovascular health).[11]
- *Arginine and ornithine*, two amino acids, are recommended by Hulda Clark to help detoxify the ammonia that is a waste product excreted by parasites.
- *Pumpkin seeds* ("pepitas") seem to be long on folklore, if not on science, as a worm remover.
- *Citrus seed extract* (often from grapefruit seed), is a powerful antibiotic that is frequently recommended for yeast infestations.

TESTING FOR PARASITES

A variety of tests point to parasites, including stool and blood tests. For example, according to William R. Kellas, Ph.D., and Andrea Sharon Dworkin, N.D., in *Thriving in a Toxic World*,[12] in a blood profile, certain liver enzymes can signal parasites:

a high SGOT may reveal parasites in the gallbladder, and a high SGPT can signal a fungus infection.

The most common means of identifying a parasite infestation is by stool sample. You collect it yourself at home, transferring a small portion of a bowel movement into containers provided by the lab, and send the containers in a prepaid mailer via an overnight delivery service to the laboratory.

In short, parasites may be an unrecognized cause of many undiagnosed problems and a legitimate focus of your detox. Speak with your health care provider about tests for parasites, or contact Great Smokies Diagnostic Laboratory, which is a lab particularly expert at diagnosing parasite infestations, for a referral to a professional near you who regularly uses their services (see "Resources").

RESOURCES

Books:

For books on chelation therapy, see "Resources" at the end of chapter 13.

Dr. Michael Colgan, *Your Personal Vitamin Profile* (New York: William Morrow, 1982). Describes different nutritional therapies for specific metals.

Anne Louise Gittleman, *Guess What Came For Dinner?: Parasites and Your Health* (Garden City Park, N.Y.: Avery, 1993). An exposé of the magnitude of parasite infestations in the general North American population, and what to do about it.

Daniel B. Mowrey, Ph.D., *The Scientific Validation of Herbal Medicine* (New Canaan, Conn.: Keats Publishing, 1986). A chapter on parasites offers herbal remedies and nutritional support during parasite detox.

William Randall Kellas, Ph.D. and Andrea Sharon Dworkin, N.D., *Thriving in a Toxic World: Tools for Flourishing in the 21st Century* (Olivenhain, CA: Professional Preference, 1996). Copies of this book can be purchased from Comprehensive

Health Centers, 4403 Manchester #206, Encinitas, CA 92024
(619/632-9042). This useful text, and its companion volume
Surviving the Toxic Crisis are clear, readable, friendly descriptions of the assaults of our modern world and what effective
remedial actions we can take to heal and protect ourselves.

Testing for parasites:

Great Smokies Diagnostic Laboratory, 63 Zillicoa Avenue,
Asheville, NC 28801 (704/253-0621 or 800/522-4762).

REFERENCES

1. Fritz L. Lorscheider et al., "Mercury Exposure from 'Silver' Tooth Fillings: Emerging Evidence Questions a Traditional Dental Paradigm," *FASEB Journal,* 1995; 9: 504–
508, as reported in *Clinical Pearls 1995,* edited by Kristine
Simpson (Sacramento, Calif.: ITServices, 1995), 194.

2. David Steinman, *Diet for a Poisoned Planet* (New York:
Harmony Books, 1990), 109–11.

3. Mau-Sun Hua, et al., "Chronic Elemental Mercury Intox-
ication: Neuropsychological Follow-Up Case Study,"
Brain Injury 1995; 10(5): 377–84, as reported in *Clinical
Pearls 1996,* edited by Kristine Simpson et al. (Sacramento,
Calif.: ITServices, 1997), 196.

4. Carolyn Reuben, *Antioxidants: Your Complete Guide*
(Rocklin, Calif.: Prima, 1992), 171.

5. Personal communication with Greg Kelly, N.D., technical
advisor at Thorne Research, Sandpoint, Idaho, March 1997.

6. Agatha Thrash, M.D., and Calvin Thrash, M.D., *Home
Remedies* (Seale, Ala.: Yuchi Pines Institute, 1981), 143.

7. Thrash and Thrash, 147.

8. Morton Walker, D.P.M., "You Can Eliminate Parasites to Cure all Diseases," *Townsend Letter for Doctors and Patients*, February/March 1997, 64.

9. Gary Null, Ph.D., *The Woman's Encyclopedia of Natural Healing* (New York: Seven Stories Press, 1996), 285.

10. Hulda Clark, *The Cure for all Cancers* (San Diego, Calif.: New Century Press, 1993).

11. Paul Bergner, *The Healing Power of Garlic* (Rocklin, Calif.: Prima, 1996).

12. William Randall Kellas, Ph.D. and Andrea Sharon Dworkin, *Thriving in a Toxic World* (Olivenhain, Calif.: Professional Preference, 1996), 208.

TWELVE

HOME SWEET, NONTOXIC HOME

If you are going to go to all the trouble of detoxifying your body, you don't want to repollute it by living in a toxic home. You don't think yours is toxic? Right now, walk over to your kitchen sink, and look beneath it. You are staring at what is probably the most dangerous four square feet in your house. Notice how many skulls and crossbones there are?

One research team studied Oregon housewives and found them twice as likely to die from cancer as women working outside the home. These scientists blamed chronic exposure to carcinogenic materials in cleaning supplies, including petroleum distillates, benzene, naphtha, chlorinated hydrocarbons, and ammonia.

Furniture, carpets, and structural elements are also blamed as health hazards. Formaldehyde is one of the most common indoor offenders. It is known to cause cancers of the respiratory tract and liver, yet it is found in the particle board, paneling, and plywood covering walls, ceilings, cabinets, and floors; it outgases from drapes, upholstery, and carpeting; and it is part of urea-formaldehyde foam insulation.[1]

Those particularly sensitive to formaldehyde don't have to wait years for a degenerative disease like cancer to develop—they quickly begin to notice symptoms like headaches, watery or irritated eyes, rashes, fatigue, and chronic respiratory ailments. Worse yet is that people sensitive to formaldehyde, when chronically exposed to this chemical, are sensitized to other chemicals so that smaller and smaller exposures result in dramatic discomforts of many kinds. This is called the "spreading phenomenon" and it basically means that you develop more and more allergies over time so that the sicker you get, the sicker you get.

You probably haven't considered the numerous sources of pollution in the average home. Gas ranges, for example, are the source of sulfur dioxide, carbon monoxide, and nitrogen oxides in your home air. In fact, after cooking with a gas stove at 350 degrees F, a poorly ventilated kitchen can contain as much carbon monoxide and nitrogen dioxide gas as a smoggy day in Los Angeles.

The typical furniture polish, for another example, is made from petroleum distillates and other dangerous chemicals, and warns you right on the label it is "harmful or fatal if swallowed." Annie Berthold-Bond, author of *Clean and Green*,[2] wants to know if your furniture polish is under the sink, with all your other toxic cleaning supplies. Is this what you want to be inhaling every time you do the dishes, she asks, with even more wafting into the room from the furniture itself? And if the container is recyclable, when you wash it out, is this what you want to be adding to the community's wastewater? (In Sacramento, California, there's a fish stenciled on curbs next to street drains and beside the fish are stenciled these words: NO DUMPING. I LIVE DOWNSTREAM.) If the container isn't recyclable, and it ends up in a landfill in your town, do you want the residue of these toxic ingredients leaching down into your area's groundwater, to reappear in your tap water one day?

If you have been suffering from undiagnosed ailments, you might consider the possibility you need a serious review of sources of chemical exposure in your home and office. You will find a nontoxic solution to just about every cleaning and housekeeping need in the books listed in "Resources" at the end of this chapter.

Let's take a tour of your home, and figure out the best way to keep it, and you, clear of toxins.

NONTOXIC AIR

When researchers from the Environmental Protection Agency studied indoor air some years ago, they concluded that the worst household dangers included air fresheners, moth crystals, aerosol sprays, and stored paints and solvents. They also blamed smoking and living with a smoker, but these exposures aren't as easy to replace! As for the others, this chapter is packed with suggestions for simple and inexpensive alternatives.

For starters, though, to improve air quality throughout your home, you'll do well to cultivate some live houseplants.

B. C. Wolverton, Ph.D., is a Picayune, Mississippi, environmental scientist who discovered that the chemical wastes we humans create as indoor pollution is delicious food for the bacteria that live in the soil around plant roots. In turn, the waste formed when these bacteria die is consumed by the plant roots as food.

In *How to Grow Fresh Air*,[3] Wolverton evaluates fifty indoor plants for ease in growing and maintenance, resistance to insect infestation, effectiveness as a pollutant eliminator, and ability to provide you with moist clean air. Following is a list of some of the best plants he found for you to clear your home and office air of the most common indoor pollutants, including benzene (from cigarette smoke), formaldehyde (from carpets, drapes, noniron fabrics, particleboard and pressboard furniture), acetone (from nail polish and remover), and TCE and PCE (from dry-cleaned clothes), among others.

PLANTS USEFUL AS CLEAN AIR MACHINES

The very best: lady palm
Second: arica and other varieties of palms
Third: gerbera daisy, rubber plant, peace lily, azalea, poinsettia, dieffenbachia (beware of small children chewing leaves, as they burn the mouth and can paralyze vocal cords—ergo its common name, dumb cane), spider plant, philodendron, golden pothos, Dendrobium orchid, chrysanthemum, corn plant (*Dracaena fragrans*), *Dracaena marginata,* mother-in-law's tongue, and English ivy

---

Although the best choice is a variety of plants, you don't have to live in a veritable jungle to have clean air. Wolverton estimates two to three potted plants for one hundred square feet in a home with an eight-foot ceiling.

THE NONTOXIC KITCHEN

You don't usually think of your dishwasher as a source of pollution, but the vapors from unfiltered tap water can contain trihalomethanes, dangerous chemicals that are formed when chlorine meets with organic material. Be sure your kitchen is well ventilated when you run the dishwasher. For hand washing, put an aerator in your faucet at the sink; you can stop the water midflow while you soap up individual dishes, then easily flip it back on to rinse, reducing the amount of water vapor you inhale.

COOKWARE

Pull out every piece of aluminum you own, including stirring spoons, and all your Teflon or Silverstone cookware. Make note of what you have, and begin to replace them with glass, cast iron, porcelain-enamel–coated cast iron, terra cotta clay, or stainless steel. Aluminum is considered a toxic metal, with possible effects on brain function, including poor memory and visual/motor coordination. Eating food cooked in aluminum can also contribute to gastrointestinal disorders like indigestion, headaches, constipation, and gas. The "no-stick" cookware scratches with use, contaminating your food with particles of plastic.[4]

GAS STOVE

- Turn on your exhaust fan and open a window when cooking.
- Place a cookie sheet or aluminum foil below food to catch spills to reduce use of an oven cleaner.
- Wipe clean as soon as the insides are cool enough to touch, using Bon Ami cleanser (contains no chlorine) or a paste of baking soda and water or a nontoxic commercial

formula, such as Nature Clean's Nontoxic Oven Cleaner.
· Make sure you don't have a gas leak.

SINK

· Use a cleanser without chlorine, such as Bon Ami.

WALLS AND FLOOR

· Add a teaspoon of borax and a small splash of vinegar to a pint of hot water in a glass jar, instead of using ammonia-based cleaners. Shake the borax-vinegar mix until the borax is completely dissolved.
· Use nontoxic cleaners, like SafeChoice Super Clean or Neo-Life's Rugged Red.

FRUITS AND VEGETABLES

What could be healthier than fruits and vegetables? The answer: *organically grown* fruits and vegetables! Fruits and vegetables that are contaminated with chemicals to control insects, fungi, and unwanted plants, can cause cancer and damage the nervous system, respiratory system, reproductive system, endocrine system, and immune system. Since cancer commonly takes ten to twenty years to develop, why put yourself at continuing risk?

· Support organic growers by buying organic produce whenever your local markets offer it.
· Tell your market's produce buyer you would buy organic produce if it was available.
· Develop a relationship with a local grower who does not spray his crops, and purchase baskets of seasonal produce as a participant in the adopt-a-farmer program (in California it's called Community Supported Agriculture (CSA). My family pays $12 a week for a box of organic vegetables, delivered to a central pickup site fresh from the farm).

- If your town has a food buying club, food cooperative, or health food store that sells organic produce, join the group or shop at that market. If organic produce is more expensive, buy it anyway—and buy less red meat and fatty, salted, exhorbitantly packaged (and priced) snack foods. The savings may show up in lower doctor's bills.
- It may be organic, but it still will need to be washed before being consumed. You don't want insects, worms, bacteria, parasites, and dirt in your salad!

If you must purchase produce contaminated with herbicides, pesticides, and fungicides and packaged with gas (apples, pears, bananas), wax (apples, cucumbers, eggplants, peppers, and citrus, among others), or dyes (cherries, Irish potatoes, and citrus) at least wash off what you can from the surface.[5]

Purchase a vegetable oil–based liquid soap such as Dr. Bronner's Pure Castile Soap, Edcor's Fruit Wash, Granny's E-Z Maid or any other good quality soap (see "Resources" at end of this chapter for others). Add one teaspoon to tepid water in a large ceramic or glass bowl. Soak your fruits and vegetables for up to fifteen minutes, then hold each fruit and vegetable individually under running water while you scrub those that can stand the pressure (not your strawberries or lettuce) using a vegetable scrub brush (available at health food stores).

Peel all produce that has been waxed.

THE NONTOXIC LIVING ROOM

CARPETS

When Anderson Labs of Hartford, Vermont, forced mice to breathe air samples from several local kindergartens, the mice died. According to lab owner Rosalind Anderson, Ph.D., this result may be random, but it also may be due to toxic chemicals outgassing from the classroom carpets.

Some of the chemicals commonly outgassing from the fibers and adhesives of carpets include formaldehyde (which causes respiratory ailments of all kinds and is thought to cause cancer), toluene, xylene, styrene, tetrachloroethylene (TCE), ben-

zene, and other potential carcinogens and irritants. "The EPA
has published a list of four hundred chemicals identified from
carpet," says Anderson. And they stay around for a long, long
time. Anderson Labs has found toxic chemicals in a carpet
twenty years old. And then there's the outgassing characteristics of the pad beneath the carpet, including the adhesive
used to connect the carpet material to its own backing, and the
other adhesives that connect the whole piece of carpet to the
floor.

It is possible that the kindergarten problem was more than
the carpet itself. "One explanation may be that kids in kindergarten wet on the rug," Anderson suggests. "Some of the
products that are used to clean up urine spots are fierce."
When the cleaning product evaporates, it pollutes the air in
the classroom.

Can you get rid of outgassing chemicals by cleaning the
carpet? John Bower is the author of *The Healthy House* and a
design consultant for nontoxic homes. He points out that cleaning a carpet cannot remove the chemicals outgassing from the
floor covering, since the chemicals are not water soluble, and
in fact some carpet cleaning products will leave an added residue of chemicals of their own, including pesticides.[6]

Besides chemicals, carpets are the happy homes of an amazing variety of microorganisms (molds, yeasts, fungis, bacteria,
dust mites) and synthetic particles of deteriorated carpet material which, when burned in the home furnace, emit extremely
low doses of toxic fumes. The threat isn't the same as when
you are exposed to these same fumes in higher doses, but over
time, the accumulated exposure may still affect your health.

- If you have chronic respiratory ailments or other chronic
  and debilitating conditions unyielding to medical treatment, consider as part of your detox plan pulling up your
  home carpeting.
- Seal plywood and particleboard subfloors using AFM Water Seal, Livos Trebo All Purpose Shellac, Safecoat Hard
  Seal, or other nontoxic sealants to severely reduce formaldehyde emissions.
- Install hardwood, ceramic tile, hard vinyl tile, brick, stone,
  or terrazzo floors.
- Use woven grass, cotton, Oriental wool rugs or other nat-

ural fiber floor coverings that can either be thrown in the washing machine or taken outside, hung over a line, and beaten until clean.

- If you have wall-to-wall carpet and you want a nontoxic cleaner, Annie Berthold-Bond suggests borax to clean up mold and disinfect, baking soda to absorb odors, and zeolite for chemicals, wood smoke, and pollutants.
- Zeolite is a powdered mineral that absorbs air pollution, and according to Berthold-Bond Zeolite is so powerful it can clear the smell of smoke damage from an entire house in three days. What is more, if you put your zeolite in the sun, the absorbed fumes will disappear and you can use the mineral again and again. (See "Resources" at the end of this chapter for source information.)
- Use nontoxic carpet shampoo, such as AFM's SafeChoice, Nature Clean's Carpet & Upholstery Cleaner, or Granny's Karpet Kleen.
- Prevent the outgassing of carpet with AFM's SafeChoice Carpet Guard or its dirt/odor/stain–repellent called Lock Out.

WALLS

The most outrageous wallpaper cleaner I ever read about was Annie Berthold-Bond's suggestion to use one or two slices of white bread to rub away dirt and smudges on wallpaper.[7]

- Nontoxic all-purpose cleaners include AFM's SafeChoice Super Clean, Neo-Life's Rugged Red, or Heartland Labs' Omni Kleen.

FURNITURE

- To dust, polish, and shine, Annie Berthold-Bond combines one-quarter cup vinegar or lemon juice with one-half teaspoon olive oil. Apply to wooden furniture with a soft cotton rag.
- Wipe furniture with mayonnaise (really!) or a cloth dipped in cool tea (so claims the queen of environmental cleaning

herself, Debra Lynn Dadd, in her opus *Nontoxic, Natural, and Earthwise*).[8]

- Use a nontoxic product like Earth Rite's Furniture Polish.

THE NONTOXIC BEDROOM

Your body regenerates and repairs itself during sleep. This is the time for rest in a peaceful and healing environment.

CLOSET

- Reduce the number of clothes that need dry cleaning by purchasing those that can be machine washed.
- When you bring dry cleaning home, leave it on a porch or in a back room with good ventilation for several days before hanging it in your bedroom closet. You don't want to be breathing the toxic, carcinogenic fumes from dry-cleaning solvents, such as trichloroethylene (TCE). One breast-feeding mother used to visit her husband at lunch at his workplace, a dry cleaner, until her baby developed liver disease from the TCE that absorbed through her breath and skin into the breast milk. After the mother stayed home at lunchtime for several months, the baby's liver healed.
- Be aware that any material not needing ironing has been treated with formaldehyde. That includes anything labeled "permanent press" or "crease-resistant" such as poly-cotton blends in bedding, curtains, and clothing.

BEDDING

- If you're sensitive to eggs you may also be sensitive to feathers. Change a down pillow for a hypoallergenic one. Some people do better with polyester, some with cotton. A good source of cotton pillows is KB Cotton Pillows (see "Resources" at the end of this chapter).
- Cotton is highly sprayed with pesticides, so if you can't

handle cotton it may be the pesticide, not the material, that is causing your symptoms.

• If you have a stuffy nose every morning, think about clearing your nights of allergens, starting with your bed. At your local department store, you can purchase covers for your pillow and your mattress that prevent infestation of the microscopic mites that live off your shed skin and other goodies in your house dust. Mites are a major cause of allergic reactions.

THE NONTOXIC BATHROOM

Consider alternatives to the numerous chemicals in cosmetics, shampoos, deodorants, hair sprays, window cleaners, mold removers, and the like. Read labels! If you can hardly pronounce the ingredients, be suspicious.

COSMETICS

Methylene chloride is a solvent used in hair sprays. Formaldehyde may be in your mascara. Polyvinylpyrrolidone plastic (PVP) and artifical colors may be in your lipstick. Why put yourself at risk of immune assault and possible cancer down the road, when attractive and affordable alternatives exist on any health food store counter, or by mail order from responsible and environmentally friendly manufacturers?

• You may not find an alternative to nail polish, but because it can contain phenol, toluene, and xylene, which are toxic when inhaled or absorbed, be sure to give your nails a break as often as you can, and when you do apply the color, do so in a very well ventilated space.

• Any health food store carries natural cosmetics from such reputable companies as Rachel Perry, Jarrow, and Aubrey. I have used two additional sources of natural, healthy, skin care products. Mariana Chicet, a Roumanian aesthetician (skin care specialist) has created a line of products that are based on integrity, quality ingredients, and results. She has a loyal following in Los Angeles, where she runs her own facial salon, and does lively mail-order business with customers who move away or go on vacation. Mariana shuns petroleum products, such as mineral oil, perfumes, alcohol, or colored dyes. Her moisturizers and revitalizing creams do contain animal products such as beeswax, bone marrow oil, elastin, and collagen. Mariana Chicet Natural European Skin Care Products, 8238 W. 3rd Street, Los Angeles, CA 90048 (800/995-4490). Pam Benet is an artist, gardener, bodyworker, and a cosmetics manufacturer. All of her Echo line of massage oils, soaps, foot soaks, and nourishing skin creams are made individually to order, and artistically packaged for unique gifts to those you love, including yourself. Echo, Pamela Benet, Sacramento, CA (916/498-9809; e-mail 6echo@CWIA.com).

SHOWER

According to Julian B. Andelman, Ph.D., Emeritus Professor of Environmental and Occupational Health at the University of Pittsburgh, the chlorine that controls bacteria in your city water supply is transformed when heated into another chemical substance, called chloroform, which combines with organic material, like leaves, to form trihalomethanes (THMs). THMs are associated with rectal and bladder cancers.

Although major city water supplies are usually carbon filtered, when you linger in a hot, steamy shower, or stick around in the same room while the dishwasher and washing machine are cycling hot water through your dishes and clothes, you are putting yourself at risk of overexposure to these dangerous compounds. And it isn't only you. The steam from your shower and the vapor from the washing machine waft through the house affecting all the people and animals who live and breathe there.

- Take a hint from Dr. Andelman and use tepid water in a short shower.
- To clean the shower and tub, use nontoxic cleaners like AFM's SafeChoice Super Clean or Safety Clean, Earth

Rite's Tub and Tile Cleaner, Descale-It's Bathroom Cleaner, and Ecover's All Purpose Cleaner Concentrate.
- To clean the mirrors, use ammonia-free, perfume-free products, such as AFM's SafeChoice Glass Cleaner or Nature Clean's Window & Glass Cleaner.

SINK

- Clear stopped-up sinks with natural enzyme action, in Heartland Labs' Build-Up Remover and Clog Gone.

TOILET

- Use Ecover's Toilet Bowl Cleaner, Earth Rite's Toilet Bowl Cleaner, Descale-It's Toilet Bowl Cleaner, Harmony's (formerly called Seventh Generation's) Toilet Bowl Cleaner, or AFM's Safety Clean.

THE NONTOXIC GARAGE

'Fess up! Did you clear your living space of gunk and poisons by dumping them in your garage? Get rid of them!

Richard Conlin and Jane Dewell claim that leftover paint comprises fully 80 percent of household hazardous waste.[9] You're probably keeping it for future touchups that will never be done. Did you know latex paint will spoil, particularly if it freezes? Or that petroleum distillates in oil-based paint and thinner, and chlorinated solvents in strippers contribute to air pollution and global warming when they evaporate? Or that chlorinated solvents cause damage to the nervous system and kidneys?

Solvents and strippers left over from refinishing jobs also kill living organisms used in your community sewage treatment plant as well as those in the river, lake, or ocean into which your household water eventually flows.

Homes painted before 1980 may have lead in the paint. Since lead affects the nervous system and even in small quantities lowers intelligence, you will want to prevent anyone from coming into contact with lead-based paint chips and dust. You can test for yourself with kits purchased at hardware stores (also see "Resources" at the end of this chapter). If your home has lead-based paint do the following:

- Cover the paint with an appropriate seal rather than removing it and exposing yourself and others to lead dust.
- Plant bushes and ground cover around the edges of your home, not food plants.
- Keep a good-quality industrial mat at your front and back doors, and/or make everyone take off their shoes upon entering. And vacuum often with a HEPA filtered good-quality vacuum. HEPA (High Efficiency Particulate Arrestance) filters are best because they can trap minute size dust, and even pollen and mold spores. These steps are among the most useful in avoiding traipsing lead dust into the home (particularly important if you have animals, toddlers, or young children who spend a lot of time on the carpet).

If you have leftover paint and solvents in your garage, take them to your community's household hazardous waste collection site. Call your local solid waste or health department for drop-off location or to arrange for pickup.

If your washer and dryer are in the garage, read the section "Shower," above, regarding trihalomethane production in chlorinated water. Make sure the door to the outside is open and the garage is well-ventilated when you use the washing machine.

THE NONTOXIC YARD

Your needs are so simple: remove aphids from your roses, snails from your strawberries, and Bermuda grass from your lawn. You don't think about birds dying while garden pests multiply,[10] your kids developing cancer and you yourself suffering so low a sperm count you have trouble having more kids.[11]

Pesticides, even those banned years ago, like DDT, stick around in the fat cells of our bodies, influencing the health and the brain function of our own and future generations. That lawn spray used by your neighbor up the street drifts in the wind to your yard, where your son and you are practicing lay-ups while waiting for your spouse to finish preparing lunch. The longer you shoot baskets while inhaling those neurotoxins, the more his school and sports performance and your reproductive health are threatened.

"Pesticide poisoning can lead to poor performance on tests involving intellectual functioning, academic skills, abstraction, flexibility of thought, and motor skills; memory disturbances and inability to focus attention; deficits in intelligence, reaction time, and manual dexterity; and reduced perceptual speed. Increased anxiety and emotional problems have also been reported," according to the Congressional Office of Technology Assessment. And that's not mentioning the increased risk of cancer, during childhood or many years hence, from exposure to pesticides applied to lawns, to pets, to garden plants, and found in the child's everyday diet. According to the New York Coalition for Alternatives to Pesticides, "In households where lawn and garden pesticides are applied, children are 6.5 times more likely to develop leukemia." [12]

As for you adults, chemicals in pesticides are nicknamed "gender benders" because they mimic the female hormone estrogen. For females, it means increased danger of breast cancer. For males, increased numbers of boys with undescended testicles, increased risk of testicular cancer, and decreased number of sperm. [13]

- Let your Congressional representatives know you support organic farming. (It *is* financially justifiable: Gallo Vineyards is now the largest organic farmer in the United States!)
- When you encourage the produce man at your local market to provide organic fruits and vegetables, mention that Danish men who consumed organic foods had twice the sperm count of men eating nonorganic food.
- Make sure your diet is rich in health-enhancing, cancer-preventing foods, like soy products, cruciferous vegetables (broccoli, cauliflower, cabbage, Brussels sprouts), dark greens (kale, mustard greens, and collards), and fiber (raw

fruits and vegetables and, if you can digest it, whole wheat, oats, and barley).

- Add garlic, blue-green algae tablets, seaweeds, vitamins A, C, and E, and the mineral selenium to your regular menus, to up your antioxidant levels (antioxidants protect you against the marauding molecules called free radicals that cause heart disease, cancer, and other common degenerative diseases). You need to supplement your diet, because even a vegetable-rich diet today is mineral-deficient, as we discussed in chapter 8.
- Recently I began distributing a product called Juice Plus+, which is a source of fruits and vegetables, juiced, powdered, and capsulated in a way that preserves the food's natural enzymes. Anyone who can swallow a capsule can have a daily serving of beets, carrots, kale, cabbage, spinach, tomatoes, parsley, and broccoli without turning on the stove, opening the fridge, or complaining about having to eat vegetables. Adults take two capsules of the fruit blend in the morning and two of the vegetable blend in the evening. Children take one of each. Contact me for a monthly supply. Carolyn Reuben, P.O. Box 254531, Sacramento, CA 95825.

RESOURCES

For information on environmental health:

Environmental Health Clearinghouse, (800/643-4794 9am-8pm, EST; e-mail Envirohealth@niehs.nih.gov). Free source of information on issues related to environmental health.

International Institute for Baubiologie and Ecology, Helmut Ziehe, director, P.O. Box 387, Clearwater, FL 34615 (813/461-4371; Internet http://www.baubiologieusa.com).
   Baubiologie is the study of how to create an environment that is nontoxic, ecological, and natural. Ziehe offers a correspondence course on how to create a safe home or office for yourself, and how to become a baubiologie inspector qualified to charge others for identifying problems with indoor air quality.

American Academy of Environmental Medicine, 10 E. Randolph Street, New Hope, PA, 18938 (215/862-4544; fax 215/862-4583). A 30-plus-year-old international association of physicians and others concerned with the relationship between the environment and human health. Provides continuing education for physicians and referrals.

National Center for Environmental Health Strategies, Mary Lamielle, director, (609/429-5358; e-mail wjrd37@prodigy.com). A clearinghouse for referrals, advocacy, technical services and information regarding chemical sensitivity. The *Delicate Balance* newsletter focuses on indoor pollution and related environmental health issues.

Environmental Education and Health Services, Mary Oetzel, president, (512/288-2369; fax 512/288-9538). Consultation on indoor air quality for home owners, architects, builders, schools. Can identify appropriate building materials ahead of construction, or recommend steps needed for improvement of current conditions.

Human Ecology, Action League, (404/248-1898; fax 404/248-0162). Publishes the *Human Ecologist* newsletter and numerous information sheets, bibliographies, and resource lists related to the connection between chemical exposure and health. Regional chapters of its Support Service Project offer a network of volunteers to discuss individual concerns.

American Environmental Health Foundation, (800/428-2343; 214/361-9515). Source of a variety of supplies for the highly allergic individual. Associated medical clinic is one of the most experienced in treating multichemically sensitive patients, and includes an in-bed facility for allergy evaluation and treatment.

For environmentally safe cleaning supplies detailed in this chapter:

AFM Enterprises, (619/239-0321; fax 619/239-0565).

Nature Clean and Heartland Labs, Products available from "Catalog of Environmentally Safe Product." (800/428-2343; fax 214/350-8896).

Descale-It, (520/293-4825).

Ecover Products, (714/556-3644).

Earth Rite, RCN Products, 5 American Lane, Greenwich, CT 06831-2561.

The Living Source, (254/776-4878).

Granny's Old Fashioned Products, (818/577-1825).

Life Tree Products, (707/588-0756).

Natural Choice Catalog, (505/438-3448; 800/621-2591).

For zeolite, a negatively charged mineral that sucks up odors and pollutants from the air:

Dasun Company, (800/433-8929; fax 619/746-8865).

For building supplies:

Varathane (a wood finish), The Flecto Company, (510/655-2470).

For wood finishes:

Auro Organics Natural Plant Chemistry/Sinan Company, (916/753-3104; Internet http://www.dcn.davis.ca.us/go/sinan). Wood finishes, paints, stains, wood glues, glazes, waxes, thinners, lacquers, artists' supplies, insulation, books.

AFM, (619/239-0321; fax 916/239-0565). Safecoat enamels and semigloss paints, stains, primecoats, wood seals, tile and concrete seals, adhesives.

Livos and BioShield, "Natural Choice" Catalog Echo Design, (505/438-3448; 800/621-2591). Two German brands of non-toxic interior building supplies: paints, stains, thinners, and waxes.

For bedding and personal items:

KB Cotton Pillows, (800/544-3752; 214/223-7193). Truly comfortable, well-stuffed, entirely cotton, handmade pillows in sizes from kid/travel to king.

Nontoxic Environments, Inc., (800/789-4348; 603/659-5919; fax 603/659-5933). Mattresses, futons, and cotton pillows of organic cotton.

Garnet Hill, (800/622-6216). Cotton sheets, natural fiber blankets, sturdy wooden beds, and clothing for adults and kids.

Auro Organics Natural Plant Chemistry/Sinan Company, (916/753-3104; Internet http//www.dcn.davis.ca.us/go/sinan). Rye-straw mattresses, wooden bedframes, cotton futons, pillows, and comforters.

Janice's, (800/JANICES; fax 201/691-5459). Mattresses, mattress pads, box springs, sheets, spreads, natural fiber clothing, and organic fabric sold by the yard. No synthetics are used in shipping materials.

The Heart of Vermont, (800/639-4123; 802/476-3098). Natural fiber bedding, futons, bed frames.

The Natural Bedroom, (800/365-6563). Cotton beds and all-hemp mattresses and futons plus other chemical-free, nontoxic inner-spring mattresses, futons, comforters, pads, and pillows. They also carry products for those allergic to natural fibers! Their products are available in 265 stores nationwide. Call for a store near you, or to order from the factory.

For environmentally friendly catalogs:

Harmony (formerly called Seventh Generation), (800/456-1177; fax 800/456-1139). Earth-friendly products for kitchen, laundry, pets, personal care, garden, and bedroom, as well as for gifts, for wearing, and for home energy efficiency.

Allergy Relief Shop, (800/626-2810; 423/522-2795; Internet http://www.allergyreliefshop.com; e-mail ggraham1@ix. net com.com). Paint, personal care, bedding, air and water filtration, and other items.

The Cutting Edge Catalog, (800/497-9516; 516/287-3813; fax 516/287-3112; Internet http://www.cutcat.com; e-mail cutcat@ i2000.com). Equipment for full-spectrum lighting, electromagnetic field testing and protection, water and air purification systems, magnets, books, and more.

Nontoxic Environments, Inc., (800/789-4348; 603/659-5919; fax 603/659-5933). Building supplies, organic cotton bedding and futons, books, health hazard test kits for mold, pesticides, lead, radon; EMF detectors, air and water purification systems.

N.E.E.D.S., (800/634-1380; fax 315/488-6336). Air and water filters, nutritional supplements, shower curtains, paints, personal care products, bedding, and other allergenic and environmentally safe products. An M.D. and pharmacist on staff answer questions and connect medical professionals with people in need.

Real Goods, 555 Leslie Street, Ukiah, CA 95482 (fax 707/468-9486; Internet http://www.realgoods.com; e-mail realgood@realgoods.com). Eclectic, artistic, and practical, from woodstoves to radiation-free gyroscopic razors. Reading the catalog is an education in itself.

For carpets:

Auro Organics Natural Plant Chemistry/Sinan Company, (916/753-3104; Internet http://www.dcn.davis.ca.us/go/sinan). Plant-dyed or undyed wool carpets.

Colin Campbell & Sons, Ltd., (604/734-2758). Biodegradable wool carpets without toxic adhesives, chemical dyes, or pesticides in the backing.

Hendricksen Natürlich, (707/824-0914; fax 800/329-9398; e-mail nathome@monitor.net). Natural-fiber carpet of wool, sisal, or seagrass (a reedlike plant growing along the shore in China), area rugs, and nontoxic linoleum and cork floor coverings.

For air filters:

AllerMed Corporation, 31 Steel Road, Wylie, TX 75098 (972/442-4898; fax 972/442-4897). Variety of air filters, from car-size to whole home systems.

For lead testing:

Hybrivet Systems, P.O. Box 1210, Framingham, MA 10701 (800/262-LEAD). Makers of the Lead Check Swabs to detect lead on any surface.

   N.E.E.D.S., 527 Charles Avenue 12A, Syracuse, NY 13209 (800/634-1380). M–F 9am–7pm, Sat. 9am–5pm. Lead testing kits for water.

Clean Water Lead Testing, UNCA, One University Heights, Asheville, NC 28804-3299 (704/251-6895; fax 704/251-6913). Testing for lead in paint, soil, dust, and water.

National Testing Laboratory, 6555 Wilson Mills Road 102, Cleveland, OH 44143 (800/458-3330).

Suburban Water Testing Laboratories, 4600 Kutztown Road, Temple, PA 19560 (800/433-6595; fax 610/929-8321).

For information about lead poisoning:

National Lead Information Center, 1019 Nineteenth Street NW 401, Washington, DC 20036 (800/424-5323). Public education about causes and prevention of lead poisoning.

Contact your local health department for information about blood testing for lead if you suspect you or family members have been exposed through water, paint, or other sources.

Books:

Harold Buttram, M.D., and Richard Piccola, *Our Toxic World: Who Is Looking After Our Children?* (Quakertown, Penn.: Foresight America Foundation for Preconception Care, 1996). 5724 Clymer Road, Quakertown, PA 18951. Coauthor Buttram is a pioneer in the field of preconception care, and he lays out the ominous trend he finds between parental exposure to the toxins of American life and the deteriorating health of our children. Just because chemicals are in common use doesn't make them safe or desirable.

Ruth Troetschler et al., *Rebugging Your Home and Garden: A Step-by-Step Guide to Modern Pest Control* (Los Altos, Calif.: PTF Press, 1996). An uncommonly thorough guidebook to deal with garden insects and indoor pests, improve vegetable garden and orchard yield, deal with plant diseases, and use pesticides safely. The philosophical underpinning of this useful work is Integrated Pest Management.

David Steinman and Samuel S. Epstein, M.D., *The Safe Shopper's Bible: A Consumer's Guide to Nontoxic Household Products, Cosmetics, and Food* (New York: MacMillan, 1995). Extremely useful lists of dangerous and safe products, such as cosmetics, auto products, pets supplies, cleaning products, food, and water. Includes explanations for their recommendations. I have photocopied numerous times their list of safe and dangerous hair coloring agents, to give to friends and relatives.

Debra Lynn Dadd, *Nontoxic, Natural, and Earthwise: How to Protect Yourself and Your Family from Harmful Products and Live in Harmony with the Earth* (Los Angeles: Jeremy P. Tarcher, 1990). Dadd is one of the pioneer writers in this field, providing the research to back up her recommendations and adequate information to make informed choices.

David Steinman and R. Michael Wisner, *Living Healthy in a Toxic World* (New York: Perigee, 1996). Steinman and Wisner are alternately irreverently funny or groaningly corny as they explain the most important sources of toxins and offer simple actions to take to avoid them.

Natalie Golos and William Rea, M.D., in *Success in the Clean Bedroom*, describe a step-by-step removal of all toxic elements, beginning with the bedroom and progressing through the home. Available for $15.95 from Dr. Rea's "Catalog of Environmentally Safe Products." American Environmental Health Foundation, P.O. Box 29874, Dallas, TX 75229 (800/428-2343; for information 214/361-9515; fax 214/361-2534).

Nina Anderson and Howard Peiper, *Are You Poisoning Your Pets?* (East Canaan, Conn.: Safe Goods, 1995). The authors point out how pets can sicken from exposure to toxins around the home, and offer simple alternatives.

Dan Stein, *Dan's Practical Guide to Least Toxic Home Pest Control* (Eugene, Ore.: Hulogosi, 1991). For orders, call 503/688-1199. I loved this small book so much I bought a case and gave them away as gifts for several years. For example, do you know you don't have to douse yourself with toxic pesticides like Lindane to eliminate lice? Or that talcum powder kills ants? Or that a 2 percent solution of Safer's Soap can be used against fleas on carpets and floors?

Household Hazardous Waste Project, *Guide to Hazardous Products Around the Home: A Personal Action Manual for Protecting Your Health and Environment*, 1031 E. Battlefield, Suite 214, Springfield, MO 65807 (417/889-5000). For $9.95. This booklet is a project of the Environmental Improvement and Energy Resources Authority, an agency of the Missouri Department of Natural Resources, administered through Southwest Missouri State University's Office of Continuing Education. It aids you to detect hazardous substances, teaches you to read labels and catch the signal words that highlight the toxicity of products, and advises you how to dispose of materials and choose safer alternatives.

David Rousseau, W. J. Rea, M.D., and Jean Enwright, *Your Home, Your Health, and Well-Being* (Berkeley: Ten Speed Press, 1990). This book offers a room-to-room, roof-to-basement, front-to-backyard survey of health factors and possible environmental problems. Coauthor William Rea, M.D., of Dallas, Texas, was a cardiovascular surgeon who developed severe environmental illness after having pesticide applied to his own home. In learning how to heal himself, he has become a major figure in environmental medicine, running one of the few inpatient allergy testing/treatment clinics in the country.

John Bower, *The Healthy House* (Secaucus, N.J.: Carol Publishing Group, 1991). For $16.95. Written by a "healthy house" consultant, it covers the important basics in a useful and thorough manner.

David Pearson, *The Natural House Book* (New York: Fireside, 1989). A luscious-to-look-at, coffee-table-quality paperback with *National Geographic*–style color photos of each element of an ecologically harmonious, healthy building, accompanied by thought-provoking, dream-evoking text. If there isn't a lump in your throat reading this book, you must already live in the perfect residence.

For pesticide management:

The Bio-Integral Resource Center, (415/524-2567). Offers material on Integrated Pest Management (IPM), which encourages the use of natural enemies of unwanted pests, the planting of pest-resistant varieties, plant rotation, soil management, and many other low-tech, proven methods to control, rather than eradicate, the insect world.

National Coalition Against the Misuse of Pesticides (NCAMP), (202/543-5450; fax 202/543-4791; e-mail ncamp @igc.apc.org). Information clearinghouse on the hazards of pesticides and least toxic pest control. Small fees for booklets and fact sheets.

Washington Toxics Coalition, (206/632-1545). Fact sheets on pest management and lawn care, as well as safer household cleaning methods.

REFERENCES

1. Jack Thrasher, Ph.D., and Alan Broughton, M.D., *The Poisoning of Our Homes and Workplaces: The Truth About the Indoor Formaldehyde Crisis* (Santa Ana, Calif.: Seadora, 1989), 67.

2. Annie Berthold-Bond, *Clean and Green* (Woodstock, N.Y.; Ceres Press, 1990).

3. B. C. Wolverton, Ph.D., *How to Grow Fresh Air* (New York: Penguin, 1997).

4. Debra Lynne Dadd, *The Nontoxic Home* (Los Angeles: Jeremy P. Tarcher, 1986), 139.

5. Doris J. Rapp, M.D., *Is This Your Child's World?* (New York: Bantam, 1996), 58.

6. John Bower, ''The Floor Plan for Health,'' *East West Journal* July 1989.

7. Berthold-Bond, 102.

8. Debra Lynne Dadd, *Nontoxic, Natural, and Earthwise* (Los Angeles; Jeremy P. Tarcher, 1990), 151.

9. ''In Search of Green,'' *YES! A Journal of Positive Futures*, Winter 1997, 62. P.O. Box 10818, Bainbridge Island, WA 98110-0818.

10. Ruth Troetschler, *Rebugging Your Home and Garden* (Los Altos, Calif.: PTF Press, 1996), 8.

11. Carolyn Reuben, *The Healthy Baby Book: A Parent's Guide to Preventing Birth Defects and Other Long-term Medical Problems Before, During, and After Pregnancy* (New York: Jeremy P. Tarcher/Perigee, 1992).

12. *Solutions* vol. 1, no. 2, Summer 1996, 48. NYCAP, 353 Hamilton St., Albany, NY 12210 (518/426-8246).

13. David Steinman, "Gender-Bending Foods," *Natural Health* January–February 1997, 48–52.

COMMITMENT REQUIRED

THIRTEEN

LETTING OTHERS HELP

Be aware that a diamond is nothing more than a lump of coal that stuck with it.

—Dr. John W. Apsley II

This section of the book begins the detoxification programs which demand the most from you. They demand more of your money, your time, and your commitment to the process. This isn't the section for those wishing to continue business (and life) as before. You will need to make deep changes, and yet, you may find that as with so much of life, the return is equivalent to the quality and quantity of your investment.

CHELATION THERAPY

Chelation therapy (from the Greek word *chele*, meaning claw) is the use of an amino acid solution (EDTA, a weak organic acid), which, when given intravenously, combines with any mineral in your bloodstream and holds it in an electrochemical grasp until it is excreted in your urine. The therapy has Food and Drug Administration approval to treat lead poisoning, and it has been used for that purpose since just after World War II. It is also used to remove other heavy metals.

The FDA approved the use of EDTA chelation therapy to treat arteriosclerosis in the early 1950s, but removed that approval in 1962, when it was decided that due to the widespread incidence of arteriosclerosis, more double-blind studies of the procedure's safety and effectiveness were needed. Ross Gordon, M.D., of Albany, California, was part of one study that fizzled due to lack of enrollment of patients by surgeons in the several study sites. One major barrier to creating a convincing body of research, Gordon says, is the simple economic fact that the amino acid combination used for chelation, EDTA, (ethylenediaminetetraacetic acid) is in the public domain, having moved out of patent around the time the FDA withdrew its approval of chelation for arteriosclerosis. Thus, drug companies have no financial incentive to fund research. Since pharmaceutical industry funding is the power engine behind research in this country, chelation advocates are somewhat cornered research-wise.

As a treatment for arteriosclerosis, chelation therapy has strong opinions on both sides. Proponents say the procedure opens blood vessels down to the most minute capillaries, improving blood circulation throughout the body: some recipients report their joint pains disappear. Others, that their eyesight improves. According to the National Heart Lung and Blood Institute, all these benefits in cases other than lead removal are suspected of being a placebo reaction (a common experience of feeling better after having a dramatic intervention, regardless of the intervention).

When asked for information on chelation, the Institute includes a copy of the *Harvard Health Letter* of January 1995, which describes a New Zealand study using thirty-two patients over ten weeks, treated with chelation twice a week. There was a small improvement in the pulsations in the arteries of the legs of those receiving chelation, but the patients themselves did not feel any different from those who received only saline solution (the control group). The *Harvard Letter* concluded, "This study did not prove that chelation therapy is worthless and did not indicate that it is dangerous. However, it did not show the types of dramatic benefits that are sometimes cited by chelation's advocates."

Chelation's advocates, on the other hand, say that someone needing a heart bypass operation would probably be given closer to fifty treatments, and criticize the New Zealand study as too brief. However, because the number of studies that are scientifically sound are small and those that have been done have not shown clear benefit, the National Heart Lung and Blood Institute, the American Heart Association, the Federal Drug Administration, the American Medical Association, the American College of Cardiology, and the American College

of Physicians believe chelation therapy is of no proven benefit
in the treatment of atherosclerosis.

Gordon, a founder of the American College for Advancement in Medicine which trains physicians in chelation therapy,
points out that "no proven benefit" is not the same as no
benefit. He, himself, has been using chelation in his medical
practice for thirty years, and there are over 1,000 other physicians who use the technique. If it was merely placebo that
was causing their many thousands of patients to feel relief of
symptoms, Gordon suggests, these physicians would have been
out of business long ago.

HOW MIGHT IT WORK?

According to Gordon, one result of deficient research is that
no one has yet proven how chelation therapy works. He suggests one potential mechanism of action, an elegant orchestra-
tion of calcium and the hormone parathormone. Calcium is a
sticky mineral and it is the linchpin of the fatty plaque that
builds up on artery walls blocking blood flow. Parathormone
is the hormone secreted by the parathyroid glands and its main
purpose is to keep calcium levels normal in the blood. When
EDTA appears in the blood, ionizable calcium in the blood
hooks on to it. If the body didn't replace this calcium, the
heart would stop beating. So, the parathyroid glands quickly
release parathormone, which pulls calcium out of the plaque
to replace the calcium that has attached to the EDTA. The rest
of the plaque loses its firmness, dissolves, and flows away in
the blood to eventually be eliminated in bowel movements.

In addition to the plaque in arteries, parathormone pulls calcium out of the lens of the eye, the eyeball, the skin, tendons,
and anywhere else it has accumulated. This is why, explains
Gordon, that some patients report improved sight and relief
from muscle and joint pain after chelation therapy. However,
although all this is happening in a nanosecond, the amount of
parathormone is very small compared to the level of calcium
that needs to be withdrawn before change is noticed.

INVESTIGATING SIDE EFFECTS

Recently, a group of medical doctors in São Paulo, Brazil, at the Centro de Medicina Preventiva (CMP), decided to analyze the side effects most criticized by those opposing EDTA chelation therapy. The most often mentioned side effects include kidney damage, heart failure, thrombophlebitis (blood clots), osteoporosis, other signs of deficient calcium, and hypoglycemia (low blood sugar). They did find a few patients with diabetes and severe atherosclerosis who could not continue therapy due to its effect on their kidneys. Two patients showed signs of hypoglycemia out of 545 patients treated one year, but the doctors suggested this might have resulted from having been chelated with an especially fast drip (less than fifty minutes). During the past eleven years, two out of twenty thousand patients treated at CMP developed blood clots.

However, no osteoporosis was measured, no lowered calcium was measured, and of the eleven patients studied who had previous heart failure before chelation (all were on heart drugs and diuretics), all showed improvements in both kidney and heart function after chelation.[1]

THE PROCEDURE

Chelation is painless and relaxing. You sit in an easy chair chatting or reading while the EDTA drips into your arm. To protect your kidneys, chelation proceeds slowly, over several hours for each session.

COST

Two British hospitals and one Dutch hospital use chelation in their cardiovascular outpatient departments. However, chelation is not covered by insurance in the United States, and it's not available in a hospital, even though, according to the New Zealand Medical Journal, chelation "costs approximately one-sixth that of coronary artery bypass grafting and one-third that of percutaneous coronary angioplasty."[2] In the United States, chelation costs around $100 per treatment, with $5,000 probably topping the cost for cardiovascular therapy, compared to over $50,000 for a bypass operation.

REPLACING MINERALS

The chelating agent pulls necessary minerals out of your body along with those you want removed. Be sure that anyone giving you chelation therapy has been properly trained to replace those needed minerals. In addition, a well-educated practitioner will give you nutritional counseling, says Dr. Gordon, and most likely put you on a low-fat, high-fiber natural foods diet and exercise program.

Trained chelation doctors are certified by the American Board of Chelation Therapy, and probably belong to the American College for the Advancement in Medicine.

HEALTHMED: THE HUBBARD METHOD OF DETOX

Your body uses fat tissues like you use a bank account. Just as you both deposit and withdraw from your bank account, your body is at this moment adding and subtracting chlorinated pesticides, industrial chemicals, drugs, and other poisons held inside your fat tissues. Missing a meal, the natural fast of nighttime sleep, illness, emotional stress, exercise, and even hot weather releases fat back into the bloodstream. Since over three hundred foreign chemicals have been identified in human fat, and since most Americans have dozens of these contaminants in their fatty tissue, you may need help divesting yourself of your chemical account.

Researchers have found that without special effort, it takes the body from ten to twenty years to reduce its toxic load of industrial chemicals by half. In 1979, researchers announced that after six years they could still find no noticeable reduction in the amount of PBBs in the blood and fat of Michigan residents who had been accidentally exposed to PBBs in contaminated dairy products, meat, and other foods.[3]

In contrast, when a detox protocol called the Hubbard Method was used with Michigan residents, researchers found that over 21 percent of the stored chemicals were eliminated within a couple weeks, and four months after treatment ended, the average reduction of the sixteen chemicals studied was over 42 percent! In another incident, a man was found to have dropped his tissue level of DDE (a breakdown product of DDT) 29 percent immediately after undergoing the Hubbard regimen, and after 250 days, his toxic load had dropped 97 percent! In addition, servicemen exposed to Agent Orange in Vietnam and chemical weapons and medical vaccines in the Persian Gulf report relief from their various health problems.

The Hubbard detox protocol was created by L. Ron Hubbard, the founder of the Church of Scientology. During the 1970s, Hubbard observed people who had used drugs. He saw that their problems persisted long after their drug use ended. He also knew that many others have unhealthy levels of pollution within their fat cells from prescription drug use and from home and work exposure to preservatives, plated metals, plastics, petroleum products, radioactive materials, electrical equipment, dyes, perfumes, cleaning solvents, pesticides, and herbicides.

The Hubbard detoxification protocol involves exercise, heat, niacin (vitamn B_3), fluid and electrolyte replacement, cold-pressed unsaturated oils, and nutritional supplementation. The purpose of it all is to mobilize the fat and get it to release its contents into the bloodstream so the toxins can be washed away in sweat and urine, and to do it in the most gentle, least harmful way. At this time, the only outpatient medical facility using the Hubbard Method is HealthMed in Sacramento, California.

Hubbard made no medical claims for his purification program. He focused on the technique as a removal of barriers to spiritual development. However, a medical evaluation (including an electrocardiogram to check for heart health) is necessary before undertaking the protocol. Good kidney function is also necessary. Pregnancy, anemia, kidney disease, breast-feeding, or a weak heart will keep someone out of the HealthMed program.

The medical director of HealthMed is David E. Root, M.D., M.P.H. Root is a retired colonel from the U.S. Air Force, and board certified in both occupational medicine and aerospace medicine. His particular expertise is in the medical consequences of exposure to chemicals and drugs. In a 1987 issue of the *Journal of Toxicology—Cutaneous and Ocular Toxicology*,[4] Root describes the removal of black toxic material through the sweat glands of a twenty-three-year-old woman who had worked for six months washing down the exhaust stack and filter pads on an oil-fired electrical generator. When she came to HealthMed, she had been unable to work for nearly a year due to symptoms of fatigue, swollen lymph glands, eye and throat irritation, and "feeling terrible." After thirty-one days of the Hubbard detox protocol, the black substance stopped oozing from her pores, almost all her acne cleared, and she no longer felt fatigue, hoarse, or had problems sleeping.

Sweating is the cornerstone of the program, but first you exercise. You will probably use the machines in the gymlike clinic to exercise for twenty to thirty minutes, then hop into the sauna in your bathing suit, where you are going to do most of your sweating. You spend your treatment session in and out of the sauna, drinking water to replace what you're losing. The program requires daily attendance, from two and a half to five hours a day, for two to three weeks. It is over when the participant feels great and has no further symptoms of toxic residues.

"Anything which is scarce becomes valuable," writes L. Ron Hubbard in *Clear Body, Clear Mind*,[5] "so the body holds onto something in demand, and will resist eliminating it. To eliminate it, provide an alternative supply of the substance." HealthMed provides the body with an alternative blend of oils, containing soy, walnut, peanut and safflower oils, which are fresh, cold-pressed, and carefully refrigerated to prevent rancidity. Lecithin, an emulsifying agent (something that breaks up fat into small, easily digested globules) is also taken daily.

Niacin (vitamin B_3) causes people to flush with a red, prickly heat. This flushing mechanism is part of the protocol, and so niacinamide, which is a form of the vitamin that doesn't cause flushing, is not used. Hubbard found niacin particularly effective for flushing out LSD crystals, marijuana, and other drugs. Hubbard also found that people taking niacin sometimes experienced symptoms from past diseases or drug use, anything from a repeat LSD trip to skin disease. Yet, if they kept taking the vitamin dose, the symptoms of distress disappeared.

A general vitamin and mineral supplement is also taken to make sure the nutritional needs of the individual are met.

THE ANN WIGMORE PROTOCOL

Our simple remedy for helping people is the God-given chlorophyll of the wheat grass. Nature uses it as a body cleanser, rebuilder and neutralizer of toxin.

—*Ann Wigmore*

When Ann Wigmore was a child in Lithuania, her grandmother told her that she "had a God-inspired certainty" that Ann was "destined to be a means whereby humanity would be bettered, physically and spiritually." Apparently her grandmother was right. Wigmore had been a sickly child who had overcome enormous hardships both in Eastern Europe and in America, where she moved as a teen. In adulthood, she became a Christian minister and was propelled into a ministry of healing by the influence of that grandmother, who raised her to appreciate nature's medicines by having the child help her when she used herbs and other natural methods to treat injured soldiers during World War I.

Wigmore spent years studying on her own, observing the food preferences of injured animals of many kinds, questioning experts in the field of agronomy, and collecting seeds from around the world and growing them herself as part of her research. Then, beginning in 1961 at age fifty-two, first in a century-old farmhouse outside Boston named the Homestead and soon thereafter at her Hippocrates Health Institute in Boston's Back Bay, Wigmore began treating the "untreatables" (and all others who were willing to receive her assistance). She used a simple diet of mostly uncooked produce, sprouts of many kinds, and her gift to the world, wheat grass juice, which G. H. Earp-Thomas, a world-renowned expert on grasses, called "the richest nutritional liquid known to man." With these, she taught, she was replenishing missing nutrients from her charges' high-fat, white flour, refined sugar, animal flesh, chemical-laden diet, and giving the body what it needed to self-repair.

In addition to administering to the physical self, Wigmore believed in the power of thought. "Health is what one makes of it," she wrote in *Why Suffer?* "It requires a mature attitude and self-discipline to rebuild failing health. . . . In fact," she continued, "if my years of training and experience in working with thousands of people have proven one thing, it is that we can learn to control our level of health and the course of our lives if we choose."[6] In her books, Wigmore shares many anecdotes of people brought back from the edge, even with diagnoses of diabetes, malignant tumors, leukemia, multiple sclerosis, arthritis, asthma, emphysema, and other difficult conditions.

Although Ann Wigmore died in 1994 at age eighty-five in a tragic fire that destroyed the original Hippocrates Health Institute, she left behind a strong legacy of many thousands of people aided by her unswerving dedication to natural healing, and her ability to communicate what she knew. Brian Clement, who was on her Board of Directors in Boston, founded a new Hippocrates Health Institute (now called Hippocrates Health Lifechange Center) in West Palm Beach, Florida. On the West Coast, Raychel Solomon was inspired to found Hippocrates West (now called Optimum Health Institute) near San Diego, California. At these institutes and through her writing, Ann Wigmore's work continues.

HIPPOCRATES HEALTH LIFECHANGE CENTER: A BANQUET OF CHOICES

Clement broke away from the Boston-based Hippocrates Health Institute a little more than a decade ago to found his own center in a tropical thirty-acre woodland area in West Palm Beach. There is room for sixty guests, though usually they host around forty per week. There is a large main building, a major guest house, and smaller cottages on the institute grounds, with four other guest houses off-site. The grounds are lush not only with vegetation, but with facilities: four ozonated pools, one with Dead Sea salt minerals; whirlpool; hot tub; sauna; fitness center; and vibrational machine. The institute offers a cornucopia of therapies: reflexology, massage, colonic irrigation, magnetic therapy, bioelectric therapy, mind-body therapy, facials, and others. Food is a take-as-much-as-you-want buffet of more than a dozen different dishes.

Clement and his wife, Anna Maria, altered the original Hippocrates protocol somewhat, eliminating the rejuvelac (a fermented grain drink used to enhance digestion), adding their own line of supplements to the supplies available at the institute store, and changing the name to Hippocrates Health Lifechange Center. They kept the core of the program: the emphasis on education through daily classes and lectures, the inclusion of the emotional and spiritual dimensions of wellness, the living foods diet, the wheat grass therapy, and the focus on the health of the colon as a key to overall well-being.

Cost for a shared bedroom and bathroom off the premises is $1,500 for a one-week stay and $3,250 for the full three-week program; for a private room and bath on the premises it is $3,500 for one week and $7,500 for three weeks.

OPTIMUM HEALTH INSTITUTE: "COLON CAMP"

My first impressions of the Optimum Health Institute are of crisply clean buildings, a sundial perched on a white cement pedestal in the center of a manicured lawn, and a patio cooled by overhanging branches of an unfamiliar species of tree. I do recognize a carob tree across the patio, heavy with dark pods. Inside the main office, I receive a friendly greeting and am handed a clipboard and paperwork.

The sign-in sheet offers directions for a successful visit, including the following: "It is important that guests leave all problems and worries at home. When this is done, this adventure into a new beginning will be fruitful." I wince at the redundancy. Is there any other kind of beginning? We are twenty minutes from San Diego in clean, clear air and peaceful surroundings. New or old, at least the intake form calls it an adventure. Like all adventures, I don't know what to expect.

Soon, I am in a chair on the lawn outside the office, sipping rejuvelac, a fermented wheat berry drink that tastes like a cross between beer and dishwater. (Later, at home, I will make my own rejuvelac, which will taste like a cross between beer and lemonade.) On one side sits an Asian man reading a Chinese book. On my other side is a California motel owner, a bleached blond, attractive woman with severely tanned skin, a pile of silver bracelets at her wrist, and air-brushed art on exquisitely long fingernails.

In the week to come, I will meet people from Taiwan, Israel, the Philippines, Ireland, Canada, England, and at least eight American states. There is an Iraqi woman who came in from London, and an Iranian from L.A. A number have been here before. One man has been here every few months for nineteen years! People return, we are told, not because the system doesn't work, but "because they know we've got the answer, so they do what they want in their lives back home, then return here to make things right."

"Here" is the dream manifest of Raychel Solomon, who was in her early sixties in March 1976, when she learned a friend had cancer. She'd already lost two sisters to cancer. She decided she had to do something, but didn't know what that something should be. She fasted and waited for a sign. In April, she decided to attend a lecture by a woman who claimed she had survived terminal breast cancer after drinking wheat grass juice, becoming vegetarian, cleansing her colon, and radically altering her life. First, Solomon read the woman's book. In *How I Conquered Cancer Naturally*, Solomon learned that the author, Eydie Mae Hunsberger, had been taught her self-care cancer treatment at the Hippocrates Health Institute in Boston.

Raychel Solomon decided she had to open a Hippocrates Health Institute West. She announced this to Hunsberger at the author's lecture. She also announced this to Ann Wigmore, when Wigmore came to town soon thereafter. Wigmore, the pragmatist, suggested Solomon first experience Hippocrates for herself.

Solomon did, but she'd already picked out her property. With grace from the universe and Solomon's incredible sense of purpose, a three-bedroom home she called Hippocrates West opened its doors in September 1976 in El Cajon, east of San Diego. Within two months the place was too small.

Two years later, Solomon moved to the current site in Lemon Grove. It was originally a retirement home, now refurbished and expanded. There are singles, town houses, and small apartments available, with prices ranging from $400 to over $600 each, per week. The fee for room and board and classes is less than a third of the Florida site, but this operation runs a simpler ship: There is a jacuzzi, and there is the lawn to relax on in lounge chairs. There are some crossword puzzles in the den. And there are a chiropractor, a massage therapist, and several colon therapists who are independent contractors whose services are paid for separately. One of the apartment buildings off the grounds has a pool, but it isn't used much. That's it.

The week I spent there in August of 1996, they had 194 paying guests, the most they had ever hosted in their twenty-year history. In addition, there were a handful of worker-guests whose fee was reduced. (You must complete your basic three-week program here before being allowed back as a worker-guest.)

Raychel Solomon was dedicated to goals similar to Wigmore's. However, over the years a rift developed and Hippocrates West became a separate entity called the Optimum Health Institute.

Each Sunday, Sam Dunbar takes a group of guests on tour. He is the institute's seventy-nine-year-old organic gardener, who, with his wife, has lived here for nineteen years. "The lifeblood of this place is the wheat grass," he says, showing us the Crystal Cathedral, an enormous greenhouse. The inside is climate-controlled for optimum growing of wheat grass and sprouts. Inside are sprouts from buckwheat, sunflower, alfalfa, fenugreek, rye, lentil, and mung beans. Dunbar tells us they place fermented seeds in a bread pan in the sun or under a light bulb, and dye them pink with beet juice for special occasions. It tastes, he insists, like turkey, tuna, or salmon. I don't believe him, but then, it is only my first day.

We pass a hedge, and beyond it I see a scarecrow guarding the organic garden. Behind us is the laundry, and the rooms for colonics, massage, and chiropractic.

On the side of the building that faces the street is a short, man-made stream, a horizontal fountain, really, meandering through a lovely garden dedicated to the memory of Solomon, who died at age eighty-one in 1993. The garden fronts the entrance to the institute's library and rooms for meeting and meditation.

People come here for many reasons: cancer, heart disease, arthritis, weight loss, or just to feel clean, inside and out. There are thirty-five classes during a three-week stay, including a gentle exercise time each morning. One week is the minimum stay allowed.

The lessons include mental and emotional detoxification, self-esteem, communication, relaxation, pain control and sleep technique, beauty care, food combining, human digestion and elimination, how to give yourself an enema (washing out the bowel), and how to grow and prepare wheat grass and sprouts.

You are expected to drink at least a quart of rejuvelac (you have your choice of either wheat or another grain berry, slightly sprouted and fermented) and a quart of water each day, to improve intestinal function. You are asked to keep your vitamins, minerals, and other supplements at home.

This is not your "put up your feet and relax all day" kind of spa, although there is plenty of time for making friends and resting in your room, in a chair on the lawn, on the patio, or in the jacuzzi protected from the sun beneath a white lattice-work cabana. It's a place where the term "veg out" takes on new meaning as you eat two meals of vegetables (and a breakfast of fruit) each day and have no access to any other food; where you learn to redefine what is a meal, and how much you need to eat to feel well; and where you are introduced to your digestive tract with intimacy that you have never known before.

What you discover is, you don't need to eat between meals; what they give you as a portion is really adequate; and your energy increases along with your tolerance for conversations about enemas and implants (they call them "E's and I's" around here). You learn that an implant has nothing to do with breasts and everything to do with your colon. It seems everything does around here, which is how OHI got its nickname of "Colon Camp."

In addition to water, wheat grass goes in both ends of you, daily. At OHI, two ounces of wheat grass are consumed twice a day, and three ounces are implanted in the colon twice a day, one immediately after a water enema, and one about an hour later. No one demands to know if you've done it, but most people seem to figure, if they came for the program, why not do the program?

We are told that we drink wheat grass juice because it is loaded with amino acids, which help the body rebuild; antioxidants, which help the body resist disease; and chlorophyll, which helps the body cleanse and detoxify. The purpose of the wheat grass juice implant is to rid the bowel of impactions and to enhance nutrition. We are also encouraged to use the pulp that comes out of the extractor machine when we juice the grass. The pulp is used as a poultice on the skin to remove toxins, reduce pain, and cleanse the skin of unwanted cells. It is the universal panacea: You can stick it in your ear or up your nose, you can put it in an eye cup and wash out your eyes (and tap the eye lightly with a towel afterwards, to stop the burning sensation!). You can put it on a tooth abscess, or on warts. Wherever it goes, we are told, it helps clear out mucus or pus or unwanted cells.

The rules of consumption are rigid: no diluting, no drinking wheat grass juice within an hour of eating or drinking anything else, and consume it within twenty minutes of juicing it. If two ounces is nauseating, we're told, start with half an ounce, but take it.

Releasing emotional baggage

The sundial on the lawn is used midweek, or rather its pedestal is used, with the sundial lifted off. Therapist Morley Tadman, M.A., M.S., who teaches a class in self-esteem, collects us on the grass and hands out paper and pencils. We write down things that don't serve us, and with appropriate ceremony Tadman burns them in the pedestal's bowl-like top.

Emotional detoxification is almost as big a focus here as physical elimination. We have "health opportunities," not diseases. We "get rid of weight," we don't "lose" it (because something lost is found). "Our thoughts," we are told, "are purchase orders to the universe." Our own negative thoughts and negative messages from others are deflected with "Cancel! Cancel!"

Psychiatrist Garry White, M.D., reminds us that stress kills. "Not occasional irritations like losing your keys, but subclinical chronic stress." Instead of putting up with it, he says, "examine your life, find out what situations or people are causing you stress, and get rid of them!"

A detox success story is Jayne de Felice, who supervises

the colonic hygienists at the Optimum Health Institute. A graphic designer and commercial artist, de Felice became so ill she had to stop working. For two years she searched for help within the medical community, without success. After ten days at OHI, all the symptoms she had been suffering those two years disappeared. She later learned her condition was caused by toxic metal poisoning from her art. She returned to OHI three times during the following two years, reevaluated her life, and left the high-pressure world of commercial art to become a colonic specialist. You just never know where these green paths will take you.

MAX GERSON PROTOCOL

When someone has a successful program, others take it and re-create it according to their particular biases and personalities and, as years pass, as new research appears. This inevitable transmutation of treatments has happened to the nutrition-based detoxification program of Max Gerson, M.D. He had phenomenal success curing cancer in the late 1950s, and although he was rebuffed by the medical establishment and his methods were derided and ignored, his work continues in two separate and distinct institutions.

One, the Gerson Institute in Bonita, California, is run by his daughter, Charlotte Gerson, who toes the traditional Gerson line. The other is the Gerson Research Organization (GRO), run by epidemiologist Gar Hildenbrand in San Diego, which has added over a half dozen other modalities to the basic Gerson protocol. In late 1996, an acclaimed German cancer researcher named Josef Issels, M.D., joined the staff at the hospital associated with GRO, which is called CHIPSA (Centro Hospitalario Internacional Pacifico, S.A.) in Tijuana. Issels's innovative approach looks for simultaneous multiple causes of the body's immune suppression. Although Issels died in 1998 his brief association with CHIPSA enhanced the hospital's credibility as a scientific medical institution.

The foundation of both the Gerson Institute and the Gerson Research Organization is Gerson's belief in the self-healing potential of the sick body, when that body is properly nourished and supported while the immune system does its job.

Like Ann Wigmore, Gerson recognized the importance of enzymes in uncooked food, and the powerful uses of vegetables
and vegetable juices to fuel immune competency. Gerson originated the use of the coffee enema to more quickly release
toxins accumulated by the liver in the gallbladder (see "Implants" in chapter 7), which proved to be a potent pain reliever. He documented his successes in books, such as *A
Cancer Therapy: Results of Fifty Cases.*

Although the most publicized cases were cancer (with particular success for malignant melanoma and lymphoma), the
Gerson protocol is used for rheumatoid arthritis, lupus, and
other chronic degenerative diseases. No matter what the official diagnosis, the underlying problem is a need for getting the
toxic clutter out of the body and giving it the tools it needs to
heal.

Each facility now has a research and educational arm in or
around San Diego, and a clinic, which for political reasons is
in Mexico, where the cancer establishment of the United States
cannot close it for using nonstandard therapies. In addition, the
Gerson Institute bravely opened an American clinic in early
1997, in Sedona, Arizona.

THE CLEAN-ME-OUT PROGRAM

Naturopathic physician Richard Anderson created a highly reg-
imented protocol you do yourself, at home, with products you
purchase either from his company, Arise & Shine, or from
your local health food store. The protocol involves daily urine
monitoring to make sure you have an alkaline pH (see chapter
4 for information on this testing procedure); decreasing consumption of food over several weeks to a climactic week of
fasting, and regularly spaced consumption of water, bentonite
powder (to absorb toxins in the bowel); psyllium seed husks
(to collect and move feces along), liquid minerals, and three
separate herbal tablets to detoxify and stimulate the bowel, replenish it with helpful intestinal bacteria, and provide healing
nourishment. Daily enemas during the fast are recommended.

This program is tailored to the level of toxicity of the user,
which is evident to a great degree by the pH reading. It
stretches from three weeks of preparation to a week or longer

of two and a half meals a day, to two a day, to one a day, to the fast, with the individual choosing to move back and forth from one phase to another as needed.

One useful service provided by this company is free advice and support by phone for people on the program. I began the program while writing this book and found it too disruptive to have to consume the right substance at the right time on a rigid daily schedule. I can see doing it when you have time set aside for little else but detoxification and self-care. However, I do know people who claim even an abbreviated version modified for their schedule was useful in clearing the head, brightening the complexion, and improving their energy.

Following are a few other facilities for detoxifying the body. I have not visited them, nor spoken with anyone who has been a resident. Thus, I cannot testify as to their worth, only that they are available for your investigation.

THE HEALTH OASIS

HC 33, Box 10
Tilly, Arkansas 72679
501/496-2364

Supervised water fasting, uniting the spiritual and physical with morning Christian bible study, afternoon lessons on health and healing. The director, Bernice Davison, is a retired nurse, but there are no medical treatments, and enemas are not a part of the program. Guests are encouraged to bring their own enema equipment, if they desire to do so.

Davison has supervised fasting for twenty-seven years. Among those she advises not to fast are insulin-dependent diabetics and anyone with severe liver problems. She prefers to have only eight guests at a time, though the facility can hold twelve. They have an exercise room with exercise equipment. Those who are ready to return to eating enjoy the bounty from their organic garden, tended by Davison's husband, Harley.

SCOTT'S NATURAL HEALTH INSTITUTE

Institute:
19160 Albion Road
Strongsville, Ohio 44136
216/238-6930

Office:
Dr. David J. Scott
17023 Loraine Avenue
Cleveland, Ohio 44111
216/671-4800

Closed Thanksgiving through January.

Dr. D. J. Scott founded this facility in 1957. It follows the Natural Hygiene philosophy with a Christian bent, offering a place for rest and fasting. Scott is a chiropractor and founding president of the International Association of Professional Natural Hygienists. His facility is particularly geared to those wishing to lose weight as well as to heal.

The institute houses from fifteen to eighteen guests, who are expected to spend much of their time lying down resting or drinking distilled water. A minimum stay of two weeks is required.

There are probably other healing programs around the United States that deserve mention, and with your help they will be in future editions of this book. Please send information about those you wish to see added to the revised text to Carolyn Reuben at P.O. Box 254531, Sacramento, CA 95825-4531.

RESOURCES

For information about chelation therapy:

The American College for the Advancement in Medicine (800/532-3688; 714/583-7666; fax 714/455-9679). Practitioners can contact them at 23121 Verdugo Drive, Suite 204, Laguna Hills, CA 92653. The public can receive a free list of doctors using chelation by sending 55¢ postage on a self-addressed envelope to P.O. Box 3427, Laguna Hills, CA 92654.

American Board of Chelation Therapy, Jack Hank, executive director, 1407 B North Wells, Chicago, IL 60610 (800/356-2228; e-mail jackhank@mcs.net).

Book on chelation therapy:

Elmer Cranton, M.D., *Bypassing Bypass: A Non-surgical Treatment for Improving Circulation and Slowing the Aging Process* (Troutdale, Virginia: Medex, 1997).

Morton Walker, *Chelation Therapy* (New Canaan, Conn.: Keats, 1997).

Arline Brecher, *Forty Something Forever: A Consumer's Guide to Chelation Therapy and Other Heart-Savers* (Herndon, Va.: HealthSavers Press, 1992).

H. DeWayne Ashmead, *Conversations on Chelation: Mineral Nutrition* (New Canaan, Conn.: Keats, 1989).

Books on the Hubbard Method and facilities that use it:

L. Ron Hubbard, *Clear Body, Clear Mind: The Effective Purification Program* (Los Angeles: Bridge Publications, 1990). The text in which Hubbard details his detox program.

Theron G. Randolph, M.D., *An Alternative Approach to Allergies: The New Field of Clinical Ecology Unravels the Environmental Causes of Mental and Physical Ills* (New York: HarperCollins, 1990). Theron Randolph, M.D., was the father of environmental medicine in the United States. In sections of this book he discusses details of the Hubbard protocol and its usefulness.

HealthMed Detox, James Woodworth, director, 5501 Power Inn Road, Sacramento, CA 95820 (916/387-8252; fax 916/

387-6977; e-mail hmdetox@aol.com). Members of the Church of Scientology can receive the Hubbard method of detox at any of their churches; Narconon, a secular, inpatient drug rehabilitation organization, also provides the Hubbard Method of detox in its facilities worldwide. HealthMed is the only site in the United States that offers the protocol under medical supervision, and has been offering the Hubbard Method of detox since 1981.

Books on the Ann Wigmore protocol and facilities that use it:

Ronald L. Seibold, M.S., ed., *Cereal Grass: Nature's Greatest Health Gift* (New Canaan, Conn.: Keats, 1991). Crisply written, giving the science behind the use of cereal grasses for healing and nutrition, including a description of Ann Wigmore and her popularization of wheat grass.

Eydie Mae Hunsberger with Chris Loeffler, *How I Conquered Cancer Naturally* (Garden City Park, N.Y.: Avery, 1992). Eydie Mae's story of her seemingly hopeless case of breast cancer and her return to health after revising her life under Ann Wigmore's direction.

Ann Wigmore, *Be Your Own Doctor* (Wayne, New Jersey: Avery, 1982). A short paperback that gives the justification for her wheat grass therapy and natural foods diet, with specific directions for preparation, including recipes and testimonials.

Ann Wigmore, *The Wheatgrass Book* (Wayne, New Jersey: Avery, 1985).

Raychel and Mark Solomon, Ph.D., *Coming Alive with Raychel* (San Diego: Raymark Books, 1986). In a ''conversation'' between Raychel and an anonymous guest, she lays out her philosophy and offers a quick overview of her mental, physical, and spiritual detoxification techniques. If unavailable near you, it can be purchased from Optimum Health Institute. Call them at 619/464-3346.

Brian R. Clement with Theresa Foy DiGeronimo, *Living Foods for Optimum Health* (Rocklin, Calif.: Prima, 1996). The how and why of uncooked foods from the founder/director of Hippocrates Health Lifechange Center in West Palm Beach, Florida. More than one hundred recipes.

Hippocrates Health Lifechange Center, 1443 Palmdale Court, West Palm Beach, FL 33411 (407/471-8876; fax 407/471-9464). The institute's store has all the supplies you need to follow the Wigmore protocol, plus books, tapes, and videos about the program.

Optimum Health Institute, 6970 Central Avenue, Lemon Grove, CA 91945-3346 (619/464-3346; fax 619/589-4098; store 619/589-4091). The OHI store sells all the supplies you need to follow the Wigmore protocol, plus numerous books, tapes, and videos of the program.

   I feel grateful to have spent a week at the institute. I'd been waiting for over twenty years to experience the Hippocrates program, having heard Ann Wigmore speak in Los Angeles in 1976. I wasn't disappointed. Now I know why my sister-in-law feels "renewed" after her yearly visit to OHI.

For wheat grass:

Growing your own wheat grass is absolutely the cheapest way to go. One tray of wheat grass gives around sixteen ounces of juice. (It costs $3 for the soil to grow fifteen trays' worth of grass.) The biggest expense is the juice extractor, unless you don't mind grinding away by hand with a metal meat grinder. For directions, see *The Wheatgrass Book* by Ann Wigmore (Wayne, New Jersey: Avery, 1985). Or I'll share the directions on how the Optimum Health Institute taught me to grow it: send a stamped, self-addressed envelope and $2 to Greensland Publishing, P.O. Box 25431, Sacramento, CA 95825-4531.

Juice bars are sprouting up everywhere. Some include an ounce of wheat grass juice, freshly squeezed, on their menu. In Sacramento, one ounce costs $1. Check the Chamber of Commerce for a location near you.

Health food stores in your area may also provide fresh-squeezed juice (it ought to be consumed within a half hour of being squeezed). Or the store may sell you a small amount of wheat grass ready for you to harvest. Again, you'll need a metal meat grinder or a juicer built especially for wheat grass to grind it.

Sungrown Organic Distributors will deliver organic wheat grass to your door for $11.25 a pound. A pound of the grass should yield ten to fifteen ounces of juice, which should last you about ten days, says Sungrown president Ken Taylor. Sungrown will also supply you with sprouts. Sungrown Organic Distributors, 2325 Hollister Street, San Diego, CA 92154 (800/995-7776).

Books on the Max Gerson protocol and facilities that use it:

Max Gerson, M.D., *A Cancer Therapy: Results of Fifty Cases* (Bonita, Calif.: The Gerson Institute, 1990). One of Gerson's most influential books, documenting the successful outcomes possible with his therapy.

Burton Goldberg Group, *An Alternative Medicine Definitive Guide to Cancer* (Tiburon, Calif.: Future Publishing, 1997). This encyclopedic view of the alternative playing field includes Issels and Gerson.

The Gerson Institute, Charlotte Gerson, director, P.O. Box 430, Bonita, CA 91908 (619/585-7600; fax 619/585-7610; 888/4-GERSON for 24-hour information; Internet http://www.gerson.org).

Gerson Association for Natural Medicine / Gerson Centers of America, 78 Canyon Diablo, Sedona, AZ (888/GERSON-8).

Gerson Research Organization (GRO), Gar Hildenbrand, director, 7807 Artesian Road, San Diego, CA 92127 (619/759-2966; fax 619/759-2967).

For Information on the Clean-Me-Out Program:

The Clean-Me-Out Program, Arise and Shine Herbal Products, P.O. Box 1439, Mount Shasta, CA 96067 (916/926-0891).

Richard Anderson, N.D., N.M.D., *Cleanse and Purify Thyself* (self-published, 1994). For a good overview of the clean-yourself-out philosophy and procedures, I recommend you read this manual before starting the program.

REFERENCES

1. Efrain Olszewer, M.D., et al., "Side Effects on Patients Treated with EDTA," *Townsend Letter for Doctors and Patients* August/September 1996, 92.

2. M. E. Godfrey, *New Zealand Medical Journal*, May 24, 1996 (vol. 195J) as reported in *Clinical Pearls*, edited by Kristine Simpson et al. (Sacramento, Calif.: ITServices, 1996), 102.

3. M. Wolff et al., "Equilibrium of Polybrominated Biphenyl (PBB) Residues in Serum and Fat of Michigan Residents," *Bulletin of Environmental Contamination and Toxicology Contam. Toxicol.* 21: 775–781 (1979).

4. David E. Root, M.D., M.P.H., and Gerald T. Lionelli, B.S., "Excretion of a Lipophilic Toxicant through the Sebaceous Glands: A Case Report," *Journal of Toxicology—Cutaneous and Ocular Toxicology* 6(1) : 13–17 (1987).

5. L. Ron Hubbard, *Clear Body, Clear Mind* (Los Angeles;

Bridge Publications, 1990), 75. 4751 Fountain Avenue, Los Angeles, CA 90029.

6. Ann Wigmore, *Why Suffer?* (Wayne, New Jersey: Avery, 1985).

FOURTEEN

ADDICTION AND SUBSTANCE ABUSE DETOX

Nutritional support is the missing component in most conventional recovery programs in the United States today.
—*Ann Louise Gittleman*

In the October 1996 issue of *Let's Live* magazine, nutritionist and author Ann Louise Gittleman suggests that in addition to an inward look with the help of a counselor, people addicted to caffeine, alcohol, nicotine, marijuana, amphetamines, heroin, and cocaine must reach beyond the psyche to the cell. According to Gittleman, satisfying the cells' need for vitamins, minerals, amino acids, and other critical nutrients will correct imbalances of brain chemistry and allow long-term recovery to be maintained.[1]

You may not have heard of using nutrition for addiction, but it is already a part of recovery programs in Amityville, New York; in Minneapolis, Minnesota; and in Mill Valley, Burlingame, and West Covina, California.

When you walk into the offices of Recovery Systems in Mill Valley, California, for example, the staff wants to know not only your life experiences, not only family patterns of eating, drinking, drug use, and medications, not only the standard laboratory tests, but also whether you are deficient in amino acids and other nutrients. They know that amino acids create brain chemicals called neurotransmitters which are of critical importance in regulating your cravings and your mood.

If your daily diet has been the usual multiple servings of white flour, white sugar, and hydrogenated fat washed down with alcohol or soda pop (and, if your cells are really lucky, a lettuce leaf once in a while or a tablespoon of ketchup as your nod to the vegetable kingdom), cravings for your drug of choice are really a red neon sign announcing malnourishment.

If you used stimulants, Recovery Systems staff looks especially carefully at how your thyroid functions. The thyroid gland, located in your throat, secretes hormones that control your energy level and your metabolic rate (how fast your body does everything it does). If you've been using stimulants, your thyroid gland probably needed help long before you began feeling the need for drugs.

Nutritional relief of substance abuse is a godsend for many closet addicts, who no longer have to suffer shame, because now they know their cravings don't come from lack of willpower. And, though getting out one's feelings and straightening out one's emotional turmoil is important, the treatment isn't *only* to white-knuckle it through yet another group.

ALCOHOLISM: NOT WILLPOWER BUT BIOCHEMISTRY

Back in 1962, nutritional biochemist Roger Williams stated, "alcoholic craving . . . has its origin in the deficient nutrition of the cells."[2] Williams further observed that "rats on high quality diets voluntarily consume far less alcohol (also less sugar) than those on deficient diets. In individual rats it has been possible to shift their alcohol consumption up and down at will by deliberately making them deficient in specific vitamins, and then supplying the missing nutrients."[3]

According to Joan Mathews Larson, Ph.D., director of the Health Recovery Center in Minneapolis and author of *Seven Weeks to Sobriety,* there are "three different body chemistries that underlie vulnerability to alcoholism (and one type that may lead to a mistaken diagnosis of alcoholism)."[4] These types are as follows:

First is someone who drinks a lot for many years, enjoying alcohol without feeling drunk. This type of person is born with a certain liver enzyme called II ADH (alcohol dehydrogenase) that allows his liver to metabolize alcohol efficiently without problems for quite some time. Then, often in his forties, he discovers that he needs alcohol just to feel normal. Without it he feels hyperactive, shaky, irritable, and unable to concentrate.

In a nonalcoholic person, alcohol is converted to acetaldehyde, which is converted to acetic acid (vinegar), which is converted to carbon dioxide and water, which is exhaled and urinated away. In contrast, a II ADH kind of alcoholic doesn't completely convert acetaldehyde to vinegar. Some goes straight to the brain and is deposited there as THIQ (tetrahydroiodoquinolone), a morphinelike biochemical that is among the most addictive substances ever isolated.

THIQ creates the craving for alcohol. It can also be involved in attention deficit disorder, hyperactivity, and many other mental and psychological problems.

Second is someone who has always felt sick from alcohol, yet after a couple days of abstinence, strong cravings drive him back to drinking. When he drinks he becomes disruptive and argumentative. This person is allergic to alcohol.

When this person drinks, it creates a biochemical cascade of alarm reactions. The drinker becomes addicted to these changes in his biochemistry. When he stops drinking, his body biochemistry shifts again, creating withdrawal symptoms that include depression and erratic behavior.

Third is a person who feels depressed until he drinks alcohol and then he feels normal and happy. This person has to keep drinking to stay happy, although eventually the drinking ruins his relationships and work life. A "successful" treatment means suffering deep depression.

One important nutritional solution that helps eliminate this no-win situation is consumption of evening primrose oil or borage oil, which contain omega-6 essential fatty acids. These provide this drinker's brain chemistry what it needs to free him from depression permanently, without alcohol. (This also works for people suffering the depression that follows cocaine withdrawal.)

Fourth is the person who feels ill from alcohol, but craves it (in women, particularly before their menstrual period), who is actually hypoglycemic, not alcoholic.

During the week before menstruation, women's blood sugar is especially low, causing some women to crave chocolates, some to crave alcohol, and some to crave both. Those who consume alcohol feel a faster sugar high, for alcohol doesn't have to be digested. It slips immediately through the stomach lining into the bloodstream and is carried, as glucose, to the brain. For glucose to be used, the pancreas has to secrete insulin into the blood, and with the help of the insulin the glucose moves out of the blood, and into brain and body cells, where it is used for energy.

The more alcohol the person drinks, the more insulin is secreted. Sometimes the pancreas overshoots how much to secrete, and too much glucose is pulled out of the blood. The person feels weak, tired, irritable, maybe even dizzy. And the craving for another quick "fix" returns. Yet, a hypoglycemic person who craves alcohol will feel drunk after one or two drinks.

BIOCHEMICAL RECOVERY

Joan Mathews Larson recommends the following nutrients to halt withdrawal symptoms, eliminate cravings, and help begin the work of detoxification. (I purposely don't include dosages. If you are interested in this program, read *Seven Weeks to Sobriety* for program details. The book is available from local bookstores for $10.95 or from the author for $14.95 including shipping and handling, through Bio-Recovery Inc., 3255 Hennepin Ave. South, Minneapolis, MN 55408 (800/247-6237). You can also purchase the exact dosages of all the nutrients you need for a six-week program, for $263.15 (compared to over $600 if you buy each supplement yourself from each company individually).

The Larson Nutritional Detox Formula

- Glutamine (the one amino acid most associated with eliminating alcohol withdrawal symptoms and cravings)
- Free-form amino acid (a variety of amino acids that erase depression and anxiety and improve memory and thinking ability)
- Phenylalanine (sometimes abbreviated DLPA) (the amino acid that by itself erases depression and chronic pain)
- Vitamin C (proven since the 1950s to reverse addictive states, in studies with heroin, PCP, and other drugs)
- Calcium/magnesium (these two minerals reverse muscle spasms, including seizures and tremors in alcoholics, in-

crease feelings of relaxation and calm, support heart function, and prevent delirium and insomnia)
- Essential fatty acids (Larson uses borage oil now, though in the book she calls for evening primrose oil. These oils provides the brain with gamma-linolenic acid (GLA), which is converted to prostaglandin E_1, which prevents withdrawal symptoms, including seizures, and helps repair liver damage)
- Multivitamin/minerals (Larson uses Multi Vi-Mins from Allergy Research Group of San Leandro, California, but any formula containing a strong B complex will help prevent the neurological and psychological symptoms of B deficiency)
- Pancreatic enzymes (taking all the proper nutrients is useless if the body can't pull them from the digestive tract into the bloodstream, a process assisted by digestive aids such as pancreatic enzymes)

Other useful supplements for drug addiction treatment include milk thistle (a liver-repairing herb discussed on page 175), glutathione (a powerful antioxidant), and coenzyme Q-10 (which helps increase energy and protect the heart). Other treatment programs have found the amino acid tyrosine to help, too, particularly with the depression following withdrawal of cocaine or other stimulants.

Julia Ross, director of Recovery Systems, suggests the following nutritional therapies for some of the specific physical and emotional effects of long-term drug use:

Complaints	*Supplements*
Agitated depression, low self-esteem, irritability, and sleep disturbance:	*L-tryptophan* (available from a compounding pharmacy by prescription). In addition, you may use natural sources of L-tryptophan, such as algae, kelp, other seaweeds,

milk, sunflower or sesame or pumpkin seeds (and pumpkin pulp), banana, and turkey. For sleep disturbance, you can also use *melatonin*. For mild depression, you can also use the herb *St. John's wort*.

Sugar cravings: *Chromium, L-Glutamine.*

Over sensitivity: *DL-Phenylalanine (DLPA)*

Anxiety, insecurity, fear, panic, and an inability to relax: *GABA, L-Taurine with L-Glycine*

No ambition, depression, and low energy: *L-Tyrosine and/or L-Phenylalanine*

Note: All amino acids should be taken with vitamin B$_6$.

Adapted with permission from Recovery Systems, 147 Lomita Dr., Mill Valley, CA 94941 (415/383-3611).

TREATING SUBSTANCE ABUSE WITH FOOD

Can you keep people clean and sober without expensive supplements, if you control the quality of food they eat? Officials in San Mateo County, California, were willing to find out.

Food is core to the successful program that Kathleen DesMaisons, Ph.D., president and CEO of Radiant Recovery in Burlingame, California, designed for a select group of San Mateo County's multiple DUI (driving under the influence) offenders.

Like Joan Mathews Larson, DesMaisons views drug dependence as inextricably connected to malnutrition. DesMaisons's program also addresses a "sugar sensitivity" that involves an abnormal response to carbohydrates. She encourages eating protein meals three times a day, including meat, cheese, eggs, tofu, and even peanut butter, along with beans, vegetables, and wholesome grains. Clients are taught to recognize and avoid eating the wide variety of sugar sources in commercial foods (anything in the ingredient list ending in -*ose* or -*ol*) as well as the sugar in grapes, watermelon, cherries, carrot juice, and all fruit juices.

Good compliance begins with breakfast: what DesMaisons calls her "power shake," a nutritious and tasty drink. Then, nourishing food at regular intervals helps clients maintain a steady blood sugar, improving their mood and self-control, and assuring them adequate levels of important neurotransmitters, such as beta-endorphin and serotonin. These biochemicals move messages from one nerve cell to another and control mood and sensitivity to pain.

Radiant Recovery has been open to the public since 1989, but it has been the San Mateo protocol that has really placed DesMaisons program on the treatment map. From May 1994 through May 1995, the Radiant Recovery program required twenty-nine multiple DUI offenders to participate in both individual and group counseling sessions, complete homework assignments, maintain a food journal, attend twelve-step meetings, and consume a diet designed to fit each participant's budget and life situation. According to DesMaisons, "it's really about creating a biochemical environment that allows behavior change." Counseling and a specially designed educational program helped participants learn and practice their new relationship with food. Notably absent from the equation were expensive nutritional supplements.

At the end of the year, 90 percent of the participants had completed the program. San Mateo County found that nonparticipants received four times as many criminal charges, and the charges were more severe than those participating in the Radiant Recovery program. The cost to the county of the nonparticipants in jail time alone, not including court costs and booking fees, was ten times that of the participants ($1,575 compared to $150 for participants). What the Criminal Justice Council of San Mateo County concluded from the results of this one study was a potential to reduce by 80 to 90 percent the number of drunk drivers traveling on their streets, with all the social and financial benefits that that would entail.[5]

AURICULAR THERAPY FOR DRUG ADDICTION

In addition to counseling and biochemical restoration, participants in the drug treatment programs at Recovery Systems in Mill Valley, California, and Radiant Recovery in Burlingame, California, receive acupuncture. The Chinese discovered some four thousand years ago that inserting needles into the skin at specific sites could make organs and glands work better, helping the body heal from disease. In recent decades, Chinese surgeons discovered that acupuncture could also be used as an adjunct or even an alternative to anesthesia during some surgeries. It was only by accident, early in the 1970s, that a neurosurgeon in Hong Kong named Hsiang-Lai Wen discovered the powerful benefit of acupuncture for drug detoxification.

Dr. Wen was preparing a patient for brain surgery, using hair-thin stainless steel needles in the patient's ear and hands to eliminate pain. The needles were stimulated by a minute electric current, too low to give the man a shock, but strong enough to induce analgesia. The patient was an opium addict, and after a while he happily reported to a nurse that his drug withdrawal symptoms had disappeared. Dr. Wen cancelled the operation. When the man's withdrawal symptoms returned, he was again given acupuncture. Again the symptoms disappeared. Dr. Wen was inspired to begin researching this phenomenon with animals as well as humans, and proved that acupuncture can be used as an adjunctive treatment for addiction.

Michael Smith, M.D., director of a drug treatment program at Lincoln Hospital, a city hospital in the South Bronx, New York, trained with Dr. Wen, and in 1974 began using acupuncture in his clinic, first for opiates, and then for all drugs. When his electrical stimulator broke, he discovered he didn't need to use electrical current to help patients detox. He also winnowed down the treatment to four or five main points in each ear. The protocol that Smith developed is now used in the majority of acupuncture detox programs.

In 1985, Smith and others he trained at Lincoln Hospital's

acupuncture clinic founded the National Acupuncture Detox-ification Association to carry on training and certification of acupuncture detox specialists across the country and around the world. The NADA protocol involves treating as many addicts as can fit comfortably in the treatment room at the same time, each person sitting upright in a chair for about forty-five minutes, with four or five acupuncture needles sticking out of each ear. The needles influence the lungs, the liver, and the kidneys, and relax the nervous system. If needed, additional points are used on the hands and feet for specific problems unique to an individual, but mostly the treatment focuses on detox, not general health complaints.

In addition to acupuncture, the NADA protocol includes an herbal tea, called Sleep Mix, composed of chamomile, catnip, peppermint, skullcap, hops, and yarrow. In some clinics, tea is given out for free while people receive acupuncture and given in bags to take home for later use. As its name implies, it is particularly effective as a relaxant at bedtime.

Today, over seven hundred drug treatment centers use ac-upuncture as a part of their protocol, including programs in Germany, Great Britain, the former Soviet Union, Hungary, Saudi Arabia, Sweden, Spain, Nepal, France, and Trinidad. Several dozen in America are part of county court–mandated drug diversion programs. Others are based in mental health facilities, and prisons.

One young female addict, when asked if acupuncture has made a difference in her recovery, answered, "It doesn't seem to [be] making much difference." Then added, "Wait, yes, it has. Yesterday I was stressed. Yet, I didn't do any [drugs]." This is typical. There isn't a fireworks display in the addict's head when the needles are in place, just a slow, gentle change inside that moves the person in the direction of inner quiet instead of turmoil, relaxation instead of irritability, and the eventual realization that he or she isn't arguing with family members as much, is able to listen and comprehend and feel what is going on in counseling more, and in general finds it easier to move farther along on the road to recovery. It is important to realize that acupuncture is added to everything else the addict is doing for detox and recovery. Smith insists that those receiving acupuncture for detox also attend twelve-step meetings and, if possible, receive individual or group counseling. Acupuncture helps stop the headaches, the muscle aches, the nausea, the insomnia, the depths of depression, and other disruptive discomforts of withdrawal that so often drive the person back into drug use. But acupuncture detox doesn't teach the person to live life differently, which only education, self-knowledge, and enlightened guidance can do.

THE HOLDER PROTOCOL

In Miami, Jay Holder, D.C., M.D., Ph.D., has discovered a new point (which he says controls the limbic system) and a new protocol for auricular therapy, which earned him the Albert Schweitzer Prize in Medicine in 1991 for his pioneering work in addiction treatment.

The Holder protocol is drug-specific, based on the particular receptor sites in the nervous system used by each drug. For example, the neurotransmitter dopamine is involved in cocaine use, while gamma-aminobutyric acid (GABA) is involved with alcohol. The treatment is also specific for the organ targeted by each drug. To reach those organs, Holder uses auricular therapy. For example, each person receives acupuncture first on the "zero point" in the center of the ear, which helps harmonize all organ systems, then the kidney point, then the limbic system, then the point which in English is called "Spiritual Gate" (but which is often called by its Chinese name, *Shen Men* (this point initiates the release of natural opiates called endorphins). Next is the sympathetic point (which relaxes the nervous system). Then, if the person's most-used drug was alcohol, the liver point will be used. If the person mostly used cocaine, the heart and brain points will be used. There is some evidence from the work on the brain receptor cascade by Dr. Kenneth Blum of the University of Texas in San Antonio, that brain neurotransmitter receptor defects not only influence the development of drug addiction, but also many compulsive disorders, such as attention deficit hyperactivity disorder (ADHD), and Tourette's syndrome.

HOW OFTEN, HOW LONG?

Acupuncture, with both NADA and Holder protocols, is used five to six days a week during the first couple weeks of detoxification. In some severe cases, particularly with methadone, it is best used twice a day. Then, as the withdrawal symptoms abate, the treatment is cut back to two or three times a week, and then even less often. The ideal program is patient-driven, meaning the acupuncture is available on an as-needed basis. This is useful for people who have successfully passed through the program and are suddenly confronted with a stressful situation that might otherwise tempt them to reuse during the first couple years of recovery.

HOW DOES AURICULAR DETOX WORK?

On the body, acupuncture involves the movement of messages along specific channels which may be some form of electromagnetic resonance. In the ear, the message moves from needle to neuron. Studies show that the mechanism for auricular acupuncture is totally different than that for the rest of the body.

Auricular therapy is based on four cranial nerves distributed throughout the ear: the vagus, glossopharyngeal, trigeminal, and facial, with the second, third, and fourth cervical nerves (called ganglions) having some influence, as well. According to Dr. Holder, "these four cranial nerves and cervical ganglions go to certain areas of the body as if mailed to specific zip codes, each nerve influencing a specific body system." It is this cranial nerve distribution, he says, "that allows us a portal of entry from the ear directly to the brain and therefore to body function."

CHIROPRACTIC FOR DRUG ADDICTION AND COMPULSIVE DISORDERS

Perhaps the most astonishing discovery of Dr. Jay Holder (who was named Chiropractor of the Year in 1992 and Chiropractic Researcher of the Year in 1995) is his discovery that chiropractic adjustments on a regular basis, using his Torque Release Technique, improve outcome of drug detox on both psychological and physical dimensions and keep patients in treatment longer than not using chiropractic.

With a grant from the Florida Chiropractic Society, Holder hired biostatistician Robert Duncan, Ph.D., of the University of Miami School of Medicine, to design and analyze the results of a randomized, placebo-controlled, clinical trial of ninety-eight inpatients at Exodus Treatment Center. One group of addicts received the usual individual and group counseling and twelve-step programs. A second group received the same counseling and group work, plus subluxation-based chiropractic (the chiropractor treats the person for alternations in the normal relationship of one vertebra to another along the spine). For this study, Holder invented a handheld device, the Integrator, that reproduces in a standardized way the treatment usually done by hand. The Integrator is FDA-approved to treat subluxations (vertebrae out of place). The third group received the same counseling and group work, plus placebo chiropractic (no true correction of any out-of-place vertebrae).

At the end of eighteen months the results were tabulated: In terms of depression, four weeks of true chiropractic care equalled what was usual to expect after about a year of recovery work. In terms of anxiety, four weeks of chiropractic equalled what usually took six months with only conventional talk-therapy anxiety intervention. In terms of retention in treatment, compared to the national average of 72 percent of patients staying in a program for thirty days, among the group receiving true chiropractic treatment at Exodus, retention was 100 percent! In terms of patient visits to nursing stations, there was less utilization of medical services by patients receiving chiropractic care. According to Holder, it all adds up to regular chiropractic adjustments being about thirteen times more successful at improving drug treatment outcomes than conventional drug treatment without chiropractic. A truly revolutionary result.

WHY CHIROPRACTIC HELPS DRUG TREATMENT

According to the pioneering work of Candace Pert, Ph.D., and others at the Institutes of Health in 1976, there are opiate receptors of the limbic system (the part of our brain controlling smell, anger, fear, sex, and other core survival-related emotions) located in the dorsal horn of the spinal cord. Subluxations interfere with these receptors, and chiropractic adjustments that eliminate the subluxations help this intimate communication system to function normally.

RESOURCES

Treatment centers using nutrition among other techniques:

Recovery Systems, 147 D Lomita Drive, Mill Valley, CA 94941 (415/383-3611; fax 415/383-1089). Treats both chemical dependency and eating disorders. Following Joan Mathews Larson's view of drug addiction as neurochemically based, Director Julia Ross, M.A., M.F.C.C., has built her program on a multifaceted approach using nutritional support, acupuncture, counseling, education, and long-term monitoring. Located across the Golden Gate Bridge from San Francisco.

Radiant Recovery, P.O. Box 1144, Burlingame, CA 94011 (415/579-3970). Kathleen DesMaisons uses biochemical restoration, with particular emphasis on foods that help prevent low blood sugar and maintain sobriety.

Comprehensive Medical Care, 149 Broadway, Amityville, NY 11701 (516/598-2960). Intravenous vitamin-based therapy.

Lakeside Milam Recovery Program, 12845 Ambaum Boulevard SW, Seattle, WA 98146 (206/241-0890). This center particularly focuses on adolescents. Milam has an adult inpatient facility in Kirkland, Washington. Nutrition is included as a part of the treatment.

Forest Tennant, M.D., 336½ S. Glendora Avenue, West Covina, CA 91790 (818/919-5807). Dr. Tennant uses amino acids and other nutritional supplements in his treatment protocol. He owns over thirty-five medical clinics catering to substance abuse, compulsive disorders, and weight management.

Health Recovery Center, Joan Mathews Larson, Ph.D., director, 3255 Hennepin Avenue South, Minneapolis, MN 55408 (612/827-7800; 800/24-SOBER for nutritional supplies). Intravenous and oral doses of nutritional supplements, including amino acids, vitamins, minerals, herbs, and other substances as per her book (see below).

Books:

Joan Mathews Larson, Ph.D., *Seven Weeks to Sobriety* (New York: Fawcett Columbine, 1992). A step-by-step, week-by-week how-to based on the successful program at Health Recovery Center in Minneapolis.

John Finnegan and Daphne Gray, *Recovery from Addiction* (Berkeley: Celestial Arts, 1990). Comprehensive discussions of supplements and foods for addiction relief, along with other methods to release cravings and rebuild your life.

Alexander Schauss, *Diet, Crime and Delinquency* (Berkeley: Parker House, 1980). Chapter 5 is "Alcoholism, Addictions and Diet."

Spencer Shaw and Charles S. Lieber, "Nutrition and Alcoholism" in *Modern Nutrition in Health and Disease*, ed. Robert S. Goodhart and Maurice E. Shils (Philadelphia: Lea & Febiger, 8th ed., 1994).

Ann Louise Gittleman, M.S., C.N.S., *Get the Sugar Out: 501 Simple Ways to Cut the Sugar Out of Any Diet* (New York: Crown, 1996). Why and how to eliminate sugar from your everyday menus. A big step to regulating biochemistry in direction of wellness, even-keeled emotions, and a reduction in cravings of all kinds.

Ellinor R. Mitchell, *Fighting Drug Abuse with Acupuncture* (Berkeley: Pacific View Press, 1995). Beginning with a roundup of the grim statistics on America's failure to control drug addiction, Mitchell covers the history of acupuncture's use for addiction, its beginnings at Lincoln Hospital in Bronx, New York, and its spread across the world to over seven hundred clinics and community programs.

Kenneth Blum, Ph.D., and Jay Holder, D.C., M.D., Ph.D., *Handbook of Abusable Drugs* (Mattituck, N.Y.: Amereon Press, 1997). A new paradigm of using auricular therapy and chiropractic, among other treatments, for drug addiction and substance abuse.

Kenneth Blum, Ph.D., and Jay Holder, D.C., M.D., Ph.D., *Reward Deficiency Syndrome* (Mattituck, N.Y.: Amereon Press, 1997). Explains the biological system at the heart of drug addiction and compulsive disorders.

Acupuncture Recovery Information and NADA Literature Clearinghouse (360/254-0186; 888/276-9978; fax 360/260-8620; e-mail acudetox@aol.com). Jay and Mary Renaud edit *Guidepoints,* a newsletter for people using acupuncture for alcohol and other drug addiction treatment. They also control the NADA (National Acupuncture Detoxification Association) Clearinghouse, from which you can obtain scientific papers, reports, videos, tapes, and other material on the subject of acupuncture detox.

Alex G. Brumbaugh, *Transformation and Recovery: A Guide for the Design and Development of Acupuncture-based Chemical Dependency Treatment Programs* (Santa Barbara, Calif.: Stillpoint Press, 1994). The bible for those eager to create a successful acupuncture detox program in their community. Brumbaugh directs the highly successful and multifaceted Project Recovery in Santa Barbara.

For treatment and referrals:

National Acupuncture Detoxification Association (NADA),

3220 N Street NW #275, Washington, DC 20007 (503/222-1362). Call or write for a list of NADA trainers near you. The local trainer will direct you to the nearest NADA-certified detox specialist.

Exodus Treatment Center, Jay Holder, D.C., M.D., Ph.D., Director, 5990 Bird Road, Miami, FL 33155 (305/534-3635; fax 305/538-2204). Holder, an Orthodox Jew, has a 350-bed inpatient facility, and an outpatient treatment program that is divided into two, one secular and one religious. They treat all drug addictions and all compulsive disorders, using chiropractic, nutrition, and ear acupuncture with needles, laser, and microcurrent stimulation, among other approaches.

American College of Addictionology and Compulsive Disorders, same address as Exodus, above (800/490-7714; 305/535-8803). Dr. Jay Holder is president of this six-year-old educational institution, which trains and certifies C.A.P.s (certified addiction professionals) in different sites around the country.

Holder Research Institute, same address as Exodus, above (800/490-7714; 305/535-8803). Call for referrals to chiropractors in your area who are trained in Torque Release Technique.

Studies:

D. S. Lipton et al., ''Acupuncture for Crack-Cocaine Detoxification: Experimental Evaluation of Efficacy,'' *Journal of Substance Abuse Treatment* L205–215, 1994.

A. Margolin et al., ''Acupuncture for the Treatment of Cocaine Dependence in Methadone-Maintenance Patients,'' *American Journal of Addiction* 2: 194–201, 1993.

Milton L. Bullock et al., ''Controlled Trial of Acupuncture for Severe Recidivist Alcoholism,'' *The Lancet* 1: 1435–1439, June 24, 1989.

Pierre De Vernejoul et al., "Investigation of Acupuncture Meridians by Radioactive Tracers," *Bulletin of the National Academy of Medicine* (Paris) 169(7), 1985.

REFERENCES

1. Ann Louise Gittleman, "How to Kick the Habit: Nutritional Fixes for Common Addictions," *Let's Live*, October 1996, 26.

2. Roger J. Williams, *Nutrition in a Nutshell*, (Garden City, N.Y.: Doubleday, 1962), 60.

3. Williams, 85.

4. Joan Mathews Larson, Ph.D., *Seven Weeks to Sobriety* (New York: Fawcett Columbine, 1992), 46.

5. "Evaluation of the Biochemical Restoration Program for Multiple DUI Offenders," May 1994–May 1995, Criminal Justice Council of San Mateo County, October 1995.

APPENDIX

GENERAL REFERENCES

1. FINDING A NUTRITION-ORIENTED DOCTOR

"There have been a few brave, caring doctors that ventured out of the mainstream of traditional medicine and are seeing their patients get well using natural procedures, but it's been expensive for them," says Bernice Davison, director of the Health Oasis in Tilly, Arkansas, in her audiotape titled "Prevent, Eliminate, or Halt Disease." "They have received a lot of opposition from their medical peers and organizations that lay down the rules for doctors. Their business has not diminished. Instead, they are as busy as ever, because people want to get well and they will go wherever true healing is offered."

As you search for true healing, interview potential health care providers about their experience and training. Don't take anyone as your consultant just because he or she has a degree and happens to be in your neighborhood. If your community has licensed naturopathic physicians, then you are particularly lucky. These doctors have been trained to use clinical nutrition as the cornerstone of their healing practice. Many chiropractors are astute at using nutrition for healing biochemical imbalances, but some are more interested in this aspect of chiropractic than others. Ask.

For a medical doctor, start by looking under Nutrition in the "Physicians" listing in your local Yellow Pages. Before making an appointment, ask the physician what post-graduate training he or she has undertaken in the field of nutrition. Ask if the physician has attended seminars or bought audiocassette tapes from Alan Gaby, M.D., Jonathan Wright, M.D., or Jeffrey Bland, Ph.D., or if he or she is familiar with the work of Roger J. Williams, Ph.D. (a nutritional researcher who wrote books on nutrition for the public) and Carl C. Pfeiffer, M.D., Ph.D. (who ran the Brain Bio Center, where nutrition solved health and learning difficulties), or uses herbs and supplements in addition to pharmaceuticals, you know that person is truly interested.

- Jonathan Wright, M.D., is in full-time practice at Tahoma Clinic, Kent, Washington. He is a frequent magazine columnist and the author of several self-help books, such as *Dr Wright's Natural Hormone Replacement for Women Over 45* (Health Freedom Publications, 1997), *Dr. Wright's Guide to Healing With Nutrition* (Keats, 1990), and *Dr. Wright's Book of Nutritional Therapy* (Rodale, 1979).

- Alan Gaby, M.D. is medical editor of the *Townsend Letter for Doctors and Patients,* a major communication link for medical professionals (and patients) concerned with clinical nutrition and all other nontoxic, nonsurgical methods of healing mind, body, and spirit (911 Tyler Street, Port Townsend, WA 98368-6541; 360/385-6021; ten issues for $49). Dr. Gaby also coedits *Nutrition and Healing* newsletter with Dr. Wright (P.O. Box 84909, Phoenix, AZ 85071; 800/528-0559; fax 602/943-2363. Twelve pages, $49/year for 12 issues; sample issue available). He is the Endowed Professor of Nutrition at Bastyr University, Seattle, Washington, and the author of *Preventing and Reversing Osteoporosis* (Prima, 1995) and B_6: *The Natural Healer* (Keats, 1987).

After Wright and Gaby educated themselves about nutrition, they eventually began educating other medical doctors interested in using nutrition in their practice. Available are audiotapes, reference manual, and handouts from the 1996 Wright-Gaby Seminar, a four-day program for medical professionals. Call for information about upcoming seminars. Wright/Gaby Seminars, 515 W. Harrison Street, #200, Kent, WA 98032 (206/854-4900 ext. 166).

- Jeffrey Bland, Ph.D., HealthComm International, P.O. Box 1729, Gig Harbor, WA 98335 (253/851-3943; 800/843-9660). Bland, one of the "points of light" within nutritional medicine, has produced a monthly audiotape on clinical nutrition for sixteen years. It's a great way to keep up with the field while commuting to and from work. He is also the author of numerous books and pamphlets, including, with Sara Benum, *The 20-Day Rejuvenation Diet Program* (Keats, 1997), which is an excellent guide to detoxification, improving immunity, combating aging, and pain relief using the scientific application of current research in nutrition.

REFERRALS

You can receive a referral to the closest doctor who has experience ordering and interpreting laboratory tests for heavy metals, allergies, and other related conditions and who probably uses nutrition in his or her practice by contacting the organizations listed below:

The American College for the Advancement in Medicine, P.O. Box 3427, Laguna Hills, CA 92654 (714/583-7666; 800/532-3688; fax 714/455-9679). Send 55¢ postage on a self-addressed envelope.

American Academy of Environmental Medicine, 10 E. Randolph Street, New Hope, PA 18938 (214/862-4544; fax 215/862-4583).

The American Holistic Medical Association, 4101 Lake Boone Trail 201, Raleigh, NC 27607. Send $5 check or money order (no credit cards, no phone orders) for national referral directory. Physicians interested in membership can call 919/787-5146 or fax 919/787-4916.

International Academy of Nutrition and Preventive Medicine, P.O. Box 18433, Asheville, NC 28814 (704/258-3243). Nonprofit organization publishing *Journal of Applied Nutrition*. Sample copy available for $10. Newsletter, "Your Health," available for $3. National referral available for free with self-addressed stamped envelop.

2. POLITICAL ACTION

American Preventive Medical Association, 459 Walker Road, Great Falls, VA 22066 (800/230-2762; 703/759-0662; fax 703/759-6711). A lobbying organization for health care practitioners who use preventive medical techniques, including nutrition and other complementary therapies. The APMA Legal and Educational Foundation sells books and directories listing physicians across the United States who practice alternative medicine.

CCHW: Center for Health, Environment and Justice, P.O. Box 6806, Falls Church, VA 22040-6806 (703/237-2249). Founded sixteen years ago by Lois Marie Gibbs, who helped organize her Love Canal neighborhood into a powerful, successful grass-roots movement to continue fighting toxic waste dumps and other environmental and health issues. A great part of their work is educating and training local people to deal with local issues.

3. USEFUL DETOX SUPPLEMENTS

Just as you wash off surface dirt as-needed (probably at least once a day), your body will appreciate being cleansed on a regular basis at the cell level, too. For example, you may decide to do a short detox with each change of season, or around New Year's, your birthday, the equinox, or some other recurring point on the calendar. In this case, you can compare one detox formula with another, one method with another, over the years to come.

Following are a few good formulas that weren't included in the main body of the book. For more suggestions of supplement manufacturers, see the Resources section of Doris Rapp, M.D.'s *Is This Your Child's World?* (New York: Bantam, 1996). Regarding the following formulas, each company has several excellent detoxifying formulas and products. I have picked just one to talk about here. For example, lipoic acid, a fat- and water-soluble antioxidant that chelates out heavy metals, is widely available, and so are good multiantioxidant formulas.

SLF PLUS. A two-week detox protocol of capsules containing silymarin, turmeric, artichoke, choline, B_6, and B_{12}, iodine from kelp, magnesium, inositol, dandelion root, DL-methionine, Russian black radish, beet leaf, and celandine. According to Herbert Schuck, a naturopathic physician in Tukwila, Washington, "This formula has some of the major detox herbs. Patients notice a difference. If they feel tired and run-down, it gives them energy."

NF Formulas, 9775 Southwest Commerce Circle, Suite C-5, Wilsonville, OR 97070 (800/547-4891).

Detoxification Factors. The printed description reads "Nutritional support for Phase I and II detoxification pathways" (as described in chapter 2 of this book) and includes a dozen of the most powerful antioxidants, conjugating agents, and nutritional cofactors that fuel the liver's work. I've used this formula with patients who have livers needing a lift, and found it quite successful in improving function.

Tyler Encapsulations, 2204-8 NW, Birdsdale, Gresham, OR 97030 (503/661-5401).

S.A.T. Silymarin, artichoke, and turmetic

Thorne Research, P.O. Box 3200, 901 Triangle Drive, Sandpoint, ID 83864 (800/228-1966; 208/263-1337; fax 208/265-2488).

NESS (Nutritional Enzyme Support System). Enzymes are the key to the proper absorption of the nutrients you consume. NESS products follow the work of Dr. Edward Howell, a physician and researcher who wrote the influential *Enzyme Nutrition* (Wayne, N.J.: Avery, 1985) detailing the critical importance of enzymes in health. NESS products provide active enzymes for the person whose cooked-foods diet has created enzyme deficiencies.

NESS, 100 NW Business Park Lane, Riverside, MO 64150 (800/637-7893; 816/746-0110; fax 816/746-8387).

4. LABORATORIES TO ANALYZE YOUR NEED TO DETOX

Be advised: your medical provider must be the one to order the test, but you could ask the lab to send information about its tests to the provider. (For more good laboratories, see the Resources section of Doris Rapp's book *Is This Your Child's World?* (New York: Bantam, 1996).

Omegatech King James Medical Laboratory, 24700 Center Ridge Road 113, Cleveland, Ohio 44145 (800/437-1404; 216/835-2150). The best deal in the country! At this writing, a hair analysis for heavy metal toxicity and a report detailing the significance of the findings, is only $30. (Prices are certain to rise! The next least expensive lab I found was $50.)

Aeron Life Cycles, 1933 Davis Street 310, San Leandro, CA 94577 (800/631-7900; fax 510/729-0383). Saliva test for sex hormone levels, DHEA, and melatonin.

Great Smokies Diagnostic Laboratory, 18A Regent Park Boulevard, Asheville, NC 28806-9901 (800/522-4762; 704/253-0621; e-mail cs@gsdl.com). Excellent results from stool analysis for parasites, yeast, abnormal bowel flora, problems with digestion and absorption; intestinal permeability, lactose intolerance, functional liver detoxification profile, and immunodeficiency (by testing secretory immunoglobulin A [sIgA]).

SpectraCell Laboratories, 515 Post Oak Boulevard 830, Houston, Texas 77027 (800/227-5227; 713/621-3101; fax 713/621-3234). Separate panels for various combinations of vitamins, minerals, and heart risk factors.

Chiralt Corporation, 15466 Pomerado Road F-S, Poway, CA 92064 (888/244-7258). Providers of the NutriProbe sublingual swipe test done in the doctor's office and analyzed in the company's lab for individual levels and ratios between magnesium, calcium, potassium, sodium, chloride, and phosphorus.

Diagnos-Techs, Inc., P.O. Box 58948, Seattle, WA 98138 (800/878-3787; 206/251-0596; fax 206/251-0637). Saliva test for sex hormone levels, DHEA, and melatonin. Liver detox profile, yeast screens, gastrointestinal efficiency and pathogens.

Meridian Valley Clinical Lab, 515 W. Harrison Street 9, Kent, WA 98032 (206/859-8700; fax 206/859-1135). The lab is associated with the medical office of Jonathan Wright, M.D., and offers stool analysis for parasites, yeast, and digestive factors, hormone profiles, allergy screening, mineral analysis, and the D'Adamo Serotype Panel (see chapter 5 for information on the D'Adamo blood typing).

MetaMetrix Medical Laboratory, 5000 Peachtree Ind. Boulevard 110, Norcross, GA 30071 (800/221-4640; 770/446-5483; fax 770/441-2237). Tests for food allergies, heavy metals, fatty acids, amino acids, homocysteine (a marker for heart disease), bone resorption, and other metabolic functions.

Aatron Medical Services, 12832 Chadron Avenue, Hawthorne, CA 90250 (800/367-7744 national; 800/433-9750 California; 213/675-1272). Amino acid assay.

Immuno Laboratories, 1620 W. Oakland Park Boulevard 300, Ft. Lauderdale, FL 33311 (800/231-9197; 954/486-4500; fax 954/739-6563). Elisa Immuno 1 Bloodprint Test for revealing 102 IgG mediated food allergies.

Vitamin Diagnostics, Rt. 35 and Industrial Drive, Cliffwood Beach, NJ 07735 (908/583-7773). Standard profile of twelve vitamins available in fluids and tissues.

National Medical Services, 2300 Stratford Avenue, P.O. Box 433A, Willow Grove, PA 19090 (215/657-4900; 800/522-6671; fax 215/657-2972). Occupational, industrial, environmental, and clinical toxicology (testing for toxic chemicals of all kinds in body tissues).

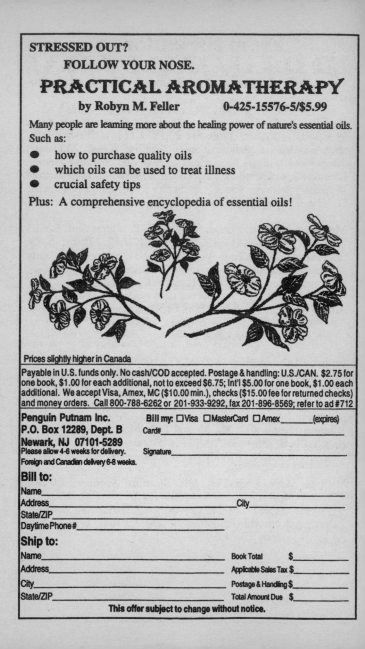